'/21 gale 340

LOVE, DEATH & RARE BOOKS

LOVE, DEATH & RARE BOOKS

ROBERT HELLENGA

THORNDIKE PRESS
A part of Gale, a Cengage Company

Thorndike Press® Large Print Bill's Bookshelf.
The text of this Large Print edition is unabridged.
Other aspects of the book may vary from the original edition.
Set in 16 pt. Plantin.

LIBRARY OF CONGRESS CIP DATA ON FILE.
CATALOGUING IN PUBLICATION FOR THIS BOOK
IS AVAILABLE FROM THE LIBRARY OF CONGRESS

ISBN-13: 978-1-4328-8095-8 (hardcover alk. paper)

Published in 2020 by arrangement with Delphinium Books, Inc.

Printed in Mexico
Print Number: 01   Print Year: 2020

To the Memory of Robin Metz,
who inspired us all
1942–2018

■ ■ ■ ■

PART ONE:
CHAS. JOHNSON &
SON, LTD.
ANTIQUARIAN
BOOKSELLERS

■ ■ ■ ■

I. The Fur Coat
(1970–1971)

My grandfather and my father ran an old-fashioned bookshop on Fifty-Seventh Street in Hyde Park — CHAS. JOHNSON & SON, LTD. ANTIQUARIAN BOOK-SELLERS — not far from the University of Chicago. At the time I started "working" in the shop in the seventies, at age twelve, we stocked about fifteen thousand rare books on the second floor and about two hundred thousand used books on floors one, three, and four; so you won't be surprised to learn that most of our family stories were about books: books that Grandpa Chaz brought with him from New York's book row when he came to Chicago in 1931; books from the Bruneau estate on the North Shore that gave Grandpa Chaz a leg up during the Depression; books that Grandpa Chaz and Dad bought at estate sales in the forties, after the war, probably the best time in history to buy rare books; books bought for $5 and sold for $10, later bought back for $100 and sold at auction, after another ten or fifteen years, for $1,000; books that got away and books that we couldn't get rid of.

But the story that sticks in my imagination is not about a book; it's about a fur coat. Not the raccoon coat in the front of the shop that Saul Bellow used to admire, the coat that Grandpa Chaz had stolen from Harry Gold — the man who engineered the theft of Edgar Allan Poe's *Al-Aaraaf* from the Reserve Book Room in the New York Public Library. It's about Mamma's fur coat.

But it's about a book too.

It's shortly after Christmas, five months before Mamma disappears. The tree is still up; I can smell it in my bedroom, where I sleep with our dog, Punch — short for Pulcinella — a stray dog that Mamma brought home one day. Mamma comes up to say good night. She stands in the doorway for a few minutes while we talk, and when she leaves, she says, *"Beh, ce l'abbiamo fatta, sani e salvi." Well, we made it through, safe and sound.* Mamma was Italian and always spoke Italian to me when we were alone, and sometimes when we weren't.

But I think maybe we haven't made it

through safe and sound, because after Grandpa Chaz goes to bed, I hear Mamma and Dad, who've been doing some drinking, arguing about something in the kitchen. I wrap my book around my thumb — my favorite Hardy Boys mystery, *Hunting for Hidden Gold* — and listen at the top of the stairs.

I'm trying to figure out what's happening. Mamma wanted a fur coat for Christmas but she'd gotten a rare book instead — a first edition of an Italian translation of Montaigne.

"Why would I want to read Montaigne?" she says.

"It's in Italian. I thought you'd like it."

Dad says more, but I can't make out the words. Then I hear Mamma say, "I want to live life, not read about it."

After a mysterious silence, Dad says — his voice different, lower — that he'll buy her a fur coat if she'll run around the house outside, stark naked, three times.

"Deal," Mamma says, laughing, "I'll do it." When Dad starts to protest, to say he's only kidding and that it's too cold to run around outside naked, Mamma won't hear of it. She's made up her mind. She wants a fur coat.

Ice cubes rattle in the sink, and then Dad

comes up the stairs. I get into bed and pretend to be asleep. He comes over to my bed, turns off the light, then stands there for a moment. After he and Punch are back downstairs, I go to my window. From my dormer I can look out at the houses across the street, at the lighted Christmas decorations in the front yards and the flicker of televisions in the downstairs windows. I don't understand what's going on. I'm embarrassed. But I'm excited too. No other mother on our block will be running outside naked in six inches of snow. I can hear them laughing. Then the kitchen door opens and closes.

About thirty seconds later I see her, down below me. She's going counterclockwise, lifting her knees in the deep snow and hugging herself, covering her breasts. She's white as snow, beautiful as an angel. But naked. I try to look away, but I can't. Another two minutes and I see her again and watch her disappear, and I know she's running through the narrow space between our house and the Harringtons', which Grandpa Chaz calls a "ginnel."

Mamma appears a third time, a ghostly figure suddenly emerging into the light and disappearing again, and then I hear her pounding on the back door and Punch barking and Dad shouting, "Who is it? What do you want?" before finally opening the door and letting her in.

I run downstairs. Dad has wrapped Mamma's robe around her and is holding her in his arms. Both of them are laughing and I start laughing too, and we all drink a glass of prosecco and something called crème de cassis.

Two days later we go to McElroy's in Winnetka. It's a sunny winter morning and we drive along the lake all the way. The sky is blue, the lake blue-green. DuSable Harbor is empty, but the water intake just beyond the breakwater looks like a giant rowboat.

I know from the way the salesman greets us at McElroy's that Dad has already spoken to him. The salesman brings a coat out of a climate-controlled vault and Dad nods. Mamma tries it on, but then she asks to see a different coat. She keeps asking to see more coats until she finds what she wants: mink (I'm too young at the time to disapprove), black, full length, and sheared. The salesman holds it up and Mamma steps into it and walks up and down, admiring herself in various mirrors.

The coat is beautiful, but it isn't a magic coat, and it doesn't keep Mamma and Dad

13

from sitting up late, drinking and talking softly. I listen as hard as I can, but I can't make out what they're talking about. I sit at the top of the stairs or at the cold air register till I hear the clatter of ice cubes in the sink, and then I get back into bed.

Mamma wears the coat all winter, wears it to the grocery store, wears it when we go with Dad and Grandpa Chaz to Maxwell Street, on a Sunday morning, where we eat Polish sausage sandwiches and listen to the Mississippi Blues Band, and Mamma gets her fortune told by a gypsy on the corner of Maxwell and Halsted. She wears it when she walks me to school with Punch on his leash. She wears it to my birthday party in April, when all the other mothers are in lightweight linen jackets or windbreakers.

But she doesn't take the coat with her when she disappears in May.

The morning she disappears is like most mornings. She poaches eggs for us, and then Dad and Grandpa Chaz leave for the shop. I drink a glass of milk with a little coffee in it, and then we walk to school. It's May but chilly — Mamma is in her fur coat, of course, and I'm in my Cubs sweatshirt. Thin clouds hang high in the sky, like hooks or tufts of hair. As we approach the corner of

Blackstone and Fifty-Eighth Street, Mamma shouts, *Ci stiamo avvicinando all'angolo della cacca numero uno — We're approaching Poop Corner Number One* — and we stop to give Punch a chance to do his business.

I'm twelve years old, just finishing my last year at William H. Rey Elementary, so when she puts her arms around me in front of the gate, I'm embarrassed. And that day it's worse because I can see she's crying. *"Mi trovo un po' in difficoltà,"* she says. *I'm in trouble.* But instead of listening, I run off to join my schoolmates, who are crowding around the front door.

When Dad and I come home from the shop that night, she's not there. There's no note. Punch is in the backyard. Grandpa Chaz is taking a nap. Her car isn't in the garage. When she doesn't come home for supper, Dad calls Mrs. Ogilvie, who owns the cabin — the Loft — in St. Anne, Michigan, where we vacation every summer, but she isn't there either. Dad doesn't do anything else the first night — she's disappeared before — but when Mamma doesn't come home by morning, he calls the police. The police won't declare her missing for a week. She's an adult and there's no sign of foul play. By then Dad has telephoned all of her friends and hired

15

a private detective. But two weeks after she disappears, a letter comes to the shop. Mamma has fallen love with another man, Dad tells me as we walk home together. She's gone to live with him in Rome.

"Do you know who it is?" I ask.

"I have a pretty good idea," he says.

Mi trovo un po' in difficoltà, she'd said to me the last time she walked me to school. I want to tell Dad, but I think that he's in a little difficulty too, and I don't want to make things worse.

A few minutes later, as we turn onto Blackstone, Dad says, "She wants to live life, not read about it."

Dad doesn't show me the letter, but I have one of my own waiting in the mailbox when we get home. Dad goes to his room, and I go to mine. We both need to be alone. She's sorry, she says in her letter, *molto spiacente* — she loves me and she hopes I will forgive her. I crumple up the letter till it's the size of a Ping-Pong ball and throw it into the wastebasket. I get my bike out of the garage and pedal down Fifty-Seventh Street, under Lake Shore Drive, and out to the Point, and sit on the big rocks and throw stones into the lake until I can't see them hit the water anymore.

When I get back home, Dad and Grandpa

Chaz have already eaten. Dad offers to fry me a hamburger, but I'm not hungry.

"What the hell is the matter with that woman?" Grandpa Chaz says, setting his glass of bourbon on the kitchen table and struggling to get out of his chair. He's a little unsteady. "You buy her a goddamn fur coat," he says, "and the next thing you know, she leaves us high and dry."

In August, Dad and Grandpa Chaz and I go to the Loft in St. Anne for three weeks and I take sailing lessons. In September, I start seventh grade at the Lab School — Latin, earth science, American history, English, algebra. After school, I go straight to the shop and take Punch for a walk. Amos, our third-floor manager, takes him out at noon, but he spends most of the day in Dad's office. I do my homework at the library table on the second floor. At six o'clock or so, Dad and Grandpa Chaz and I walk home with Punch. I always listen for Mamma's voice as we enter the empty house, and Punch runs through all fifteen rooms looking for her.

On Christmas Eve, Dad and I go to the four o'clock service in Rockefeller Chapel, and afterward we skate on the Midway. It feels

17

good to glide with him on the ice as it gets dark, and then sit together in the warming house.

Does he expect something to happen? Does he think, or hope, as I do, that Mamma might come back for Christmas? They've been divorced since Thanksgiving in the United States, but Dad says he and Mamma are probably still married in Italy, because Italy won't recognize an American divorce.

I had swallowed my anger and answered Mamma's letter — which I'd retrieved from the wastebasket — begging her to come home. Dad and I don't talk about the possibility. We're afraid to jinx it.

I help make dinner that night while Grandpa Chaz sits at the kitchen table drinking bourbon. We boil some small potatoes and make a salad. I set the table in the dining room while Dad sautés three small steaks. Dad opens a bottle of red wine and we sit down to eat. We don't talk much. I think we're all waiting for something to happen. Afterward we sit in the living room and wait some more. The tree looks nice, but it doesn't have Mamma's touches. Dad sits in his chair with his eyes closed, a book on his lap, while I wrap a couple of presents at the glass coffee table and fill out the tags.

I haven't wrapped any presents for Mamma, but I have a couple of things in reserve, just in case — some earrings and a small leather wallet. I assume Dad does too.

"High and dry," Grandpa Chaz said. "I'm going up to bed."

Dad opens his eyes and picks up his book again. We read in front of the fire for another half hour, and then Dad unplugs the tree and says good night. I'm halfway through a boy's version of *Sir Gawain and the Green Knight,* which I've read before. The Christmas festivities are over and Gawain is about to set out on his quest to confront the mysterious Green Knight. I try to imagine him in his gleaming, golden-bright armor, but I get lost in my fantasy and keep picturing him in Mamma's fur coat. I close the book, and then my eyes. But I don't fall asleep. I'm waiting, as if for Santa Claus — or Babbo Natale, as Mamma called him — and watching the shadows from the last embers move along the ceiling. After a while I go upstairs. I take Mamma's coat out of her closet, still in its protective garment bag, and drag it down the stairs. I plug in the tree and unzip the bag and pull out the coat and, slip it on. It's incredibly warm. I turn up the collar. There's a blue plastic poop sack in one of the pockets.

19

I turn on a light to keep myself awake, but then I lie down on the couch and after a while I fall asleep. I'm still there, wrapped up in Mamma's coat, when Dad and Grandpa Chaz come downstairs in the morning. Dad shakes me and says, "Merry Christmas."

"How much did you pay for that goddamned coat?" Grandpa Chaz asks. "And she didn't even take it with her."

"The best money I ever spent," Dad said. "I don't want to hear any more about it." He gets that look he sometimes gets and leaves the room.

At ten o'clock, Dad and I take Punch for a walk. Along the way, Dad points out the site of the old Stineway Drug Shop on Fifty-Seventh and Kenwood. The owner, he tells me, once asked three men to leave because they came in every morning and never ordered anything except coffee, and later the busboy told him he'd just kicked out three Nobel Prize winners.

Back home, Dad puts a precooked turkey from the Co-op in the oven to warm up, and together we peel the potatoes and put them on to boil. We open a can of cranberry relish and put it in a cranberry glass bowl on the dining room table. I set the table and Dad opens a bottle of wine. We take the turkey out of the oven and put in an apple pie, also from the Co-op. There are none of Mamma's fried artichokes. There's no pasta. From my seat I can see Mamma's fur coat, folded over the back of the couch.

II. FIRST LOVE

(1974)

After Mamma went away, I started walking to the shop with Dad and Grandpa Chaz early in the morning. Punch would go with us, and I'd shout out, *Ci stiamo avvicinando all' angolo della cacca numero uno,* and then, depending, *numero due.* I'd sit in Dad's office till it was time to walk to school, reading a book or adding up columns of figures on the old Victor adding machine — one that had been "retired" — with two black columns for the cents, three white columns for the tens, and three more black columns for the hundreds — as I waited for the tap tap tap of Miss Sullivan's flats on the stairs and the smell of her perfume. She and her sister, Estelle, who worked the register at the counter by the front door, wore different perfumes. Equally expensive and equally offensive. Dad kept them both supplied at Christmas and birthdays. They were always carefully made up, eyes dark (greenish blue) with mascara, their hair — already thinning and turning pale — held in place by tortoiseshell combs.

Afternoons Punch and I "worked" the first floor selling children's books to young readers — readers my own age — and to their mothers. In those days, the first floor was like a conveyor belt. On Tuesday and Thursday afternoons, people could bring their used books to the shop, and Archie Blair, who came from Belfast and spoke with a heavy Ulster accent, would go through them — history and philosophy, religion, literature, science, travel, cookbooks, children's books — and quote them a price. If the price was acceptable, he'd put them on a cart, and a day or so after they'd been processed, they'd emerge at the front of the shop, where they would wait for buyers for a few days before being shelved.

At six o'clock, we'd walk home. I still listened for Mamma's voice as we entered the empty house, and Punch continued to run through all fifteen rooms looking for her.

By the time I was fourteen, young adult literature was beginning to emerge as a distinct genre, and I was beginning to feel the pangs of adolescence. Used copies of

The Catcher in the Rye and *Are You There God? It's Me, Margaret* and *Charlie and the Chocolate Factory* started showing up in the shop, and I was happy to recommend them. But by the time I turned fifteen, I was looking for something more, which I seemed to find in poetry (Tennyson's *In Memoriam,* for example) and in long walks with Alex, with whom I was doing independent reading in Latin; and in long bike rides. We walked the boundaries of Hyde Park (Lake to Cottage Grove). We biked along the lake, sometimes all the way up to Loyola. Alex's mother was a warm, loving woman, and we sometimes did our homework together in her kitchen, but more often we worked at the shop, at the library table on the third floor, between "Psychology" and "Philosophy."

We read everything we could find about sex for our library project in science — everything from Krafft-Ebing's *Psychopathia Sexualis,* in a translation of the seventh enlarged and revised German edition (1894) by Charles Gilbert Chaddock (on a shelf next to the library table), to Nancy Friday's *My Secret Garden: Women's Sexual Fantasies.* And our joint report on *Psychopathia Sexualis,* which contains a total of 238 case histories of human sexual behavior, created a sensation at the Lab School, especially the account of the man who drank the urine of a nine-year-old boy after performing fellatio on him. Parents complained to the director, who complained to our parents, and there was a fuss about First Amendment rights and freedom of speech.

Krafft-Ebing gave us a lot to wonder about, and the report made us heroes of a sort. Our classmates started coming into the shop to have a look, some of the girls, too, including Alice Archer, the only girl I'd ever kissed, though I'd often undressed her in my imagination. We tried not to draw attention to our gatherings at the long table, but either Dad got wind of them, or else he simply stumbled upon us by accident. It was an interesting moment. We froze. But Dad didn't scold us. Instead of scolding, he talked about the publication history of the book. We had four different editions in the shop, including the first German edition (in "Modern Firsts" in the rare book room). Later editions, he explained, were quite different from the first, and some of the bindings were very interesting, but by this time, the report on Krafft-Ebing was behind us and we had moved on to other things — our French teacher, for example, Mademoiselle Arneau. *What would it be like to put your hand up Mademoiselle's Arneau's skirt?* Alex wondered. *How about dropping your pencil on the floor so you could at least look up her skirt?*

"But she sits at her desk in the front," I objected, "so you'd have to drop your pencil at the front of the classroom, and she'd have to come around the desk."

Pretty tame after Krafft-Ebing. Most things, including *Playboy,* seemed pretty tame after Krafft-Ebing. There was still plenty to wonder about, of course, especially a woman who came to the shop once a week, around closing time on Thursdays. Shirley. Alex thought she might be a Playboy Bunny. Or at least she could have been. She was small and curvy and had long blond hair, like a movie star. Alex said she probably glowed in the dark. In summer she wore a wide straw hat and in winter a pillbox fur hat like the hat Geraldine Chaplin wears in *Doctor Zhivago.* Dad said it was fox fur.

I tried to connect her visits with some of the words we'd learned in Krafft-Ebing: *coitus, fellatio, cunnilingus, sadism, masochism, fetishism, imitatio coitus inter femora viri, frottism* — not words, really, but *counters* that I understood only dimly.

Dad usually sent me home with Grandpa Chaz, but I started pretending to be busy with my Latin homework. We were reading Ovid. Alex and I were working on a translation of Amores 3.14, which was not actually on the reading list, but which, like Krafft-Ebing, stimulated our imaginations: *"Spondaque lasciva mobilitate tremat." Let the bed shake with your trembling motion. Or, Shake the bed with your lascivious movements.*

"She's got great legs," Alex said. "Knockers too. Stick right up there. Do you think he's putting it to her?"

"No way," I said. "In the shop? That'd be like doing it in church."

"It happens. Jerry Holsinger told me that Father Donovan likes to touch the altar boys. He's got some magazines he says will keep you going all night. But we'd have to rent them."

I was curious but not ready to jump.

Sometimes I'd stay at the shop and walk down Fifty-Seventh Street to Blackstone with Dad and Shirley, who took the IC from the Fifty-Seventh Street station. One night Dad came to get me earlier than usual. I had my books spread out on the library table. Dad was alone. I'd been translating a difficult passage in the *Metamorphoses* about Actaeon, and Dad startled me as

27

Actaeon must have startled Diana. I looked up. The sight of him was reassuring.

"Dative of passion," I said, and he laughed. The "dative of passion" had been invented by Alex. I started to pack up my books, but he told me to wait.

"Shirley's coming to the shop," he said. "Later. There's a present for her on my desk in the office." He handed me a ring of keys. "Just lock up, and be sure to reset the alarm."

Shirley? By herself?

I said okay and turned back to Ovid, to the Latin textbook and the Loeb I was using as a crib, but the words on the page were out of focus. The shop was empty, quiet. My heart was ramping up, the way it did before an exam in precalculus or when doing a difficult problem at the board, in front of the class.

Shirley arrived just before we locked up at eight. I heard Oscar speaking to her and then I heard the elevator trundling up to the second floor, where I was working at a table between the elevator and "Banned Books." I wasn't sure what was happening and held my breath till she appeared. Immediately, she pulled out a chair and sat down next to me. She was a beautiful woman. I tried, unsuccessfully, to slow my breathing. She looked at all the books spread on the table.

"You take up a lot of space," she said, and asked what I was reading.

I tried to explain: "Precalculus, Latin, history . . ."

"Would you like to come to your dad's office with me?"

"Do you want me to help you find something?"

"He said it would be on his desk."

I started to say that I needed to get home, but she smiled and put her hand on my arm. "You don't need to be afraid." She nodded her head toward the office in the back.

Why would I be afraid? I asked myself. Maybe, I answered, because I was thinking of the horror stories in Krafft-Ebing.

"Well," she said. "Maybe it's good to be a little bit afraid."

I started to tell her about Actaeon. "He saw the goddess Diana naked and she turned him into a stag. He didn't mean to see her. It just happened. Out in the woods. He was hunting. And then she turns him into a stag and sets his dogs on him, and they tear him apart."

She gently tugged on my arm. As I followed her through the open stacks, my body seemed to be pulling me back — my hands were sweating and my feet seemed to be sinking into the floor at each step. Shirley turned: "Better to walk behind a lion than behind a woman." She laughed. "I promise I won't turn you into a stag," she said. "Cross my heart."

I often thought of this moment, in later life, walking behind a woman in the Co-op, or on Fifty-Seventh Street, or on Michigan Avenue. *Better to walk behind a lion than behind a woman.*

The key to Dad's office on the second floor, next to the rare book room, was on the key ring he'd given me earlier. I had trouble opening the door. It was a nice room, but nothing fancy. Books everywhere, of course. Wherever Dad sat down, you'd be sure to find a pile of books.

She took her clothes off. I'd never seen a naked woman before, except in *Playboy* — or the time Mamma ran around the house starkers. I'd never seen the hair between a woman's legs. She unbuttoned my shirt and I didn't stop her. She leaned over and touched my chest with the tip of her tongue, and I was no longer afraid.

Dad didn't have a regular bed in his study, but there was a comfortable sofa. I didn't understand that I was supposed to come in her mouth. I was super aroused, of course, but I was young and had a lot of staying power and used the occasional thought of Krafft-Ebing to put a brake on things. After a while she asked me if I'd like her to use her hand, and then I understood. I thought I didn't have a word for it, but I did: *fellatio.*

We lay on our backs next to each other in silence. The couch was barely wide enough for the two of us.

"I told your dad he should get a real bed in here."

"What would people think?"

"They'd think he likes to entertain pretty women up here."

I'd crossed a line, but really it was more like straddling a line. I wasn't sure how to ask for what I wanted. What I wanted was the real thing. The thing itself. *Coitus,* not *fellatio.*

"Is that all?" I asked.

She laughed. "No," she said. "There's more."

"You do these things with my father?"

"Yes. And did he tell you not to give me all your money?"

"Nooo," I said. "He didn't tell me *that.* I don't have any money anyway. Maybe three dollars." She laughed again.

She lay down and opened her legs, though

not too wide, because the couch was narrow, and pulled up her knees. I was ready. What I experienced was not the moving and shaking I'd been wondering about in Ovid; it was more like a slow easy roll. But enormously gratifying. I felt as if I were drifting above the clouds, or skating on the Midway.

The present for Shirley was on Dad's desk. It was a book — of course it was a book — wrapped in custom tissue paper with the shop logo on it: CJ&S. I waited for her to open it, but she slipped it into her large purse, and we took the elevator down to the first floor.

I reset the alarm, double locked the big front door, and we walked out onto Fifty-Seventh Street. "Are you coming to our house?"

"No," she said, and took my arm. We were in front of the Medici. Shirley's purse banged between us and she shifted it to her other shoulder.

"Will I see you again?"

"Probably not in this life."

"Are you going away?"

She nodded. "I'm going to Vegas with a girlfriend. She's got a job in a casino. I'm going to look for one too. Change my luck."

"Have you had bad luck here?"

"No, Gabe," she said. "I've had pretty good luck here, but it's time for a change."

"Are you a Playboy Bunny?"

"Not anymore."

"Was it fun?"

"It was the opposite of fun."

"Did you meet my dad at the Playboy Club?"

"No. We weren't allowed to date the patrons. Besides, I don't think your dad ever darkened the door of the Playboy Club. I met him at Kroch and Brentano's on Wabash."

"So, you like books?"

"Not really," she said. "I was shopping for a present for my girlfriend, and she likes books. I've always wanted to live life, not read about it. Your dad was talking to Mr. Kroch. Or maybe it was Mr. Brentano."

I wondered about the book that Dad had given her. She still had my arm in hers. She held it tighter. We got to Blackstone, but I wasn't ready to go home. I walked her all the way to the Illinois Central station and waited with her for the train that would take her wherever she was going.

I offered her the three dollars that I had in my wallet, and asked her to place a bet for me on number 108.

She laughed. "The numbers don't go up

33

that high," she said. But she took the money and slipped it into her purse.

By the time I got home, Grandpa Chaz had already gone up to his rooms on the third floor, but Dad was waiting for me in the kitchen. I handed him the ring of keys. He was reading *To the Lighthouse* and drinking some of Grandpa Chaz's Jack Daniels.

"Books," he said, looking up, "are a bulwark against time, against human ignorance. For most people they're ornaments, decorations hung on the tree of life." He turned to a page he'd marked in the book and read aloud: " 'He' — Mr. Ramsay — 'would argue that the world exists for the average human being; that the arts are merely a decoration imposed on the top of human life; they do not express it. Nor is Shakespeare necessary to it.' But we know better, don't we," he added.

We had a drink together. Another first. In those days. Dad rarely drank hard liquor. There was always beer in the refrigerator and wine in a small wine-storage rack in the butler's pantry, and sometimes champagne and crème de cassis for special occasions. But that night he was drinking Jack Daniels. Bourbon.

He poured me some in one of the multifaceted almost unbreakable French Duralex glasses that we used for just about everything. Almost unbreakable, but not quite, and when one did break on the tile floor, it didn't just break. It exploded.

"Well," he said. "Did she like her present?"

"I think so," I said. "But she didn't open it."

"You didn't fall in love with her, did you?"

"No," I said, though it wasn't true. I had fallen in love with her. "She's going to Vegas," I said.

He nodded. I took a sip of bourbon. It tasted mysterious and exciting, like the mysterious words in Krafft-Ebing. It was good to be sitting in the kitchen drinking bourbon with my father, sitting in the circle of his love, remembering the night he promised Mamma he'd give her a fur coat if she'd run around the house naked. And it was below zero. And how playful and happy they'd been. His face looked naked now. As if he'd removed a mask, or had been asleep and had just awakened. He rubbed his forehead. I suddenly realized that he loved Shirley too, and this made me happy and sad at the same time.

"She said she wants to live life and not just read about it."

35

"That's what your mother used to say." He paused. "Do you think that's what we're doing? Reading about life instead of living it?"

I said I didn't think so, though I wasn't really sure.

"You read to get things into words. You remember how Helen Keller felt when she figured out what Annie Sullivan was doing?"

"Spelling out *w-a-t-e-r* on her hand with her fingers?"

He nodded. "Everything had a name," he said. "The world blossomed for her. 'Mother,' 'Father' . . . and not only that. She saw with a strange new sight. Without the words, she couldn't see anything. Do you see what I mean?"

"Can you get *everything* into words?" I asked. Remembering how my swollen penis had felt in Shirley's mouth, and then inside her.

"Bedtime," Dad said. Putting the cap on the Jack Daniels.

I wanted to remember him this way. And I do, just as I remember Shirley, standing in the Illinois Central station with her big purse slung over her shoulder, her big straw hat floating on her head, laughing as she holds out her hand for my three dollars.

But what had I learned? How had I been

changed? I'd been through a rite of passage, but where had I come from and where was I now? And what did it mean? And what did it mean that my father loved Shirley too? I wanted to put my answers to these questions into words, but I couldn't do it. And I thought of the words in Krafft-Ebing: *Sadism, masochism, fellatio, cunnilingus, fetishism, frottism, coitus, imitatio coitus inter femora viri, necrophilia, copraphilia, voyeurism* . . . These were great words, mysterious words, secret-cult words. But they didn't name my experience.

III. Second Love

(1984)

I didn't fall in love again, really in love, till the spring of 1984. I was twenty-five years old. I'd majored in classics at the University of Chicago. I'd served my apprenticeship in Americana with Grandpa Chaz, who had helped build the rare book collection at St. Anne College — the Ogden Collection — into an important collection for the study of the Upper Midwest and the Great Lakes Region; and my apprenticeship in Modern Firsts and British and American literature and history with Dad. I'd taken courses in descriptive bibliography and Early Printed Books at the new Rare Book School at Columbia University and had started cataloging some of our Early Printed Books in Latin — and a few in Greek — books that Joe McDowell and Grandpa Chaz had bought in the thirties and forties and had never cataloged because they didn't know Latin or Greek. That was going to be my job.

But on Saturday, May 26, 1984, my agenda was to put together an Orwell exhibit. June 8 was the thirty-fifth anniversary of the pub date of Orwell's novel and Dad wanted to have an Orwell display in place. There was a lot of hoopla in the papers about the novel and about the Michael Radford film that was scheduled to open in the United States in December with Richard Burton as O'Brien, John Hurt as Winston Smith, and Suzanna Hamilton as Julia.

Olivia Bennison, who worked at the shop on Tuesday and Thursday afternoons and who helped Dad organize readings and talks, had been drafted to help me. Dad thought it was time for me to get married, or at least to think about getting married, and had fixed on Olivia. This wasn't the first time he'd put us together. "She's very open," he said to me, more than once, "but she's not naïve. You don't have to explain things to her."

She was waiting for me at the door of the shop, talking to a young man who was listening attentively. She was wearing a suede coat, long but lightweight. She held a cup of coffee in one hand, a book in the other. I was twenty-five. She was twenty-one. She'd been working at the shop for almost a year and was just completing her junior year at the University of Chicago, my alma mater. The young man, who was wearing a long maroon and gray U of C scarf, smiled at me as he lit a cigarette and walked west on Fifty-Seventh Street. I thought about digging my own U of C scarf out of the back of the front hall closet.

"What's a 'quagga'?" I said.

"Some kind of horse," Olivia said. "Extinct. I read the article too."

"Dad didn't say anything about getting married, did he?" I said as I unlocked the front door.

"He didn't set a date," she said. "There's plenty of time; a lot of things could happen — Relax," she said when she saw the expression on my face. "I'm just kidding."

She laughed and tossed her head like a pony and opened her mouth, as if I'd offered her a carrot, but she didn't blush. Her front teeth overlapped just slightly. "Well, not exactly," she added.

Her aunt, who was a buyer for Marshall Field, had given her a pair of orange Ferragamo shoes and a matching orange Balenciaga handbag — a "city bag" — for her birthday. Olivia was wearing the shoes and was holding the city bag as if she knew who she was. She was wearing a purple sweatshirt that said MY SOUL IS AN ENCHANTED BOAT across the front in white letters. At the moment I thought I knew who I was too. I'd survived several romances with girls who were probably attracted to me because I always had something else on my mind, something more important than they were, like writing up a catalog description of an Aldine Aristotle. But seeing Olivia in orange shoes and her ENCHANTED BOAT sweatshirt, I suddenly thought Dad might be right, that Olivia was just what I'd been looking for all along, though it had taken me a while to figure it out. She had my full attention.

Our stock of Orwells included two first editions, published in London by Secker and Warburg, one with a red dust jacket and one with a green. No one was sure, as is sometimes the case with identical twins, which was born first. Both were slightly faded at the extremities.

More interesting, and more valuable, was a Russian language first edition. "It was printed in Germany," I said, "and smuggled behind the Iron Curtain." Next to it was a 1947 Ukrainian translation of *Animal Farm,* also printed in Germany. "All the copies were seized by the U.S. government and handed over to the Soviets." And then there was my personal favorite, the pulpy 1950 Signet Giant edition (#798) with a muscular Winston Smith and sultry Julia backed up against each other — Winston in a sleeveless top and Julia in a blouse with a plunging neckline with an ANTI-SEX button pinned to the lapel, while a poster of Big Brother O'Brien glares down at them from a wall: BIG BROTHER IS WATCHING YOU!"

On Friday afternoon, Stuart Kaminsky read the "newspeak" passage from *1984*. After the discussion, which went on till six o'clock — in which no one agreed about anything — Dad took Kaminsky out to dinner, and Olivia and I finished a bottle of white wine in Dad's office and sat next to each other, without actually touching, on the comfortable couch where Shirley had taken me by the hand and led me across the border into a new country.

Olivia touched her nose with the tip of her finger. "Why is there a dog bed on the floor?"

"That was for my mother's dog, Punch."

"What happened?"

"She went away."

"Punch?"

"My mother."

"She just went away? Just disappeared?"

42

I nodded.

"You can't just disappear."

"Well," I said, "there was a visiting art history professor at the university who used to spend a lot of time in the shop. He was an Italian, from Rome, and liked to talk to Mamma in Italian. Mamma went to some of his lectures. She went with him to Italy."

"I'm sorry," she said.

"Punch disappeared too," I said.

"He went with her?"

"Died. Later. We were never sure how old he was, but he'd be at least sixteen or seventeen by now, maybe older."

We sipped our wine.

"What about the sign on the door: I'D TURN BACK IF I WERE YOU? Do you think it's aimed at us? Doesn't sound like your father."

"I don't think so. That sign's been there so long, I don't even see it." But I saw it now, though it was on the other side of the door. A clipping from the *Trib,* a photo of a sign — the letters wood-burned into an old barn board: I'D TURN BACK IF I WERE YOU. I don't think either one of us wanted to turn back, but something kept us from going forward. Maybe we were too timid, or too shy. Or maybe we were just drawing back in order to spring forward with greater force at a later date. Maybe we just wanted to go slowly. Maybe we felt awkward about my father's crude attempts at matchmaking. In any case, we did turn back.

One night at Jimmy's, just before the end of the fall quarter, she laid out her senior honors thesis on the Romantic Imagination. By this time I was definitely in love. I always liked the way she kidded me, but she never kidded about her thesis. "The Romantics," she said, "were the first generation of writers to write in a universe that didn't have a built-in meaning. They were the first generation of poets who had to create their own meaning."

"And how did they do that?" Olivia rubbed her finger around in a circle in some beer on the tabletop, hesitating, as if reluctant to reveal a state secret to someone she couldn't fully trust. "Imagination," she said. "Not Reason. Imagination. How do we grasp reality? Not through Reason, but through Imagination. It doesn't just record the external world, it transforms it. 'What the Imagination seizes as Beauty must be Truth.' " I could feel her capitalizing the big words. "Letter to Benjamin Bailey," she added. "November 1817."

"What is your imagination seizing on right

now as beauty?" I asked.

Olivia looked around. "I don't know," she said. "You?"

"The bottles lined up in front of the mirror behind the bar are nice," I said. "Lots of interesting shapes and colors, the reflections in the mirror, like an Impressionist painting."

"You'll have to do better than that."

"Is this some kind of test? Checking out my imagination?"

"I'm sorry," she said. "I'm sure your imagination is working just fine, just like Coleridge's great esemplastic power — the living power, with a capital P. The prime Agent of all human Perception, and as a repetition in the finite mind of the eternal act of creation in the infinite I AM."

"You're kidding. That's what it really is? Actually I was imagining what it would be like to kiss you."

"And put your hands on my butt?"

"That too," I said, "but you're sitting on it." The palms of my hands tingled. I could feel a pulse beating along my throat. And beyond that the kind of excitement you feel as you're setting out on a long journey and aren't quite sure where you're going.

"That's just 'fantasy,' " she said, "not 'Imagination.' The word the Romantics used was 'Fancy.' It's mechanical. When a man and a woman start talking trash, pretty soon they both want to jump into bed. That's Fancy, not Imagination."

"Give me an example of Imagination, something 'esemplastic.' "

" 'Esemplastic' is from a Greek word meaning 'to shape.' To mold things into a unity. Do you remember 'The Eve of Saint Agnes,' she said, "when Porphyro sneaks into Madeleine's room and watches her undress?"

"Vaguely."

"Do you remember what happens?"

"I can guess."

"No you can't. Nobody could guess. Just Keats."

"What happens?"

"Madeleine's dreaming about him — about Porphyro — but when she wakes up and sees him, he looks sick, pale. She thinks he's dying. She's desperate. He doesn't match up to her dream. You see what I mean? Doesn't match up to her Imagination."

"And?"

"So she takes him up into her dream. 'Into her dream he melted, as the rose blendeth its odour with the violet.' That's Imagination!"

46

I took a minute to marvel at the transformative power of words. I thought that the real seduction was just beginning. But then I said, "Does she get pregnant?"

She laughed, friendly and generous, open but not naïve. "Would you like to come up to my room?"

I was as nervous as I'd been when Shirley asked me if I'd like to spend some time with her. But of course I said yes. We went up to her room in Snell-Hitchcock. I may not have measured up to her imagination, but like Madeleine in the poem, she took me up into her dream.

Olivia was planning to stay in Hyde Park over the Christmas break to work on her honors thesis and finish her grad school applications, which were due at the end of December. The dorms were closing. She needed a place to stay. I said she could stay with us.

"What about your dad?" she asked.

Dad wanted me to get married, wanted me to marry Olivia, in fact. "He won't mind," I said.

"You sure?"

"What about your aunt?"

"She won't mind either. In fact, she'll be in London. If I stay with you, I won't have to go back and forth to Evanston. But what about your grandfather?"

I laughed. "I'll give him a heads-up," I said. Grandpa Chaz wanted me to get married too, wanted another generation to carry on the shop. I felt a current of happiness running through my entire being — firing neurons, tripping synapses, lighting up nerve endings.

The dorms closed on December fourteenth. Dad and I picked Olivia up in front of Snell-Hitchcock in Grandpa Chaz's 1977 Cadillac, which had only thirty thousand miles on it because it almost never left the garage. Around town we usually drove our thirteen-year-old Chevy van, but Dad had just traded the van for a first edition of Jack Kerouac's *On the Road* and we hadn't replaced it yet. The Cadillac was a formidable car — a Fleetwood Brougham. Olivia put her things in the back seat, and we drove to the Midway to go ice skating. People were leaving or getting ready to leave, or looping around one last time. I was wearing my good Italian sweater, black with a black leather panel in the front. Dad had brought my mother's old Jackson Glacier skates, which he'd had sharpened for Olivia. We put our skates on in the warming house.

"I'm such a klutz," Olivia said as I helped

her on with Mamma's skates. "Really clunky."

The clicking of skates outside on the ice sounded like someone dropping ice cubes into an empty glass. I held Olivia's elbow to guide her, but the moment we pushed off, I understood that she would be taking me wherever she wanted to go. We skated arm in arm, and then Dad, who was an expert skater, joined us. Our skates dug into the ice, which was cold and fast, but soft enough to plant your toe pick for a jump, not that I was planning to execute a double axel. But Olivia's skates seemed to skim over the ice, the way the warrior Camilla skims over the waves in the *Aeneid* without getting her feet wet.

We made several loops, carried along effortlessly in the slipstream that circled the rink, floating past snow-suited children staggering around like drunks, girls holding hands, guys showing off their moves. Dad veered off after a while, and I had the uneasy feeling that Olivia and I were skating not on the Midway but on a thin layer of ice that covered a deep lake and that might crack open at any minute. All the other skaters were ignoring the danger, so I ignored it too. Olivia pulled me along, applying gentle pressure when needed, till she broke away and started to spin, faster and faster, while I circled her.

"It's like standing still," she said, coming out of the spin, "with the whole world spinning around you."

The Midway was not too crowded, so we could go pretty fast without knocking into anyone. We raced around the perimeter, skating with the traffic, staying out of the center, where there were people practicing jumps, spins, and footwork. They stayed out of our way, and we stayed out of theirs. "It's not a race," she shouted, turning her head as she picked up speed. But of course it was a race. I thought I could catch her by concentrating, but concentrating didn't make me go any faster. Maybe even slowed me down. Finally she stopped abruptly, next to Dad, in front of the warming center.

As we were taking off our skates, Dad said, "Did you know that ice skating was invented by the Finns five thousand years ago?"

And Olivia said, "I wish I had a cigarette."

"You're right," Dad said. "Now would be the perfect time for a smoke. But we don't have any."

"Do you want me to see if I can bum a couple?" She didn't wait for an answer, and soon they were lighting up. They both surprised me by smoking. Like characters

50

in an old movie. I'd never seen either one of them smoke before. I didn't know what they were thinking as they savored and tasted. I imagined how they might look walking down Fifty-Seventh Street, or sitting across from each other at a table in a restaurant, sharing a tranquil moment, and I knew that Dad loved her too. But I never saw either one of them smoke again. Not for a long time.

Olivia tucked one leg under her and sat on her skate.

"I hadn't known that," she said. "About the Finns. That they used bones for skates. For the blades."

We took off our skates and walked down Fifty-Ninth Street to the car and drove home. Seeing our fairy-tale house, Olivia was charmed.

"It's just like a bookstore!" she said, looking around as she hung her coat up in the front hall closet.

"It is a bookstore," Dad said. "Everything's for sale. "Well, almost everything," and I remembered how Grandpa Chaz had sold my Winnie the Pooh books.

"I'll have to look around," she said. "Where should I put my suitcase?"

"You can put it in Gabe's little apartment over the garage," Dad said, "or you can have your own room."

Mornings Olivia worked at the Regenstein on her senior thesis and her graduate school applications; afternoons she worked in the shop; late afternoons we went skating; evenings, after supper, we read to each other in the living room, while Dad and Grandpa Chaz sat in the kitchen, and she schooled me in Keats's Imagination and Wordsworth's Correspondent Breeze. Nights we melted into each other's dreams. Or were they just fantasies? Either way, I thought, we were embarking on a life together.

By this time our curiosity about our bodies had been satisfied though not exhausted, and we were open to curiosity about our lives, which we offered to each other. Olivia, who came from Goshen, Indiana, which was named after the land of Goshen in the Bible, remembered that her mother always said "yes" and her father always said "no," and that her father didn't like the way she made her M's because the tops of her M's resembled women's breasts, and he didn't like the way she made her W's because the bottoms of her W's resembled women's buttocks; and that they lived across from a cemetery, where her grandparents, who'd been killed by a tornado that killed 147 people on Palm Sunday 1965, were buried. She'd been two years old. She'd attended Jefferson Elementary School and remembered her fifth-grade teacher and kids coming in from other classes to see the volcano they'd built. She remembered that she hadn't been allowed to see the movie *Grease* in the summer of 1978, when she was fifteen, and that she'd gone to see it anyway, with a friend, and then in November her parents were killed in an auto accident and she came to live with her aunt in Evanston. Her aunt had taken her to Paris the next spring on a buying trip for Marshall Field, and she'd missed two weeks of school.

I told her the story I've told you — about Mamma's fur coat that she'd left behind when she went to Italy, and the Italian translation of Montaigne that she'd taken with her.

"Real fur?" she said. "It's probably beautiful, but I don't want to see it."

On Christmas Eve, we went with Dad to the afternoon service in Rockefeller Chapel and then Olivia and I took the Jeffrey Express downtown to go skating at Navy Pier. We joined Dad and Grandpa Chaz later and ordered pizzas, which we ate at the kitchen table, and drank a bottle of red wine.

■ ■ ■ ■

When I woke up on Christmas morning, Olivia was not in the bed beside me. I tried not to panic, tried to stay in the present moment. As I understood it. Of course, the present moment consists of memories and anticipations, so it's hard to stay in one place. But when I got out of bed and went to the top of the stairs, I could hear Dad's voice in the kitchen. And Olivia's too. And when I went downstairs, Olivia was opening the present I'd left for her on the dining room table — the first publication of Keats's "Eve of St. Agnes," in *Lamia, Isabella, The Eve of St. Agnes, and Other Poems.* Printed for Taylor and Hessey, London, 1820, a small duodecimo in dark red morocco that you could hold in one hand. It was a fabulous book that included the "Ode to a Nightingale," the "Ode on a Grecian Urn," "To Autumn," "La Belle Dame sans Merci." It was expensive, but Dad had encouraged me to give it to her.

"You need to inscribe it," she said.

"Already inscribed a card," I said.

"I'm afraid to look," she said.

There were ten of us at the long table with

serpentine ends — some members of the old guard, the generation that was passing away — and some new blood too. Old leaves and new leaves. What they had in common was that they all loved books and bought them at the shop, and they all had book stories.

This was our extended family, at least for the day. I was afraid that Olivia would be bored, but she jumped right into the conversation and even proposed the first toast: "Oh, for a beaker full of the warm south," she said, lifting her glass of French Bordeaux that Alice Ramsbotham had brought, "with beaded bubbles winking at the brim."

Glasses were raised and soon the wine began to lubricate the conversation.

Olivia wasn't bored at all. She exhibited a nice mix of awe and skepticism when it came to rare books, and pretty soon everyone was angling for her attention. Even the women. Sitting across the table from me, she filled my field of vision.

When Alice Ramsbotham, who was supervising Olivia's honors thesis, invited Olivia to explain her big idea, Olivia didn't hesitate: "The Romantics," she said, "were the first generation of writers to write in a universe that didn't have a built-in meaning. When Alexander Pope went out in the woods, he didn't see trees. He saw history, and politics, he saw the great chain of being, he saw a hierarchy that started with dirt and stones, went up to plants and then animals — with the 'half-reasoning' elephant up near the top of the heap, just below human beings — and then angels, of course. But when Wordsworth went out in the woods, he saw . . ." She paused and looked around. "What?"

"Daffodils," Alice said, and everyone laughed. This was spontaneous laughter induced by the feelings of goodwill that sometimes come just from being together with other people — not exactly strangers, not exactly old friends, but people who are prepared to be interesting and agreeable, just happy to be sitting at the same table with each other, listening to a beautiful young woman outlining the new sources of meaning ushered in by the Romantic Movement: Nature (Wordsworth and Shelley), Art (Keats and Coleridge), the Romantic Hero (Byron). And the odd thing is, I don't need a glass or two of wine to experience those same feelings when I think of that dinner — the turkey that Olivia and I roasted, the cranberry-horseradish relish that we made in the blender, Nora Chapman's tossed salad and Alice's mince pies, the

French Bordeaux and Ben Warren's bottles of Michigan sauvignon blanc made with grapes from his own vineyard west of St. Anne, Mark Ramsbotham's explanation of *libration* and the phases of the moon, Olivia passing around the copy of *Lamia, Isabella, The Eve of St. Agnes, and Other Poems,* blushing when Alice Ramsbotham read the inscription aloud: *Into her dream he melted.*

That night, after the leftovers had been put away and the dishes had been put in the dishwasher and the dishes that wouldn't fit in the dishwasher had been washed by hand, Olivia read "The Eve of St. Agnes" to us — to Dad and Grandpa Chaz and me — in the living room. Dad and Grandpa Chaz sat in two armchairs on either side of the fireplace. I sat on one end of our dark red — almost black — leather sofa. Olivia on the other end, holding the book of poems on her lap in a circle of light cast by a floor lamp with a parchment shade. It's a long poem — 42 Spenserian stanzas, 378 lines. Olivia read confidently, without letting her own emotions get in the way of the words. Keats's words didn't need any extra help:

St. Agnes' Eve — Ah, bitter chill it was!
The owl, for all his feathers, was a-cold;
The hare limp'd trembling through the

frozen grass,
And silent was the flock in woolly fold;
Numb were the Beadsman's fingers,
  while he told
His rosary, and while his frosted breath,
Like pious incense from a censor old,
Seem'd taking flight for heaven, without a
  death,
Past the sweet virgin's picture while his
  prayers he saith

Grandpa Chaz didn't get up to go to bed. Dad didn't get up to pour another glass of wine. We let the old words wash over us, let them mingle with our own secret thoughts and name our own deepest longings, let them open our eyes so we could see the world with a strange new sight.

We all stood up at the same time, and Grandpa Chaz and Dad both touched Olivia, as if to release us from a magic spell. The fire in the fireplace had died down, but we didn't poke at it. We could have made some popcorn, but we didn't. We were all tired, ready for bed.

Lying next to Olivia in the narrow bed up in my little apartment over the garage, I almost proposed. I would have proposed, but I didn't want her to feel trapped, and we were both too tired anyway.

■ ■ ■ ■

At the beginning of January, Olivia moved back to Snell-Hitchcock. I hadn't proposed to her — the time had never been quite right — but I was expecting to marry her, expecting her to do her graduate work at the University of Chicago. But she had a different agenda. She'd been accepted at both Princeton and Yale in March — Chicago, of course, and Stanford. This good news didn't dispel my fantasy. I had waited with her for the results of her GREs; I had read her applications; I had walked with her to the post office on Ellis Avenue when she put them in the mail; I had helped her celebrate her letters of acceptance, and the generous offers of financial support.

She decided on Yale. She wanted to go out East. I thought she'd be better off at Chicago, which was more historically oriented than Yale, where she'd have to deal with the all the deconstructionists, but she wanted to go where the action was; she wanted to start deconstructing things herself. She showed me pictures of the university apartment she planned to rent on Chapel Street in New Haven, across from Vanderbilt Hall, a women's dorm.

The knowledge that she was actually going to leave Hyde Park didn't become really real — "Felt in the blood, and felt along the heart," as Olivia liked to say — till I looked through the window of car number 8406 on the Lake Shore Limited and saw her sitting by herself. She was looking at a twenty-two-hour trip with forty-six stops. She'd have to change trains twice. I'd offered to pay for a sleeper between Chicago and New York, but she was planning to sit up and read all night. She already had a book in her hand. "What are you reading?" I shouted, but she couldn't hear me. Her lips moved. She was shouting too, but I couldn't hear her reply. The train started to move into the darkness at the end of the platform. I walked alongside her car as far as I could. It was almost ten o'clock at night. I watched the red lights on the back of the train till they disappeared into the tunnel, and then I walked to the IC station on Randolph Street and took the train back to Hyde Park. I reminded myself that she had her own way of being in the world, her own memories and experiences, her own history, her own story to write. I could go back to Hyde Park, but I didn't think I could go back to being who I was before Olivia. I could no more imagine a

future without Olivia than I could imagine
Fifty-Seventh Street without Chas. Johnson
& Son, Ltd. Antiquarian Booksellers. I'd
thought all along that she was Madeleine
and I was Porphyro, but now I thought that
she was La Belle Dame sans Merci, and I
was her knight at arms, alone and palely
loitering.

When I got to the shop the next morning,
Delilah, who was in charge of our large
mystery section on the first floor, was making coffee in the staff room next to the
freight elevator.

"You put her on the train?"

"Yeah." I sat down at the wooden table.

"You look like you got *hit* by the train.
You expect her to change her mind at the
last minute and say she's going to stay in
Chicago instead of going out East?"

"Of course not."

"Then why the long face?"

"I think I need a philosophy of life. I
didn't think I needed one, but now I do."

"You mean like Plato — getting out of the
cave?"

"I thought I *was* out of the cave, but
now . . ."

"Your dad got a philosophy of life?"

"I don't know"

"How about your grandpa?"

61

"I think so, but I don't know what it is. How can I look for answers when I don't know what the questions are? Why is there something rather than nothing? Does God exist? Do we have free will? Can we ever see things as they really are? Are moral values just opinions? What happens when we die? None of these questions interest me. They're good questions, but they aren't *my* questions."

"What are *your* questions?"

"Is the coffee ready?"

"If that's your question, the answer is 'yes.'" She filled two ceramic mugs.

"Have *you* got a philosophy of life?"

"Yeah: 'Get your stuff up off the floor and don't feel sorry for yourself.'"

"When you love someone —" I said, but she interrupted.

"You want to melt into her dream, right? She told me about that."

That stopped me. "Go to hell," I said.

She laughed. Delilah was loud and always spoiling for a fight. "I need more space," she said. "You know those shelves under the stairs on the west wall? Let's get all those civil war books up on the second floor, where they belong. Those books must have been shelved downstairs by accident."

"You always want more space."

"That's because I know what people need to read if they want to get out of the cave. They need to hear tough working class voices that tell the truth about the class struggle in this country. They need to read about people who find meaning and purpose in their work, people who actually do stuff as well as thinking about stuff — tracking down witnesses, getting physical with the bad guys, casing crime scenes, bedding femmes fatales, or hommes fatales, whatever. They need to read Dashiell Hammett and Raymond Chandler, and now you've got some strong women muscling their way onto the stage: Sara Paretsky, Marcia Muller, Sue Grafton. They want to hear some black voices. Don't get me started: Pauline Hopkins, J. E. Bruce, Charles Chestnut, Rudolph Fisher, Chester Himes, Ann Petry, Ishmael Reed. We got a good start right here, but we could do more. And we'd have to do some rearranging. Make use of that space under the stairs. You want to see what I mean? Let me show you. I'm thinking we could have a whole section called 'Black Noir.' "

"I'll talk to Dad about it," I said.

"I already talked to him. He said okay."

"I guess that settles it."

"Gabe," she said. She put her hand on

mine, then wrapped her fingers right around my wrist. "I'm sorry about Olivia. But I've got stuff to do." She was wearing a blue bookman's jacket that Grandpa Chaz had brought back from the Loudermilk sale in Philadelphia, back in 1971. She wore it over a yellow dress that picked up the highlights in her dark skin and swished as she left the room.

Delilah had written her PhD thesis at Chicago on the hard-boiled detective novel and was pretty hard-boiled herself. She never *left* a room, she broke away; she never recommended a book to a customer, she pitched it; she never beat the traffic, she slapped it aside; she never walked anywhere, she hoofed it or cabbed it. Her dad collected Langston Hughes and ran a funeral home on Sixty-Third and Cottage Grove and three or four more in different parts of the city. Like Dad and Grandpa Chaz, he was a member of the Caxton Club.

IV. THE BOMB

(1989)

When Olivia left for New Haven in August 1984, she took with her the volume of Keats's poems that I'd given her for Christmas, and the association copy of Wordsworth's *Prelude* — it had belonged to Wordsworth's neighbor — that Dad had given her. We corresponded for a while for the first year — I proposed to her twice in letters that she didn't answer, at least not directly. I suppose I was just writing the same words that other disappointed lovers had written before. I had trouble ending my letters: "All the best"? "Sincerely"? "Love"? After a while she stopped writing, so there weren't any more letters to answer.

What I knew about Olivia's life at Yale came mostly from her aunt — Aunt Fern — who had sold her house in Evanston and moved into the 1700 Building in Hyde Park, across from the Museum of Science and Industry. Olivia was struggling at Yale —

didn't like her seminars, didn't like her professors. Talked about transferring back to Chicago, but this was complicated. Then she found a mentor, a thesis advisor, and was ecstatically happy. And then she was miserable again.

I saw her briefly, once a year at Christmas, but I didn't really *see* her again till March 1989. I was standing on Fifty-Seventh Street in front of the shop. It was six o'clock in the morning and I'd been standing there for two hours. The shop had been bombed in the middle of the night. Police cars, blue lights swirling, blocked the street. The police had called about 3:30. I didn't wake Dad and Grandpa Chaz, I just threw on a pea coat and left the house. It was cold, there were still piles of snow in shady corners and in the ginnel between our house and the Harringtons'. Signs in the little grocery store on Fifty-Seventh Street advertised the specials in Spanish and English. The sidewalks were empty, though a crowd had gathered up ahead, on the south side of the street, opposite the shop.

I felt sick to my stomach. But excited too.

Salman Rushdie's *Satanic Verses,* which had been published in September, had been banned in India, Sudan, South Africa, Bangladesh. By October, Viking had been pressured to withdraw the book. In December, seven thousand Muslims demonstrated in Bolton, England. In January, a public book burning had been staged in the city of Bradford. In February — February eighteenth — Ayatollah Ruhollah Musavi Khomeini had issued a fatwa against Rushdie, encouraging Muslims to kill the author of *The Satanic Verses.* Ten days later Cody's in Berkeley had been bombed for displaying the book. The Riverdale Press in the Bronx had been bombed after publishing an editorial defending the right to read the novel. We'd displayed an illegal Iranian translation of the novel that Dad and I had picked up at the New York Book Fair, along with a signed first edition in English, printed on vellum.

The whirling lights were making me dizzy. I wanted to speak to the officer who had called me, but I was reluctant to cross the crime scene tape. I could see that one of the front windows of the shop had been completely shattered, the one with *The Satanic Verses* on display in several languages, including the illegal translation into Persian that had been printed in Germany. The sidewalk sparkled with broken glass. A fire hose snaked into the building but I couldn't see anything through the smoke —

no flames, no lights. Two firemen in black and yellow helmets vanished completely as they entered the shop. I needed coffee, but the Medici didn't open till seven o'clock. I needed to go home to tell Dad and Grandpa Chaz, but I couldn't tear myself away. I wanted to be on the scene.

When I was finally able to speak to an officer, I told him I was the owner. He said someone would come to talk to me. I was not to go away. I tried to tell him about the man who'd come into the shop two days earlier, but he told me to wait. As I was waiting, I was aware of a woman standing next to me. I first saw her reflection in part of the shop window across the street that hadn't been shattered by the bomb. I couldn't make out her face in the reflection, but I could see that she was a little bit pregnant and I knew without turning to look that it was Olivia.

I was stunned. I could see Olivia stretching her legs out in a booth at Jimmy's, proposing a toast at our Christmas dinner, sitting alone in Car 8406 as the Lake Shore Limited pulled out of Union Station. And now she was standing right next to me. I turned to her. "Will you marry me?" I said, almost (but not quite) without thinking, because I thought that all of a sudden I understood the truth about love, as if my mind had just opened up to drink in the early morning sunlight, as if I'd just stepped out of Plato's cave into the sun, as if I'd just discovered a new planet.

She laughed. "I'm not looking for someone to rescue me," she said.

I started to protest.

"I've made enough mistakes in my life," she said. "I don't want to make another one." She took a sip of coffee. "But I am looking for a job."

"What are you doing here?"

"I heard about the bombing on WBBM. I couldn't sleep."

"Where'd you get the coffee?"

"Medici."

"Not open yet."

"I know someone. If you go round to the back door . . ."

She offered me a sip of her coffee, and I put my lips where her lips had been. I was thirty-one years old. Too old to be knocked on my ass like that, but that's the way I felt.

"I meant," I said, "when I asked what you were doing here — I meant, what are you doing here in Hyde Park?"

"Let's go to the Medici," she said. "It'll be open by now."

I looked at my wrist. I hadn't put on my

watch. "I'm supposed to wait for the officer in charge. I've got a pretty good idea about who threw the bomb."

"You know who did it?"

"Not exactly, but — We had an Iranian translation of *The Satanic Verses* in the window. The Ayatollah issued a fatwa in February."

"I know about the fatwa, Gabe."

"You know about the bombing at Cody's too? And the Riverdale Press in New York?"

She nodded. "And you know that *The Satanic Verses* was burned in public in Bradford, England, and seven thousand Muslims demonstrated in Bolton?"

This she didn't know.

I called Dad from a pay phone at the Medici. It was hard for him to believe that this was more than a prank, or petty vandalism.

"It wasn't a brick," I said. "They're saying it was a Molotov cocktail." I wasn't really sure what a Molotov cocktail was, but that's what the newspaper had called the bomb at Cody's.

In a booth at the Medici, I told Olivia about the waiter from the Middle Eastern restaurant on Fifty-Fifth Street who'd come into the shop a week before the bombings in San Francisco.

"Right after we put up the display. He wanted to buy the Iranian translation. But he wanted to buy it so he could burn it. I wouldn't sell it to him. 'If that man Rushdie comes into my restaurant,' he said, 'I will kill him.' You think this is normal? You think it's acceptable?"

"I think he was upset."

"These people are insane."

"These people," Olivia said. "Listen to yourself. *These people.* They're just people."

"I suppose the Nazis were *just people* too."

"Rushdie attacked their deepest beliefs, he insulted their religion. The Koran. He made fun of Mohammed, represented him as a brothel keeper. It's like burning the flag in this country, or pissing on it. No wonder *these people* got pissed off. The reason we don't get pissed off about literature in this country is not because we're good and tolerant; it's because we don't care enough about literature to get riled up about it. It's lost its power to get our most important experiences into words."

"People got upset about *Piss Christ*," I said, "and about the Mapplethorpe exhibit. But they didn't lynch Andres Serrano or Mapplethorpe."

"No, but they sent them death threats."

"And you think that's acceptable?" I was

pretty stunned by this position. "You don't like a book or a work of art so it's okay to murder the author, or the artist? Okay to send death threats? How many of the people who are so riled up about *The Satanic Verses* do you suppose have actually read it?"

"Probably not very many."

"Have *you* read it?"

"No."

"There you go."

"How about *you*?"

"I couldn't get through it. I don't think it's a very good book. It's like trying to read Tolkien's *Silmarillion*." We both laughed. "Before the fatwa it wasn't selling very well. The week after the fatwa it sold seven hundred fifty thousand copies.

"Maybe I could get the Ayatollah to issue a fatwa against my dissertation."

"Finished?"

She shook her head and patted her stomach. The curve of her stomach wasn't much more than a little bump, but it struck me as a great mystery, like one of the mysterious mathematical curves that I'd learned to map in Miss Hackberry's geometry class, or was it algebra? — circles, ellipses, parabolas, hyperbolas, and that was only the beginning. I could do the numbers, plot the curves, but I never understood what I was doing, or why. "I'm sorry," I said.

"It's a baby, Gabe. No reason to be sorry. I'm going to keep working on it."

"The baby?"

"The dissertation. I don't need the degree to turn it into a book. I never could figure out how the *Prelude* deconstructed itself, so I went back to my original idea."

"The Romantics," I said, "were the first generation of writers to write in a universe that had no built-in meaning."

"Very good, Mr. Smarty Pants."

I didn't ask her more questions at the time, didn't ask her if the baby had a father. Maybe I didn't want to know.

When I finally talked to the investigating officer, I told him about the waiter from the Middle Eastern restaurant. It was hard for him to believe that someone would bomb a bookshop because of a book.

I told him about the fatwa and the bombings in Berkeley and New York.

"If the book is such a problem," he wanted to know, "why did you put it in the window?"

Three days later no trace remained of the Persian translation or the signed first edition, but they had been replaced by editions in several different languages. The police tape was gone. The smoke had been more or less cleared out by an ozonator. The arson investigators were long gone, the cleanup crew, in yellow hard hats and brown uniforms, were finishing up. The mysterious waiter had been arrested, But a new development took place: Miss Sullivan discovered a pipe bomb in a wastebasket outside the rare book room. She handed it to me as I was coming up the stairs. Dad was in the office, Grandpa Chaz in the catalog room. I was paralyzed. The bomb was in a paper sack, a full-sized grocery sack. Miss Sullivan had opened the sack to show me. In the bottom of the sack you could see two lengths of pipe stuck together with duct tape. There was no sign of a fuse, and I didn't hear any ticking. She told me to put it in the dumpster in the alley. I told her to call 911.

I hadn't had a lot of experience with pipe bombs, but I'd seen Kyle Reese and Sarah Connor assembling pipe bombs in *The Terminator,* so I knew better than to put it down. I went down the stairs and out the back of the shop, out the shipping-and-receiving door, into the alley, cradling the bomb in both hands while I waited for the police, or the bomb squad. The police arrived first. I don't think they'd had much experience with pipe bombs either. They stayed in their cars, lights flashing, blocking both ends of the alley. An officer spoke to me through an electronic bullhorn. "Don't drop it," he said. "We're going to evacuate the area. The Cook County Sheriff's Police Bomb Squad is on the way. Everyone on the squad has completed eight weeks of intense training at the United States Army's Hazardous Devices School in Redstone Arsenal in Huntsville, Alabama. They're going to load a robot that can dismantle a pipe bomb without destroying the evidence by detonating it."

It wasn't easy to master my emotions while holding the pipe bomb. I wasn't even sure I could have put a name on my emotions. Anxiety? Anger? Paranoia? But also the feeling that I was at the center of the universe. Maybe that was it. The feeling probably wouldn't last very long, but I was enjoying it.

Wake up, I thought. *Open your eyes. Olivia is back. I don't know what happened at Yale, and I don't care.* I started to entertain a fantasy about family life that took me a long way into the future. I was imagining that I was holding a child in my arms when Grandpa Chaz came out the back door and started walking toward me. He used a cane now and was hunched a little.

The police yelled at him to go back, and Dad and I yelled too.

"I'm eighty-one years old," he shouted. "Give me the fucking bomb."

"Grandpa, no. Stay back." I hugged the bomb tighter. The eyes in his old face glowed like coals.

He kept coming, but just before he reached me, two police officers converged on him and wrestled him back to the loading dock. I was stepping backward all the time, trying not to trip on the uneven bricks in the alley. Grandpa Chaz kept shouting: "I'm eighty-one years old, give me the fucking bomb."

The robot finally arrived, delivered in what looked like an oversize UPS truck. It had been developed in Northern Ireland, where pipe bombs were the order of the day, and was operated remotely by a technician who watched it on a closed-circuit TV screen as it trundled over the rough bricks in the alley. It was bright yellow and looked like a small tank with jaws on the end of a long robotic arm.

"Take the bomb out of the sack and place it gently in the jaws."

He had my attention now. The bomb was becoming more real, if there are degrees of reality. I was having trouble breathing. I looked into the sack and then at the jaws and then back again. "It's not going to fit," I said. "There are two pipes."

"Fuck."

The bomb squad conferenced.

Time passed. A rat ran out from under the dumpster behind Benny's Steakhouse, where we sometimes ate supper after an especially long day, took one look at the situation, and turned around. For one second I forgot about the bomb, but I didn't drop it.

After a while two bomb squad guys in bomb suits, looking as if they were getting ready to land on the moon, came lumbering toward me with an X-ray unit. "They're going to take a picture of the bomb." The electronic megaphone made the speaker sound like an old gramophone. "The cable they're dragging will link the pictures to a Telex screen."

It took a long time for the two men to reach me. I could see the rat, under the dumpster, watching us.

"You said they're two pipes? How big?" I held up thumb and first finger in a circle.

"Jesus," he said. "Don't let go of the sack. Two pipes, about two inches in diameter."

They set up a real-time X-ray camera on

a tripod, aiming it at the package cradled in my arms. "Hold real still now. Smile. It works like a scanner at the airport. There's no balance switch on the bomb, or it would have gone off when you picked it up in the store."

They took several shots at different angles.

Another bomb squad guy shouted from the van: "It's a bomb all right, but it looks like the timer's maybe fucked. It's in the bottom of the sack."

The robot was standing by.

"Looks like a kid's alarm clock."

"You're going to hand me the sack now. Real easy. Make sure I've got it."

I handed over the sack.

"Now get the hell out of here."

I got the hell out.

Dad was talking to someone through the window of a police car at the end of the alley. Grandpa Chaz was standing with his back against the loading dock. "You stupid son-of-a-bitch," he said when I reached him. "I'm eighty-one years old."

"You wanted to be the hero, didn't you?" I said.

He looked surprised and then he laughed. "So did you!"

"The bomb failed to explode," I explained

to Olivia on the following Monday, "because the pressure buildup from the chemical reaction had not exceeded the casing strength of the two-inch wrought steel pipes. At first they thought there was a problem with the alarm clock — a 'Tiny Tot' alarm clock. But the alarm clock was working just fine." We were standing in front of the shop. "If I'd dropped it, though, the shock would have ruptured the statically pressurized casing. If the bomb had gone off, it would have destroyed all the rare books and killed everyone in the shop. Well, it would have killed me."

"Then you'd be a martyr too — Hyde Park's first Salman Rushdie martyr."

"Jesus, Olivia. You're a piece of work."

"What exactly does that mean, 'you're a piece of work'?"

"I means that you're an interesting person but difficult to get along with. You complicate the simplest thing, set yourself in opposition to the clearest things."

"Okay. I can accept that."

"Good," I said. "We've reached some common ground."

"Are you going to offer me a job?"

"Of course. We need someone to work the first floor and keep an eye on the children's books. Janice Holmes is not coming back.

She's the only one, though."

"I can handle that. One more thing, though. How did the pipe bomb get into the wastebasket on the second floor? You wouldn't throw a fire bomb through the front window and *then* go into the store and put a pipe bomb on the second floor. Whoever put it there must have left it in the shop the day before. He may be coming back."

"Right," I said. "He or *she.*"

"Right," she said. "*Or she.* Then we'll all be martyrs."

"The waiter from the restaurant's still in custody, but he's got a solid alibi for the Molotov cocktail. The pipe bomb's more problematic. The lead detective said they're going to hold on to the waiter for a while and take a good look at the mosque on Stony Island, and all the other mosques too — especially out in Devon — but they can't patrol the shop."

"Mosque Maryam," Olivia said. "That's the Nation of Islam. They don't have much truck with Muslim Muslims. Or vice versa."

"But it's right around the corner."

"That's like looking for your keys under the streetlight," Olivia said, "instead of looking where you think you dropped them."

Dad put on a good front, but Grandpa Chaz was shaken and insisted on hiring a night watchman. The Sullivan sisters' hair turned white over the next two weeks. The waiter was released from custody. He'd been at work on the night of the bombing, and the fingerprints on the dismantled pipe bomb belonged to somebody else.

Every morning the floor staff patrolled the aisles, reshelving books that had been left on tables or on the floor, restoring the world to order in a rough approximation of the Dewey Decimal System: philosophy, psychology, religion, social science, languages, science, history and geography, literature, the arts.

Olivia continued to work at the shop until the end of August. She went into labor on a Friday morning, September 15. Aunt Fern called me at the shop and wanted me to come to the hospital. I walked to Bernard Mitchell Hospital on Fifty-Eighth Street. Aunt Fern was waiting for me in the second-floor lobby.

"I told them she was waiting for her husband," she said. "So you'll be able to be

81

with her."

I was surprised but not annoyed. In fact — catching a glimpse of my subconscious — I realized I was secretly pleased.

"I'm not the father. You know that."

"Of course I know that, but it doesn't matter now, does it?"

"I'm not sure she'd want me there, to see, I mean . . ." I didn't really know what I meant.

"That doesn't matter either. Just go to her."

There was some coming and going in the maternity ward. A nurse led me into a tiny bathroom to change into a hospital gown and told me to scrub my hands, really scrub them. Which I did. "She's already in stir-rups," the nurse said when I came out of the bathroom. "The cervix must be one hundred percent effaced and ten centime-ters dilated before a vaginal delivery. You're here just in time."

In the birth room Olivia was completely exposed. Her legs forced apart. The insides of her thighs smooth and shiny and white as eggs.

"She's already at six centimeters," the nurse said. "You can put compresses on her face. Here. Just wipe her forehead."

Olivia noticed me for the first time. "I

didn't expect to see you here."

"Your aunt called me."

"She wants to marry me off. She wants someone to look after me. Someone else. Someone not her. But don't worry. I don't need anyone to look after me."

She went into a contraction and started to scream.

"Do you want me to call a nurse? What about your doctor?"

"He was here earlier," she said when she stopped screaming. "I was on my way to the shop when my water broke. It didn't really 'break.' I thought I'd peed myself."

"You're sure you don't want me to go out in the hall and call someone?"

"It's all right, Gabe," she said. But then she started to scream again as another contraction came on.

"When my water broke," she said again, "it wasn't like the movies — a water balloon hitting the sidewalk. It went on for hours. And I didn't have to rush to the hospital right away. I went into the Medici and called my aunt. She called the doctor and picked me up in a taxi."

The nurse came in and cuffed her and pumped up the cuff. "I want you to close your eyes and imagine your cervix opening up like a flower," she said to Olivia. "You too," she said, nodding at me.

"I don't have a cervix," I said. I wasn't sure what a cervix was. I didn't *think* I had a cervix. But maybe I did. "Do I?"

She laughed. "Just use your imagination."

I imagined a cervix opening up like a flower. I could feel it. Could feel myself turning inside out.

"I want you to keep putting these cold compresses on her forehead," the nurse said.

"Talk to me, Gabe. A poem, anything." Olivia wanted a poem? What poem? Keats? Part of "The Eve of St. Agnes"? I didn't have a copy. Why hadn't I memorized it? Well, I had memorized the part about Porphyro melting into her dream, but it didn't seem appropriate right now. All I could think of was Yeats's "Long-Legged Fly" — a series of private moments: Caesar in his tent before crossing the Rubicon, Helen of Troy practicing a tinker's shuffle, Michelangelo up at the top of the Sistine Chapel. These were great mysteries, but not as great as the mystery I was watching. And Olivia's mind wasn't moving upon silence, like Yeats's daddy longlegs. She started to scream again. I wiped her forehead. "I didn't want it to be easy," she said when the contraction had run its course.

"Things were too easy for us," I said, lean-

84

ing over her. "Dad wanted us to get married. Your aunt too. And I didn't have a wife to get in the way . . . Maybe that was the problem. We needed an obstacle. A naked sword in the bed between us." She started to scream again.

An hour later the nurse handed me a baby. *The* baby. Baby Saskia, eight pounds four ounces. Holding her in my arms was like holding the pipe bomb, but even more frightening. Even more dangerous.

V. 100,000 Books

(JANUARY 1990)

I was on a high. I'd been right there in the delivery room at Bernard Mitchell when Baby Saskia was born. I'd stepped into the role of surrogate husband and father. I began to fantasize about marriage and family life, and Aunt Fern encouraged these fantasies. In her eyes I was a hero. In my own eyes too, I suppose.

Olivia, on the other hand, was suffering from postpartum depression and needed cheering up. I invited her to drive out with me to Cardinal Newman College in Lake Forest to look at a large cache of books. The college had been founded by Monsignor Joseph Reitman back in the sixties. Monsignor Reitman had a pal in the Vatican Library who'd hung on to a lot of duplicates that had been withdrawn and books that had never been cataloged in the first place. When Monsignor Reitman went to Rome to get the charter for the college, he bought them all and had them crated up and shipped to Lake Forest. Now that Monsignor Reitman was dead and the college had closed, the diocese wanted to unload the books to pay off creditors. They needed someone they could trust not to rip them off, and they wanted to avoid publicity. They had a potential buyer for half the campus and were in a hurry to get the books out of the old library. Ben Warren, one of our collectors and a member of the Caxton Club, was on the board of trustees. His brother was an editor at *Commentary,* and Ben had given them my name. In 1990, it was easier to sell good material than to buy it, so I was eager to look at the books.

Olivia was waiting for me in the turnaround in front of the 1700 building, where she was living with her aunt, who was going to look after Baby Saskia, who was now almost five months old, not able to sit up on her own yet, but able to recognize my voice and to play peek-a-boo.

It was January 1990. Ice was chunked up around the edge of the lake. The heater in the van wasn't quite enough to keep our feet warm. I took the Outer Drive all the way to Green Bay Avenue. We passed McElroy's, where Mamma got her fur coat. I reminded Olivia of the story.

"The coat's still in her closet," I said. "Would you like it?"

"Mink?" she said. "Are you kidding?" But at least she smiled. "Where did you say we're going?" she asked.

I had to remind her that we were going to Cardinal Newman College in Lake Forest.

"I thought it was closed."

"It is," I said, "but the trustees still have a boatload of books from the Vatican on their hands that they want to turn into cash."

"Are you going to buy them?"

"We'll see what there is. We'll buy some. Maybe a lot. There's bound to be a lot of junk that's not worth the cost of shipping."

We followed Sheridan Road through some of the wealthiest suburbs in the United States: Evanston, Wilmette, Winnetka, Kenilworth, Glencoe, Highland Park. We didn't talk about the Romantics, about the new sources of meaning — Nature, Art, the Romantic Hero. Olivia was done with the Romantics. She sat in the passenger seat staring out the window, when I asked her what was the matter, she said: *angst, nausée, ennui* — and winter in Chicago. She was in the passenger seat and her face was in the morning sun, turned away from me, but I could tell she wasn't smiling.

In front of the Administration Building, a

red brick Victorian relic, originally part of a seminary, we were met by a priest, a handsome man in black clericals. Father Gregory, SJ.

We introduced ourselves and shook hands. His black robe gave me a little frisson, because it made me think of the stories that Grandpa Chaz and Clare Duval told about the Jesuit fathers who'd been tortured by the Iroquois.

"I've never shaken hands with a Jesuit before," Olivia said.

Father Gregory laughed. "Let's get some coffee to take with us," he said. "I've got some water going in the staff kitchen."

We never got an exact count of the books, but Father Gregory thought there were well over a hundred thousand. I was astonished. The college had been closed for almost a year. The college library had been moved to a seminary in Wisconsin, and most of the Vatican books had been put on the shelves in the old library, in no particular order. Others were in boxes on the floor in the unheated basement of the Administration Building, or piled on trestle tables in the old gymnasium. Some were still in crates covered with colorful stamps and stamped *Poste Vatican* in the basement of one of the dormitories.

■ ■ ■ ■

By four o'clock in the afternoon, we were frozen. We'd probably looked at — or walked past — twenty thousand books, and that was just the beginning. Father Gregory boiled more water in the little kitchen and spooned some instant coffee into Styrofoam cups. "A lot of dealers would give their eyeteeth to have a look at these books," he said.

"Then you should have invited a lot of dealers at the outset, which is what I suggested, instead of asking me to look at a hundred thousand books. What exactly are you trying to accomplish here anyway? Do you want to start a bidding war? I could arrange a shelf auction or a bulk auction. Invite dealers to bid on two or three hundred books at a time. All or nothing."

"All right," he said. "Forget about other dealers. What we want is to turn these books into cash without making a lot of noise. St. Mary's College got a lot of bad press when they sold off their rare books. Like Ronald Reagan wanting to sell off the rare book collections in the Bancroft Library at the University of California. The bishop doesn't want that to happen to us. The main thing is to make sure we're not unloading something really valuable, like a Gutenberg Bible or a Shakespeare First Folio."

"Unlikely," I said. "Most of these books are going to wind up in the landfill."

"The landfill!" Father Gregory was indignant. But I was right, most of these books were going to wind up in the landfill. On the other hand, there were some treasures here too, and I wanted to get my hands on them. I'd seen too much to turn back. It was a huge opportunity for the shop, but I didn't want to be too obvious about it.

"What if we just sent the books to Christie's or Sotheby's?" Father Gregory asked.

"Father Gregory," I said. "Christie's and Sotheby's are not going to sell any lots under five thousand dollars, and they're not going to sort through a hundred thousand books."

Olivia hadn't touched her coffee. I'd drunk about half of mine. It wasn't any better than it had been in the morning.

"Here's what I suggest," I said. "I'll pick out some books for the shop and offer you a fair price. I'll box them up and send a truck to pick them up. Then we'll pick out a couple thousand books and I'll arrange to sell them at auction at Swann's. You've got to understand that you won't get market value from a dealer. Any dealer. You won't get market value from me, but you'll do better if I go through them first. You might see your fifth edition of Burton's *Anatomy* in a catalog for four or five thousand, but that doesn't mean that a dealer will give you four or five thousand. It means that a dealer might give you a thousand, if you're lucky."

"All right," he said. "All right."

We'd walked the stacks for six hours. We hadn't eaten. I was ready to go home, but Olivia had disappeared. Father Gregory and I started to look around. After a few minutes we started shouting: *Olivia, Olivia, Olivia.* We were starting to retrace our steps when she came out of the bathroom in the administration building. She'd been crying. Father Gregory and I crowded around her. I thought she looked beautiful.

She turned to Father Gregory. "Before we go," she said, "there's something I'd like to ask you."

"Ask away."

"This is kind of private," she said, turning to me.

I was taken by surprise. Father Gregory too. He pulled a package of cigarettes from a pocket under his Jesuit robe.

"Could I have one?" she said.

I backed away. I didn't want to hear this, didn't want to intrude. It was embarrassing. Well, of course, I did want to hear, didn't want to miss anything, but I thought backing away was the right thing to do. Was there something about Father Gregory that I'd missed? Something that invited this sort of confession?

"What would you say," I heard Olivia ask, "to someone who was thinking of becoming a Roman Catholic?"

Father Gregory tapped the pack of cigarettes expertly against his wrist and offered one to Olivia. Olivia said something I couldn't make out. Father Gregory lit their cigarettes and the smoke curled up and disappeared. "I would say," he said, inhaling deeply, "if someone were to ask me . . . I would say . . . I would want to know what's troubling you right now, at this moment in your life? As you're standing here with me."

I couldn't hear Olivia's answer.

"You're turning everything inward," I heard the priest say. I remembered Olivia smoking with Dad in the warming shed at the ice rink. Dad smoking too.

"Like a teenager," I heard, or thought I heard, Olivia say.

The priest shook his head.

Olivia's back was toward me. The priest

kept his head down. He touched her shoulder, her arm. She kept her head down too. I was thinking about all the books. Was it like winning the lottery? Or was I like the guy at the end of *Beowulf* who stumbles on the dragon's treasure — and unfortunately wakes the sleeping dragon. I'd have to talk it over with Dad.

Father Gregory made the sign of the cross over Olivia. It was time to go.

Instead of following Sheridan Road, we drove back on the Edens Expressway, not saying a word till we saw the sign for Highland Park. I asked her about her tête-à-tête with Father Gregory, but she didn't want to talk about it.

"Up ahead, Gabe," she said suddenly. "What's that? You'd better slow down."

It wasn't snowing, but a heavy black cloud had settled down over the highway ahead of us, stretching east to the lake and west as far as we could see. But it didn't look like a cloud. It looked like a solid mass.

"Gabe, we're driving into the side of a mountain . . ."

The cloud-mountain was outlined in black against a dark gray sky that was only slightly lighter than the cloud itself. You could see summits and peaks silhouetted, like mountain peaks. Nothing moved. It was a solid mass. It was hard not to see it as a mountain.

"Don't you see it?"

I did see it.

"Gabe, slow down."

"I'm only going fifty."

Olivia was starting to tremble. "Gabe, we're going to crash into it."

"It's just a cloud."

"It doesn't look like a cloud. You should pull over."

I knew it was just a cloud. What else could it be? But the illusion that it was a solid mass, a mountain, was too strong. I couldn't see it any other way. But I kept on driving. Other cars were driving too, disappearing. Cars were coming toward us, out of the mountain. Headlights on.

"If it's a solid mountain, where are the cars going, or coming from?"

"There must be tunnels."

"We're on the Eden's Expressway. There are no tunnels. Or if there *are* tunnels, we can go through them too."

"You see it too, don't you."

I had to admit that I did.

"Please, Gabe. Pull over."

"You want someone to run into us?"

"No, Gabe, no. It's too horrible." She

95

started to unfasten her seat belt.

"Don't do that."

"I can't help it, Gabe. You've got to pull over. I have to get out of the van. I'm going to scream." She was breathing hard, as she had been earlier. "Once I start, I won't be able to stop. I'll just keep on screaming."

I pulled over, and Olivia jumped out of the van and started to walk up and down on a paper-thin layer of snow.

More snow was starting to fall. Light snow. Out of the light gray sky. Olivia sat down. I turned the engine off and got out of the van. I was frightened too. I sat next to her on the verge, in tallish grass. About a quarter inch of snow. I was afraid to touch her. She was twitching. I got up and stood behind her. Defenseless. Her hair was tied back with what looked like an old shoelace. I hadn't noticed it before. I put my hand on her head. She didn't move. I massaged her shoulders. She was very tense.

"Think about Saskia," I said. "Think how happy she is. And your aunt. It's good to have an aunt. I've always wished I had an aunt."

When I closed my eyes, I could see her as a young girl. Before I'd known her — though I had almost no images of her child-hood apart from a few photos — holding a chicken in her arms, on a farm in Goshen, Indiana; in her prom dress in front of her aunt's big house in Evanston. I could see her standing outside the shop in her EN-CHANTED BOAT sweatshirt; sitting across the table from me at Jimmy's after we'd put together the Orwell display.

Cars disappeared into the mountain and other cars appeared. We sat in the snow till the wind started to blow in from the lake and blew the mountain away, and we got back in the van and drove off.

We didn't talk about what had happened till we were back in Hyde Park. "You were right to keep on driving," she said as we pulled into the turnaround in front of the 1700 Building. "But I was right too, to be afraid. I think the mountain was a mountain of books. Father Gregory said you could read all those books and still not under-stand. You drove right into it, but I pan-icked."

"Understand what?"

"Understand what's important. He didn't say. Maybe it's not something you can *say.* He gave me a book that he said would help me. But it's in French. How am I supposed to read it?" She produced the book from her green book bag. Yellow, soft-cover, prob-ably from the twenties: *La vie intellectuelle;*

son esprit, ses conditions, ses méthodes.
"It's by a Dominican priest."

"You can read French," I said.

"Not a whole book."

Was she joking? I didn't know what to say, didn't know what to hope for. A car was pulling in behind us, and Randall, the doorman, was opening Olivia's door. So I didn't say anything, tried not to hope for anything. I pulled out of the turnaround and drove back to Blackstone, trying to figure out what had just happened so I could explain it to Dad.

It took me six weeks, off and on, to go through the books at Cardinal Newman College. I'd take a sandwich with me and eat it in the little kitchenette. I'd make coffee in Mamma's Moka pot because I couldn't stand the powdered coffee that was the only thing on offer at Cardinal Newman.

Dad and I spent some long evenings sitting at the partner's desk in the office at the shop, sipping some of Dad's Balvenie 10, consulting Allen and Patricia Ahearn's *Book Prices Current,* going through old auction catalogs in our reference library — records for the books themselves and similar books — looking at our own records of similar books in our card catalog, filling long yellow legal pads with our calculations. Arguing about tentative prices, and about whom to quote *to,* what to put in a catalog. You're willing to spend a lot more on a book that you figure you can sell with a phone call than you are on a book that's likely to sit on your shelf for two or three years, or five or ten years. I already had two customers in mind for an early Geneva Bible, but the seven volume supplement to Diderot's *Encyclopédie*? Keep it or send it to Swann's? Today you could go online and see how many copies were owned by libraries in the United States, and that would give you a pretty good idea of how scarce it was. But in 1990? It wasn't listed in *American Book Prices Current,* but we decided to hang on to it.

At the end of February, I laid the results of these calculations out for Father Gregory in the little kitchenette, where I'd been eating my sandwiches at lunchtime. I offered him $40,000 for 2,000 books I thought I could sell for $100 apiece, and $72,000 for 600 books I thought I could sell for $600 apiece. A total of $60,000. In short, I offered $112,000 for 2,600 books. And I offered to sell the high-end items on consignment: a Wicked Bible with a famous misprint ("Thou shalt commit adultery"), a

German Bible (the only incunable), Burton's *Anatomy of Melancholy,* three books of hours, the supplement to Diderot's *Encyclopédie,* the Evelyn translation of Lucretius, and Vesalius's *De humani corporis* (seven volumes, 1568). And finally, I arranged for another three thousand books to be sent to Swann Galleries to be auctioned off over a period of two years.

He wasn't happy, but he wasn't up for a fight. He didn't want to wait two or three years for three thousand books to be auctioned off at Swann's; he didn't want to wait two or three years or more for me to sell the high-end items on commission; he didn't want to worry about separating the remaining books into sheep and goats. In the end, I agreed to take everything: I offered him four hundred thousand for the lot — for about fifty-six hundred books I hoped to sell for two and a half million, though some of those books would sit on our shelves for three or four years. Or five. Or ten. But it was good material and would sell in the end.

"It will take a few days to get the money together," I said.

"That's all right," he said. "Just get the books out of here. I don't want to see them. Or maybe I don't want them to see me. We never had any use for them."

"I'll come out tomorrow with a truck and boxes and some college kids to pack the books — books for the shop, books for Swann's, books for the landfill. It will take a couple of days."

We sealed the deal with a drink, not in the kitchenette but in Father Gregory's modest office, which was full of his own books, on collapsible folding shelves, the kind we used to display our books at book fairs.

He got two jelly glasses from the cupboard and poured us each a little Scotch, Cutty Sark. The office was cold. We kept our coats on. I asked him what he'd said to Olivia at the end of our first visit.

"You should ask *her*."

"I have." I tasted the Scotch. "What would you say to *me*?"

"Are *you* considering joining the church?"

"No."

"I didn't think so."

"What happened here anyway?" I asked.

"Monsignor Reitman," he said, "was too idealistic. We all were. A classical education in a Roman Catholic framework — a 'clear, calm, accurate vision and comprehension of all things, as far as the finite mind can embrace them.' It worked for Cardinal Newman, though he didn't actually found a university, but we couldn't make it work here. We couldn't agree on a science curriculum. We took on ten million dollars in debt thinking we could triple our enrollment by 1985, four years after we opened our doors, but we never had more than three hundred students. We needed another two million for repairs. The accrediting agency put us on probation . . ."

"O tempus, O mores," I said.

"Cicero," he said. "Cardinal Newman patterned his style on Cicero." He was sitting at his desk. He swiveled around and looked out the window. "Come over here," he said.

I stood beside his chair and looked out the window.

"When Cardinal Newman left Oxford on February 23, 1846, he recalled the snapdragons that had been growing on the wall opposite his window in his first college, Trinity College. He took them as an emblem — 'my own perpetual residence even unto death in my own University.' That's what I'm going to be doing now. Recalling snapdragons. You see where your van is parked?"

I could see the van in front of the Administration Building.

"You see those Italian pots? They look like terra cotta but they're actually plastic. If they were terracotta, they'd have cracked during the winter. They should have been taken inside anyway, but there's no one left to do that sort of thing."

I nodded.

"I filled those pots with snapdragons every spring in honor of Cardinal Newman. They're annuals. You can grow them as perennials, but not this far north."

"My grandfather planted daylilies," I said. "Our yard is full of them. They come back every year."

"Maybe that's what I should have planted," he said. "Daylilies."

VI. THE ANATOMY OF MELANCHOLY

(MARCH 1990)

I didn't know what to make of Olivia's visionary mountain, or her private conversations with Father Gregory, but I was on a high, not just because of the book deal, but because Olivia had come out of her funk. She reorganized the children's books on the first floor and started a story hour on Saturday mornings — leaving baby Saskia with her aunt, who brought her to the shop twice a day so Olivia could nurse her in the staff room. She was a little prickly, uncomfortable about accepting help, but we saw each other every day, often in intimate circumstances (nursing the baby in the staff room). Dad still wanted me to marry her. He wanted a grandson, or a granddaughter, someone who would carry the shop into the fourth generation when the time came. And Olivia's aunt, who always spoke her mind, also wanted me to marry her. "Gabe," she said one blustery winter day as she was

104

tucking Saskia's little arms and legs into a snowsuit. "Take her out to dinner. Tell her you love her. It's not that hard. She doesn't want to burden you with somebody else's child. But I don't think you're worried about that."

I no longer needed a philosophy of life because I knew what I wanted: I wanted Olivia, and I took her aunt's words to heart and took her out to dinner on her birthday. We went to a tapas bar on the near north side. Our shoulders touched as the Jeffrey Express bus jostled us along the Outer Drive.

It was a Saturday night and the restaurant was crowded. We ate olives and anchovies and serrano ham and garlic and olive oil on boiled potatoes, while we waited to order, and we drank wine out of a *porrón.*

"Remember the Orwell exhibit?" she said. "Orwell hated *porrónes.* He thought they looked like bed bottles, especially if you're drinking white wine. As soon as he saw a *porrón,* he asked for a glass." But she drank expertly, holding the *porrón* at arm's length and letting the stream of wine arc into her open mouth, saying *"Donde es Gregorio"* while drinking. She didn't even have to wipe her mouth after she set the *porrón* down.

I picked up the *porrón* but my hand was

trembling and I put it back down. "Do you remember what I wrote in the Keats book I gave you for Christmas, the Christmas you spent with us? Eighteen twenty. First edition."

"What is this, Gabe? I know what you wrote in it. You were such a Romantic, with a capital R."

Something clicked. "You don't have it, do you?"

"Gabe," she said after waiting a beat. "I had a hard time in New Haven. I was miserable, all right? It wasn't like Chicago. I didn't fit in. Nobody wanted to direct my dissertation. They were too busy deconstructing everything to worry about the first generation of writers to write in a universe that didn't have a built-in meaning. I had an affair with a professor — David — because I thought he might take on my dissertation, and he did, but he wanted me to deconstruct Wordsworth's *Prelude.* He said it would be easy because the *Prelude* deconstructed itself. I fell in love with him, actually, and his wife found out and complained to the chair of the department and to the dean and to the president and she wrote a letter to the Yale *Daily News* begging faculty members not to fuck their students while their wives were at home making coq au vin or paella."

"You didn't get kicked out?"

"No, but David did . . . Well, not exactly. They told him he wouldn't get tenure. He'd published one book — *Deconstructing Keats's Odes.* I thought it was brilliant but they said that wasn't enough. But that wasn't the real reason. He landed at the University of Michigan, so that was okay, probably better. For him. But he left before I figured out how the *Prelude* deconstructed itself."

"Do you still love him?"

"I didn't love him at first. But after a while everything changed. I thought we'd belonged together from the beginning of time. I thought he was a force of Nature. That sort of thing. That was how it started. You know what Keats wrote to Fanny Brawne?"

I shook my head. "I have no idea what Keats wrote to Fanny Brawne."

"It doesn't matter," she said, "but my thoughts flew out the window when I saw David coming down Chapel Street."

"Did he melt into your dream?"

"Don't make fun of me."

"And now?"

"I don't know, Gabe. I don't know anything."

"Did he know you were pregnant?"

107

"Yes. No. I don't know. I don't think so. I told you, I don't know anything. I was a different person then."

"Why didn't you tell him?"

"I didn't want him to feel trapped."

"I see," I said, though I didn't see. "It's all right," I said. "Are you ready to order?"

"Why don't we just sit here," she said, "and eat some more tapas and drink some more wine."

I understood then that she was going to wait for David to divorce his wife.

I hardly slept that night. In the morning I walked over to the Abrams Funeral Home to see Delilah, who was on call on Sunday mornings. It was as if the world — the banks, the churches, the Quadrangle Club, Mandel Hall, the Regenstein Library, the coffee shop on the corner of Drexel, the hospitals — had been stripped of meaning. I turned south on Cottage Grove, thinking of an old song Grandpa Chaz used to sing: "She used to live out on Indiana Avenue, moved to Sixty-Third and Cottage Grove. Used to live out on Indiana Avenue, moved to Sixty-Third and Cottage Grove. She took all of my money, stole all of my clothes." I needed to see Delilah. Delilah's dad, Parker Abrams, had buried my grandmother, and he'd bury the rest of us. I, for one, was ready. I'd recently sold him a first edition of Carl van Bechtel's *Nigger Heaven.* He was a longtime member of the Caxton Club. Dad had helped him put together a first-rate Langston Hughes collection.

I sat down in a padded chair in the funeral home office and tried to bring my thoughts and emotions into a quiet place. Delilah shoved her way through a curtain and looked up from the book she had folded around her thumb.

"How can I help you," she said automatically. And then, "Gabe, what's going on? Your dad okay?"

"He's okay. I just need a place to be quiet for a minute or two."

"You want to come in the back?"

"I think I'll just sit out here for a minute."

"What happened?"

I told her. "She's waiting for David to divorce his wife."

She nodded.

"You knew? And you didn't tell me?"

"Not my place. When a woman like that falls in love with a man," she said, "her whole world opens up like a flower, like she's discovering a new world. You've got to understand that. It's different for a man."

"What do you mean 'a woman like that'?"

"Soft on the outside; tough as old leather on the inside." I had trouble taking this in. "Maybe this'll shatter your illusions," she said. "Help you out of old Plato's cave. Like somebody watching TV so hard they can't see the real world, and then stepping outside into a sunny afternoon."

"We don't have a TV," I said.

"I forgot," she said.

The phone rang. Delilah answered, asked for information, repeated the address and the phone number as she was writing them down. "Someone will be there in a little while."

I picked up a pamphlet on grief and looked at the pictures.

"Mrs. Jackson," Delilah said, "you're going to have to call your doctor, or the coroner, or I can do that for you. And then I want you just to sit quietly for a little while. You don't have to do anything. I know it's hard, but I just want you to sit quietly for the next half hour." I thought for a minute she was talking to me. "Yes," she went on. "In the same room. It's okay . . . Go right ahead . . . Is somebody with you? . . . I see. Then my brother and another man will be on their way, but we can't bring him to the home till he's officially pronounced dead."

Suddenly I wasn't angry. I wasn't anything at all.

She hung up and turned to me. "Somebody just stepped out of the cave."

"I see you've got a new sign," I said. "A new motto."

" 'Any man's death diminishes me' — John Donne."

"Remind me," I said. "What was the old one?"

" 'Experience the difference,' " she said. "My grandfather came up with that. Never felt quite right to Daddy."

"Big difference," I said. "Big difference. You're alive and then you're dead. Hard to compare the two experiences, unless you're like Lazarus."

"Hard to know. Lazarus didn't sound too happy when he came back."

"Well, he was all bound up. Must have been uncomfortable."

"Grandpop was thinking of the quality of service we provided. He couldn't see it any other way. You want me to give you something to read, take your mind off your troubles?"

"Something to read?"

"Something to help you make it through the rest of the day. If the phone rings, don't answer it. I'll pick up in the back."

She shoved the curtain aside and disappeared. While she was gone, I started to read the pamphlet on grief. There was nothing to disagree with, but nothing that went beyond the obvious.

Delilah came back in with a book. I didn't bother to look at it. "You're going to have to let go of that woman. She's going to do what she wants to do, not what you want her to do. You've got to accept that. You get to work on the new catalog and you'll be okay. Those Cardinal Newman books are not going to catalog themselves."

I put the book under my arm and walked home and told Dad what had happened. "I'm going to lie down and read," I said.

That night Dad made a salad and cooked a couple of hamburgers. We sat in the living room and read. The book Delilah had given me was an ARC (advance reading copy) of a detective novel by Walter Mosley, *Devil in a Blue Dress.* The protagonist, Easy Rawlins, is a work in progress — an out-of-work day laborer on his way to becoming a hardboiled detective. The woman he's hired to find — a white woman, Monet — turns out to be a light-skinned black woman whose real name is Ruby.

We turned in early. I told Dad I wanted to get an early start on cataloging the Cardinal

Newman books in the morning. They were still in boxes in our cataloging room. But I stayed up and read for a long time.

It had been a long time since I'd been pulled so hard into a story. I read it the way I used to read as a child, totally absorbed. By the time Easy got things sorted out — killing a couple of people and blackmailing Ruby along the way — it was past midnight.

If Punch had still been alive, I'd have reached over the edge of the bed and scratched the top of his head, but Punch had died a long time ago.

Delilah was right. Descriptive bibliography may not seem like a lot of fun to most people, but it was exactly what I needed to do. I needed to pay close attention to something that was right in front of me. I needed to look at it the way an artist looks at a leaf or a flower or a human face. A lot hinges on descriptions. This is where a book dealer shows his stuff. The main thing, as Grandpa Chaz liked to say — and if he had a philosophy of life, this was it — is to give the book a life, make it accessible, cherished, wanted. Who owned it? When was it bought and sold? Who did the restoration? Who's ex libris is glued to the upper pastedown? Why is this book important? And like any intimate physical experience, it can be healing. You touch the body of the book: the raised bands on the spine, the smooth leather stretched over the boards, the fore edge, the endpapers, the headbands, the hinges. You hold it to your nose and smell it, you sleep with the book, so to speak. You pay close attention to every physical detail: to rubbed edges; to worm holes (tunnels created by the larvae of various kinds of beetle that may cut out letters, such as the death watch beetle or the common furniture beetle); to hinges that have been reinforced; to foxing (fox-colored spots caused by sunlight); to the sewing; to the quality of the leather — Grandpa Chaz claimed that he could feel the difference between goat skin and calf, though scientists say you can't really tell without DNA testing; you pay attention to the quality of the original binding or subsequent rebindings; to marginalia; to issue points, like the misprint in the "Wicked Bible"; to indications of provenance, like a coat of arms stamped in the compartments on the spine or library marks; to a printer's device stamped on the boards, to woodcuts, maps, illustrations (making sure all are accounted for); to owner's marks and inscriptions; to small tears; to ink holes and water stains; to the end bands, to library stamps, such as the stamp for the Vatican secret archives. To deaccession stamps too, of course. We worked in silence except for occasional eruptions from Grandpa Chaz, who was working on an eighteenth-century French cookbook and kept reading bits of the recipes aloud.

In the middle of March — we had cataloged over two hundred books — I picked up *The Anatomy of Melancholy,* which I had set aside.

THE
ANATOMY OF
MELANCHOLY
What it is, with all the kinds,
symptoms, prognostics & Several cures
of it.
To three Partitions, with their several
Sections, numbers & subsections.
Philosophically, Medically,
Historically opened & cut up.
BY
Democritus Junior
[i.e. Robert Burton]

The Anatomy was an old friend. We were glad to see each other — old friends bumping into each other in a crowded subway car — and reminisce about Dudley Sanderson's class in seventeenth-century literature, on the third flood of Wieboldt Hall.

First published in 1621, over twenty years before Harvey's *Anatomical Exercises Concerning the Motion of the Heart and Blood,* Burton's *Anatomy* looked back to the old world of the four humors — the four bodily fluids that were thought to shape our psyches, our temperaments, our personality types: blood, yellow bile, black bile, phlegm — corresponding to sanguine, choleric, melancholic, phlegmatic. At the same time, it looked forward. It was one of the first works to consider the problem of mental illness in any depth. (In those days, Love was still regarded, as it had been in the Middle Ages, as a medical illness.) As I was collating the first "book," I paused at Part 3, Sect. 3, Memb. 1. Subs. 1. "Love Melancholy," to see if I could recognize myself. If Olivia was phlegmatic — cool, calm, composed, thoughtful — I was melancholic — serious, introverted, contentious but susceptible to depression. Maybe that was the problem. Maybe not. If love melancholy was the foundation of chivalry ("heroic melancholy") and a source of poetic inspiration, it could also be a devastating illness (*ferinus insanus amor* in men, *furor uterinus* in women) that required medical treatment.

Burton likens it to the plague, to a torture so severe that "in a word, the Spanish inquisition is not comparable to it." Hmmm. What can be done?

The cure for love melancholy, of course, is marriage, a cure that brings its own set of challenges. Books are not quite as reliable, but they can help:

> And if I were not a King, I would be an Vniuer ity man; *And if it were so that I must be a Prisoner, if I might haue my wish, I would dessire to haue no other Prison then that Library, and to be chained together with so many good Authors.*

The library that Burton refers to here is the Bodleian. I was thinking of the room I was in right at that moment, between Oscar, who was still collating the plates in the Diderot, and Grandpa Chaz, who'd finished collating the cookbook and had moved on to something else.

Would I be content to stay here, to be a prisoner in this room, surrounded by these books and by my bibliographic tools? I started to answer in the affirmative, but then I thought again of Plato's cave. I had the sensation of stepping out of one cave only to find myself in another, a cave where bibliographers gather and speak to each other in their own special code. You wouldn't be able to make a lot of sense of it, so I'll mention only the fact that the copy I had in front of me once belonged to John Overton, whose papers are in the Bodleian Library at Oxford. Overton paid six shillings for his copy in 1638. In the same year he paid seven shillings for a Shakespeare First Folio, nine shillings for a pair of stockings for his wife, and seven pounds for "a seven-year old dapple gray ambling nag."

VII. HEATWAVE

(1995)

Burton was my close companion for the next four years, sitting near me on the shelf next to my desk at the shop, traveling with me to book fairs. Dad wanted me to sell it, but I turned down several good offers, couldn't let it go. I read it as Dr. Johnson read it: because it was therapeutic — a response to widespread suffering, what we call depression today. I read it because it was the first book to take psychosomatic disorders seriously. I read it because it was a bridge to an older world. You don't have to believe in the four humors — blood, black bile, yellow bile, and phlegm — to see their value as metaphors. I read it for the same reason that Burton wrote it: because it spoke to my condition — love melancholy. I thought that it spoke to Olivia's condition too, but while she was waiting for David to divorce his wife, I was waiting for Kafka's axe to break up the frozen sea inside us.

Things continued to happen, of course. The Japanese translator of *The Satanic Verses* was murdered and left in a hallway outside his office; the Italian translator was stabbed in Milan. The man who'd placed the pipe bomb in the shop was identified, but he decamped to Iran before he could be arrested. David's fill-in position at the University of Michigan turned into a tenure-track job. Dad and I continued to exhibit at all the major book fairs — New York, Boston, California — and we unloaded a lot of the Cardinal Newman books for very good prices. In 1994, we celebrated the sixtieth anniversary of the store with a new exhibit every month — books published in 1934 — starting in January with an exhibit of detective novels that ranged from *Murder on the Orient Express* ($999) to *The Clue of the Broken Locket (Nancy Drew Mystery Stories,* #11) ($400).

By this time Delilah had become our store manager, and Olivia had persuaded Dad to lay out $4,000 for a computer for the store so she could enter all our children's books in a database.

I was still waiting for Kafka's axe to fall when Mayor Daley declared 1995 the "Year of the Book in Chicago." I thought I would try to make something happen, chip away at the ice. I persuaded Olivia to go with me to the kick-off event — a black-tie dinner at the Newberry Library sponsored by the Caxton Club. Aunt Fern bought her a new dress for the occasion — one that "follows her curves without clinging to them" — and Olivia looked very elegant as we browsed through the display cases in the Fellows' Lounge on the second floor.

Our copy of Faulkner's first book, *The Marble Faun* — the only book he ever signed "Bill" — and our copy of *The Anatomy of Melancholy* — the one that I'd been lugging around for four years — were side by side in a case next to Julius Caplan's Shakespeare First Folio, in perfect condition — worth more than all the other books in the room combined.

Outside in the world of retail, the big box stores were duking it out in what became known as the Chicago Book Wars. Independent bookstores were closing right and left. Farther outside, in what we now think of as cyberspace, the Internet was just beginning to make its presence felt in the rare book trade — a huge giant stirring on the sidelines, mentioned only in whispers. But our first floor was still humming like a conveyor belt, and our rare book business was doing better than ever. Institutional buying had tapered off, but collectors had stepped up to the plate and were dominating the market, driving prices higher and higher. And inside in the Fellows' Lounge, surrounded by beautiful books, the mood was convivial. We drank champagne and ate Lake Michigan salmon tartare, with pressed caviar and tomatoes, till dinner was served in the Reading Room on the third floor. We found our places and two minutes later the waiter set down our soup — *"consommé with sorrel leaves floating on the surface."* Olivia lowered her head and reached under the table, as if she'd dropped her napkin and was having trouble finding it.

"Need some help?" I asked, pushing my chair away from the table. And then I realized that she was praying, saying grace and trying not to be observed. I wasn't *too* surprised. I supposed that, like me, she was tired of waiting and that, like me, she had her own agenda, one that ran parallel to mine. She been corresponding with Father Gregory, who was teaching at Regis College, part of the University of Toronto, and had started reading the book he'd given her — A. G. Sertillanges's *La vie intellectuale* — reading it in French. She was going to begin a serious spiritual practice; she was going to keep a journal; she was going to follow Sertillanges's advice by reading one thing at a time instead of skipping all over the map; she was going to *listen* for the truth; she was going to seek out the law within that needed to be obeyed; she started taking instruction at St. Tom's on Kimbark, where Mamma had taken me on Easter and on Christmas Eve and on her saint's day, October second — feast of the Guardian Angels.

Dad and I were planning to spend a week in July at the Loft in St. Anne, and I was going to suggest to Olivia that she and Saskia might like to come with us, but then the weather suddenly went out of control. On Wednesday, July 12, the temperature shot up to 100 degrees and kept on rising. We decided to keep the shop open, as we'd done during previous heat waves — not for business, but as an unofficial cooling center. We brought down our supply of box fans and closed off the top two floors because the air-conditioning couldn't handle the load. We arranged the fans in a circle around the perimeter of the first floors blowing counterclockwise.

The next day the temperature reached 106 degrees. Humidity was at record levels, and the heat index reached 119 at O'Hare and

125 at Midway. Bridges had to be hosed down to keep from buckling; power grids failed; many hospitals closed, unable to handle any more people. Three thousand fire hydrants were opened.

Parker Abrams, Delilah's father, and Delilah brought people in the funeral home limousines, and they brought some blankets and mats for bedding. Refrigerated trucks were brought to keep the bodies from decomposing on the sidewalks outside the morgue in the Cook County Medical Examiner's Office on West Harrison Street. The Red Cross brought sandwiches and bottled water. The bathrooms couldn't handle this many people. Men peed outside. We rented a couple of porta-potties that we put in the alley. Dad and I drove the van out to the suburbs to get bottled water. It was impossible to think.

Olivia was everywhere. She kept up morale, filling the whole shop with her energy, like a songbird — reading to children, passing around pieces of fruit and pillows and bottles of water. By Friday, there were two hundred people on the first two floors of the shop. Sitting. Leaning against the stacks. Lying on the floor. The oldest people got the few comfortable chairs on the second floor and a dozen cots that Parker Abrams brought over.

The Red Cross sandwiches were supplemented by sandwiches from the Medici and Salonica and the Café Florian. Fruit and canned goods came from the Hispanic grocery store. Saskia ran around, which was good for the old people. I could see that Olivia was enjoying herself, though "enjoying" is the wrong word. I could see that Olivia wasn't aware of herself at all. She was losing herself in this work, bossing me around, Dad too. She sent Dad to the Randolph Street market to buy crates of apricots and boxes of plums and cherries. I watched her from the landing when I went up to the second floor to check the temperature in the rare book room. She deployed her entire arsenal of smiles — shy and demure, bold and inviting, skeptical, encouraging, thoughtful; smiles that sprang from the heart, and smiles that said "you can't fool me," eyes-only smiles and now-you-listen-to-me smiles, amused smiles, naughty-girl smiles, sideways smiles for the old men, smiles with a promise of mysteries. She put things in perspective, and I could see that she was happy. She leaned forward into the heat as if she were walking into a bracing wind. She listened to her own advice as if she were learning something, or in the process of discovering something funny. And as it turned out, she was.

"The secret of life," she told me when the heatwave was at its worst, "is to live for others."

"Like one of Tolstoy's peasants?"

"You don't need to be sarcastic."

I wasn't being sarcastic.

When it was over and the shop had emptied out — the cots returned to the Abrams Funeral Home, the box fans put back in the attic — she gave me a copy of a book that Father Gregory had given her — based on the precepts of St. Thomas Aquinas — *La vie intellectuelle.* "There is a law within you," she said, as if confiding a secret. "Let it be obeyed."

"You should send a copy to the mayor," I said.

Seven hundred people died in Chicago, many of them old and alone, more on the South Side than on the North. When it was over and the temperature was back down to the lower nineties, the mayor, who'd been on vacation, pooh-poohed the crisis, said he hadn't known anything about it, denied the findings of the medical autopsies, sat on the numbers, refused to accept responsibility for the city's failure to follow its own heat-emergency guidelines, blamed the victims

— the dead — for neglecting themselves, and chided their neighbors for expecting the city to take care of them instead of taking care of their own.

Dad and I resumed our plan to go to Michigan, our first summer without Grandpa Chaz, so we'd have two bedrooms instead of just one. I caught up with Olivia on the stairs going up to the second floor. I told myself that when we reached the top step, I would speak, but before I could invite Olivia to Michigan, she told me she was giving notice. She was on her way to talk to Dad. David, she explained, had finally managed to divorce his wife. She and Saskia were going to live with him in Ann Arbor.

I was stunned. I followed her to Dad's office at the back of the second floor. She wanted to let him know first, she said.

I could see that she was elated and trying not to show it. "So," I said. "This is the law within you that needs to be obeyed?"

"I suppose so," she said without irony. Either she was obtuse; or she was cruel. Or maybe she was just happy.

She knocked on the office door. I was ready to step inside with her, but she said she needed to do this alone."

"Okay," I said. And that was better, I

thought, than breaking down and crying in Dad's office.

"I loved her too, you know," Dad said on the way home that afternoon. "Too bad she's such a cunt." Dad used a lot of profanity, but I'd never heard him use that word before. I started to argue, but there was nothing to argue about.

"Let's leave tonight," Dad said.

"Tonight?"

"Oscar's going to keep on cataloging, and Delilah's going to mind the shop. I already spoke to them." I'd lost my enthusiasm for the trip to Michigan, didn't care one way of the other, but Dad was eager to go. It took us twenty minutes to throw some clothes in a suitcase and pack a couple of knives and our big cast iron frying pan. Dad said he was too tired to drive, so I drove Grandpa Chaz's Cadillac, which was still in good shape. This was a first. Not really a shift in power, just a shift. I wasn't sure what it meant. Probably nothing, or maybe Dad just wanted me to feel useful. We headed out of Chicago on Stony Island, past Moo & Oink, past Mosque Maryam, past the old Avalon. As we approached Seventy-Ninth Street, we were passed by an old VW camper. Painted on the side, in bright colors: SOMETIMES I GO AROUND FEELING SORRY FOR MYSELF, AND ALL THE WHILE I'M BEING CARRIED BY GREAT WINDS ACROSS THE SKY. I was tempted to follow the camper, but it was too late. We were already climbing the Skyway ramp. I thought about painting that on the side of our own van, which looked a little bit like a hearse.

We were in a different world now, up in the air. Dad was snoozing, his head up against the window. He was wearing the old clothes that he always wore in St. Anne — jeans and a short-sleeved white shirt frayed at the collar. I'd made this trip alone, of course, but when we were together, Dad had always driven. Even when Grandpa Chaz was with us. It was an odd feeling. As if we'd come up over the top of an old glacial deposit that I hadn't known was there and were now speeding up as we went down the other side. And, in fact, we had driven over an old glacial deposit, the original "stony island." I was thinking that this would have been a good moment to share with Olivia. I looked at Dad, and then I looked down at the speedometer. I was going eighty-five miles an hour. I could almost hear Grandpa Chaz's voice from the backseat telling me to slow down.

I touched the brake and slowed down to seventy, and time itself slowed down. We didn't have to hurry anymore. When we crossed into Michigan, I turned the air-conditioning off. Dad woke up and we rolled the windows down. We were almost there; the familiar landmarks were overlaid with memories: Redamaks (A LEGEND IN ITS OWN TIME); Judy's Motel (AIR CONDITIONING, FREE TV); the big sign for the Simpson Boat Factory (CUSTOM WOOD BOATS, RUNABOUTS, CRUISERS, DECK BOATS AND MOTOR YACHTS, TRAWLERS AND SAILBOATS).

"Your mother always wanted a sailboat," he said. "Maybe I should have gotten her a sailboat instead of that coat."

I wasn't sure what to say. I thought Dad was opening a door that he'd always kept locked.

"You never let go of Mamma, did you?" I said, tacking into new territory.

He didn't answer at first, and then he said, "I don't know, Gabe. I can understand why she left me, but I still can't understand how she could have left you behind."

"Why would she have left *you*?" I asked.

"She was nineteen when we got married. I was twenty-eight. She was pregnant. I thought I could be her teacher, her guide, but it was the other way around. She was my teacher, my guide. In all the important things. Sex, dancing, music, food."

And I pictured her, the way she swung her shoulders when she walked across a room, or the way she raised her chin and lowered her eyes when she came into my room to read me a story and say good night.

"We used to go over to the Trianon on Cottage Grove, or we'd take the IC downtown and then the El all the way up north to the Aragon or the Edgewater Beach Hotel's Beachwalk. The jitterbug, the twist, all the new dances. She didn't have to learn, she just *knew* what to do, and she taught me. Night Clubs too. Chez Paree on the third floor of the Schatz Building, just before it closed. We heard Frank Sinatra, Louis Armstrong, Bob Hope, Milton Berle. The only thing I taught her was how to swim. She caught on right away, and we used to swim off the Point at night, late at night. The cops showed up one night. We stayed out in the water, about fifty feet out, and finally they went away. Maybe they figured that we weren't going to drown.

"I thought about going to Rome, you know. After she left. You could have stayed here with Alex. I wanted to walk around Rome, but I knew it was a bad idea."

I was usually able to stand outside myself, understand my own feelings. But I had trouble doing so as we followed Duval Street into town, past the Williams orchards and vineyards, past the Dudeck Cold Storage plant and the Catholic Cemetery and past the sign that said, ST. ANNE, POP. 10,600. I was driving back into a past where, during July and August, Mamma and I would drive to the depot in St. Anne on Friday afternoons to wait for Dad and Grandpa Chaz to arrive on the Michigan Central Train from Chicago; back into a past where the four of us would play tombola (a kind of Italian bingo, usually played at Christmas) or Vudú (Grandpa Chaz's favorite, in which you place a curse on one of the other players and make that person do funny things — trumpet like an elephant, or hold his finger on the tip of his nose — till something happens to remove the curse; back into a past where Mamma would sit on the edge of the double bed in the crowded bedroom she shared with Dad and tell me stories about Bobo, a boy my age who understood the languages of all the animals and who was once elected Pope after a dove landed on his head in Rome. She would kiss me good night, and in the morning I'd wake up in the narrow loft bed in the living room.

■ ■ ■ ■

In 1995, St. Anne was still more or less what it had been when I was growing up — a sleepy little lakeside town that had once been populated by missionaries and by French traders who ministered to and traded with warring Indian tribes: Miami, Iroquois, Potawatomi. There was a settlement at the mouth of a river, which was founded after a schooner, the *Acadia,* heading for the fort at St. Joe had been wrecked in a November storm. The crew managed to bring the lifeboat into a natural harbor, liked what they saw, and named the settlement after St. Anne, the patron saint of sailors and protector from storms. The captain, Captain Ignatius Duval, thought it could rival the port of Chicago. That didn't happen, but a lot of Chicago people kept their boats in St. Anne, in three different marinas — the Municipal Marina on Water Street and two marinas on the north side of the river.

You had your rich-out-of-sight on the bluffs along the lake, to the north — Old Chicago Money, New Chicago Money. I didn't know if the Swifts and the Armours still had summer homes here, but in the old days, Martha Swift had taken sailing lessons with us, with Toni Glidden and me, back in 1972, the first summer without Mamma, the year Apollo 16 landed on the moon. The Swift estate had stretched almost half a mile along the lake. I had no idea who lived there now, or if it even existed.

Of course, I knew Ben Warren, who lived in a fifteen-room "cottage," and a couple other collectors, and I'd been invited to parties where most of the guests kept their watches on Chicago time (Central) instead of local time (Eastern).

South of St. Anne you had your summer people renting cottages up and down the lake. You had your ordinary people, and small African-American and Italian communities. The Simpson Boat Factory was the biggest "industry," with lots of customers from Chicago. And the Whirlpool factory farther north, and a couple of tool and die places, an art supply outlet, and a gasket company.

Inland you had orchards — peaches and apples — and vineyards. Berrien County, one of the six richest agricultural counties in the United States, produces strawberries, blueberries, grapes, peaches, apples. The world's largest open air produce market is located in Benton Harbor. And out on the edge of town and beyond, east, along the St. Anne River, there were still a few people living off the grid, hunting and trapping for a living.

It was late, but Vitale's Italian grocery store on Water Street — at the center of a small Italian community anchored by the boat factory and St. Joe's Catholic Church — was still open. Signora Vitale asked about Mamma, as she always did — as if Mamma were waiting for us back at the Loft. She spoke to me in Italian. Her southern Italian accent was a little difficult to understand, but not impossible. I answered her in Italian. Dad picked out a big steak and a couple bottles of Lachryma Christi del Vesuvio, the southern Italian wine that Signora Vitale always recommended and that Mamma liked, made from grapes grown on the side of Mount Vesuvius. On his ascent into Heaven, according to Signora Vitale, Jesus had looked down on the Bay of Naples and wept tears of joy. The lava tracks on the side of Mount Vesuvius were left by the falling tears. I picked up a plastic container of Kalamata olives.

We took Schoolcraft instead of LaSalle Road and drove past traditional shingle-style "cottages," past a couple of new Palladian villas, past some houses so far back from the road that if you glimpsed one, you were probably seeing a carriage house. Farther north the bluffs were higher and the houses smaller, and you'd get glimpses of the lake, between the houses and through the trees.

I always enjoyed the crunch of the gravel under the tires on the long drive. There were ten houses along the drive, all on the south side except for Mrs. Ogilvie's house at the end, on the north — a big house with a tower. The Loft, the last house on the south, was actually built over a garage. It had a large kitchen-living area, and two bedrooms, a loft bed in the living room, a deck, and a view of the lake.

We unloaded the car and carried our stuff up the stairs. I always enjoyed the rituals — hauling our gear up the steep stairs, stowing it, setting up the kitchen, and listening to the waves.

We'd forgotten to get charcoal, so we pan-fried the steaks and drank some wine in glasses with yellow flowers on them. And then we washed the dishes and sat out on the deck for half an hour, finishing the bottle of wine, reading, and listening to the waves. We were both tired and turned in early.

I could have slept in the second bedroom,

which Grandpa Chaz had always used, but I slept in the loft bed in the living room, as I'd done since I was a boy. I was reading one of the books that Grandpa Chaz had left at the Loft years ago, and which I'd read many times — *Historical Atlas of the Great Lakes* — when Dad came out of the bathroom in his pajamas.

"I'm sorry about what I said," he said.

"What you said? About Olivia?"

He nodded.

"You mean . . . ?" I asked.

"Yes."

"It's okay," I said. But of course it wasn't okay, and I was suddenly overwhelmed, carried out into deep water by a riptide. I knew I had to swim sideways, get out of the current, but I just let myself drift.

What are these feelings anyway? What do our feelings *feel* like? Do they change over time? I mean, over historical time? Does each emotion have its own history? Do they travel in packs? Do they link us to the ancient people who once gathered around this great inland sea ten or eleven thousand years ago? Who left their points and pottery, their projectile points, scrapers? Who ate mammoth and mastodon and caribou? The ancestors of the Pokagon people who were building a casino outside St. Anne?

When I imagined Olivia lying in the narrow bed next to me, I got one kind of feeling, a disturbance in my lower body, a humming like an electric motor. And when I imagined her lying next to David in a big queen-size bed in Ann Arbor, I got a very different feeling, a disturbance in my upper body, as if my chest were tightening around my heart. And when I remembered Mamma running around naked in the snow outside our big house on Blackstone and Dad throwing his arms around her when she burst back into the kitchen, my body seemed to levitate; and when I remembered her coming to my elementary school and telling me she found herself *in difficoltà* my body seemed to sink to the bottom of Lake Michigan. And then after Mamma went away, lying in my loft bed — listening to Grandpa Chaz and Clare Duval and Dad talk as they pored over one of Grandpa Chaz's Indian books, or tried to find out where things had gone wrong, spinning out alternative histories — *What if the French and Indians had won the French and Indian War? What if the Federalists had prevented Jefferson from making the illegal Louisiana Purchase?* — waiting for them to lower their voices and say something about Mamma, or talk about Father Isaac Jogues and Father Jean de Brébeuf, who were tortured by the Iroquois, or by the Mohawks, or about the young men of the Mandan tribe, who were initiated into manhood by being starved for several days and then suspended from the roof of the medicine lodge by stakes driven through their chests and shoulders — my mouth would go dry.

These stories stayed more or less the same till I was old enough to sit at the table with the men, sipping a small glass of whiskey and asking questions: *Why did they starve them? How did they drive the stakes through their chests and shoulders?*

But now, in July 1995, I wasn't thinking about Grandpa Chaz and Clare Duval, who were both dead. I was thinking about Dad, sleeping alone downstairs, wondering what he was thinking about as he went to sleep. Was he thinking about Mamma and her Italian lover? Or maybe about Shirley, or Darlene, who came after Shirley? Or about dancing at the Trianon and at other places that didn't exist anymore? Or about swimming naked off the Point, treading water till the police went away? And I experienced a very different disturbance, one that I couldn't locate in my body. I wanted to climb down the ladder and sit on the edge

139

of the bed, tell Dad that everything was okay.

All these thoughts flowed together in me, like the great Arctic currents that had scoured out the Great Lakes basin, scouring out a great sadness. And then all of a sudden I could see clearly, could see the battered VW camper we'd passed as we were getting on the Skyway: SOMETIMES I GO AROUND FEELING SORRY FOR MYSELF, AND ALL THE WHILE I'M BEING CARRIED BY GREAT WINDS ACROSS THE SKY.

I lay on my back and let myself feel the great winds holding me up, let them carry me across the sky, taking me wherever I needed to go.

VIII. The 19th Boston International Antiquarian Book Fair

(NOVEMBER 1995)

The great winds that had been carrying me across the sky had ceased to blow by the time I drove out to Boston in November 1995 for the 19th Boston International Antiquarian Book Fair. I hadn't fully recovered from Olivia's sudden departure from my life, and Dad thought it would be good for me to handle the fair on my own, though he didn't put it this way.

Business was good, but the Internet was starting to cast its shadow over the rare book trade. I saw my first website on my way to the fair — in Helen Barstow's old barn, just outside Erie, Pennsylvania. Dad wanted me to look at a copy of the *Gettysburg Address* that she'd put on the cover of her latest catalog. I found Helen sitting in front of a computer on a trestle table. The black box next to the computer, Helen explained, was a modem that converted the analog signal of the telephone line to digital data on the computer. The computer and the modem hadn't been there the year before when Dad and I stopped by. Helen and I looked at her website on a computer monitor. You couldn't order books on the site, but you could see what Helen had in stock and give her a call, or fax her, or write her a letter. I bought the *Gettysburg Address,* and then Helen and I sat up late talking, about books and about the way Grandpa Chaz and Dad used to load up the van or truck with books to sell at the fair. I spent the night and left early in the morning. As I was leaving, I stopped the van at the end of the long driveway and looked back at Helen's old barn. Helen was waving, and I thought I was looking into the past and into the future at the same time.

And I was.

I'd been in low spirits and was glad to be sharing a booth with Marcus Cohn, my oldest friend. Marcus and I had taken classes together at Chicago, shared our notes, studied together in the shop, drunk beers at Jimmy's, eaten pizza at the Medici, attended classes together at the Rare Book School when it was still at Columbia University. Like Chas. Johnson & Son in Chicago,

142

Cohn & Son in New York was one of the last three-generation bookshops in the country. Our grandfathers had done business together, our fathers too. Marcus and I were going to be interviewed as the youngest members of the AABA — the American Antiquarian Booksellers Association.

As Marcus was helping me set out my two hundred books, I experienced the same sensation I'd experienced at Helen's: that I was looking into the past and into the future at the same time. The fair itself was the unchanging, immutable past: dealers displaying antiquarian books and buying fresh stock from each other; book binders demonstrating their craft; collectors wandering up and down the aisles, searching for treasure; book conservators offering solutions to common problems (mildew, red rot, acid migration); expert appraisers on hand for visitors who wanted to put a price on their old books. Grandpa Chaz had once been part of the immutable past too. Dealers from every quarter of the country stopped by during the course of the fair to reminisce about him and ask about Dad, and to see if I needed anything.

But something was different this year. Superimposed on an image of the immutable past was an image of a radically mutable future. I could see it in the computers sprouting up here and there, like daffodils sprouting up during a warm spell in late winter, and I could hear it in the shop talk at the end of the day — talk about websites and databases, about Telnet and Gopher and Veronica, about Amazon — which had sold its first book over the Internet on July 16, during the heatwave — and about paperless e-books that could be transmitted over the air to a computer screen. I could hear it in the jokes at the annual poker game, and in the questions posed by the reporter for the *Boston Globe* who interviewed Marcus and me on the last afternoon of the fair, and who wanted us to peer into the future: Would we live in houses with no bookshelves? In cities with no bookstores? Would we have robots doing our reading for us?

I'd had a good fair: I'd made my nut on the morning of the second day; I'd sold the three books of hours from the Cardinal Newman cache to the Morgan Library; I'd unloaded several other high-end items that had been sitting on our shelves for too long; I'd bought some new stock. But I was uneasy, ready for the closing bell to sound so I could pack up my books and head home. The glimpse into the bookless future imagined by the young woman who interviewed us for the *Boston Globe* was implausible but disturbing, and half an hour before the end of the fair, I had a glimpse into the "immutable" past that was even more disturbing. Two old grandpas in baggy suits with nests of hair springing out of the sides of their heads came to blows over our signed copy of Faulkner's *Marble Faun.* Marcus and I had to pull them apart. My asking price suddenly skyrocketed, and ten minutes later I sold the book for an outrageous price. Fifteen minutes later it was resold at an even higher price. The fight left a bad taste in my mouth. I looked around at the frantic scene in front of me with new eyes and shook my head as a professional croupier might shake his head at gamblers throwing their chips down on the roulette table. Or as a nonsmoker might shake his head at a beautiful woman lighting up a cigarette, or a nondrinker at the stupidity of a man hoisting up a tot of whiskey. "We're no better than commodity traders," I said to Marcus. " 'Getting and spending we lay waste our powers.' "

But then, just as the closing bell was about to sound — I'd already started to pack my books — something prompted me to leave

Marcus at the booth and take a last look at a copy of Montaigne's *Essais* that I'd seen earlier in Arnold Perlberg's double booth — PERLBERG RARE BOOKS, TORONTO.

Perlberg was starting to pack up his books, but the Montaigne was still open in a display case on the table: *Les Essais de Michel Seigneur de Montaigne. Cinquiesme edition, augmentée d'un troisiesme livre et de six cens additions aux deux premiers.* It was the last edition published during Montaigne's lifetime and included Montaigne's address to the reader and the detailed long preface by Mlle. de Gournay — Montaigne's *fille d'alliance* — who had made corrections in her own hand on the printed sheets before they'd been bound.

I looked at Angelier's large woodcut device within an ornate border on the title page and at the woodcut initials and ornaments. "Some yellowing and marginal repairs to final leaf," Perlberg said, but that didn't bother me. Some books want you as much as you want them, and that was the case with this copy of *Les Essais.* It had spoken to me earlier, and now it called to me over the tumult of the closing minutes of the fair, summoned me. Marcus and I had read the *Essays* in Jock Winetraub's class on autobiography, and I knew I had to have it, and suddenly everything became clear, all the crazy activity going around me — the rabid collectors, the wheeling and dealing, the getting and spending.

"Does your dad know what you're doing?" Perlberg asked, and laughed. I knew better than to try to haggle with him, and he let me have the book for eighteen thousand.

"Your grandfather," he said, closing the book in its clamshell case, "would have asked for the dealer discount. You didn't ask, but I'm going to give it to you anyway. Ten percent."

IX. Dad Orders His Tomb

(2003–2009)

I came back from the fair with a renewed sense of my vocation and a clearer sense of my purpose in life, which was to step into Grandpa Chaz's shoes. I put my oars in the water and rowed hard, buying aggressively at estate sales and auctions, horse trading at book fairs, cultivating our contacts and the collectors who relied on us. I continued to row hard for several years, and our rare book department prospered in spite of the dot-com bubble, but by 2003, the year Olivia moved back to Hyde Park, our two hundred thousand secondhand books on floors one, three, and four had become the proverbial drug on the market. The cavernous old inner-city bookshop was rapidly becoming a thing of the past, as were the old barns full of books, like Helen's, that used to dot the countryside. These old shops, which had once been cultural centers where many collectors got their start, had been undermined by Google. Readers could find what they were looking for on the Internet without rummaging through an old bookshop. Cheaper too. I didn't blame them. A couple of the behemoths would survive, like dinosaurs in a science fiction movie — the Strand in New York, John King in Detroit, Powell's in Portland — but Laudermilk's in Philadelphia was long gone; Goodspeed's in Boston was long gone; Holmes in Oakland had just closed. And they weren't coming back. Shorey's in Seattle was struggling. We couldn't blame all our problems on the Internet, of course. Inner-city rents were skyrocketing; the city was nickel and diming us to death with new regulations, new codes, new taxes. Parking had become impossible. Foot traffic was down. Our profitable rare book business could not continue to support a large secondhand book operation.

I kept on rowing, but I was rowing against the current, and every year I had to row harder and harder to keep the current from carrying Chas. Johnson & Son, Ltd., down to the sea. I kept the Montaigne on my desk at the shop and dipped into it from time to time, not looking for profound truths, just hoping for moments of clarity, stays against confusion.

Olivia came back to Hyde Park at the end of 2003 to manage the new Borders store on Fifty-Third Street. She'd been working at Borders headquarters in Ann Arbor for several years, reinventing herself as a tech person, and when she was offered the chance to manage her own store, she took it.

Her return did not upset our apple carts. We told ourselves that we were both too busy to think of romance; or maybe we were just afraid to revisit the past; or maybe we just weren't the same people we'd been ten years earlier. We'd lived through the dot-com bubble, the subprime mortgage crisis, through 9/11 and the Space Shuttle *Columbia* disaster, through the invasion of Iraq and the increasingly dominant role of the Internet in the book trade. We'd lived through death and loss: Grandpa Chaz's death had left a big hole in our lives that Dad and I had to step around every morning when we opened the door to the shop, and every evening, too, as we sat down at Mamma's old butcher's table to eat our supper. Aunt Fern's death had left a similar hole in Olivia's life; a messy divorce from

David had left her unsettled; a daughter who didn't want to move to Hyde Park and who refused to live in Ann Arbor with her father and his new wife had made her life complicated.

But we had plenty to talk about in the present without trying to revisit the past. On the one hand, Borders was flourishing — about 1500 stores nationwide, five in the Chicago area. The aisles in the store on Fifty-Third Street were crowded, and Starbucks was selling lattes and cappuccinos and macchiatos at a coffee bar on the second floor. Olivia was flourishing too. She was the captain of a brand-spanking-new ship with a first-rate, well-disciplined crew. You could walk through the new store and get a good sense of what was going on in the world. You could ask any staff member a question and get an answer.

On the other hand, at Chas. Johnson & Son, Ltd., writing had appeared on the wall: "MENE, MENE, TEKEL, UPHARSIN." Book of Daniel 5:25–26: "God hath numbered the days of your reign and brought it to an end." We didn't need a Daniel to interpret it, we needed an accountant, and we had one. Mr. Patterson, CPA. Every year he issued the same warning, but we continued to ignore him till our old landlord died in

January 2009, and the new owner wanted us out.

Mr. Patterson was sitting in Dad's reading chair in Dad's bedroom. His large battered briefcase was on the floor between his feet, like a faithful dog — Italian leather. He had stopped on his way home from his office on Woodlawn.

We knew what Mr. Patterson was going to say, but this year we had to pay attention to him because we no longer had a choice. What we needed to do, he said, was ship our used books out to our warehouse on the South Side and let Delilah set up an online site, and then set up a rare book shop on Michigan Avenue or, better, in the Monadnock Building. He happened to know there was space available. "Then you have to start selling your rare books online, like everybody else."

Dad was in bed. He was eighty-two and had suffered a TIA — a transitory ischemic attack. He was "able to sit up and take nourishment," but he was having trouble with initial fricatives, as in *pfucking* Internet or *pfucking* Amazon. He wanted to get some things sorted out before he croaked (his word). "Pfuck it anyway," he said. "We've got another year on the lease."

"And then what? The new owners have

offered to pay for the move if you agree to be out by Christmas. Take them up on it."

We sipped some Balvenie 10 in silence. There were no papers to sign, no dramatic moment, that afternoon, at which property or money changed hands, at which a firm decision was reached. The lease would expire, and one way or another, that would be it. Grandpa Chaz was dead. Helen Barstow was dead. Estelle Sullivan, who'd worked the cash register for forty years, was dead. Olivia's Aunt Fern was dead; and now our old landlord, Tommy Mariakakis, who'd actually read books, was dead, and his sons had sold the building to a holding company in St. Louis.

"I don't know how to think about these things," Dad said.

"I just told you how to think about them," Mr. Patterson said.

After Mr. Patterson left, Dad started to rant.

"Dad," I said. "Things change, but we'll be okay. The rare book market is solid. Hakluyt's *Voyages* sold last year at Christie's, at the Streeter sale, for over four hundred fifty thousand dollars. A first edition of Lewis and Clark brought almost three hundred thousand. Grandpa Chaz's copies of both those books are upstairs. Good copies too, with all the maps."

"Pfuck Christie's," he said. "Pfuck Sotheby's. Pfuck Bonham's too. Those pfuckers just want to cut out the dealers anyway and go right to the new dot-com millionaires, the new billionaires, so they can jack up the prices. They've got to muscle in everywhere. Pfuckers. They're like Wall Street. They don't give a pfuck about books. No lots under pfive thousand dollars. High spots only. People will pay anything for high spots, not because they care about books but because books are trophies, or investments — hard assets that don't go up and down with the stock market or the bond market. Pfuck. That's no way to collect books. That's the Wall Street model. Make a buck. The rare book trade depends on knowledgeable collectors and institutions — and fellow dealers — to drive sales, not dotcom millionaires who want some trophy books to go along with their trophy wives. Like that guy who bought the little Audubon from you last week, sent his secretary all the way from California to pick it up, and then she didn't even want to look at it. They're dumbing down the rare book market."

I'd picked up the Audubon at the Barstow sale in Philadelphia — Helen Barstow's inventory had been auctioned off at Freeman's — not the double elephant folio that sold for $11.5 million at Christie's in December, but a later seven-volume *octavo* edition, which actually had more prints. I hadn't intended to buy anything, but it was a way of paying my respects to our old friend Helen, and we'd made a nice profit on it.

Dad managed to pour himself another couple fingers of Scotch. The whiskey was fueling his rant. "Book collecting isn't a hobby — like collecting Hummel figurines; and it's not an investment — like putting together your portfolio. Our vocation isn't to locate high-spot books for dot-com millionaires. It's to help collectors put together in-depth collections that mean something to them, and to other people too — Al Bernstein's holocaust books for children, Ben Warren's rivers collection, Parker Abrams's African-American books and pamphlets, your grandfather's early Americana and all the books about the Midwest that he bought for the special collections at St. Anne: the Great Lakes, the Civil War, Lincoln, Chicago, the Great Migration, the Haymarket Riot, Detroit, the Mississippi River Valley, the Wisconsin Glacier. Now the high-spot collectors and the new investors are driving the prices out of sight."

"So what do you think we should do?"

"I'll tell you what *you* should do. Send your grandfather's *Americana* to Swann's — it's the only auction house that's a member of the ABAA. The others don't want to be bothered with a code of ethics. Send the rest to Cohn and Son. Marcus can sell them for you on commission. At least you know he won't cheat you. Then you'll have a healthy income stream. Marry Olivia, for Christ's sake; cocker up your genius and live free; sell this place and go to the south of France, or Italy — a rooftop apartment in the middle of Rome, by the Campo dei Fiori. Like your mother. Or buy a little villa in Tuscany or in the south of France. Some olive trees. A little vineyard. Make your own olive oil, your own wine. Live your life, don't just read about it."

"I've heard that before," I said, "but I never expected to hear it from you!"

"I need to lie down," he said, and turned over on his side.

"Marry Olivia?"

I walked over to Borders on Fifty-Third Street to see Olivia because I didn't know what else to do. It was February, but I hadn't worn a coat.

By this time — five years after she'd

moved back to Hyde Park — writing had appeared on her wall too. Borders had outsourced its online business to Amazon back in 2001 and was struggling to get it back, struggling to break free from Amazon and establish its own online presence with a new interactive browser window featuring "The Magic Shelf." But it was an uphill struggle, and Borders, which had posted a $187 million loss in 2008, was hoping for an extension on a loan from a hedge fund company — Pershing Square Capital Management — that had invested heavily in Borders stock, which was now at an all-time low.

Olivia looked up when I walked into her office. "Livy," I said, "we're going to have to close the shop," and saying those words brought me to tears. It was embarrassing, but I didn't care. I picked up a large yellow paper clip from her desk and bent it out of shape. I was aware that this kind of vulnerability brings out tenderness in women. In some women. But there was nothing I could do about it.

"Oh, Gabe," she said. "I can't tell you how sorry I am. For your dad especially."

"He's blaming the *Zeitgeist*. He's been reading *The Gutenberg Elegies: The Fate of Reading in a Digital Age*."

"Amazon's come out with a second-generation Kindle."

"Depressing. Do you think the printed book stands a chance?"

"I hope so. But I sit in front of a computer screen all day long. The Internet is only a click away. The e-mails keep pouring in. No thought goes unexpressed. There's always something else I should be doing — like cutting another staff person — and doing it faster. I need to get away from that. I need to slow down and read a book."

"What are you reading now?" I asked.

"I'm seeing through other eyes," she said. "It's not like anything." The phone rang. She answered it, asked the caller to hold, and covered the mouthpiece. "Hemingway's *Garden of Eden.* I gave your dad a copy. You should read it too."

"I thought you disapproved of Hemingway."

"This is different, Gabe. This isn't your grandfather's Hemingway. This is like — No, listen," she said (to me). "I'll bring some supper over later. I'll pick up something at the Medici."

"You don't have to do that," I said, but she pointed at the phone in her hand and waved me away, flicking her fingers toward the door. I walked home. It was February, very cold. I hugged myself to keep warm.

Dad perked up when Olivia arrived that evening with three Styrofoam containers of spinach lasagna in a large heavy-duty paper sack. I was glad to see this sign of life. Solzhenitsyn's *Cancer Ward* was folded around his thumb, but there was another book open on the bed — an Armed Services Edition of *Tortilla Flat.* Olivia noticed. "Is that your backup?"

"It's like drugs," Dad said. "You've got your downers and your uppers, your amphetamines and your opioids."

"You shouldn't be mixing downers and uppers."

"Pfuck it."

The smell of the spinach lasagna was starting to fill the room.

"If I have one more drink," Dad said, "I'll ask you to marry my son."

"Da-ad."

"He's pfifty years old. You must be pfortypfive, pforty-six. Pfuck these pfricatives. God damn it anyway."

"It's okay. It's nicer to say 'Pfuck' than 'fuck.'"

"Pfuck it. I'm serious."

"Would you like it if I said 'fuck' or 'pfuck' all the time? No. And I think Gabe can look

159

after himself."

"You mean his little guitar teacher can look after him? Athena? What's her name?"

"Atene Oikonomides," I said. "I haven't had a lesson in over a year."

"Some goddess of wisdom. What did she teach you every week? Besides *pf*ucking?"

"Dad, please, you've had too much whiskey on an empty stomach. We'd better eat something."

"What's the matter with you two? Is this some kind of pfucking comedy where the audience can see what's what but the lovers can't? Benedict and Beatrice?"

"Dad, enough."

"Mr. Johnson." Olivia sat down on the edge of the bed. "Read my lips. Watch how I do this and do what I do. Close your lips and say 'puck.' "

"What the —" But he did it. "Puck."

"Now keep your lips apart. Put your bottom lip up against your top teeth. Keep your top lip up. Open your mouth a little. Touch your lower lip to your front teeth."

Olivia was the only one who could get away with this.

"Now let your breath out: fuh fuh fuh."

"Pfuh pfuh pfuh."

"No, keep your lips apart. Fuh fuh fuh. Hold your tongue back."

Dad laughed. "Pfuck pfuck pfuck. God damn it anyway."

Olivia took hold of his upper lip with her finger and thumb and pulled it up. "Now try it."

I had to look away. It was too intimate, the sort of thing that should be done in private. But I could hear Dad saying "Fuck fuck fuck." And Olivia asking, "How does that make you feel?"

"Better," he said. "Now let me ask you something: why don't you marry my son?"

"I don't think Gabe wants to invite disaster into his life. Besides, I haven't got time."

"Livy, you were never a disaster. Besides, you're getting older. You look good, but you've got some miles on your face. Living all alone in that condo over on Hyde Park Boulevard all by yourself since you came back from Ann Arbor. I hope your aunt left you some money when she died."

"My daughter lives with me."

"When she's not in the dorm. You know she still comes into the shop. I see her studying her Arabic on the third floor. Hard to believe. She's reading bits of the Koran. We become different people when we read, you know."

"It's very difficult," she said.

"Are you religious at all?" Dad asked. "I

161

think you are."

"Do you want me to say a prayer for you? I'll do it, you know."

"That sounds like a threat," Dad said. I could see that he was a little embarrassed. "The lasagna's getting cold," he said.

"I'll get some plates and silverware," I said. "And glasses and a bottle of wine."

Olivia went down to the kitchen with me.

"*Tortilla Flat,*" she said, using two hands to hold on to three plates and three Duralex glasses. "That's one of the worst books I've ever read."

I laughed. "You just don't appreciate its mythic qualities."

And then *she* laughed. "He's just overwhelmed right now," she said.

"Me too," I said.

Back in Dad's bedroom, we dug into the spinach lasagna, which was delicious. How could they make spinach taste so good? It was good, really good, but it wasn't good enough to wash the taste of shame and humiliation out of my mouth. I couldn't imagine Fifty-Seventh Street without Chas. Johnson & Son, Ltd. Antiquarian Booksellers.

Dad wanted a poem. He'd been memorizing poems so he could say them to himself on his death bed. " 'The Bishop Orders His

162

Tomb,' " he said. "That's what I want."

He had a nice edition of Browning's *Dramatic Personae* (Chatto & Windus) next to the bed, bound in full tan morocco, but he wanted me to read it in a different edition, the edition he'd read as a boy. He wasn't sure of the title, but it had "Suitable for boys and girls" on the title page, which he found amusing. Grandpa Chaz had given it to him, and he'd given it to me, and I found it amusing too. It was in my room next to a Dover Thrift edition of Samuel Butler's *Erewhon* and Robert Browning's *Shorter Poems,* edited by Franklin T. Baker.

I went to look. When I came back into the room, they were working on fricatives. Dad pulled his tongue away from Olivia's finger and thumb and asked me to fix us drinks.

"Bourbon or Scotch?"

"Surprise us."

I went to the kitchen and brought up three Waterford tumblers, Donegal pattern, and our last bottle of Balvenie 10, though I thought there was still another bottle at the shop.

I poured him two fingers and two fingers for Olivia and two for myself. I fluffed the pillow behind his head and sat down on the edge of the bed.

"Read it with a Southern accent," he said,

flipping through the pages, so I knew he was in the mood for a laugh. He handed me the book.

"How about *faux* French?" I protested.

He shook his head.

Olivia took the book out of my hands. She looked it over for about a minute and then began to read: "Draw raoun ma bay-ed, iz Anzelm keep'n' back?"

Dad nodded his approval, and she went on.

"Nefiuz, sunz mahan, ah Gahd, I know naht.
Whale, she main wudd have t' be yer mother wonzt . . ."

The bishop can't trust his sons to build the magnificent tomb he wants. He threatens to leave everything to the Pope, but he can't trust the Pope either. Dad closed his eyes. When Olivia got to the line about horses and brown Greek manuscripts and mistresses with great smooth marbly limbs, he still had his eyes closed and I thought he might be asleep, or maybe dead, but he was smiling. She kept on reading.

When she came to the end — "Az stee-ul he envied me, so fay-er she wuz" — he struggled to sit up. "Most people think the bishop had it all wrong," he said. "But I think he got it just right. He never gave in to the shadowy world of spirit."

Dad was exhausted. He lay back down. I was glad to see him hanging on, like the bishop, rather than letting go. I sat there for a while, trying to think about what I could say. I thought Dad had gotten it right too, and I was looking for the right words to tell him, I couldn't do better than the bishop.

"Is there any more of that Scotch?" Dad asked. "You know, they're not making Balvenie 10 anymore. It's going to be Balvenie 12 from here on out."

"Just a tick," I said. I poured another finger.

"What do you think I should have on *my* tombstone? he asked. " 'Of the making of books there is no end'?"

"How about 'My soul is an enchanted boat'?" Olivia suggested.

Dad looked at her to make sure she was joking. I handed him the tumbler and he swirled the whiskey around and we admired the way the Waterford picked up the light.

"Let me see the book." Olivia handed him the book. He turned the book over in his hands. "Spine a little darkened and faded in places," he said. "Corners square but rubbed through. Front internal hinge

165

cracked. Binding somewhat loose. Some foxing throughout." He looked up as if he'd surprised himself. "That's it," he said. "That's what I want on *my* tombstone."

"Congratulations," Olivia said. "You're getting your fricatives right."

"Now I've got to pee again," he said, "and then I'm going to sleep. I'd sleep better if you two would get married."

"Good night, Dad," I said.

Why *didn't* Olivia and I get married? Marriage would have made a lot of sense. I was forty-nine years old, Olivia was forty-six. Olivia had been divorced for two years. Atene had accepted a teaching position at the Manhattan School of Music in New York and had left already.

I think we didn't get married because we'd congealed, we'd become who we were going to be. If you'd seen us drinking coffee in the Medici, you would have taken us for a divorced couple talking about the book trade, or about the Internet, or about a letter from Atene, inviting me to come to a program of Renaissance music at the school in New York, or about the latest book fair; or about David's new book — *A Symptomatic Reading of Wordsworth's Prelude* — or about the new priest at St. Paul and the

Redeemer, or about Saskia, whose child-hood had come to an end and who had switched from French to Arabic because she was in love with her roommate at the University of Chicago — Nadia, who was from Jordan — or about the books we'd been buying and selling and even reading, or talking quietly, as if we were making decisions about the kids, about money, about things in general. If you'd been sitting in the next booth, you might have heard us discussing problems in the book Olivia was writing about literary experience: *The Varieties of Literary Experience.* "Profound ideas are a dime a dozen," she liked to say. "If you're looking for profound ideas, go to the sympathy card section at Walgreens."

We walked down Blackstone, past Poop Corner Number One, and then over to her condo on Cornell. We said good night on her doorstep and I kissed her on the cheek. Dad was asleep when I got home.

X. Blessed Is
the True Judge

Mr. Patterson's advice was still on the table when Dad died in his sleep in the middle of July. Nothing had been decided, no course charted, the ship was dead in the water, waiting for a freshening breeze.

Instead of a eulogy at the funeral, there was a poetry reading — some of the poems that Dad had memorized so that he could always have them on the tip of his tongue when he needed them — but at the end, Marcus, who'd flown in from New York in the morning, stood up and said a few words about how much Dad had meant to him when he was an undergraduate at the U of C, working at the shop. Dad had been a second father. And then he said something in Hebrew that I didn't understand but that some people did, because they repeated it: *Baruch dayan emet.*

That evening Olivia asked Marcus about it: "What was it you said at the funeral?"

Six of us were crowded into a booth at the Medici — Olivia between Marcus and me on one side, Delilah, Saskia, and Nadia, Saskia's roommate, on the other.

"*Baruch dayan emet* — Blessed is the true judge."

"Which means?"

"Even when it comes to death, we need to bless the true judge."

"I think it's a way of acknowledging that death is beyond our understanding," Olivia said. "We need to accept whatever God gives us." She looked around the table as if she expected someone — me — to challenge her, but our pizzas arrived and we were hungry and we opened the second bottle of wine that we'd brought from the house, since the Medici didn't have a liquor license.

That night Marcus and I drank the last of Dad's Balvenie 10 in the rare book room at the shop, surrounded by beautiful books. "Infinite riches in a little room," he said.

I'd gone to New York to be with Marcus, right after 9/11. Marcus's wife had taken the kids up to Rhinebeck to stay with her folks, and Marcus and I were sleeping in the shop. We'd gone to the Caplan sale at Christie's in Rockefeller Center and had

169

seen a Shakespeare First Folio — the one Olivia and I had once seen displayed in the Fellows' Lounge at the Newberry Library — knocked down for a record $5.6 million (plus the buyer's premium, which put it over $6 million) to an anonymous telephone bidder. Arnold Perlberg, who'd sold me our copy of Montaigne's *Essais* at the Boston Fair in 1995, was the underbidder. A beautiful copy of Blake's *Songs of Innocence* brought over $600,000; $358,000 for a copy of Newton's *Principia;* over $200,000 for Isaac Walton's *Compleat Angler.*

"Whatever happened to the copy of Maimonides?" I asked him. "You put a copy of Maimonides in the window and taped up a sign: GUIDE FOR THE PERPLEXED."

"It's very rare," Marcus said. "There are two copies of the Arabic text in the British Library, and a couple more in the Bodleian. It was written in Arabic, but with Hebrew characters. You can't read it unless you understand Jewish Arabic — Arabic *and* Hebrew."

"People saw the sign and kept coming into the shop,' I said. "It was an oasis. People just wanted to sit quietly for a few minutes in a room full of beautiful books."

"An oasis," he said. "That's a good image. That's what you've got here, in this room."

"Marcus," I said. "I have to tell you, I'm thinking of getting out. That's what Dad wanted. Go to the south of France, or Italy."

Marcus put his hand on my arm. "Gabe, you're upset about your dad's death. I understand that. But don't make any big decisions right now, okay? Are you listening to me? Your dad was a Luddite. He didn't want to change with the times, didn't want to sell books online. I don't blame him, but — that's no excuse for you."

"Our last two printed catalogs sold ninety percent."

"That's not the point," he said. "Don't go to the south of France, don't go to Italy. Come to New York. I think that's what your dad would have wanted. My dad too. If we joined forces, we'd be a dominant force."

"I can't think about it now," I said. "You just told me not to make any big decisions now."

"But promise me you will think about it?"

"How did that go again, what you said at the funeral?"

"*Baruch dayan emet* — Blessed is the true judge."

I repeated it after him: "*Baruch dayan emet.* I don't get it."

"I don't get it either," he said.

171

"Did you ever sell the Maimonides?" I asked.

"We sold it the next week, right after Bin Laden escaped at Tora Bora."

"Who bought it?"

"Someone with a lot of money."

Marcus's flight left at five the next morning. I rode out to O'Hare with him in a Yellow Cab.

"Gabe," he said on the way, why don't you marry that woman?"

"It's complicated."

"It's not complicated," he said. "Listen to me. If you don't want to marry that woman, just tell me and I won't mention it again. I know she fucked you over a couple of times. But so what? It doesn't matter. But if you do want to marry her, you've got to step up to the plate. She has to know that Borders is in trouble, serious trouble. Borders stock is trading so low now they may take it off the New York Stock Exchange. They had to sell off all their subsidiaries. Outsourcing their online business was a huge mistake, and that wasn't the only one. It's a shame, but that's the way it is. Make her an offer she can't refuse, throw her a lifeline. She'd be a fool not to take it. She's, what, forty-four, forty-five She's got a daughter who wants to make nice with the Arabs. She's paying tuition at the University of Chicago. Looks like you get on with the daughter okay. She seems like a smart kid. She told me you give her presents, books, talk to her. You're the good uncle, right?"

A "lifeline," I thought, was what Marcus had thrown me earlier. Would I be a fool not to take it?

"She's a good kid," I said — "Saskia. You know, I was there when she was born. I was the first one to hold her in my arms."

"There you go," Marcus said. "I'll propose the first toast at the wedding."

I asked the driver to take me back to the shop. I wasn't ready to go home. In Dad's office I lay down on the couch. I woke up about an hour later and had to go to the bathroom. I thought about Montaigne, who boasted that he could hold his water for eighteen hours. Maybe I *could* start over in the south of France, or in a villa in Tuscany. Maybe I *could* live life instead of reading about it. It had never occurred to me that I could choose my own way, that I wasn't chained to old books.

When I came back from the bathroom, I booted up the computer, poured some

Scotch in my empty glass, and started searching for properties in Italy, New York too, and France — the Dordogne, near Montaigne's old estate. I thought maybe I'd crossed a line in my sleep. The more Scotch I sipped, the more I felt the need to get out of Hyde Park, away from Fifty-Seventh Street, away from the shop. The *genius loci* had gone. I was admiring a two-bedroom terraced house with a riverside garden in a popular market town (not named) between Sarlat and Bergerac.

PRÊT À EMMÉNAGER

Maison mitoyenne de 2 chambres avec jardin au bord de la rivière 45m2 au coeur d'un bourg populaire entre Sarlat et Bergerac en Dordogne Endroit charmant . . . grand investissement. 99000 € (frais d'agence inclus).

"The greatest thing in the world," Montaigne says somewhere, "is to know how to belong to oneself." That was the most important thing I remembered from Weintraub's seminar. Could I learn how to belong to myself in this two-bedroom terraced house between Sarlat and Bergerac, not far from Montaigne's old home? I was trying to picture myself in a little garden on the banks of a river when Delilah came bursting into the office. I closed the window immediately.

"Looking at pornography?" she asked. "This early in the morning? Shame on you."

"I was looking at a house in France," I said.

"Right," she said. "That typescript of a 'Simple' story you gave Daddy," she said. "Funny way to pay for a funeral. He wanted me to thank you. That's all. I didn't mean to interrupt your fantasy."

"I told you," I said. "I was looking at a house in France."

"If you say so," she said. "You don't look too good. You been sitting here all night?"

"Marcus was here," I said, "till about three o'clock. I rode out to the airport with him, got back about four thirty."

"Blessed is the true judge," she said. "Sounds better in Hebrew, but I like it. Better to bless the true judge than sit around feeling sorry for yourself."

I was too tired to argue.

"Why don't you go home? I'll look after things here."

"I'll go in a minute," I said. I clicked a computer key, but I couldn't find the site with the two-bedroom terraced house with a riverside garden. I could, however, still picture the whitewashed walls and red window. Only €99,000. I could sell Grandpa Chaz's Americana and buy a whole row of terraced houses. And then it hit me: I could do whatever I wanted to do, go wherever I wanted to go.

But now that Dad was dead, where did I want to go, and what did I want to do when I got there?

XI. THE SHOUT

(SEPTEMBER 2009)

At the end of July, the following obituary appeared in *The Caxtonian:*

Charles Johnson, Jr. 1931–2009

Mr. Charles Johnson, Jr., died at his home on Tuesday, July 6. A memorial service will be held later at the bookstore on Fifty-Seventh Street that was founded by Charles Johnson, Sr., in 1934 — one of the oldest bookstores in the Midwest.

His death signals the passing of an age in which a bookseller's inventory was recorded on three-by-five cards, not on computers; in which the bookseller knew many of his customers personally and understood their different interests; in which a bookseller often worked with individual collectors to build collections that had a clear sense of direction.

The store on Fifty-Seventh Street held

about 10,000 rare books when Charles joined his father (Chaz) in the business in 1955, at age sixteen, and now holds over 20,000 rare books and over 200,000 secondhand books.

A longtime member of the ABAA and the ILAB, Charles served for two terms as the President of the Midwest Chapter of the Antiquarian Booksellers' Association of America. He also served on the Board of Directors, the Ethics Committee and the Membership Committee of the National Chapter of the ABAA. He was an active member of the Caxton Club and regular contributor to The Caxtonian.

He is survived by his son, Gabriel, who joined his father and his grandfather in the business in 1981, after being graduated from the University of Chicago. A memorial service will be held later in September at Chas. Johnson & Son, Ltd. Antiquarian Booksellers, on Fifty-Seventh Street.

Olivia and Delilah had organized everything, even putting up copies of articles about the closing from the *New York Times* and the *Chicago Tribune.* Olivia was standing in the doorway of the shop, wearing a white silk blouse and a dark blue skirt that fell just below her knees — right where she'd been standing the morning we started putting together the Orwell display back in 1984. I didn't recognize her at first, and when I did, it was as if I were seeing her for the first time, standing in this doorway in her orange Balenciaga shoes and her "enchanted boat" sweatshirt.

"Everything under control?" I asked.

"Delilah's gone to talk to Piccolo Mondo to see about getting more wine. A lot of people are here already. I'll get the Piccolo Mondo people to help me push the chairs up. People can stand in the back. Your job is to stay here and greet them."

"Like a greeter at a funeral? My own funeral?"

"Don't be difficult, Gabe," she said.

I stepped up to the plate and greeted members of the Caxton Club, Chicago authors, patrons of the shop and U of C professors, and people who came in off the street for a free glass of wine and an hors d'oeuvre. I greeted friends and neighbors and students. Everyone kept saying how sad it was, and I had to bite my tongue. If you're so sad, I wanted to say, why are you buying your books online instead of coming into the shop? But that would have been preaching to the choir. The people who were there that night were the people who *had* come into the shop. They had a right to be sad.

I'd called Mrs. Ogilvie to make sure the Loft was free. I was planning to leave that night. I had to get away, away from the empty house, away from the doomed shop.

Some people dressed up, and some dressed down. Suits and ties, jeans and T-shirts. Parker Abrams looked splendid in a gray silk suit with a ribbed yellow tie. Delilah wore one of her yellow dresses, not bright yellow but earth-toned. Miss Sullivan, her cane hooked over the back of her chair in the front row, was all in black. Toni Glidden, the mayor of St. Anne, who still had a condo on Lincoln Park West — was looking very smart in a blue-black silk dress, the color of the ink I used in my Aurora fountain pen. A woman in the back was wearing a straw hat and a cream-colored dress. Her face glowed, like the face of a movie star. She was probably wearing some kind of expensive radioactive makeup that an ordinary person couldn't buy in an ordinary shop.

I was glad when Dr. Connor, the Caxton Club president, finally stepped up to the microphone. After the usual squawks and hums, he began by remembering Grandpa Chaz and the early days of the shop, and moving on to Dad's role in building our inventory in Modern Firsts, and then to the readings he used to organize, and his service to the Caxton Club and to other professional organizations, especially the Midwest Chapter of the ABAA.

I was supposed to bring up the rear, and it was getting late — the caterers would start clearing in half an hour, but I was disoriented and still had no idea what I was going to say. While Ruth MacDonald, the director of the library at St. Anne's, was telling a story, the woman wearing a straw hat got up to leave. She was holding a book in one hand and had slung a huge leather purse over her shoulder. She walked straight toward me, looking at me boldly as if she were trying to intimidate me. I thought she intended to walk out of the shop with the book and I was prepared to stop her, threaten her with a citizen's arrest, but when she got closer, I could see that she'd been crying.

"Gabe," she whispered, and I realized that it was Shirley. She took my arm and pulled me outside. "I'm sorry, Gabe," she said. "It's just too sad. About your dad. I have to go. I've got to pick up my son at O'Hare, and I'm already late. You know I loved him, and I think he loved me too. Maybe I didn't understand at the time, but I understand now. I saw the article about the memorial in the *Trib.*"

Up close I could see the fine lines that radiated from the corners of her eyes. "Shirley? Is it really you? Did you come all the way from Vegas?"

"No," she said, "I came from Glencoe. I'm a suburban matron now. I married Angelo Salvatore." Angelo Salvatore was a prominent defense lawyer; someone you called when you were in serious trouble. "We have two kids. One's in law school at Stanford. The other — I just wanted to see the store before it closed. Angelo's a big reader; he wanted to come, but he's in LA. But you'd better get back in there."

"Will I see you again?"

She laughed. "Probably not in this lifetime."

"That's what you said the last time."

"Unless you come to Glencoe," she said. "We're in the phone book. Or commit a serious felony. Then you'll want to talk to Angelo. He wanted to come tonight but something happened and he had to go to LA. They're probably wondering what happened to you. I'd better go."

"Shirley," I said. "What was the book Dad give you? The one he left on his desk for you?"

She looked puzzled for a minute. Then she smiled. "*To the Lighthouse,*" she said.

"Did you read it?"

She laughed. "No, but I still have it."

Olivia was coming out the door. I knew the look. She was going to scold me. But when she saw me, she said, "Gabe, are you all right? You've got to make a speech, you know. You've got to say *something.*"

Twenty-five years had passed since the Orwell display; twenty years since she'd come back from New Haven and I'd seen her reflection in the broken window of the shop, on the morning after the bombing, and thought I'd discovered the truth about love. How many times could I come back to the same point? Or was it a different point each time? Olivia was not fighting aging like Shirley, but all those years were swept away in a moment: "Will you come to Michigan with me?" I said. "After this is over? You've just signed a contract with Johns Hopkins for *Varieties.* We ought to celebrate."

"Tonight? You mean a dirty weekend?"

"We both need a dirty weekend. A little comfort. I've already reserved the Loft."

"Gabe, are you sure about this? What about Saskia?"

"She's twenty years old, and she lives in

Burton-Judson."

"Gabe, they're waiting for you."

"Will you come with me?"

"Gabe, I don't know what to say. Just get in there. We'll talk about it later."

I walked through the crowded shop to the podium. "I thought I might tell an old story," I said, "about how bits of wood (runes) and the shoulder bones of sheep and camels (the Koran), and how clay tablets gave way to paper and to the scroll, and how the scroll gave way to the codex, perhaps the most monumental technological change in the history of the book. And how the codex gave way to the printed book, and how the printed book is giving way to the electronic reader. The old order changeth, yielding place to new, and God fulfills himself in many ways. Let's hope so.

"But instead I'm going to tell you a story about the time Dad and I went to New York to bid on a Kelmscott Chaucer for Dr. Martin, a neurologist who collected arts-and-crafts-movement books from the end of the century. The nineteenth century. I was thirteen years old and was very excited to ride the Broadway Limited and stay at the Chelsea on West Twenty-Third Street, where Arthur C. Clarke and Stanley Kubrick had collaborated on the screenplay for

184

2001: A Space Odyssey. It was my first auction too, and though I know now that Swann Galleries is not as upscale as Sotheby's and Christie's, it has a special place in my heart, and I've come to appreciate the bare walls and exposed pipes, the comfortable chairs, the palpable respect for the books themselves. Books are not a sideline at Swann's.

"Dr. Martin already had a Kelmscott *Chaucer* and wanted to be sure that he was buying a superior copy. He needed someone on the ground who knew about ink and paper and decorations and bindings, someone familiar with the Kelmscott Press books, someone who knew the other dealers and the collectors or institutions they were likely representing, someone who would represent his interests in the war of all against all that is fought out on the gallery floor. You have to remember that in those days there was no telephone bidding, no Internet bidding. You could see your opponents and judge when just a slight increase or two over your limit would probably take home the prize.

"Most of the lots were going for between five hundred and two thousand, but we paid ten thousand for the Chaucer. That was in 1971. At the Garden sale at Sotheby's in

1989, a copy sold for $176,000, and another copy, in pigskin, was knocked down at Christie's last year for $140,000, and right now Cohn & Son in New York is offering a copy for $160,000, but that's one of a handful of copies printed on vellum.

"When we arrived at Union Station at eight o'clock the next morning, Dr. Martin was waiting for us. Dad handed him the book and told him that the underbidder was so-and-so, who was probably bidding on behalf of another so-and-so. I don't remember the names, but I remember that Dr. Martin was pleased when he heard them. I didn't understand these passions at the time, but the rivalry between collectors is as fierce as the rivalry between the Cubs and the Cardinals, the Yankees and the Red Sox. Fiercer.

"Over the years, Dad and I helped Dr. Martin build his Kelmscott Press collection, till he had everything. I got a call from him about a week after Dad died. He was sorry he hadn't come to the funeral, he said, but he couldn't get out anymore. Now that he'd filled out his run of Kelmscott Press books, there was nothing for him to look forward to. He wanted to sell. 'The kids don't want them,' he said. 'They won't know what to do with them when I'm gone, and I haven't got much longer to go.'

" 'You ever think about giving it to a library? The whole collection, I mean. Your alma mater? Northwestern, isn't it? Keep them all together?'

" 'The kids want the money,' he said. 'Besides, I don't like the idea of locking the books up in an institution. Let other people have a chance to enjoy them. I'm starting to think of them as old sailors returning to the sea after a spell on dry land.'

" 'That's a lovely image, Dr. Martin. I'll remember that.'

" 'I want to keep them at home,' he said, 'till I set sail myself, or whatever the hell happens at the end. I used to worry about it, but I don't worry anymore. I think I've mixed up my metaphors,' he said. 'I used to worry about that too, but I'm eighty-six years old. I guess I can do whatever I want.'

" 'How do you want to handle the books?'

" 'Gabriel, you remember when you and your dad came back from New York with the *Chaucer,* and I met you at Union station?'

" 'Of course I remember.'

" 'That was probably the happiest day of my life. I remember everything about it. Your dad was his usual rumpled self, but you were wearing a vest suit and flared

187

slacks and a wide belt. That was the year after your Mamma went away, wasn't it. They were still working on the Sears Tower. You ever hear from her?'

" 'I got a letter after Dad died,' I said. 'We always figured she was living in Rome, but she's living in Florence. She doesn't like the bread there. No salt.'

" 'I'd like to see you again,' he said. 'I'd like to see your dad again too, but I guess that's not going to happen now. But you and I can sit down together and take a last look at the books, figure out what to do with them. Just the two of us. I'd like that. Give me a call.'

" 'I'd like that too,' I said. 'Give me a week or two, okay?'

" 'We'll have a glass of whiskey and drink a toast to your dad, and we'll figure something out,' he said. And that was the last time we spoke. He was dead by the end of the week, and the Kelmscott Press books are going to return to the open market without my help. 'Old sailors returning to the sea after a spell on dry land.' It's a lovely image, isn't it? I hope you'll remember it when you think of Dad and of Chas. Johnson & Son, Ltd. Antiquarian Booksellers."

The only thing left to drink at the end of

the evening, after the Piccolo Mondo staff had cleaned up, was a half bottle of pinot grigio, which Olivia had set aside on a shelf behind the cash register. We carried the bottle with us and walked through the empty shop, drinking out of plastic cups. We walked all four floors, up and down the aisles that opened off the atrium at the front, up the spiral staircases in the back of the shop, through Children's Literature and Cookbooks and Mysteries, through Africa and Asia and the Americas, through Ancient Greece and Rome, through Art and Architecture, through Psychology and Biography, Philosophy and Religion, History of Science, Literature.

"You can feel the sadness in the old books," I said, "in their spines, in their dust jackets, in their smell. It's like feeling a glass of wine moving into your body, softening the focus."

"I suppose people didn't want to sell them," Olivia said. And I thought she was right. People sold their books when they were desperate, facing bankruptcy or illness or divorce. Or death.

Or because the next generation — like the Martin kids — wasn't interested in maintaining a private library.

Olivia pulled a book off a shelf and found

a grocery list, which she read to me: "one bottle Perrier, white wine, tomatoes, supper, apples, green peppercorns (near the hot peppers), *polpa,* tortelloni. At the end it says, 'Love — H.' And after that: 'Don't forget the cottage cheese — medium curd.' Underlined. Medium curd?"

"It's a joke," I said.

When she put the book back, I looked at the title: *Illinois Star Watching Guide.* "If you keep pulling books off the shelves," I said, "you'll find pressed flowers, love letters, strands of hair, grocery lists, bookmarks, snapshots, theater tickets, signatures and inscriptions, books inscribed to children at Christmas, book inscribed on birthdays. And sometimes drawings. Books dedicated to the dead, *in memoriam.* Once I found a letter from a pilot who'd been shot down over Okinawa in World War Two."

"How do you know he was shot down?"

"Because his wife, or his mother, wrote it on the envelope."

"It wasn't your fault," Olivia said.

"Well, somebody shot him down."

"I mean the closing. It's not anybody's fault."

"It's somebody's fault," I said. "We should have computerized sooner, we should have started selling online — at least the used books. Dad couldn't bear the thought. I guess I couldn't either. We got too far behind the curve."

I picked up a set of bound galleys. It was a translation of *The Iliad* that was lying open, spread-eagle, on the table where Alex and I used to study together and where I'd been sitting when Shirley asked if I wanted to spend a little time with her. I'd been afraid then — when I was waiting for Shirley — and I was afraid now, afraid that Olivia would turn me down, or maybe afraid that she wouldn't. I looked at the book. "This doesn't belong here," I said. "It belongs on the third floor." I didn't recognize the translator.

"Somebody loved this passage," I said. "Look how it's underlined. Book eighteen. Right after the death of Patroklus. Iris is telling Achilles to show himself to the Trojans. Athena wraps a shining cloud around him and they go to the wall. And he lets out a great shout. And Athena stands behind him and she shouts too."

I read the passage aloud. It was a prose translation, but I tried to imagine the line breaks, as if it were in verse:

Achilles halted and cried out, his voice
Like a trumpet sounding from a besieged

city, Unmanning the Trojans and terrifying their horses, so that they turned their carts. The charioteers turned pale when they saw the unearthly fire that Athena kindled around the head of Achilles. Three times Achilles shouted and twelve brave warriors were killed in the ensuing panic.

I laughed. "I know just how he feels," I said. The shop was perfectly quiet for a moment, as if it were holding its breath. Without thinking about it, I threw my head back and let out a great shout. I shouted three times, and I could hear Olivia shouting behind me. And behind Olivia, I could hear Dad shouting, and Grandpa Chaz. We filled the empty shop with our bronze voices: "AAAAAAAAAAAHHHHHH AAAAAAAAAAAHHHHHHHH AAAAAA-AAAA-HHHHHHHHHHH." And then Olivia and I looked at each other and started to laugh.

"Okay," she said. "I'll go with you." I thought maybe we had come uncongealed!

XII. Epiphanies
(SEPTEMBER 2009)

We walked over to Blackstone to get the car, Grandpa Chaz's Cadillac, which now had forty thousand miles on it.

"I don't know, Gabe," she said as we passed Poop Corner Number One. "What about clean underwear?"

"We'll only be there two days."

"As long as we don't have an accident."

As we drove past the old Moo & Oink on Stony Island — QUALITY MEAT FOR THE FAMILY BUDGET — Olivia started riffing on the radio commercials: "Give me a wave if you like catfish. Jump up if it's your favorite dish!"

I joined in: "Wave for catfish — Moo & Oink!"

"Scrrrrrrream for ribs," she sang — "Moo & Oink!"

We were quiet for a while.

"Was Stony Island ever an island?" she asked.

"Thirty-five million years ago," I said. "A coral reef. Got buried by limestone. When the glaciers receded, they left part of it behind."

"Where is it now?"

"Between Ninety-First Street and Ninety-Fourth."

"You mean it's still there?"

"It got blasted away to make room for sewer and water mains."

"That's something to think about."

I was thinking we're probably going to talk for a while without saying what was really on our minds. But maybe not. As we pulled onto the Skyway at Seventy-Ninth Street, she said, "Feeling better?" It was an invitation to open up.

"Better, but not good."

"I thought for a minute there," she added, "that you were going to faint. Afterwards, when you were shouting."

"You were shouting too."

"It felt good, didn't it? But who was the woman in the straw hat?"

"Someone I used to know. A long time ago. A friend of Dad's, actually."

We pulled off the interstate and stopped for gas at a truck stop just outside Gary, hometown of the late Michael Jackson.

Olivia used the restroom while I filled up the car and checked the oil. The Cadillac was a great car, but it was starting to burn oil. I added a quart and we were on our way.

Back on I-94, I felt agitated. I told her that Dad wanted me to walk away from the whole thing. Forget about setting up shop on Michigan Avenue, forget about going into business with Marcus. Go to Italy or the south of France.

She suddenly sat up straight and turned toward me. The idea that I could go into business with Marcus in New York galvanized her. She couldn't believe that I hadn't jumped at the idea.

"Gabe," she said. "You're sitting on eight or nine million dollars' worth of old books. You could buy a condo on the Upper West Side." She started to poke at her phone. "Let me Google 'New York condos Upper West Side.' David knew someone with a condo . . . we used to stay there . . . Here's one on Eighty-Ninth Street, right on the park, for two million three hundred ninety-five thousand. Two bedrooms, two baths."

"Whoa whoa whoa," I said.

"We used to take the train down from New Haven. We'd take the Metro-North to Grand Central Terminal and eat in one of those restaurants in Bryant Park. Or just pack a lunch and eat it on a bench."

"You and David?"

"New York is so fantastic."

"Two million's a little steep."

"Let me look for something on the East Side. New York is so fantastic," she said again. "New Yorkers are smarter, more alert, more spirited. And they stay up later. You can walk around lower Manhattan at two o'clock in the morning and there are people everywhere — people, taxies, cafés, bars, restaurants. People dress smarter too. You could get yourself some new clothes at Barney's and you'd fit right in. It's a magnet for talent too. And if you want a break from the city, you've got the Hudson River Valley, you've got the Hamptons, you've got the Jersey shore. And it's not so corrupt. At least not like Chicago. And the food. You can get anything."

"You must have spent a lot of time there."

"As much as we could. It wasn't always easy to get away."

"I suppose David's wife was a problem," I said.

Olivia flared up. "Gabe, don't judge me. I was in love. We were in love. You've got no idea."

"Maybe you're right."

"No maybes about it, Gabe."

I could think of a lot of things I wanted to say at this point, but probably nothing that Olivia wanted to hear.

She'd taken her stockings off in the restroom and put on a pair of sandals with complicated straps that she bought in the convenience store at the truck stop. I admired her painted toenails. And she'd bought a little sign that she pulled out of her purse and propped up on the dash. White background, red letters.

IF WOMEN CAN LEARN TO FAKE ORGASMS, MEN CAN LEARN TO FAKE LISTENING.

"Okay," I said. "I'm listening."

"Go, to, New, York," she said, enunciating each word clearly. "Now I'm going to take a little nap." She turned away from me and leaned her head against the window.

Was she offering to go with me? I wondered, but I didn't ask.

It wasn't till we crossed into Michigan that I began to relax. What I felt, at that moment, was relief, maybe something better than "relief" — surprise. I didn't have a clear plan, but maybe I didn't need one. I was driving down the highway at night with a beautiful woman next to me, a beautiful

197

angry woman. Angry even in her sleep. Her head leaning against the windowpane. The sign on the seat beside her.

She didn't wake up till we turned off I-94 and passed a new landmark, the Three Fires Casino. All lit up. Blazing like an enormous bonfire.

"The Three Fires," I said though she hadn't asked, "was the name of a confederacy. The Three Fires Confederacy. The Ojibwe were the Keepers of Tradition; the Odawa were the Keepers of the Trade; the Potawatomi were the Keepers of the Fire. They all got kicked out of Michigan, except for the Pokagon band of the Potawatomi. They got to stay because they were Roman Catholics, and because Leopold Pokagon outmaneuvered the federal government. But they didn't get federal recognition until a couple of years ago, and the new mayor, Toni Glidden, encouraged them to build a casino here: three thousand slot machines, one hundred gaming tables, two thousand jobs, over four hundred hotel rooms, six restaurants, fifteen thousand people a day, eighteen-hole golf course."

"Have you been there?"

I shook my head. "I don't like to gamble," I said. "Probably corresponds to a defect in my character."

"Maybe we could work on that at the blackjack table, give the three tribes back some of the money we owe them. Do they kick you out if you count cards? David and I used to go to Foxwoods in Connecticut. David got kicked out for counting cards. We had to leave."

"Too much excitement?"

She nodded.

We drove into town and stopped near the Municipal Marina and parked in the boat launch parking area. "This is a town of ten thousand people," I said, "but it's got twelve hundred slips. Three marinas, actually. Surrounded by beautiful condos. A fifty-million-dollar development. The *New York Times* called St. Anne a hot spot, but after the housing market collapsed, the development company went belly-up. The new mayor, Toni Glidden, is a friend of mine. You saw her at the memorial tonight."

"She was the woman in the straw hat?"

"No, that was Shirley, Dad's old girlfriend. Toni was wearing a blue-black dress with straps. She still has a condo on Lincoln Park West, over the zoo. You can hear the seals barking from her living room."

"Then how can she be mayor of St. Anne?"

"After her husband died, she moved to St.

Anne, but she kept the condo. She's been coming to St. Anne all her life, knows everyone, knows how to talk to people, knows where the money is. I guess after her husband died, she was looking for something to do, so she ran for mayor. People were sick of the old guys who were lining their pockets with the development money. She's been putting things back together. A lot of people are actually glad that the housing market crash put a stop to the development."

I had Olivia's attention. "How's she putting things back together?"

"She formed a corporation to refinance the Town Square development. That's what they call it. And she's managed to keep a lot of the things that the developers wanted to zone out of business: Vitale's Italian grocery, Andy's Fruit Market, Potts' Hardware, the lumber yard, the old Michigan Central Depot. You can get good espresso at half a dozen places, but you can still get a regular cup of coffee at Atkinson's. She's the one who got the grant from the state for restoring the old depot."

"How do you know this wonderful woman?"

"Summers in St. Anne. We took sailing lessons together. She married a petroleum geologist who worked for Amoco."

"Is she beautiful too?"

"Yes," I said. "And when you have a conversation with her, she makes you feel good about yourself."

"I see."

Olivia disapproved of Amoco Oil; she disapproved of the casino, and she disapproved of all the new condos, but she wasn't immune to the beauty of the lake, and of the boats: yawls, ketches, schooners, trawlers, cabin cruisers, motor yachts. I knew she was conflicted, hadn't given herself up entirely to this adventure. But I could feel her lightening up as we walked along the boardwalk and laughed at the names of the boats: *Miss Behaving, Wet Dreams, She Got the House.*

"My mother used to make up stories about the names," I said. "Just like she used to make up stories about the big houses on Blackstone."

Olivia took my arm. "Why don't *you* make up a story about one of the names?"

"Which one?"

"She Got the House."

"That's too easy, don't you think? Maybe too sad."

"A sad tale's best for winter," she said.

"I see them sitting in the kitchen," I said,

201

"in that condo, the one right across from us, by that big sailboat with the red and yellow flag on the mast. There's a light in the window, and I'm looking through the window. I see a counter with two stools drawn up. They're sitting on the stools in their bathrobes. It's morning and they're drinking coffee. I see a fancy espresso maker on the counter, not a stovetop pot, but an electric one. The kind you see in all the catalogs now."

"Are they mad at each other?"

"No. They're sad at each other. Things haven't worked out. They don't know why. They thought things would work out if they moved to St. Anne. They bought all new furniture, and the fancy electric espresso maker. They drink their coffee in little Italian cups with blue stripes around the rim."

"Is he in love with another woman?"

"No, but she's seeing another man. She doesn't want to, but she can't help herself."

"So why does *she* get the house?"

"He's going to live in Chicago," I said. "He's already made an offer on a condo in a Mies van der Rohe building on Lake Shore Drive. He's going to keep the boat here, at least for now, and rent a *pied-à-terre* in St. Anne. She's going to put their condo here on the market and find something less expensive."

"I've always wanted a *pied-à-terre.* What a nice phrase. *A foot on the ground.* Have you ever known anyone who has a *pied-à-terre?*"

"Toni. She's still got the condo by the Lincoln Park zoo. But that would be a big *pied-à-terre,* more like a *cul-à-terre.* Your whole butt on the ground."

"So what are they doing now? The couple in the story."

"Right now they're talking about the time before they had tons of money, about the time they went to Rome and got locked out of their rental apartment, about the hundred thousand lire bottle of wine they drank at a wine bar on Via Condotti, about their little girl who died when she was only three years old. Anna was her name, and she was born with a full head of red hair. They were going to try to stay together, but she's changed her mind again. He's pouring the last of the wine into her glass."

"I thought they were drinking coffee," Olivia said.

"Right," I said. "That was in the morning. Tonight they're drinking red wine. He knows now that he's got nothing left to lose, so he stands behind her and rubs her shoulders. She puts her hands on his hands as he kneads her shoulders. He leans over and puts his face in her hair."

"I think that's enough, Gabe."

"He's going to take the train to Chicago in the morning," I said. "She'll see him off at the new Amtrak station, and then she's going to meet with a real estate agent."

"I thought she got the house?"

"Can't afford to keep it."

Vitale's, across from the boat factory on Water Street, was closed. We drove past the Abrams Funeral Parlor on Duval, between the town and the mall, across from Andy's Fruit Market — "That's Delilah's uncle," I said. "His main operation is in Benton Harbor, but he owns the one here and one over in Three Oaks."

She gave me a look that said she didn't believe me.

"Why not?" I said.

"I don't know."

We drove out to Harding's Friendly Market, in a shopping center east of town, where we bought oranges, eggs, bacon, bread for breakfast, and a bottle of wine for tonight. I wasn't particular about wine, which is more expensive in Michigan than in Illinois, but Olivia was particular and picked out an expensive sauvignon blanc.

"I thought you liked pinot grigio," I said.

"I feel like something a little rougher tonight."

"My mother usually drank red wine," I said, "that she got at Vitale's, but she liked sauvignon blanc too. I used to go shopping with her. She always dressed up like an Italian woman just to go to the Co-op in Hyde Park. High heels, her fur coat."

"She *was* an Italian woman."

"St. Anne didn't have a shopping center then. Just Vitale's Market. And Andy's Fruit Market on the corner of the highway and Duval Street. You had to drive up to St. Joe to find a supermarket."

Instead of heading north on I-94, I drove back into town and crossed the river on the LaSalle Road Bridge, which everyone called the Griffon, after LaSalle's ship — the first ship to go down on the Great Lakes — and headed north on LaSalle Road. We were passing the college — St. Anne — which was on our left, on the lake side, when Olivia's cell phone rang and she turned away to enjoy some pretend privacy.

"Saskia," she said after the call.

"Everything okay?"

She nodded. "Checking up on me."

"What'd you tell her?"

"Dirty weekend."

"You told her that? What'd she say?"

"She said I deserved it. And she told me to thank you for the signed copy of *Father Melancholy's Daughter* you gave her for her birthday. And she said she thinks you ought to go into business with Marcus in New York."

"She said that, or you're just making it up? How could she know about Marcus?"

"Gabe," she said. "I'm sorry I gave you a hard time about New York." She paused. "But you really ought to think about it."

Just before we got to Ben Warren's place, we came to the sign that marked a one-mile stretch of private road: IF YOU ARE NOT A RESIDENT, TURN BACK. I suppose I'd wanted Olivia to see that sign. Wanted to see her reaction.

"That's like the sign in your dad's office," she said.

I didn't ask her if she wanted to turn back.

The Loft was unlocked. Mrs. Ogilvie had put clean sheets on the bed and turned on the electric baseboard heating. I was almost expecting to see Dad. "One year when Dad and Grandpa Chaz and I got here, the place was full of bats."

"Now you tell me."

"That was a long time ago. Haven't had any since." I looked around, just in case, inspected the curtains, checked above the windows.

"I thought it would be quieter here."

"It is quiet."

"I hear a lot of rustling, something pounding."

"The waves. After a while you won't hear them. Unless you want to."

We took off our shoes and walked down the steps to the beach. The air was warm but the sand was cold on our feet. We walked past a stretch of a dozen big houses on the bluff above us. We could just see the tops of the roofs. The moon was full and we could see slate blue waves shredded by invisible fingers as they rolled over the sand bars, and the lights of a freighter. Beyond the freighter the lights of Chicago glowed on the horizon.

"Some nights," I said, "if the weather's perfectly clear, you can make out the Sears Tower. With a good pair of binoculars."

"It's the Willis Tower now," she said.

"And Marshall Field's is Macy's."

We walked north along the shore until we came to a couple making love in the sand. On a blanket, but the blanket had scooched out from under them. The woman was on top, straddling the man, whose bottom was digging into the sand. I could almost conjure up the sensation. There was no easy way around them, but it was easy enough to imagine their story. Or maybe not. You never know. I had never actually seen two people fucking like that. Pictures, yes. But real people, no. Their clothes were spread out on the beach beside them. Bikini panties draped over a picnic hamper. An empty wine bottle by the remains of a fire. Maggio sauvignon blanc, the same wine we'd bought at Harding's. I found it easier to imagine their story than my own story.

I don't think either one of us wanted to watch, but it was hard to look away. Not even when there were so many other things to see: glow of Chicago, summer constellations, a full moon, the lights of a big laker.

"Is this an epiphany?" I asked Olivia, "or maybe a spot of time? Like Wordsworth seeing a dead body pop up out of the lake."

She suddenly stopped whispering and broke into poetry:

"At length the dead man, 'mid that
    beauteous scene
Of trees and hills and water, bolt upright
Rose with his ghastly face."

The lovers didn't hear her at first. So she spoke louder. And then she shouted: "Are you okay?"

Now I had something else to ponder.

The woman threw her head back and screamed.

"It's okay," Olivia said. "Don't mind us. We're just going for a walk."

But the lovers uncoupled themselves and took off down the beach. Their buttocks blinking like white caps.

"They left their picnic hamper," Olivia said.

"Why did you do that?" Gabe asked.

"I wanted them to have something to remember."

I looked at Olivia. "Sometimes," I said, "I look at you and think I know what you're thinking, but I'm always wrong."

"You're probably not wrong this time," she said, pulling her summer dress over her head and then waiting for me to embrace her. I could smell the heat coming off her. Her skin shone like the moon. And I was a young man again, about fifteen years old, trembling inside, not understanding, remembering the old scary words from Krafft-Ebing. But at the same time full of love and gratitude. Exempt from the universal laws that govern mortality.

"I don't have a condom. They're back at the Loft."

"I'm on the pill."

"On the pill?"

"Gabe, I'm not a nun."

"Sorry."

"It's all right, Gabe."

When I put my hands on her upper arms, I could feel the life force coursing through her and into me, breaking like the waves breaking behind us. We started out parallel to the shore, but we scooched around and pretty soon I could feel the waves caressing my feet, our feet.

Her eyes were glued shut, but she touched my face and her long fingers felt like rain. She pulled the beach blanket up over us, but not before I got a glimpse of a tattoo on her butt that hadn't been there before. It had been a long time since I'd seen her butt. Twenty years. Longer. Maybe I just didn't remember. I didn't ask. I didn't want to imagine her naked and laughing with another man, or exposing her buttocks in a tattoo parlor. How did they arrange that anyway? But when I twisted around to get a better look at it, she told me to wait till she came; then I could look at it all I wanted. I was seeing with a strange new sight.

The tattoo, a black panther, seemed to glow in the moonlight, like luminous paint. "It looks like it's digging its claws into your butt," I said.

"Just be quiet for a minute and keep moving. Like that."

I kept moving underneath her, a slow easy roll, and the waves kept breaking and licking our feet.

After a long drawn-out orgasm, she said, "The panther is supposed to save us from the Evil One. Its breath is very sweet, signifying the sweet influence of Christ."

"I thought it signified Dionysus?"

"That too."

"The tattoo was part of my spiritual journey." I looked up at her to see if she was serious. "It seemed like a good idea at the time," she said, pulling on her panties. "But if you tell anyone about it, I'll kill you."

"Orwell had tattoos," I said. "On his knuckles. I think the tattoo's a good sign, don't you? A black panther. Very suave. And the lovers too, another good sign." Olivia opened the picnic hamper and discovered another bottle of sauvignon blanc.

"Epiphany?" I said. "Or just a coincidence?"

"You know I don't believe in coincidences," she said, tucking the bottle of wine under her arm.

"Are you going to steal it?" I asked.

"It may be a 'sign,' " she said, "but it's not an 'epiphany.' "

■ ■ ■ ■

In the morning we ate toast with butter and soft-boiled eggs with salt and pepper and Trappy's green hot sauce. The eggs were double yolked, and I regarded this as still another good sign. After breakfast we stood at the top of the steps, as if about to take flight. I wasn't sure if anything had been settled, or even if there was anything to settle.

"Some of these have close to two hundred steps," I said. "The Loft has only sixty-seven. The bluffs get higher the farther north you go. There are one hundred twenty steps at the state park about two miles down the beach."

Olivia was wearing the strappy sandals she'd bought at the truck stop. Her toenails were dark purple. We walked past the spot where we'd surprised the lovers — the picnic hamper was gone — and kept going till we came to a house that I hadn't seen in years, just past the public beach that was part of Duval State Park. It was the most beautiful house I'd ever seen, and I was astonished to see a FOR SALE sign in the window. It made me think of first love, first sex, second love and second sex; it made me think of the Kelmscott *Chaucer,* and of my mother in her fur coat shouting *Ci stiamo avvicinando all'angolo della cacca numero uno.* It made me think of the time Mamma danced with the bass player outside the Rush Tavern on Maxwell Street. It made me think of Grandpa Chaz's snap brim fedora. It made me think of Olivia reading "The Bishop Orders His Tomb" in a southern accent.

I was trembling inside. "This would be a good place," I said, "to cocker up your genius and live free. That's what Dad wanted me to do. This is a place where you could be happy."

"Whoa. Slow down. *'Cocker up your genius and live free'?* What does 'cocker' mean anyway?"

"It's from Middle English *cockren,* 'to baby or pamper.' "

"Hmmm. How do you 'cocker up your genius'? I mean, What would you *do?*"

"Read Montaigne all the way through in French. Maybe do a translation. Take up drawing. I've always wanted to draw. Dig Grandpa Chaz's old Gibson out of the garage and take up the blues or *The American Songbag.* My teacher would *not* approve, but she's in New York now."

"Your little Greek Athena?"

"Atene," I said. "Her mother spelled it wrong on the birth certificate."

"You could wear your grandpa's hat," she said.

"I might reread the *Odyssey* in Greek. Marcus and I read most of it in Professor Blake's Homer class. I've still got my old onionskin Oxford text, *Iliad* and *Odyssey* in one volume, and we've got an Aldine *Homer* in the rare book room."

"You need a job," Olivia said. "You need to work, to have something you have to do when you get up in the morning. Me too. You're not the cocker-up-your-genius-and-live-free type."

"All right. But just think about it for a minute. You want to know what my ideal day would be like?" I took her by the hand. She pulled back at first, and then she relented and gave my hand a squeeze.

"Up at first light," I said, "for a swim; then breakfast; then at my desk with Montaigne till time for lunch; then an hour to read Homer; an hour to do some sketching; and hour to practice the guitar. I could get a chainsaw, look after the trees. We could sit out on the balcony, watch the sun set in the evening."

We climbed up the steps to get a better look at the house, which had big wooden shutters over the front windows. The little outbuilding, on the south side of the house, which we could barely see from the beach, wasn't locked. We went inside.

"It's a sauna," I said. "I don't know how it works, but how hard could it be?" We sat down on a wooden bench. "Look, you heat the wood in the stove, and the wood heats the rocks. I think you splash water on the rocks and that makes the steam. And a big thermometer. Look, it goes up to a hundred ninety degrees."

"That's hot."

I turned to Olivia. "What do you think?"

"What do I think? Gabe, the house looks like it's about to slide into the lake. Look at the bluff. It's been eaten away. It's collapsing. Going to collapse."

"That house has been here ever since I can remember. We don't usually walk this far, so I haven't seen it in three or four years."

"But it's not going to be here much longer. You'd never get insurance. Maybe Lloyd's of London."

"It's post and beam construction. You can see that the piers are set back from the edge of the bluff. It's not going to go anywhere."

She didn't say anything for a while.

"Do you ever wonder," I asked her, "what

would have happened if you'd said 'yes' when I asked you to marry me? After the bombing, when you came back to Chicago. I saw the reflection of a pregnant woman in the window — just starting to show — and when I realized it was you, I thought I understood what love was."

"Yes, I remember, but how did you know I wasn't married?"

"You didn't *look* married."

"Gabe, pu-leeze. How did I look?"

"You looked like you were in trouble."

She didn't say anything, but at least she didn't blow her stack.

"Gabe," she said, "how many times do I have to say it?"

"You've already made enough mistakes, you didn't want to make any more. That was twenty years ago. I've never understood that."

"I'm not sure I can explain. I was a girl then and now I'm older. Let's just leave it at that and have an uncomplicated dirty weekend? We've got one more night after tonight. Let's not spoil it."

"If we'd had children, they'd be in college now."

"I *have* a child, Gabe. She's a sophomore at the University of Chicago. She still hangs out at the shop on Fifty-Seventh Street. She studies her Arabic at the big table in the front of the second floor where you used to do your Latin homework. She still has the Big-Little books you gave here when she was just starting to read. And a copy of *Peter Rabbit* when she was six. She's got *all* her birthday books — the ones you sent her in Ann Arbor too. They're lined up in her dorm room at Burton-Judson. She wants to go to Amman with Nadia this summer, but it's too dangerous: Nadia's parents would freak out if they found out their daughter's a lesbian."

"You know what our problem was?"

"*Our* problem, or *your* problem?"

"We didn't have any big hurdles to leap over. No parental disapproval to work around. No one to defy. Dad encouraged us, smoothed the way, practically tucked us into bed. Remember how we used to go skating, the three of us? I had my own space over the garage. And you didn't have anyone keeping tabs on you. Nobody put a sword in the bed between us. Your aunt too. She called me when you were in labor. She told them at the hospital that I was your husband. 'Go to her.' That's what she said when I got to the hospital. 'Go to her.' "

"And I appreciated it, Gabe. You did good."

"You don't think it would work?"

"What would work?"

"Don't you think we could be happy here in this beautiful house? On this beautiful inland sea? Borders is in big trouble. Their stock is down to nothing. Get out now before they go under. We could sell books out of the house."

"Are you crazy? This is the sort of thing that's fun to think about when you're young, but nobody in his right mind would consider it seriously."

"Uncertainty is a way of life," I said. But the moment had come and gone. "I thought I was having a vision," I said. "But I guess it was just a waking dream."

"I'm sorry, Gabe," she said, putting her hand on my arm. "It's a waking dream, and it's a good one. But I'm applying for a job at Borders headquarters in Ann Arbor. I want to be part of the team that keeps Borders out of Chapter 11. The job hasn't been posted yet, so please don't say anything to anyone, but I've been invited to apply, and all signals are *go*."

■ ■ ■ ■

PART TWO:
THE GOOD LIFE

■ ■ ■ ■

XIII. The House
On the Lake

(2009–2010)

Saul Bellow used to say that Chicago had three great universities and that Chas. Johnson & Son was one of them. I heard him say it twice — once to Grandpa Chaz, right after Mamma went away — and once to Dad, right after Punch died in 1976. I was just finishing my junior year at the Lab School. Bellow had come into the shop to get one of his early novels, *The Victim,* and was admiring our raccoon coat while Grandpa Chaz went to look for a copy. He turned to me and asked how I was doing.

"My dog just died," I said. "My grandfather wanted to call him Edgar, after Edgar Allen Poe, but my mother called him Punch, which is short for Pulcinella."

Bellow put his hand on my shoulder. "When he was about your age," he said, "maybe a little younger — my son promised me that if he could have a dog, he'd never be sad again. But it doesn't work that way,

221

does it?"

"I understand that now," I said.

He was right, of course, and now, thirty years later, I was thinking of that conversation as I walked through the empty shop for the last time, and I wished I'd offered him the raccoon coat, which was in the back of our front hall closet, along with Mamma's fur coat.

The books from the rare book room had been crammed into the house on Blackstone — Jefferson bookcases at odd angles in every room, archival storage boxes stacked in the upstairs halls and bedrooms. Two hundred thousand used books had been moved to our warehouse on the South Side, where Delilah was setting up an online operation. The metal bookcases along the perimeter and along the load-bearing columns that ran through the center of the shop — which had originally been two buildings — had been moved too. Not a book in sight. Just crumbling brick and rough plaster.

Olivia and Saskia were in Ann Arbor.

It was already dark when I locked up and walked home. The streets had been plowed and the sidewalks shoveled. Most of the front yards along Blackstone were alight with Christmas displays. I hadn't gotten around to stringing lights around Grandpa Chaz's crabapple tree, which had weathered more than fifty Chicago winters, but the tree was still full of bright red berries, and that was enough. The house was cold, but instead of turning the heat up, I got Mamma's coat out of her closet and put it on, and suddenly I was warm. I ate some salami and cheese, being careful not to get my greasy fingers on the coat.

Life as I had known it had come to an end. I was going to have to invent a new life, one that was not rooted in the old shop on Fifty-Seventh Street, one that did not depend on Olivia.

I'd never found the Italian translation of Montaigne that Dad had given Mamma for Christmas, but the copy of the *Essais* that I'd bought at the Boston fair was sitting on my desk in my bedroom upstairs. The book had summoned me at the fair, and now it summoned me again with a sudden urgency.

How many of us, Thoreau asks in *Walden,* have dated a new era in our lives from the discovery of a book, a book that explains us to ourselves, a book that addresses the same questions that trouble us, all of us? Marcus and I had read Montaigne in Jock Weintraub's seminar on autobiography, my senior year at Chicago, and at that moment I thought that maybe Montaigne's *Essais* would be that book. Not Plato — too suspicious of pleasure, always hankering for an ideal realm beyond the world of the senses. Not Aristotle — maximizing our unique capacity for reason. But easygoing Montaigne. "The greatest thing in the world is to know how to belong to oneself." That was the most important thing I remembered from the Weintraub's seminar. I searched for the passage in the French text, but I couldn't find it and finally fell asleep at my desk, still wearing Mamma's fur coat.

In the morning — Christmas morning — I opened up my computer and managed to locate the property in France, the place between Sarlat et Bergerac that was *prêt à emménager,* ready to move into — not far from where Montaige wrote his *essais.* Ninety-nine thousand euros seemed like a real bargain. Then I Googled the Monadnock Building and imagined Montaigne in the lobby, waiting for one of the slow elevators, or buying a hat at Optimo, or a shirt at Zeglio's Custom Men's Clothing, or getting his hair cut at the Metropolitan Barber Shop, or having an espresso in the Intelligentsia Café. I Googled condos on the Upper East Side, not far from where Marcus lived with his wife and his youngest daughter, tried to picture Montaigne walking through Central Park, or standing in front of Cohn & Son on Seventh Avenue, admiring the books in the window as he might have admired the unbound sheets of Plutarch's *Lives* in the workshop of Simone Millanges on the rue St. James in Bordeaux. And then I called Mrs. Ogilvie and asked if the Loft was available, which of course it was, and would she turn some heat on. I threw some clothes in an overnight bag and drove to St. Anne.

The Loft was warm enough when I got there, but there was nothing to eat, and I was hungry. I unpacked my overnight bag and drove back to the highway, to the Casino, which I had never visited. It was pretty amazing. Huge. Over four hundred rooms and suites. I wasn't looking for the "pulse-pounding experiences" that the Casino promised: CHANGE YOUR LIFE BY WINNING $500,000 AT THE WHEEL OF FORTUNE® OR AT SUPER SPIN™. Or you could go to the SPECIALLY DESIGNED HIGH-LIMIT SLOT AREA FOR "MAXIMUM EXHILARATION." This is just like a book fair, I thought. My pulse was already pounding; I was as close as I wanted to be to "maxi-

225

mum exhilaration."

I ate a 42-day-dry-aged steak at the Copper Rock Steak House for a very reasonable price, and then I experienced *some* exhilaration by losing a hundred dollars betting on the red at the roulette table. But the sight of so many people pouring money into slot machines canceled out the exhilaration. You don't even have to put coins into the machines. You just create an account up front and then keep pushing buttons on your machine till it tells you you've run out of money. But, in fact, the Casino brought a lot of people to St. Anne, provided two thousand jobs, and put a lot of money into the Pokagon Revenue Sharing Fund.

I had to make several calls in the morning before I managed to locate a real estate agent. The woman who answered the phone at Shoreline Realty said they were closed for the long Christmas weekend; she'd just come in to pick up some files, but she agreed to wait for me. She turned out to be a very attractive woman, part schoolmarm, part night club hostess. She was dressed in jeans and a man's white shirt. Her dirty blond hair was in a tangle. "Merry Christmas," she said.

It was a medium-size office. Two desks in front. Two comfortable chairs. Maps on the walls. Cubicles farther back. Lakefront properties with photos listed on a large bulletin board.

"Nothing under half a million?" I asked.

"Not on the lake," she said. The agent was tall and blond, hadn't put on her makeup but she looked good without it. She offered coffee. "It's good coffee," she said. "Hasn't been sitting around. I made it after you called this morning."

I had trouble explaining the location. "Just on the other side of the state park," I said, and finally she said, "Oh. That must be the old Palmisano place." She laughed. "Sorry," she said. "I shouldn't laugh, but . . . I don't have that listing, and I don't know who does. I didn't even know it was on the market."

"There's a FOR SALE sign in the window."

"Are you sure we're talking about the same place? Looks like it's going to slide into the lake?"

"You could say that, I suppose, or you could say it's cantilevered out over the edge of the bluff."

"Look, Mr. Johnson. I'm not in the business of discouraging buyers, but — you're asking for trouble." She paused. "I'm in the business of selling houses. Well, it's more complicated than that. It's more like matchmaking. You want people to be happy in their new home. Let me show you one of the new condos. They're really lovely. You'd have a fantastic view of the lake. Pool, sauna, meeting rooms, doorman."

"I see where this is going."

"I see it too, and it's not what I'd like to see."

"Who has the listing?"

"I don't think anyone does. Look, you'll never get a mortgage because you'll never get insurance."

"Lloyd's of London?"

"Yes." I'd expected her to laugh at the joke, but instead she named three or four insurance companies up there with Lloyd's of London. "But you'll pay twenty-five K a year for it."

"What if I just don't get insurance?"

"You won't get a mortgage."

"What if I pay cash?"

"You're prepared to pay cash?"

I nodded.

"And if it slides into the lake?"

"Aren't there companies that stabilize bluffs?"

"Groins, revetments . . . They help, and there's new stuff coming down the pike. Ecofriendly, native plants, diverting the ground water. But you still won't get insurance."

"Can I at least look at the place? It ought to be cheap, given the housing market, all those empty condos."

"The market's coming back. The crisis has brought people together. And the new mayor has got yuppies and locals on the same side for a change. She used to be an editor at *Chicago Magazine*."

The new mayor, I explained to her, was, in fact, an old friend — Toni Glidden — but I don't think she heard me. Or maybe she didn't believe me. "What about the Palmisano Place?"

"Right. That house shouldn't be on the market at all. Did the FOR SALE sign list a realtor?"

I shook my head. "It was a hand-lettered sign in the window."

"Let me make a few calls. Old Man Palmisano's still alive. Augustus Palmisano. He's out at The Dunes. Nice place. Upscale. Top of the line, not bad at all. Good food. Car service will drive you into town. He's not going to be easy to deal with. He was a broker on the Benton Harbor Market. Indicted more than once for tax evasion, and some things worse than that. Maybe a lot worse. All kinds of rumors. His uncle

229

was Eddie from Chicago."

"My grandfather used to talk about Eddie from Chicago. You'd think the nephew'd be glad to sell."

"I don't know what to tell you."

"You want to convey my offer, or shall I find someone else?"

"Let me make the calls. I'll get back to you. Are you prepared to make an offer?"

"I'd like to sell my house first, but that shouldn't be a problem."

"So there's no rush."

"I'd like to know, that's all. Like to have a figure."

"Give me a week. I'll call you in Chicago."

"How about tomorrow?"

"Saturday?"

"Why not? I'm here now."

"Did you get a firm figure?" I asked the real estate agent — Anne Marie — on Saturday morning. I hadn't been able to pin her down on the phone. Now we were on the way to see the house. She was driving a red Jeep Wrangler, two doors with a canvas top and a tire bolted on the back. Instead of driving along LaSalle Road, she took Duval Street out to the highway and headed north.

"First you have to see it," she said. "Then we'll talk."

"You talked to someone."

"Not exactly."

"How can you 'not exactly' talk to some-one?"

"I talked to a lawyer."

"I see."

"But you have the key? So you must have been out to see Signor Palmisano?"

"Yes. But he's not sure he wants to sell."

"Who put up the sign in the window?"

"It's not clear."

"Is it for sale or not?"

"You won't know till you make an offer."

"I could stop by The Dunes and talk to Signor Palmisano."

"I wouldn't do that."

"Why not?"

"Not professional."

"What do you know about the house?"

"It's Finnish. Originally. The original own-ers were Finnish, moved down here from the UP in 1939. The house was built with precut, machine-planed logs. I guess you could say it captures the drama of the forest on the east and the drama of the lake on the west. At least that's what I'd say if I were the acting agent. The logs for the sauna house were trucked down from the Upper Peninsula."

"It's beautiful, whatever it is."

"And the sauna's a plus. You can't really see it from the beach. Everybody in Finland has one. But then the husband died and the wife moved back to the UP. Go figure."

"It doesn't look like a house with a lot of secrets. Except for the sauna. That might have a few secrets. It's not locked. My friend and I went inside. I'd be moving from a house with a lot of history to a house with no history."

"It's got plenty of history, though it's hard to sort out the facts. Well, it was owned by Signor Palmisano, but it was his uncle who put up the money. "Eddie from Chicago. He was involved in some kind of feud with the New York Mafia. Quite a legend. No one ever saw him. They say he was at the going-away party for Al Capone at the Hotel Vincent in Benton Harbor. Signor Palmisano says he was there too, but he was pretty young, so he doesn't remember much, but he's got a lot of stories."

The driveway, originally an extension of Pier Road, was bordered by huge maples and oaks. It had curved off to the north and then zigzagged down the bluff to one of the lumber piers that had been built out into the lake. We crossed a culvert over a small stream, frozen now, that flowed into the park and emptied into the lake. The road

232

had been plowed up to the property line and no further. "Signor Palmisano wanted to sell the house for a teardown, but the lot isn't deep enough to build a McMansion. You can't build that close to the bluff now. He tried to sue the state to get a variance, but he didn't get anywhere."

The yard hadn't been mowed in the fall, and dry weeds stuck up through the snow cover.

"From here," I said, "the house looks just like a house. From the beach it looks like it's getting ready to step down the bluff, like that painting *Nude Descending a Stairway.*"

"I think it's *Staircase,*" the agent said. "*Nude Descending a Staircase.* And in the painting the nude is already halfway down the stairs, or staircase."

"Post and beam construction," I said. "It's not going to go anywhere. You can see the piers are sunk back from the bluff. I love the wide overhangs, the old-fashioned Finnish wooden shutters on the outside to protect against storms. A person could be happy here."

"It's going to be dark inside," she said, "unless you go around and open those shutters on the lake side."

"The electricity's on, right?"

"So we can turn the lights on."

The house was beautiful — a big kitchen with a restaurant stove, a balcony that ran the width of the house, a billiard room in the back (or the front, depending). A reading nook at the northwest corner of the living room, cantilevered out over the edge of the bluff. " 'Cantilevered' is a good word," I said. "You could sit here and look north and south as well as west. There's room for a low bookcase and two comfortable chairs."

I liked the word "cantilevered" and used it several times.

"It's not really cantilevered," she said. "And it's not exactly sticking over the edge, not yet. But the bluff has been eaten away underneath."

"I prefer 'cantilevered.' "

"I think he's asking half a million."

"Offer him fifty thousand."

"I'd be embarrassed to do that. Besides, he'd think you're joking."

"Do you think I'm joking?"

"I don't know enough about you to venture an opinion."

"So you're not prepared to convey my offer? He probably wants to get out from under. And aren't you obligated to convey my offer? Like a lawyer. A lawyer has to advise his client that the prosecution's put

234

an offer on the table, right? Even if the lawyer's going to advise his client not to take it."

"I'm not a lawyer, and no, I don't have any legal obligation to convey your offer. And you're not my client anyway, not till you sign a contract."

"You don't think you're under an obligation?"

"You're prepared to pay cash?"

"Cash as in used hundred dollar bills?"

She laughed. "No. Cash as in a certified check or a bank transfer. I can't advise you to make this offer, and I couldn't advise Mr. Palmisano to accept it."

"I won't have the money available till I sell my house. You don't want me to talk to Signor Palmisano?"

"That's *my* job."

"I've got a lot to think about," I said. But it seemed to me that I was contemplating the implications of a decision that had already been made.

I spent a week at the dining room table with the books from Grandpa Chaz's North Americana collection spread out in front of me, arranged in chronological order. These books had come from the estate of Henri Bruneau, who'd died of heart failure during the banking panic of 1931. Dealers and collectors who'd been paying top-drawer prices for books and whole libraries at the end of the twenties were forced to sell. Grandpa Chaz had been scouting for Frances Hamill and Margery Barker, whose shop on Michigan Avenue contained the best rare book inventory in the Midwest, and with some help from these two women, he put enough money together to buy Bruneau's entire library. He'd been going through the rare books collection, which wasn't all that he'd hoped for, when Bruneau's sister, who'd come from France, said, *"Hey, wasn't there another house? Where Papa was cared for while he was dying?"* Only she said it in French. Grandpa Chaz, who spoke Canadian French, liked to imitate her when he told the story: *Hé, il n'y a pas une autre maison? Où Papa été soigné pendant qu'il mourait?* There was, in fact, another, smaller, house on the edge of the property, where two servants had cared for M. Bruneau as he was dying, and that's where Grandpa Chaz found a copy of the *Al Aaraaf* — in a locked vault, a big metal door in the wall, like something you'd see in a movie — and about three hundred other high-end books. All these books were sold years ago, of course, except for Grandpa Chaz's private cache of Americana, which was now spread out on the table in front of me.

These were important books, several of them worth more than the *Al Aaraaf,* which is now in the rare book collection in the Regenstein Library — the early voyages of discovery, the Native American portfolios — portraits of Indian chiefs, accounts of dress, of customs, of treaties, maps of the Mississippi and Ohio river valleys. The earliest attempts to honor and preserve Native American culture, or cultures. I didn't think there was a single library, apart from the Library of Congress and the Newberry, that owned *all* these books, and I wasn't one hundred percent sure about the Newberry.

I looked at some of the asking prices on ABE: $78,000 for the Melchisedech Thévenot; $100,000 for James Otto Lewis's *Aboriginal Portfolio;* $420,000 for a copy of the Champlain's *Voyages* with a rare double sheet engraved map (missing from our copy): "Add to basket." "Free shipping."

"Free shipping"?

There were only three or four Americana dealers in the country who handled books like these. I knew them; we spoke to each other at book fairs. But I wasn't one of them. I thought of a television show that I used to watch with Mamma up in her little sewing room. *The Millionaire.* A man in a suit and tie would show up at someone's front door with a cashier's check for $1 million, tax free, and by the end of the show, whoever got the $1 million would be miserable. I would have to watch my step.

On Monday morning I called the real estate agent — Anne-Marie — in St. Anne and told her to offer Signor Palmisano $50,000 for the house on the lake. She wouldn't do it. "Offer him a hundred thousand," I said.

"Okay," she said, "but you're going to have to do better than that, and you're going to have to start thinking about a private mortgage. I can help you with that."

"Call me," I said.

That afternoon I walked over to Borders to see Olivia, back from Ann Arbor. She was at her desk. She held up the book she was looking at: *No Fear Shakespeare.*

When I told her what I'd done, she said, "Gabe, you need a minder, or a psychiatrist." But she didn't say it in a mean way. She wished me luck, she touched wood, and she put *No Fear Shakespeare* on a cart next to her desk.

The first agent I talked to — from Hyde Park Realty — told me to get rid of all the books. The next day I found a more congenial real estate agent, and two weeks later, I had a tentative offer from a Mr. Al-Dajani, who was going to be the new head of cardiology at Bernard Mitchell. I never met Mr. Al-Dajani, but Mrs. Al-Dajani came from Cleveland to look at the house and fell in love with it right away. A week later we had a deal. The Al-Dajanis wouldn't be moving to Hyde Park till the first of June. They were both from Amman, Jordan, but they'd met in Cleveland and had lived in Cleveland for forty years. They had three children, a son and two daughters, and several grandchildren, who liked to visit. Which was why, she explained, they needed such a big house.

The closing on the house on the lake took place at The Dunes on March 15, the Ides of March. It was cold, bleak, brutal, but beautiful too. Anne-Marie drove. Ice caves had formed on the lake, and frost flowers that had been extruded from the plants along the road. The piers were still covered with thick layers of ice. The marina was empty, the boats in storage barns or shrink-wrapped and left in lots south of town, along Water Street, or on the other side of the river.

Signor Palmisano had his lawyer at his

side; I had Anne-Marie. It was a decent room, with heavy drapes admitting shafts of gray light, maps of Berrien County and of the Great Lakes on the walls.

Signor Palmisano's lawyer had drawn up a private mortgage — which I'd had vetted by our attorney — that would be held by the Fifth-Third Bank of St. Anne, which had a branch in Hyde Park: a $50,000 down payment, and $50,000 a year for the next three years. Signor Palmisano was not a happy camper. His lawyer had to restrain him.

The first thing Signor Palmisano said was: "You're the man who wants to steal my house. You're a thief, *un ladro*. There's a special place for you in hell. With Vanni Fucci. You make figs at God." He made a "fig" at me, his thumb sticking out between the second and third fingers of his clenched right fist.

"Signor Palmisano," I said. "You and I both know that the house could fall into the lake. I can't get insurance. I can't get a regular mortgage. The housing boom in St. Anne is over. There was an article in the *New York Times* about it. I can't even get an appraiser to look at it."

He bared his lips: "*Cazzata.* You can get an appraiser to look at anything. Besides, that house has stood there for seventy years. Hasn't moved an inch."

"The house hasn't moved," I said. "But the lake has. The bluff." I wasn't sure just what had moved. There was only one way to deal with people like Signor Palmisano. But I wasn't sure what it was.

"The wood alone is worth fifty K. Those beams are solid spruce. I could make a call," Sig. Palmisano said.

"Is that a threat?"

The lawyer intervened. "Augie, you don't have to go through with this. You haven't signed anything."

"If I live another five years, I'll be broke and they'll throw me out on the fucking street. Ah, t' hell with it. With any luck I'll be dead by then." He gestured with both arms this time, holding his thumbs between his first and middle fingers and shaking them at the heavens, or maybe at me.

We signed the papers, each of us initialing every page. I signed with my Aurora fountain pen, which had a black cap and a green barrel. Augie signed with the lawyer's silver ballpoint pen.

"My dad had a pen like that," Augie said.

"It's Italian," I said. "Aurora. Aurora Optima. Take it." I held out the pen. "It's yours. I've got another one. Almost the same, but the cap is green and the barrel's black. This one's got a broad italic nib. The other one's got a fine nib."

"Why is the barrel green and the cap black?"

"Something's wrong with the threads in one of them. The black cap screws on tight on both pens, but the green cap only works on the black pen."

Signor Palmisano hesitated. "I don't want to give you the satisfaction," he said. But he wanted the pen. And I wanted him to have it. It was the least I could do. I didn't think it was polite to laugh, but I was laughing to myself anyway on the drive back to the Loft with Anne-Marie. Laughing at the memory of Sig. Augustus Palmisano making figs at me. I was tempted to buy Anne-Marie a glass of wine at Stefano's, but Stefano's wasn't open yet, and I decided to head back to Hyde Park.

I picked up my car at the real estate office and headed for home. On the way I stopped at the marina. All the boats were in dry dock, but I remembered the story I'd told Olivia about the couple having coffee, or was it wine, and talking about their marriage. Maybe I hadn't been passionate enough for Olivia? I felt a kind of coldness toward her now, and this was a terrible feeling, like losing an arm or a leg.

When I got back to Hyde Park that night, I looked up Vanni Fucci in the Samson edition of the *Inferno.* Canto 25. Poor Vanni is bitten by a snake, then incinerated, then he regains his human form, and then he's bitten again. Hmmm. His crime? Stealing holy objects from the cathedral in Pistoia. At the end, Vanni directs his anger at God, making figs with both hands. *"Togli, Dio, ch'a te le squadro!"* he shouts. "Take these, God. Up yours."

On the morning of the move, March 2, Delilah stopped by on her way out to The Warehouse. Then Olivia and Saskia. We stood in the kitchen. The packers had packed everything up the week before. The kitchen was empty except for a small espresso pot and a single cup with two blue stripes just under the rim. No saucer. Through the window you could see Grandpa Chaz's daylilies, about ten different kinds, which he'd divided every three or four years till they filled most of the small yard. I'd removed the dead leaves and fertilized the plants at the end of March. The scapes that produce the buds had begun to shoot up above the leaves. In the fall I'd raked leaves over the small tomato patch, but I wasn't going to plant any new toma-toes.

Delilah gave me a hug and banged out the door, swinging her big purse. Olivia picked up the little espresso cup and examined it.

"Nadia and I are coming this summer to lay out on the beach," Saskia said. "If the house hasn't fallen into the lake by then. We'll bring Mom with us."

"It should still be there in July."

"You look sad," Olivia said.

"Look at this," I said, holding up a black urn. "Punch's ashes. I just found it in the garage. You didn't know Punch, did you."

"No, but I remember the dog bed in your dad's office. And the sign." She turned to Saskia. "Gabe's dad had a sign on his office door that said I'D TURN BACK IF I WERE YOU."

Saskia laughed. "Do you wish you could turn back now?" she said to me. "I mean right this minute?"

" 'Two roads diverged in a yellow wood,' " I said, turning to Saskia. "Your mother doesn't think it matters which one you take, but I think it makes all the difference. In any case, I'm ready to move on." And I *was* ready to move on.

Saskia looked at her mother: "That's ridiculous. That's like saying it won't make

244

any difference if I move to Ann Arbor and live with Dad and pay instate tuition, or if I stay right here."

"You're not moving to Ann Arbor," Olivia said. "Don't even think of it."

And I realized that Olivia had not been offered the job at Borders headquarters.

Later that morning I shared a cup of coffee with our cleaning lady, Mrs. Farmer, in the kitchen. She'd brought her own thermos, and I fixed an espresso. She had spent most of the month in the house, arriving at eight and leaving at five, taking an hour for lunch, which she ate with me in the unreconstructed kitchen. She'd brought a sandwich, which she offered to share. I didn't feel like eating, but I chatted with her while she ate.

"You'd better get going," she said. "You want to be at your new house when the movers get there."

"They've got to drop some stuff off at The Warehouse on Eighty-Seventh Street," I said.

One of the movers came out of the house with two coats slung over his shoulder — Mamma's fur coat and raccoon coat I should have given to Saul Bellow. "You don't want to forget these," he said.

"I'll put them in the van," I said. "With

Punch's ashes." I'd sold the Cadillac to a vintage car dealer in Tinley Park.

I signed a form clamped to a clipboard and made sure the movers knew how to find The Warehouse and the house on the lake. And then I offered Mamma's fur coat to Mrs. Farmer.

"I remember your Mamma used to wear this coat everywhere. It never made sense that she left it behind."

"It should have been stored professionally," I said.

"I told her a hundred times she should leave it at the dry cleaners over the summer, but I guess she wanted it close to hand. She didn't want it cramped in either. And she had this special bag."

I was still holding the coat. "Try it on," I said.

We unzipped the special breathable long-garment storage bag. I held it up so Mrs. Farmer could slip her arms into the sleeves.

"Look at you," I said. "Look at yourself in the mirror."

She stood in front of the large mirror in the front hall. She turned around and looked at herself over one shoulder, then over the other shoulder.

"You look beautiful," I said. "I want you to have it."

"It ain't right, Gabe," she said. "What if your Mamma comes back and is looking for her coat?"

"Then I'll buy her another coat," I said.

"It's beautiful," she said.

I walked through the house one last time. All fifteen rooms. Built for comfort, not for speed. And then I said good-bye to Mrs. Farmer, who was still wearing Mamma's coat. She was going to spend another week going through the empty house, cleaning the attics and the closets, dusting, mopping the floors, washing the windows on the inside. She'd be there when the electrician came to replace the old knob-and-tube wiring in the attic, which was part of the contract with the Al-Dajanis. Then she'd lock the doors and drop the keys off at the real estate office on Fifty-First Street.

On the way out of town, I stopped at the cemetery to say good-bye to Dad and Grandpa Chaz. And my grandmother, too, whom I barely remembered. There were four plots. My French Canadian grandmother was on the right: ET DIEU ESSUIERA TOUTES LES LARMES DE LEURS YEUX. Then Grandpa Chaz: BOOKMAN. Dad's stone wasn't in place yet. On Dad's left was a plot for Mamma, or maybe for me.

I told them that the shop had closed and that I'd bought a house on the lake, not far from the Loft, and then I drove to the monument company on Cottage Grove to see why Dad's tombstone wasn't in place. They were very busy, they said. People kept dying. They couldn't keep up.

What could I say to that?

XIV. The Good Life

Montaigne was thirty-eight when he retired to the country. I was fifty. Montaigne had his library — about 1,000 books — in a tower on the family estate; I had my library — about 20,000 books — in a house overlooking Lake Michigan.

Four o'clock in the morning, Thursday, April 22, my fifty-first birthday. It was the end of my third week in St. Anne. Everything that needed to be done had been done — two loads of gravel spread out on the drive, the restaurant stove hooked up, the dark green shutters given a fresh coat of paint, a new gas dryer, the septic tank pumped, the well shocked — and I was sitting in my study, which, like every room in the new house — except for the kitchen and bathrooms — was chock full of books. The auction houses had all been eager to handle the sale of Grandpa Chaz's Americana — I'd had several calls, in fact — but I'd been busy and had missed several consignment deadlines. Now I'd have to wait for Swann's Printed & Manuscript Americana sale in November, but that was fine. Grandpa Chaz had been a friend of Arthur Swann back when he (Grandpa Chaz) was scouting for Harry Gold on Book Row, and we had a long history with Swann's. I'd been feeling good about the estimates — over two and a half to three and a half million for eighteen books and two maps. It would be a big sale for me, huge, and a big sale for Swann Galleries. Toby Arnold, who managed the auctions, was eager to get his hands on the books and offered to cut me a little leeway on the consignment deadline for the November auction.

I was waiting for first light, waiting for the sun to come up, waiting for my new life — the good life — to begin. My MacBook Pro was at the ready. My Aurora Optima, the one with the black barrel and fine nib, loaded with fresh Aurora black ink, was at the ready. My deep red Claire Fontaine notebook was at the ready. My Old French dictionary — Randle Cotgrave's seventeenth-century *Dictionarie of the French and English Tongues* — was at the ready. My copy of Montaigne — *Les Essais, edition nouvelle.* Paris, Abel L'Angelier, 1595

— was at the ready, the boards supported on two tightly rolled towels to prevent it from lying flat. It looked like a bird spreading its winds as it's about to take flight. I sat there in the dark. Waiting. Excited, but frightened too.

I'd learned enough about happiness to know that you can't aim at it directly. You have to sight off to one side. But what are you supposed to aim *at* in the first place, before you sight off to one side? "Reason and sense remove anxiety," Montaigne writes in "Of Solitude," quoting Horace, "Not villas that look out upon the sea." This was one of several warnings that seemed to be directed at me, but I wasn't worried, because I already had a feeling that I was going to have a good day. I just had to figure out how to cooperate with this feeling.

"Reason and sense" was only one target. I had several others in mind. My new how-to-draw book, for example — a "complete course" — promised to teach me to connect my mind to my hands and eyes like never before! To teach me to see in the light of reason and measure. To teach me to make marks with vitality and freshness. And to draw the human figure and discover new depths to my own humanity! I was skeptical but excited. My old guitar teacher, Atene, had made similar claims for music: "Music is the greatest good that we can experience. It's beyond words, beyond thought, beyond language. It brings us into harmony with ultimate reality. The music of the spheres is a metaphor, but it's not *just* a metaphor. It's a metaphor at the edge of language. Language can't take us any further. That's why we need music."

But what I was going to aim at was something more modest — a working, or at least workable, conception of the good life.

At first light (6:12 a.m.), I took off my shoes and rolled my pants up and climbed down the sixty-seven stairs to the beach. The water was still too cold to swim, but it felt good on my feet. The wind was coming off the lake and I listened to the sound the waves made as they collapsed upon themselves, listened to the waves themselves, not representations of waves, not recordings of waves (like Dad's sleep machine). My eyes took in the beauty of the lake, the silvery lakelight, the dunes, the gulls, the sturdy beach grasses that held the dunes together. Beauty itself, not representations of beautiful things, not photographs or paintings, but the things themselves.

Was it overwhelming? Yes, but was it

enough? Would it be enough? Would translating Montaigne's *Essais* — my immediate agenda — be enough? Or would I wind up like a priest who's abandoned his vocation and is searching for ways to distract himself?

I climbed back up the steps to the top of the bluff, rinsed my feet off in the shower outside the sauna, wiped them on the front door mat, and made my way from the front door to the kitchen. It was like negotiating a maze. My study was the only room in the house not choked with books (though it was *full* of books).

Jefferson bookcases in front of Jefferson bookcases lined the walls in the large living room and in the bedrooms upstairs. I hadn't removed the boards that covered the books, so I wasn't one hundred percent sure what order they were in, if any, and of course, there were boxes of books everywhere. The reference library was in the billiard room, along with more books from the shop. The old card catalog was in the garage. The entryway and the upstairs hall were full of boxes of books. I'd calculated that I had about 550 linear feet of wall space in the house, excluding windows and doors. I thought the house could handle 20,000 books. If you figure 8 books per foot of shelf space, 8 books times 6 shelves is 48 books.

For 20,000 books, you need about 500 feet of wall space. And of course, some books won't fit on the shelves and will have to be shelved separately, but that's par for the course.

I made a large caffè latte the way Mamma used to make it, in a Neapolitan pot, and carried it upstairs to my study. My intention was to start at the beginning — Book I, Chapter 1 — and translate them myself, for myself, one page a day. It would be a way of shaping my day, like a real job. Even if I took a day off now and then I'd be done with a draft in two years.

But instead of starting on page 1, I turned to my favorite chapter — "Of Solitude" — in which Montaigne compares his own study to an *arrière boutique* — a back shop or room behind the shop, "in which one can withdraw and enjoy real liberty, in which we can converse with ourselves without family, servants, possessions."

What would I talk about with myself in this *arrière boutique*? Would I bring my thoughts and desires and fears into the light of consciousness? Would I learn to accept things as they are and not wish them to be some other way? Would I put aside what Montaigne calls *"conditions populaire"* —

ambition, greed, fear, irresolution, lust (*les concupiscences*) — and learn to belong to myself? Or would I take my chains with me?

Bookselling, of course, is a less exalted vocation than that of the artist or musician, than that of the statesman or the diplomat, than that of the priest or the philosopher, than that of the deep sea diver or the mountain climber — just as Montaigne is a less exalted philosopher than Plato or Aristotle. But it had been *my* vocation for many years. And now? I could almost hear my books in the living room, boarded up in their Jefferson bookcases, crying out to me, like someone stuck in an elevator, or a coffin: "Let us out of here. We're suffocating. Let us out. Let us OUT!" And I started to laugh. "I'll be down in a minute," I said.

I located Grandpa Chaz's tool box in the garage and spent two hours removing the boards from the front of the bookcases. I pried out the nails and put them in a Duralex bowl and stacked the boards in the garage. When I came back inside, the house was redolent with the smell of old books. I took a moment to savor it before going back up to my study, my *arrière boutique.* I was just settling down with Montaigne when I heard a gonging I hadn't heard before — the doorbell.

I capped my pen, put my computer to sleep, and went downstairs. My first visitor was Anne-Marie, the real estate agent. She was wearing a striped linen shirt over a dark blue T-shirt, white jeans, a pair of large-lens sunglasses pushed up onto her forehead, and I recognized an invitation. I asked myself, "What would Montaigne do?" And I answered, "Why not?"

"I just came by to see if the house was still standing," she said.

"Coffee?" I said.

She took one look at the bookcases surrounding the room, the Jefferson bookcases two deep, and at the books spread out on the table and said. "You used to run a bookstore in Chicago, isn't that right?"

"In a former life," I said.

"I love the smell of old books."

"Hundreds of volatile organic compounds," I said, "released from the decaying paper and the ink and the adhesives. My grandfather could make a good guess at a book's age simply by smelling it."

"Like a wine expert," she said, reaching for a copy of Laura Ingalls Wilder's *Little Town on the Prairie* on the top shelf of one of the bookcases. I almost stopped her, but she knew enough not to tug the book off the shelf by the head-cap. "I thought it was

Little House *on the Prairie,"* she said.

"*Little House* was the first of a series," I said. "*Little Town* came later."

She held the book to her nose and sniffed it. "Grassy notes," she said. "Hints of vanilla and almonds, acidic finish."

"I'll make a pot of espresso," I said.

"I'm thinking I could show you some properties," she said, putting *Little Town* back on the shelf. "There's still space in the old depot, but there won't be for long. That would be ideal for a bookstore. There's already a coffee shop lined up, and an art gallery. You need to speak to the mayor, but she's in Chicago right now, and I think she's planning to go to Nepal to stay or sit for a while in a Buddhist monastery. Sounds crazy to me, but who knows. Maybe there's something to it. I can't picture Toni in a Buddhist monastery."

"I can," I said.

"That's right," she said. "I keep forgetting that you already know her."

It was easy to picture Toni in a Buddhist monastery, and it was easy to picture the depot too — an old-fashioned red brick Michigan Central station, sprawling out along the tracks, with narrow windows and separate waiting rooms for men and women. Separate baggage rooms too, though men and women were no longer separated. Mamma and I had waited on Friday afternoons to pick up Dad and Grandpa Chaz. The depot had been built at a time when St. Anne dreamed of competing with Chicago, but it lost out to St. Joe farther north because the St. Joe River was more navigable than the St. Anne.

Amtrak, unwilling to maintain the building, had sold the depot to the city for $10, and it had become part of the development project.

"What do you do all day?" she asked.

"I'm working on a translation of Montaigne."

" 'To study philosophy is to learn how to die.' Reverend Sarah has a sign in her office at the Episcopal Church. It's on her bulletin board."

"Yes, but that's Montaigne quoting Cicero."

"This town needs a bookstore," she said. "Walden Books closed out at the mall. The college bookstore doesn't have any books. Just textbooks. And they rent them. Can you believe it? The nearest Barnes & Noble is in South Bend. I could show you some properties."

"These are 'rare' books," I said. "It's a different kind of business."

"Duh!" she said. At least she didn't say she'd rather live life than read about it. "Let me at least show you the depot. I'll pick you up in the morning."

The restoration of the old depot, on Duval and Merchant in the center of town, was being funded largely by a grant from the state. I didn't have to look too hard to see that it was a wonderful space, something I hadn't thought about as a child while Mamma and I were waiting for Dad and Grandpa Chaz. There was a central corridor or atrium. The framing was already in place for a coffee shop and an art gallery. Workmen were installing a new cabin in the old elevator shaft, by the front door, so we had to enter through the side door. If you picture the depot as a cathedral, the wide aisle that runs from the east side (the parking lot) to the tracks on the west side would be the nave. The longer, narrower corridor that bisects the nave would be the transept.

"My mother and I used to ride up and down in the elevator," I said. "She'd say, *'Primo piano, per favore,'* if we were going up, or *'Pianterreno, per favore,'* if we were coming down," and I'd push the right button.

"She was Italian?"

"Right, and she always spoke to me in Italian."

"So you're half Italian. What about the other half?"

"A mix. My father's mother was French Canadian. What about you?"

"Look," she said. "They're testing the elevator."

We watched as the elevator door closed. In about sixty seconds we heard the door open on the second floor.

"A law firm has already rented the north half of the second floor," she said. "You want to see if we can ride up in the elevator?"

"I can wait," I said. "You're handling all the rentals?"

She nodded. "I just poked around on the web a little," she said. "Googled 'rare bookstores.' There are some pretty fancy bookstores out there."

"Right," I said, "but mostly it's mom-and-pop operations."

She dropped me off at home and waited for me to invite her in. I walked around the Jeep to the driver's side and stood outside her window and we chatted for a minute. I was tempted. It was time to cocker up my genius and start living free, but I was feeling shaky.

■ ■ ■ ■

Anne-Marie picked me up at home again a week later, and we visited the depot a second time. It was coming right along. We rode up and then down in the elevator. Work had not begun on the second floor — office suites — but on the ground floor you could see the shape of the coffee shop, and the art gallery, and a jewelry store, and a children's clothing store. Anne-Marie had more information. And she said she knew for a fact that I wasn't the only party interested in the space — three large rooms on the east side, along the tracks. "Two guys from Chicago are interested in opening a brewpub," she said. "And it's an ideal site for a new community center. But nothing's going to happen till the mayor gets back from Nepal."

She drove me home. It was five o'clock. I offered her a glass of wine.

Inside the house she headed straight for the books spread out on the library table, and I didn't blame her. They weren't the most beautiful books in the room, but they were interesting, powerful. All twenty volumes of Edward S. Curtis's *The North American Indian* were stacked on one end of the table. I showed her the signatures in

Volume I, Curtis's and Theodore Roosevelt's. And we looked at some of the photographs.

"What did your grandfather want with all these books?"

"You mean, why didn't he sell them? I think he was looking for accounts of the Garden of Eden. Before the white men destroyed it. He and his pal Claude Duval."

"Did they find it?"

"Yes and no. Their real animus was against the British. They thought that the French were in tune with the natives in the Ohio Country — everything between the Great Lakes and the Appalachians. The French respected the Indian customs, they adopted native diplomatic protocols, they understood ritual acts of reciprocity, they understood the importance of kinship networks and extended kinship ties, they accepted the sovereignty of the different nations: the Potawatomi, the Odawa, the Ojibwa, and about half a dozen others. The British not only trampled on all these things, they used biological warfare. Blankets infected with small-pox."

"And if the French had defeated the British?"

"In the French and Indian War? We'd probably be speaking French," I said. "Or

Algonquin. An Algonquin Grammar sold at Sotheby's last March for over five hundred eighty-five thousand dollars."

She opened her eyes wide and then closed them tight and then opened them again. "You're kidding," she said.

I shook my head.

"Well, that would probably rule out teaching Algonquin in the public schools."

"It went way over the estimate," I said.

I showed her the first mention of Lake Michigan in print — *"Lac de Michigami oú Illinois"* — in Melchisedech Thévenot's *Recueil de Voyages* (Paris, 1682). "Thévenot invented the spirit level," I said, "and wrote the first book on how to swim. It's here. Somewhere." I opened James Otto Lewis's *Aboriginal Portfolio* to a hand-colored drawing of Me-No-Quet in full regalia. "He was a Potawatomi chief," I said. "Lewis painted this at the Treaty of Fort Wayne. Three million acres ceded to the federal government."

"You ought to sell it to the Casino," she said. "The Pokagon Band was part of the Potawatomi. The Pokagon Fund spreads a lot of money around this town, five or six million last year. They could display it in the Casino."

"That's not the worst idea I've ever heard," I said. In the kitchen I opened the refrigerator and poured two glasses of pinot grigio from a bottle that was already open.

"I'm just telling you," she said, carrying her wine back into the living room and starting to pick up, with one hand, the copy of the *Gettysburg Address* I'd bought from Helen Barstow.

"Careful," I said. "Let me take your glass. There's no place to put anything down in here," I said. "Not till I get the books sorted out. I'll put our glasses down in the kitchen."

"Is this the *Gettysburg Address*?" she asked.

"Lincoln's part is at the end," I said. "Last two pages. The rest is Everett's speech."

"Huh," she said, turning to the back of the book. " 'Four score and seven years ago,' " she read. She read it to herself, all the way to the end. "Where's 'With malice toward none'?" she asked.

"That's in the *Second Inaugural Address*," I said.

"I've always liked that," she said. " 'With malice toward none.' "

We had a second glass of wine and went up to my study to look at the Montaigne. I told her about buying it at the Boston Fair.

The Montaigne was on my desk, where I'd been working. She touched one of the raised bands on the spine with a fingertip. I opened it to the *arrière boutique* passage, which I had bookmarked.

She looked at me. "Is this some kind of a test? Because if it is . . ."

"Of course not," I said. But I suppose it was. In a way.

"I can read it, you know . . . Four years of high school French, three years in college, junior year abroad." She started to read: " *'Il se faut reserver une arrière boutique toute nostre, toute franche, en laquelle nous establissons nostre vraye liberté et principale retraicte et solitude.'* "

She read confidently, voicing her *r*'s in the back of her throat.

"Very nice," I said.

"I can understand it," she said, "but the spelling's funny."

"It's 'Middle' French," I said. "But it's closer to Modern French than Chaucer is to Modern English."

She sat down on the old sofa that I'd salvaged from Dad's office and tucked her knees under her. I sat down next to her. "There's something sexy about French," she said. She raised one shoulder and then the other, not a shrug but a little dance.

"My dad had a sign on his office door," I said. " 'I'D TURN BACK IF I WERE YOU.' I have it here somewhere. To remind me."

"Je ne veux pas revenir en arrière."

"Moi non plus," I said. "We'll have to use this sofa for a bed. The bedrooms are too full of books. You can't get to the beds."

"Where do you sleep?"

"Right here," I said.

The next morning I translated several pages of the *Essais,* not moving steadily from page to page as I had planned to do — the argument didn't go in a straight line, so why should I? — but jumping around from chapter to chapter, just translating whatever matched my mood, becoming a different person in the act of reading each chapter.

In the afternoon I drove into town. I wasn't a stranger in St. Anne, of course. I enjoyed mixing with the first of the summer people, down by the marina — young mothers with children, people like me in the middle of their lives, older people too, all of us admiring the beautiful boats in the water and dreaming. I enjoyed fantasizing about the used catamaran at the Boat Factory, like the one I'd learned to sail on when I was a boy. I enjoyed drinking a cup of coffee at Atkinson's, listening to Jack Donnelly, the harbor master, tell astonishing stories about the corruption in the Department of Harbors and Marine Services in Chicago, where he'd worked for years. The last four directors he'd served under, before he became the director himself, had wound up in federal prisons, the last two on his testimony. He'd been terminated in 1993 for stepping on too many toes, but he hadn't been indicted! I enjoyed dropping by the college library and chatting with Ruth MacDonald, or stopping on the way home to pick up a bottle of wine at Vitale's, where Signora Vitale always asked about Mamma. I enjoyed drinking a glass of Michigan wine with Ben Warren, who had collected all sixty-five books in the *Rivers of America* series, published between 1937 and 1974, and was working on his own book about the St. Anne River. And I enjoyed Anne-Marie's visits. She always took me by surprise.

My good life was taking shape: a beautiful house on the lake, a library full of rare books, meaningful work (Montaigne), plenty of money, a girlfriend (so much less complicated than loving Olivia).

It was the good life, but was it good enough? *Je ne creins point à dire,* Montaigne writes at the end of the essay "On Cruelty": "I am not afraid to admit that my nature is so tender, so childish, that I cannot well refuse my dog the play he offers me or asks of me outside the proper time." Even though I'd been looking for it, the passage took me by surprise. Like a poem that puts something into words for you, something you've known all along. How could you live the good life without a dog? I still had Punch's vet records in my file. The black urn holding his ashes was in the garage.

I drove to the animal shelter on Duval, halfway to Harding's Friendly Market, and came away with a medium-size black-and-tan German shepherd–Lab mix named Bowser and a supply of HeartGard for heart worms and Frontline for fleas and ticks. The HeartGard he could have with his food. The Frontline I would have to rub into his fur between his shoulder blades. I wrote everything down.

At the pet store on Merchant Street, I bought a large bag of expensive dog food, an expensive leash, an expensive collar, and an expensive Kong toy. I figured I had enough bowls at home for food and water.

I didn't care for the name "Bowser" and spent the rest of the day trying to discover the name of Montaigne's dog. I searched through the French in a PDF file that I'd downloaded, searching for *chien.* Then I paged through Donald Frame's translation. No luck. Most of the references to dogs were in the form of historical anecdotes or of general truths. I telephoned the French Department at the University of Chicago — an important center for Montaigne studies — and spoke to the secretary. She laughed. Five minutes later I got a call from the head of the department. Professor Marchand. He laughed too. "Montaigne didn't have a dog," he said. "He had a cat, but the cat didn't have a name. He had hunting dogs, but he didn't have a pet dog, and the hunting dogs didn't have names."

I read him the passage in French.

"You've got a decent accent," he said.

"I spent a summer in Bordeaux," I said. "With the family of a school friend. This passage doesn't sound like he's talking about his hunting dogs. You're *sure* Montaigne didn't have a dog?"

"I'm sure," he said.

"Okay," I said. "I'll figure out something."

I tied a red bandanna around Bowser's neck and we went down to the beach for the first time. He was very handsome in the soft light, filtered through a thin ribbon of clouds just above the horizon in the west. I took his collar off and we had a serious talk.

I'd thought I'd change his name to Book-man, which was on Grandpa Chaz's tomb-stone, but then I thought "Booker" sounded better. And Booker it was. "Booker," I said. "I'm not going to keep you tied up, so you're going to have to make a choice. You can stake out your territory. There's plenty of room. You can come down to the lake. You can mess around, play with other dogs on the beach. But if you run away, I'm not going to chase after you. Do you under-stand?" I repeated it in French. *"Je ne vais pas courir après toi."*

"D'accord," he said — two quick barks — and took off running on the hard-packed sand, heading north. "Booker," I called after him, but of course he wasn't used to his new name. "Bowser," I shouted, but he was gone.

He came back in fifteen minutes and we walked south together all the way to the Loft, about two miles, so I thought we had a good understanding. On the way back, as we approached our own stairs, Mrs. Ogal-vie's dogs — a big brown Lab named Barley and a big poodle, Whitefoot, who had not been shaved, and who'd been following us at a distance — joined us. They touched noses with Booker and sniffed butts. I thought they might be planning to get together in the morning.

It was six o'clock when we walked into the kitchen. I fed Booker and he cleaned his bowl. We looked at each other. I gave him a couple of baby carrots, tossing them into the air. Neither one hit the floor. He investigated the house while I cooked some pasta. I still had Mamma's only cookbook, *Tavolo d'Oro,* and thought I could learn to make some of the southern dishes that Mamma used to make. Tonight it was *spaghetti cacio e pepe* — Romano cheese and lots of pepper. I mixed the cheese and pepper in with some thick spaghetti and added a little of the hot pasta water to bind everything together. It wasn't my favorite dish, but made me feel at home.

Booker patrolled the house a second time, and didn't come back to sit with me until he had completed a thorough inspection. I put the leftover pasta in his bowl and he wolfed it down.

I'd forgotten to buy a dog bed. That night I spread out a blanket on the floor. Booker managed to wrap himself up in the blanket so that he was totally covered, except for his long snout.

The next morning Booker rendezvoused on the beach with Barley and Whitefoot, herding them this way and that, like a true

German shepherd. I walked along the beach by myself and was relieved when, after twenty minutes or so, he joined me. I walked behind him. He kept looking back over his shoulder to make sure I was still there. The water was too cold for me, but not for Booker, who plunged right in to retrieve the piece of driftwood that I tossed into the incoming waves. Back in the kitchen, he stood very still while I toweled him off. I filled his bowl, poached an egg. I translated a page of the *Essais* and then we drove into town and walked along Water Street to look at the boats in the Municipal Marina. It was the end of May. Summer people were starting to arrive and the boat ramp was busy. I sat on a bench in front of a store called Inner Peace and watched a police cruiser — a converted bass boat — taking on fuel at the gas dock and thought about the passage I'd translated that morning: "One man who was being led to the gallows said they must not go by a certain street, since there was a danger that a certain merchant might have him collared for an old debt." *Well,* I thought, *we're all in the same boat,* but I didn't pursue this thought because Booker had attracted a handful of children and their athletic mothers. After half an hour, Booker indicated that he was ready to go. At home we ate a snack and then followed an unmarked trail into the woods. The forest floor was covered with old leaves, cast down by the wind; but the trees were leafing out, bringing forth a new generation to replace the old. Wildflowers too, blue and white. I had Grandpa Chaz's *Michigan Trees: A Guide to the Trees of Michigan and the Great Lakes Region,* by Burton V. Barnes and Warren H. Wagner, Jr., University of Michigan Press, Ann Arbor, Michigan, 1981. But I didn't open it. "Everything has a name," I said to Booker, "I should have listened to Grandpa Chaz when he tried to teach me, but right now I'm going to make do with the little store of names I'd picked up on Blackstone, between the Midway and Fifty-Seventh Street: oak, hickory, maple, gingko."

"D'accord," he said, a sort of stutter-bark.

Some of these trees had been standing at the time of the American Revolution. They had survived the first wave of logging in the nineteenth century because the loggers had been looking for white pine, not hardwoods. They had survived the second wave, in the thirties and forties, because the Duval family had gone bankrupt in the Depression and couldn't afford to pay the real estate taxes on the land, and so had given every-

273

thing north of Pier Road to the state for a state park — everything except the plot of land at the end of the road that they'd already sold to the Finnish people from the UP.

Booker was waiting for me every morning when I got out of the shower, eager to lead me down to the beach. He would press his shoulder against my leg as I pulled on my pants, and bang my knees with his pointy snout as I put on my shoes, and we soon developed a comfortable routine that gave me a reassuring sense that time was going in a circle. At the bottom of the stairs, he would exercise his free will. If he pooped right away, he would turn to the left, toward St. Anne. Otherwise he'd turn right, toward St. Joe.

Montaigne was waiting for me too, after breakfast. Montaigne and Seneca and Lucretius, and Pliny the Elder, and the rest of the gang I'd invited into my library. We were like a gang of booksellers talking shop before the opening bell of a book fair, wondering if there was time to grab another cup of coffee. Or enjoying a glass of whiskey after the closing bell.

ברוך השופט האמיתי
XV. You Can't Always Get What You Want
(JUNE 2010)

I'd made the mistake of telling Anne-Marie — pillow talk — about the estimates from the auction houses for Grandpa Chaz's Americana, and Anne-Marie told Reverend Sarah — the "dynamic" priest at St. Anne's Episcopal — and Reverend Sarah told others, and by the end of the summer, Anne-Marie was not the only one who thought it was my civic obligation to open a bookstore in the old depot. Space was still available.

Mayor Toni proposed a dinner at Stefano's — three formidable women and one formidable man, and me. Toni, Ruth MacDonald, the head of special collections at the college library, Reverend Sarah, the dynamic priest at St. Anne's Episcopal, and Ben Warren, the former chair of the Chicago Board of Trade. Ben was a family friend, a member of the Caxton Club, and someone who knew a great deal about the rare book business, so I was sorry to learn at the last

275

minute that he wouldn't be able to make it.

On my way to the restaurant, outside a bar on the corner of Marquette and Indiana — the Corner Connection — I heard a woman cry out: "You can't always get what you want." I thought she was shouting at me, taunting me about Olivia. Her voice was high pitched but not quite a screech. "Speak for yourself," I shouted through the open door.

Reverend Sarah was standing in front of Potts Hardware, next to the restaurant, looking at something in the window.

"Reverend Sarah," I said. "Reverend" didn't sound comfortable. What I knew about her, I knew from Anne-Marie, though she had paid a pastoral visit back in April to invite me to become a part of the St. Anne (Episcopal) family. "May I ask you a personal question?"

"Go ahead."

"How did you decide on 'Reverend' Sarah?"

"As opposed to what?" she said. " 'Father' Sarah? 'Mother' Sarah?"

"How about 'Sister' Sarah. That has a nice ring to it."

"I'm not a nun. Actually, it was a choice between 'Reverend' and 'Pastor.' I chose 'Reverend.' "

I wasn't sure how to move the conversation forward. "I planted eight tomato plants back at the end of May," I said. "They already have a lot of blossoms. My grandfather always said that the sandy soil in Michigan was good for tomatoes. Sandy and acidic."

"We've got about twenty plants at the church," she said.

I had a feeling that something was wrong.

"I buy all my nails and screws here," she said, nodding at the display window. "I'm looking at the rolling tool chest. It's beautiful, isn't it."

"You have to do your own repairs?"

"My father was a carpenter," she said.

"Doesn't the church have a custodian?" I asked.

"Yes, we've got one, and we've got a sexton too, but I like the physical work. I feel that I know what I'm doing when I'm patching drywall or changing sash weights, or putting a new door on a kitchen cabinet. I'm in my area of competence."

"And your mother?"

"A seamstress. Made all my clothes. Now I have to do my own repairs and make my own clothes."

"I thought they had special stores for priests' clothes."

She laughed. "Not if you want a blouse with breast darts or curved panels."

I didn't know what "breast darts" were, and I didn't ask.

"Are we waiting for Toni and Ruth?"

"Actually," she said, "Ruth is already inside. Toni's late, but she's always late. I was waiting for you. I wanted to have a word with you. I even thought of making another pastoral visit." She looked me right in the eye. "This is a little awkward, and I hope you won't take it in the wrong way, but I just wanted to be sure that you know that Anne-Marie is married."

"Anne-Marie?"

"The real estate agent who sold you your house. The woman you've been bonking."

Whoa, I thought. "Of course," I said. "Yes," I said. "She's a big fan of yours. But why are you telling me this? What business is it of yours?"

"I just wanted to be sure," she said. "That you understand what you're doing. She's not very stable, you know. But you've probably figured that out for yourself."

"Maybe we should go in," I said.

"It may be fun for you, but you're not doing her any favors. There are plenty of eligible women in this town, especially in the summer. Divorcees crawling all over the

278

place, looking for men like you. You don't need to prey on married women. Anne-Marie and her husband are trying to sort out their marriage, and you're not helping. And you're not the only one either. You should leave her alone."

"You don't beat around the bush, do you."

"Just looking after my flock," she said. "I've already spoken to her. She and her husband are coming in for counseling."

"You're a good shepherd," I said. She had some nerve poking her nose into my business, but to tell you the truth, I was a little relieved.

In the restaurant Sarah sat down opposite me and ordered a bottle of wine while we waited for Toni. I sat next to Ruth. I started to tell them about the voice: "You can't always get what you want."

"That's a line," Sarah said, "from a Rolling Stones album, *Let It Bleed*. They're riffing on the Beatles' 'Hey Jude.' "

"Oh," I said. "I thought it was from Montaigne."

"But maybe she *was* yelling at you. That would make a better story, wouldn't it? As far as you knew, she was. Yelling at you."

The wine arrived and Sarah filled our glasses. We tasted it, and it was fine. It tasted expensive, northern Italian.

"Your real estate agent," Sarah said, "says you're translating Montaigne's essays. How's that going?"

"One day at a time. One page at a time. When I sit down at my desk in the morning, after a swim, Montaigne is there, waiting for me. I translate a page and then I read it aloud to the dog, Booker. He's good company. I'm not trying to nail down the big picture. I'm going to let the big questions get sorted out without my help. Two or three pages a day, that's all. I'm in no hurry. After that, after lunch . . . Doing a little drawing, practicing my guitar. Rereading Proust. Tony Hillerman too. Walter Mosley. I'm halfway through Arnold Bennett's *The Old Wives' Tale.* No one ever said anything about that book that made me want to read it, but it's a great book. Totally absorbing."

"That's it?"

"Isn't that enough?"

"Go off by yourself in the country, cultivate your modest talents, appreciate the beauty of nature, enjoy the servant girls, have sex with cripples. It's too easy."

I was relieved to see Mayor Toni walking across the room toward us, brushing something off her linen jacket, stopping at every table — the restaurant was full — touching everyone she talked to. She was one of those women who come trailing clouds of gestures and touches and smiles.

"What are we talking about?" she asked when she got to our table and sat down at the end of the table.

"Having sex with cripples," Ruth said, "and translating Montaigne."

"Sounds like fun."

"What I meant to say," Sarah said, "was that Montaigne's essays have been translated several times. There's no point in translating them again. And Montaigne's a lightweight anyway."

"Did he like to have sex with cripples?" Toni asked.

"Well," I said, "he quotes an Italian proverb: 'You can only taste *Venus en sa parfaicte douceur* in the bed of a cripple.' "

"You need to surrender to something larger than yourself," Sarah said.

"Like what?" I said. "The church?"

"We always need help in the kitchen at St. Anne's. We serve a meal for the community every Thursday and a dinner once a month after the service on Sunday."

"Don't let her get her hooks into you," Toni said. "She'll have you protesting the power plant and the dune mining, and the next thing you know, you'll wind up on the vestry."

Sarah started to protest.

"And don't give her all your money!"

Sarah continued to protest, and then she laughed. "Gabe heard a voice on his way to the restaurant," she said. "Shouting 'You can't always get what you want.' "

And Toni said, "I intend to get what *I* want."

"What's that?"

"Something to eat."

"You've come to the right place," Ruth said.

Toni ordered a *tris* for all of us — three pasta courses served family style — and we talked while we ate. Each woman had her own idea of what a bookstore should look like. Ruth had in mind a really good academic bookstore, full of books that would support the curriculum — the Midwest Studies Center and the Great Lakes Study Center — instead of sweatshirts and beer mugs and key chains. Like the old Bryn Mawr college bookstore before it was turned over to Follett.

Sarah had in mind the small bookstore in the Newberry Library, where, she said, "every book counts."

Toni was still thinking of the store on

Fifty-Seventh Street, where she and her husband had been regulars. A store where you could find a cheap copy of *Anna Karenina* in maybe two or three different translations.

"What is it that *you* want, Gabe?" Sarah asked.

"Now that I've got a dog?" I said. "Nothing." And it was true.

XVI. THE SAUNA
(SEPTEMBER 2010)

I was able to resist Reverend Sarah and
Ruth and Mayor Toni, and Ben Warren too,
who'd dropped by the house to have a look
at Grandpa Chaz's Native American books,
but I couldn't resist Signor Palmisano, not
that Signor Palmisano gave a fig about a
bookshop. He was interested in getting the
second mortgage payment nine months
early. I agreed to talk to him — not that I
intended to advance the money, but because
I had some questions about the house.

According to several articles in old issues
of the *St. Anne Examiner,* Eddie from Chicago — Augie's uncle — was a real person,
though some thought he had been more or
less invented by Joe Valachi when Valachi
testified against the Mafia in October 1963,
just before the Kennedy assassination. I was
thinking of putting together some books on
Berrien County. Not only the Mafia presence, but the literary presence too. Carl

Sandburg, Ring Lardner, James Fenimore Cooper, Michigan writers. But, in fact, I was curious about the history of the house.

The Dunes wasn't a bad place. It didn't have a bad smell. The hallways were wide, the floors buffed and full of light, the bulletin boards papered with notices: a guitar player coming for a sing-along; "Dog Days" — relatives could bring their dogs to visit — were going to be celebrated in the Common Room; a reading by a local poet; trips to different malls and to the library. The door to Signor Palmisano's suite was open. I could hear the TV. I knocked on the open door.

He took one look at me and struggled out of his chair. "That fountain pen you gave me," he said. "It leaks. You gave me a fountain pen that leaks."

"Let me have it," I said. I took my second Aurora fountain pen out of the carrying case in my left pants pocket — the one with the green cap and the black barrel as distinct from the one with the black cap and the green barrel. I gave it to Signor Palmisano. "I'll get yours fixed," I said. "It's probably the pump. I'll send it to Fahrney's. This one's got a fine nib. I hope that's okay."

"You'd do that?"

"Tell me a little bit about Eddie from

285

Chicago," I said. "Your uncle, right?"

"Yeah," he said. "Eddie was a virtuoso with a machine gun. He could shoot from every angle."

"Funny you should say that. I read the exact same words about three times in different newspaper articles. He was 'a virtuoso with a machine gun.' "

"Well, it was true. He could shoot with a pistol too, and a sawed off shotgun, and probably a bow and arrow too if you gave him one."

"Whom did he shoot?"

"He shot a lot of people. You heard of the Castellammarese War. Joe Masseria and Salvatore Maranzano. It was Eddie who gunned down Masseria's lieutenant, Giuseppe Catania, on Belmont Avenue, in Brooklyn. It was Joe Valachi picked him up in a car afterwards. Eddie was talking to a cop on the street, telling the cop there'd been a shooting. He put Catania away, but didn't hit his wife. That's how good a shooter he was."

"Valachi said Eddie was killed in a fight over a craps game. At least that's what I read."

"That's what Eddie wanted people to think. He didn't trust the New York mob and they didn't trust him. He went to

California for a while, then came back here."

"Why did they call him Eddie from Chicago?"

Augie shook his head. "Because he was from Chicago."

"They don't call you 'Augie from Chicago.' "

"I'm not from Chicago. I'm from Cicero. Four-story walk-up on South Forty-Ninth Street. By St. Anthony's. Besides, they needed to tell him apart from 'Eddie the Clutching Hand.' "

"Who was Eddie the Clutching Hand?"

"You don't want to know."

"Eddie from Chicago was your uncle, right? How did you wind up here?"

"I fell and broke my hip."

"I don't mean *here*. I mean in St. Anne."

"Eddie brought me with him when he bought your place. The family still had a farm — thirty acres, vineyards — over by Coloma. Made a lot of wine during Prohibition. Still producing grapes. Eddie always liked this area. A lot of the old mob guys did. Killer Burke had a place up in Stevensville. It's still there. It's a real estate office now. A lot of other guys too. Louis 'Little New York' Champagne, Philip D'Andrea, Jake Guzik, Edward Konvalinka, and Paul 'The Waiter' Ricca. DeLucia was his name.

Ricca-DeLucia. There was a regular Little Italy up in Benton Harbor. Capone liked to come down and play golf, he'd stay at the Whitcomb in St. Joe, or the Vincent in Benton Harbor. Eddie come down for his going-away party, you know. When he went up for tax fraud."

"Eddie was your uncle?"

"How many times do I got to tell you? You don't believe me? Eddie took care of me. I was twenty-one when he bought this place. Eddie took care of me and I took care of him. We had a lot of good times in that house. Eddie bought that big restaurant stove in the kitchen and I did the cooking. We always had a dog. Big German shepherds, the German kind, not the American. Big Tony, Hootie, Lucky, Rosetta. That one was named after Raffaele Cutolo's sister. Nothing was gonna get by those dogs. Rosetta — that was the last one — used to come in the sauna with us. Take a steam. Lie on her back and wave her paws in the air. If I hadn't broke my hip . . . God damn it anyway. I'd still be living in that house, and you'd be . . . living somewhere else."

"I've got a dog now, a German shepherd–Lab mix."

"Yeah?" he said. "What are you doing right now?"

"I'm on my way home."

"I'll come with you," he said. "I want to see this dog, and I want to see if the old place is still standing. Before a big storm washes it into the lake. Serve you right."

"Did you do anything to stabilize the bluff?"

"You didn't see the groins and vaults and those big things like giant pillows, full of cement? The seawall?"

I nodded.

"They don't do much good," he said. "Enjoy it while you can."

Booker greeted us at the door, and sniffed Augie's shoes.

Augie looked around. *Porcamadonna,*" he said. "You could open a bookstore." He leaned over to scratch Booker's ears.

By this time Saskia and Nadia, who'd come down several times to lie out on the beach, had helped me shift books. The house was still choked with books, but at least you could move around.

We walked through the house together. Augie pointed out this and that. "It's a Finnish house," he said. "That why you got no closets. You still got our big wardrobes upstairs? I should've sold those separate. I should charge you for them. And for the sauna too. And for the stove.

"Eddie set up a billiard room in the back," he said. "Brunswick billiard table. Inlaid solid mahogany, steer horn diamond shape rail sights, custom cloth, matching cue rack. Three-cushion billiards, that's all Eddie ever wanted to play. I never got the hang of it myself, though I tried hard enough. Eddie had to pay a couple of guys from Chicago to come down to play against him. Poker, though. That was another story. Big eight-sided poker table too, at the other end of the room. All gone now, but let's take a look, I'll show you."

The "billiard room" was at the back of the house. Or the front, depending. I opened the door.

"What's in the boxes?" he asked. "More fucking books? You read all these books?"

"Most of them." Not quite true, but not really false. I knew what they were.

"Where you got that big table now, that's where the poker table was. We used to clean up. Me and Eddie." He stopped suddenly, and I realized how sad he was. But trying not to show it. We walked back to the living room. I'd opened the shutters and the room was filled with light.

"Fucking books everywhere," Augie said.

Grandpa Chaz's Americana were on a couple of Jefferson bookcases, covered with

290

a sheet, in front of the windows that looked out on the lake. The library table in the living room was covered with books from my old room that I'd been sorting into small piles. Augie picked one up and opened it at random.

- If there is a cat on the roof and if I stand in the garden and look toward the roof, then I will see something that I will take to be a cat.
- I am standing in the garden and looking toward the roof.
- I see something I take to be a cat.
- Therefore, in all probability, a cat is on the roof.

"Jesus Christ, what the hell is that supposed to mean?"

Roderick Chisholm's *Theory of Knowledge.* I wasn't really prepared to defend Chisholm. "It's about theories of knowledge."

"That's what it says on the cover. It don't look to me like this guy's got a very good grip on reality. I see that you paid fifty cents for it. What're you going to do, sell it for twenty bucks?"

"If I can find someone who wants to pay twenty bucks for it. These are books I'm getting rid of. It's yours if you want it."

"You know what you should do with it?" he said, not really a question. "Give it to the dog here. Booker. Good name. A dog likes to have something to think about." He picked up another book. "This one's got a little more heft to it." He was holding a Bollingen edition of Plato's *Dialogues*.

"About two years ago," I said, "I sold a copy of the first English translation of Plato for fifteen thousand dollars. One of the most important books in the Renaissance, in the Western world."

Augie looked up at me and then back at the book, which he'd opened. "*The Apology.* What's he apologizing for? I knew a guy named Plato. Greek guy. Used to peddle plum tomatoes on the market — Benton Harbor — plum tomatoes and olives. Used to buy raw olives in Chicago and cure 'em himself. Pretty good too. Those big Greek olives, you know what I mean? Not my favorite, but pretty good. You planning to sell all these books?" He waved an arm at the books on the shelves.

"A lot of these were our personal books," I said. "Most of the books I need to sell are still on these bookcases or in boxes."

"Who's gonna buy them?"

"Collectors, dealers, libraries."

"Collectors?"

"There are some high-end collectors right here in St. Anne — at least four. Ben Warren, Al Bernstein, Ed Janacek, Susan Reynolds, Carl Abrams. That's five. These are good people. They tell you right up front what's on their mind: they want the book, they buy it; they don't want a book, they don't. They want the book on approval. Okay. They pay right away. It's always a pleasure to pass on something nice to them."

"Carl Abrams," Augie said. "*L'imprenditore negro?* I remember when he bought the Compton Funeral Parlor. Some folks blamed the Comptons for selling, but I guess it worked out all right. He lives up in Benton Harbor, right?"

"He collects books about death," I said. "He bought a lot of Civil War books from us. That's when they started embalming, you know. Get the bodies back to the families. Rival undertakers setting up shop right on the battlefields. His brother's got three or four funeral homes in Chicago."

"Al Bernstein I know," he said. "Got a place on the lake by Grand Mere. Used to hustle high-end bonds. Hunh." He picked up another book: *Intimacy: Sensitivity, Sex, and the Art of Love* and started to read: " 'The authors explain the use of the bioloop — the recently developed method of controlling mentally what had previously been thought of as autonomous bodily functions.' What the fuck. You're telling me that Al Bernstein's going to pay money for a book that's going to tell him how to fuck? You must be thinking of a different Al Bernstein from the one I know. Well, maybe he's too old now. Maybe that book would help, I don't know."

"He's moving to Israel."

"Son of a bitch."

"That goes with the books I'm throwing out. I don't even know where it came from."

"Like hell you don't."

"Here's one you ought to like," I said. "*The Boy's King Arthur*. Worth about five hundred dollars. This one I'm keeping. My mother used to read it to me in an Italian translation: *Re Arturo*. I've got it somewhere."

"He wants five hundred dollars for a book about *Re Arturo*," he said, addressing Booker, "and he wouldn't give me a decent price for this beautiful house." He examined the picture on the cover — two knights whaling on each other. "Yeah, I heard of *The Boy's King Arthur*. Kind of like the South Brooklyn Boys, right?"

"Kind of," I said.

294

Augie pulled a chair out from the table and sat down. Booker sat next to him so that Augie could scratch behind his ears. "But you know something? If I was you, I'd want to live life, not just read about it. Take someone like Eddie. Now Eddie knew how to live. And he had a high opinion of himself. Liked to put on a new silk shirt and admire himself in the mirror. We both did in the old days. And the women all liked him, even when they saw through him. We laid enough pipe to reach to Rio de Janeiro and back, and if I was you, I'd be doing the same thing. You got a woman?"

I didn't know what to say.

"How about that real estate broad? She's a looker, but you want to be careful. Let me tell you a few things about her."

"I'm not sure I want to hear them."

"So, you got something going with her? I'll keep my trap shut."

I didn't say anything.

"And a couple other broads too, laying out on the beach with their tops undone."

"How do you know about that?" I asked.

"I hear things."

"That was my old girlfriend's daughter," I said, "and her roommate from the University of Chicago."

He touched his cheek with his thumb and

twisted his fist. "You should bring them over to The Dunes next time."

"They're lesbians," I said.

"Too bad." He shrugged. "What happened to your old girlfriend?"

"She turned me down."

Augie nodded. "You know, Chicago's full of women. If I was you . . . Eddie used to make a call and in about two hours a whole carload of women would show up. Chicago, Cicero, Cal City. I'd get the sauna cranked up, and by the time they'd get here, it would be ready to go. We'd hop in the sauna. You got to be careful, though. Take a shower first. Otherwise your skin can get funny. I guess the bacteria can go crazy in the heat. And no booze either — before the sauna, maybe one drink. But afterwards — nothing but the best. Canadian Club and ginger ale. That was Eddie's drink. Me, I liked Scotch." He looked around. "We didn't need a book to teach us how to live."

"So, you're not much of a reader?"

"Never saw the need. I never saw nothing like this. What's the good? What do you know from a book that I don't know? Tell me one thing."

"I don't know where to begin," I said. "Take your idea of the good life. Drinking whiskey, laying enough pipe to reach to Rio de Janeiro. Most philosophers would say it's a wasted life. Plato would say it's like the life of an oyster, not a man."

Augie shook his head. "Yeah? Well, I'd rather go to bed with a woman than read a book about going to bed with a woman, I can tell you that. And I don't think you can convince me different. You ever hear of an oyster fucking a woman? Or a man fucking an oyster?" He waited for the thought to sink in. "I didn't think so." *Another pause.* "You want me to make a call?"

"Who you going to call? A pimp in Chicago?"

"Nah." He looked out the window at the lake. "I don't got the number anymore. I'm lucky if I get a hand job from one of the nurses out at The Dunes. I got to sit down."

"You want a cup of coffee?"

"You got any whiskey?"

"Beer and wine, that's all I've got."

"I got a better idea. You know what we ought to do?"

"What?"

"Crank up the sauna."

"I don't think that's a very good idea. I doubt it's working."

"Why wouldn't it be working? I had the chimney cleaned every month. Creosote. You don't want a fire. At first, Eddie didn't know what to do with it. He was gonna use it to store the booze. But then a guy from the UP come down to take care of some business and showed us what to do. We cleared the booze out. You just got to be careful not to overheat it. I like it about a hundred and sixty degrees. That's what you call 'mellow' heat. Eddie, he liked to crank it up higher. He could take the heat."

"Might be a bird in the chimney?"

"You know something? You worry too much. There's a screen over the top."

"It's September, for Christ's sake. Seventy degrees out. You don't take a sauna when it's seventy degrees outside."

"That's a popular mistake."

"Look . . ." I was reluctant. I didn't really want to see Augie naked, didn't want Augie to see me naked. Didn't want to sit next to him on a wooden bench moist and slick with steam. "You sure know how to work it?"

"I did it for almost fifty years and then I kept doing it after Eddie passed in 'eighty-six — till I broke my hip and couldn't live out here by myself. Me and Eddie used to sit out there. Colder than hell outside. Hotter than hell in the summer. Didn't matter. And then with the women. You could get eight, ten people in there. A little tight, but that was okay. Good for my sciatica."

"In the sauna?"

"The rocks there on top of the stove," Augie said. "The Finnish guy trucked them all the way down here from up by Lake Superior. That was before Eddie bought the place. We used to take a steam at a place over in Benton Harbor — but then Eddie got somebody to show him how to work the sauna, and we never went back. You got an extra robe, or a big towel? The outside shower working okay? It's got a special faucet so it don't freeze. If not, there's another shower in the *stanza di fango.* First we got to get some steam."

Augie was a little unsteady on his pins. Some old newspapers were stacked next to the woodstove in the sauna and some kindling in a bucket on the floor. "Crumple up those newspapers," he said, "and add some of that kindling. Looks like there are a couple of those birch logs left. Not in the best shape. They'll burn quick, but that's okay."

It took half an hour for the rocks to heat up. We sat facing each other in two Windsor chairs in the living room. "You want to let it go full blast for about fifteen minutes. No more. Then you got to slow it down. Close the vent a little. Nice steady heat. Soft heat too."

We sat there in the living room. Augie was easy to talk to. Or rather to listen to. Like some women I knew, like the mother of my Polish girlfriend when I was in high school. Nonstop. It was like standing in the rain. It felt good.

"Where did Eddie get his money?" I asked.

"Here and there. He had a finger in a lot of pies. We had to lie low for a while."

"What I read in the papers," I said, "was that a lot of people thought Joe Valachi was laying off a lot of his own crimes on Eddie."

"Valachi was a bullshitter, but that was okay by us as long as New York thought Eddie was dead. Eddie bought the house in 'forty-nine, Harry Truman was in the White House. Then the Kefauver Commission started poking its nose into everything. That's why we had to lie low. Then later on there was more trouble with New York. They got long memories. Fifteen years later they send two guys to off Eddie, wearing top coats and fedoras. Dumb as stones."

"What happened?"

"We sent 'em away. We let the dog out the back to come running around and distract them, and then Eddie sent them away. Then they sent two more, and Eddie sent them away too. Four guys, each one dumber than the last. What did they think, they could ring the doorbell and we'd invite 'em in for a shot of Canadian Club and a glass of ginger ale?

"Eddie did some bootlegging too after he come back from New York. You know, all the fruit grows right here. Plus, the family still had the thirty acres of grapes up by Coloma. Making wine. Some guys got drowned in a vat . . . that's why I don't care for wine. Prohibition was good for Eddie, good for everybody. Capone had a place up by Berrien Springs where they made whiskey. They used to bring the fast boats right up the river. That was before my time. Sold the whiskey in Chicago, said it was from Canada. He had a big going-away party up at the Hotel Vincent."

"You couldn't have been very old?"

"I was four years old, still living with my folks in Cicero. But Eddie, he told me all about it."

Augie took my arm. We left our robes in the house and walked together down the covered walkway that ran along the side of the house. Between house and garage. Booker declined to join us.

Augie held on to me in the outside shower.

He was all sagging skin, except for his buttocks. I was uncomfortable.

"Now run some water into that bucket," he said. "To throw on the stones."

The biggest stones were the size of softballs, or grapefruit. The big thermometer showed 130 degrees and rising. We sat for a while. It was hard to breathe at first, but then I started to get used to it and relaxed a little.

"We'll let it go full blast for about fifteen minutes," he said. "No more. Then we'll slow it down. Nice steady heat," he said again.

"My first sauna," I said.

"You're supposed to say SOW-nah," Augie said, "not SAW-na. Say it. Make the first part two sounds, like *SAU*erkraut. Ah-oo, ah-ooo."

I said it. "SOW-nah."

"One time there was these three girls from Calumet City. Beautiful. Just me and Eddie and these three girls . . . Talk about the good life."

The big thermometer was up to 140. Too hot for me.

"You want to adjust the damper," he said. "Just turn that little knob at the bottom to the right. And then throw some water on the stones, like I showed you. Just dip the ladle in the bucket. Not too much. About half. You get too much and it kills the steam." I followed his instructions. "Now don't this feel good?" he said. "They got a word for it — *löyly.* Say it: 'loo-loo.' Say it."

I said it: "Loo-loo."

"Like getting your rocks off, but maybe better. This Finnish guy from the UP, he said it a little different, but that's as good as I can do. Loo-loo. Eddie asked him to say it over and over but we could never get it quite right. You know, people used to be born in the sauna. And they laid out the dead too. Not around here, but in Minnesota and the UP, up around Lake Superior, and in Finland too. All these logs were trucked down from the UP."

At 150 degrees I'd had enough. Augie picked up the ladle and, as we got out, splashed some water on me. Outside, we took turns standing under a cold shower.

"Now don't that feel good?"

It did feel good. My core temperature must have been up so high that the water from the shower didn't feel cold at all.

"Don't you feel *smagliante,* clean?"

"That's what my mother used to say," I said, "when I was in the bathtub, but I thought it meant 'floating.' "

"No," he said. "Clean, dazzling." He

303

laughed. "Eddie was a great guy. He'd put his hand on my shoulder and say, *La vita non è inesauribile? Non è bello essere vivi?* Only after a while he didn't have to say the words out loud. Just put his hand on my shoulder, like I'm putting my hand on your shoulder. Isn't life inexhaustible? Isn't it good to be alive?"

I gave Augie a couple of ripe tomatoes from the side of the house, and then Booker and I drove him back to The Dunes, and when we got home, I called Anne-Marie at Shoreline Realty and set things in motion.

"I thought you'd be mad at me," she said. "Reverend Sarah said —"

But I interrupted her. "Isn't life inexhaustible?" I said. "Isn't it good to be alive?"

I talked to the contractor who was in charge of the remodeling about what was possible and what was not possible. The coffee shop ("Innkeepers") and the children's clothing boutique ("Ducklings") had been framed in. The space on the south side — the old ticket lobby, the old men's waiting room, the men's baggage room — had been roughed in. The old waffle radiators had been torn out. Overhead pipes for heating and cooling were in place. It would have made more sense to sell books out of my house — how hard could it be? I'd just have to clear some space — but I could already see the books on the shelves in the shop — Chas. Johnson & Son, Ltd. Antiquarian Booksellers. *Isn't life inexhaustible?* I thought. *Isn't it good to be alive?*

■ ■ ■ ■

Part Three:
"At Least"

■ ■ ■ ■

XVII. Dejection
(CHRISTMAS 2010)

By December — in time for the Christmas season — Innkeepers was serving espresso and cappuccino and caffè latte; the art gallery was hanging pictures by local artists and some Chicago artists too; Ducklings was having an opening sale. You could buy a nice watch at Workman Jewelers, or pick out your china and tableware.

The new shop was still a work in progress, but I hoped to move the books in January, as soon as the new shelves, which were being built from the shelves in the old shop, had been installed.

I was planning on spending a quiet Christmas at home and then flying to New York for a week, staying with Marcus and his family, taking in the Davidson sale at Christie's, talking shop, schmoozing with dealers we'd done business with over the years, conferring with Toby Arnold at Swann's, spreading the word about the new/old shop in St. Anne, and interviewing two bright young booksellers, Adam Byrd and Carla Berkhof, who'd been recommended by Marcus. I'd schmooze with dealers and buy some stock just to let the world know that Chas. Johnson & Son, Ltd., was back in business.

I was about to take Booker out to the rectory — he was going to stay with Reverend Sarah while I was in New York and I wanted to introduce him to her cat before I left — when Saskia called. It was the Tuesday before Christmas.

"I'm worried about Mom," she said. "Something's wrong. At first the doctor thought appendicitis, then she thought ovarian cyst, but now she's worried that it might be irritable bowel syndrome or worse — non-Hodgkin's lymphoma, which is hard to diagnose because it mimics other diseases."

The doctor was going to run some more tests, but not till after Christmas. Saskia wanted to know if she and her mother could come to St. Anne for Christmas. My heart did not leap up — Olivia wasn't the only one who'd made mistakes — and I almost said "no."

"There's something else too," she said. "Borders is closing the store in Hyde Park.

It's not official yet, no one's supposed to know, but Mom had it from an inside source. She sort of knew anyway, when she didn't get the job in Ann Arbor."

I wasn't surprised. The writing had been on the wall.

"She's going to lose her insurance," Saskia said. "And if she's got non-Hodgkin's lymphoma . . . I don't know what we'll do."

"She'll keep her insurance as long as Borders stays in business," I said. "They're not going to close *all* the stores. Not yet."

"They've offered her a job in Houston," she said. "As an assistant manager."

"Does your mom want to come to St. Anne for Christmas?"

"I haven't told her yet."

"You'd better speak to her. She won't want to be rescued, you know."

"Maybe *she* doesn't want to be rescued, but *I* do. If it's okay with her . . . ?"

The time to say "no" had passed. Besides, I was enjoying an unmistakable sense of triumph. "Okay," I said.

I called Marcus to apologize.

"Maybe something will come of this?" He inflected the last sentence as if it were a question.

Booker and I picked out a Christmas tree

that afternoon in the parking lot in the marina and spent an hour looking for the old stand in the garage, which was still full of moving boxes. We found the stand and our old ornaments too. I put the tree up but didn't decorate it. I didn't feel like decorating it. I was restless. As if I'd turned a corner and found myself on a strange street where nothing was familiar. *Jamais vu.*

Booker was restless too. He was asleep on the couch, but his legs were twitching. On the beach that afternoon he found a dead herring gull. I shouted at him to drop it, but he carried it off and disappeared into the dunes and didn't reappear.

I walked on till I could see the plume of smoke rising from the power plant. A stiff onshore breeze was pressing down the waves and flattening the dune grasses: marram grass, American beachgrass, beach pea. Booker was waiting for me at the top of the stairs when I got home. I didn't ask him what had happened to the gull.

Saskia and Nadia had come down several times during the summer to *lay* out on the beach, but I hadn't seen Olivia since we'd said good-bye in the kitchen of the old house on Blackstone. My bedroom, like every room in the house, was full of books, but you could get to the wardrobe and to the bed itself. The same was true of the room that the girls had shared. They spoke Arabic to each other when they were alone. At first it sounded fierce and warlike, lots of glottal and guttural consonants, but after a while it started to sound like wind chimes.

I shifted some boxes of books in the extra bedroom, cleared a path to the bed, and then I tried to distract myself by reading the morning paper, the *St. Anne Register-Mail,* which was still folded up on the kitchen table. Last week I'd read an article indicating that the country was entering a period of growth that would top three percent, and I'd felt pretty good for the rest of the day. This morning's paper, however, indicated that the U.S. economy, as if responding to the bad news about Olivia, was going to be stuck in the slow lane for the foreseeable future. Job reports were sluggish. Demand for durable goods was weak and growth was slow. Businesses were slashing their average work week to thirty-two hours. People were downshifting careers. Detroit was in financial trouble but had not yet filed for Chapter Nine. Wayne County was heading for a demographic cliff as baby boomers retired in greater numbers. It wasn't good news, but I didn't feel much worse. I was seriously annoyed, however, to read that CC Sabathia had earned $23,000,000 in his second season with the Yankees. I did the math. If Sabathia had pitched, say, 33 games and had thrown, say, 100 pitches per game, he'd have thrown $33 \times 100 = 3,300$ pitches over the season. $\$23,000,000/3300 = \$6,969.70$. Almost $7,000 a pitch. If I skipped 10 stones a day, which I did regularly on my walks with Booker, I'd skip $10 \times 365 = 3,650$ stones a year. If I got $7,000 every time I skipped a stone, I'd get $3,650 \times \$7,000 = \$25,550,000$. I'd be making about the same amount as Sabathia. A little more, unless Sabathia had pitched 35 games, not 33.

But when I thought about it, I realized that I *was* in the same position as Sabathia, though of course, I was playing in a different league.

I got out my Claire Fontaine journal and my Aurora italic fountain pen — which had been repaired at Fahrney's — and wrote a note to Olivia in which I tried to explain. We were old friends and I would stick by her through the illness and the Borders closing. I thought of the voice crying out of the tavern: "You can't always get what you want." But I already had what I wanted. I wasn't planning to actually send the note, but even so I tore the pages out of my note-book and crumpled them up and threw them in the wastebasket. I had no idea what Olivia wanted.

I read about the cold front that was roar-ing down from Canada like a runaway freight train; I could feel it in the weight and smell of the air when I went outside to bring in some firewood. The sky was low and dark. I lit a fire in the woodstove and started moving books around, clearing a larger space in front of the woodstove. By the time Olivia and Saskia arrived, I was exhausted, and it was starting to snow.

Olivia didn't look sick when she got out of her little blue Mazda. She looked beauti-ful. Her see-through skin was pale but not sickly. She looked younger, as if some kind of inner beauty was making itself felt. Or maybe I was romanticizing illness. You could romanticize TB, but there was nothing romantic about an ovarian cyst or irritable bowel syndrome or, for that matter, non-Hodgkin's lymphoma, which I'd looked up on the Internet. Non-Hodgkin's lymphomas are any cancers of the lymphocytes that are not Hodgkin's lymphoma. Duh. I could remember a time when cancer was spoken of only in whispers, as if it were a personal failure, but now it was shouted all over the

Internet.

Olivia didn't look sick, but she looked nervous. I looked at Saskia for clues, but her face revealed nothing other than she was relieved to be here. She helped her mother off with her long black cloth coat.

I'd always been on good terms with Saskia. I was the good uncle, as Marcus put it — the confidant, the one who poured her a glass of wine at the dinner table and remembered her birthdays. Last year's birthday present had been especially successful: Frank Baum's *Wizard of Oz*. A special edition, University of Kansas Press, 1999. Twenty-five drawings numbered and signed by Michael McCurdy, the illustrator. Foreword by Ray Bradbury. A beautiful book in a beautiful green silk folding box.

Olivia'd brought a case of Clos du Bois — pinot grigio and pinot noir — in the trunk of her Mazda Protégé. She thought I didn't spend enough on wine. And a case of Perrier. Our repeated blind tastings had failed to persuade her that the eighty-five-cent two-quart bottles of seltzer from the grocery store were just as good as — better than — the three-dollar sixteen-ounce bottles of Perrier. She chose the grocery store seltzer almost every time. That was years ago, and she still wanted her Perrier. I carried the wine in from the car. The chat was normal. *How was the trip? Fine. You beat the big storm. We made good time. Saskia drove all the way.* I didn't know whether I wanted to break through or not, but it was awkward with Saskia there. I'd made up beds for her and Saskia in the bedrooms upstairs.

We continued to talk for a while without saying what we really meant, and then I said, "I'm going to go to the store — to stock up before the storm. Would anyone like anything?"

"Don't look so worried, Gabe," Olivia said. "Ovarian cysts go away by themselves. 'Watchful waiting,' that's what the doctor said."

"Mom," Saskia said. "You wouldn't get an ovarian cyst if you're on birth control pills. It has to be something else. That's what Dr. Matthews said. You take birth control pills to *prevent* ovarian cysts. She said it might be non-Hodgkin's lymphoma. That's why she wants to run some tests."

Olivia started to protest.

"Mom, we've got to face facts. We might as well get this out in the open. We've got some things to settle."

Was she asking me to step up to the plate?

" 'Watchful waiting,' sweetie. That's what the doctor said. We just got here. And it's

317

Christmas. Why don't you go to the store with Gabe and I'll lie down for a little while."

"I want to go down to the beach before we go," Saskia said, shaking her hair out of her eyes. "I want to make sure the house isn't going to slide into the lake while we're here." She disappeared out the front door (which was on the north side of the house). We watched her walk to the steps.

Olivia and I looked out the window at the weather. "Maybe we *should* stay in a hotel," Olivia said, as if someone had already suggested it. "Just in case."

"This isn't like you," I said. "I didn't think you were afraid of anything."

"I'm a little upset, that's all," she said. "I need a friend. How could Borders close the shop in Hyde Park? What went wrong? Our numbers were good. We were making money. What are they thinking? It doesn't make sense."

I carried her suitcase upstairs and put it in her room in the back (or the front, depending) of the house. I turned back the covers. She didn't wait for me to leave before starting to undress. She lay down on the bed. I sat on the edge of the bed and put my hand on her forehead.

"It's not a fever," she said; "it's an ovarian

cyst. Put your hand on my ovary."

"Which one, right or left?"

"I feel full all the time. Bloated."

I rubbed her stomach, below her stomach. I wasn't sure where her ovaries were.

"Saskia wants to go to Jordan."

"Next fall?"

She nodded.

"You don't want her to go?"

"I do, but I don't. It's so far away. And expensive."

"Nothing is easy."

"I'm sorry, Gabe."

"Your mom says you want to go to Jordan," I said to Saskia as we pulled out of the drive onto the highway.

"Early days," she said.

"Going to stay with Nadia's parents?"

"I want to take a class at Princess Sumaya University in Colloquial Jordanian, but I'll have a real job too, at the Ministry of Water and Irrigation. Nadia's father can arrange it."

"Did you read about that suicide in Tunisia?" I asked. "Last Friday, I think it was."

"Mohammed Bouazzi? Nadia thinks it's going to have repercussions all over the Arab world. Maybe even start a revolution or two."

319

"What would *you* do?" I asked. "Or what would you advise King Abdullah to do?"

"I was at the doctor's office with Mom when he called my cell phone."

"What?"

She gave me a smile. Like one of Olivia's mysterious smiles.

"Does he consult you regularly?"

"Only when there's trouble."

"What do you tell him?"

"I tell him the same thing I tell President Obama and all the rest of them. Crack down on corrupt politicians. Start giving breaks to the poor instead of to the rich. That sort of thing."

"What do they say?"

"They say they'll do it, but then —"

"Nothing happens?"

"Nothing happens. But I think King Abdullah's a good guy. He's stuck to his Decent Housing for Decent Living program; he's pushed the parliament to work on press reforms and publication law. He's worked for the Israeli-Palestinian peace process."

"Do you think the king will be able to sort things out? With your help, of course."

After a short silence she said, "I don't think things are going to get sorted out. I was a delegate at the Model Arab League last March in Georgetown. It's too depressing." She ticked off a list of problems: Iran seizing an Iraqi oil well on the border, civil war in Syria. More suicide bombings in Afghanistan. Car bombs in Iraq. "And now," she went on, "the collapse of TIBC in Bahrain has destabilized the whole banking system in the Middle East."

"What's TIBC?"

"The International Banking Corporation in Bahrain. They'd extended twenty billion dollars in credit, but when the CEO died, it turned out there wasn't a real bank. Just a bunch of computers. The customers were fictitious, the loan agreements forged, the records faked. They took a lot of other banks — real banks — down with them. I definitely want to go to Jordan, but I'm thinking I might switch my major to linguistics. I'd be in a good position to get a job. How many people know Arabic?"

"A lot of Arabs," I said.

"Right," she said. "I forgot about the Arabs."

Vitale's was closed, so we drove out to Harding's Friendly Market. She talked all the way, explaining the differences between Modern Standard Arabic, which everybody learns in school, and colloquial Arabic, which they speak at home, and everywhere else. Nadia's parents speak English, but at home they speak colloquial Jordanian. And then she explained the course requirements at Chicago. We drove a couple of miles in silence, and then she said as we crossed the bridge over I-94, "Borders will stay open awhile, but not for very long; that's why Mom doesn't want to take the job in Houston. She doesn't want to go to Houston anyway. What's going to happen to her? What's going to happen with her insurance? What if it *is* non-Hodgkin's lymphoma? COBRA's expensive, and I don't think she can get it if Borders really shuts down all the way. Maybe she could come and live with you? You have insurance, don't you?"

I started to laugh, but it wasn't very funny. "My insurance wouldn't cover her."

"It would if you married her."

This time I did laugh: "How much do you know about love?"

"More than I know about insurance."

"She can sign up for Affordable Care if the Republicans haven't managed to trash it. What about your dad?"

"He's a full professor now. His wife's the problem. Maybe not for too much longer, though."

"His first wife or his new wife?"

"Either one. Both."

322

Saskia was quiet for a while. "I'm thinking of a Joan Baez song that Mom used to sing — along with the record. 'The water is wide, I cannot cross over, And neither have I wings to fly. Give me a boat, that can carry two, And both shall row, my love and I.' She'd sing along and cry. But that was a long time ago."

"Do you know the rest of the song?"

She nodded. " 'Love grows old, and waxes cold, And fades away, like morning dew.' "

"Do you think that would happen if your mom came to live with me?"

"I don't know. Mom always says that living together is a sure cure for love."

"Is that what happened with your dad? David?"

"I was too young. I don't know what happened. But I'm scared now. I don't know what's going to happen now. I think Mom's scared too, but she won't admit it. Maybe we could go into Chapter 11, or file for it, like Borders. What's Chapter 11 anyway?"

I explained Chapter 11, and I explained Chapter 7 too.

"Mom has always seemed like she was getting one step closer to something she wanted, but not now. It's like she's walking backwards, or trying to walk up a down escalator."

People were worried about the storm. The shelves were emptying rapidly. There was no bread. The bottled water was almost gone. But we had the case of Perrier.

"Get a cart with a prime number," Saskia said. "That's what Mom always does."

"How about one nineteen?" I said.

"Divisible by seven," she said. "I've got a list in my head. Here's one thirty-one; that'll work."

I bought steaks, shrimp, scallops, a pork roast, bacon, eggs. As if good food were the solution.

I'd laid in a full cord of wood and had stacked it outside the sauna house. Saskia and I carried in armfuls of small logs, cut short to fit in the sauna stove and in the woodstove in the living room. I fixed spaghetti with scallops. I opened a bottle of Olivia's pinot grigio and a bottle of Barefoot, for comparison. The Barefoot was slightly effervescent. We listened to NPR while we ate. Olivia didn't eat very much. She was worried about the house. After supper I tried to get her to sit in Dad's comfortable club chair in the reading nook, with windows on three sides, while Saskia and I did the dishes, but she was too nervous.

We decorated the tree that I'd put up

earlier. New lights. Boxes of old family ornaments were set out on the library table, along with wrapping paper, tags, ribbons. We wrapped presents, pretending to hide them from the person they were for. By "presents," of course, I meant books. I wrapped up a nice copy of Coleridge's poems for Olivia, and set up Mamma's Italian crèche at one end of the library table and arranged the little figures around the manger.

At first the storm looked like a black band that had been wrapped around the horizon, like a ribbon stretched tight, or a thick rubber band. And then the ribbon came loose, the rubber band snapped, and we watched the storm come rolling across the lake, rolling toward us like a big wave. The black band disappeared. Then the gray clouds disappeared. Then we couldn't see the lake, couldn't see anything except flashes of lightning, followed by claps of thunder. I should have closed the big shutters. Too late now.

"I thought it didn't thunder in winter," Saskia said.

"That's what Gurov's daughter says in 'The Lady with the Dog,' " Olivia said. "Gurov explains it."

"What's the explanation?"

"Chekhov doesn't give it. He just says Gurov explains it."

"It was a dark and stormy night," I said.

Booker was snoozing on his rug between the couch and the coffee table. Olivia was pacing up and down. "Why has that line gotten such a bad rap? I think it's a good opening."

"Bulwer Lytton," I said. "Have you ever read Bulwer Lytton? We've got a first edition of *Paul Clifford,* but it's boxed up now. Three volumes. Dad liked it."

"The pen is mightier than the sword," Olivia said.

"He said that too?"

"And 'the pursuit of the almighty dollar.' In *The Last Days of Pompeii.* I thought it was pretty good. It's scary, though, but what's really scary is that he was one of the most popular writers of the nineteenth century, and now he's a joke, reduced to one line."

We talked about storms — the storms in *Gawain and the Green Knight,* in the *Odyssey,* in *King Lear,* in Kate Chopin's "The Storm."

"How about *Moby Dick*? There must be a big storm in *Moby Dick*?"

"There's a huge storm," I said. "Ahab tells the helmsman to sail right into it."

"Those storms were all the work of the gods," she said. "Divine punishments or warnings. Nowadays storms are just storms. Cold air colliding with warm air. You don't need the gods to explain them."

"The Arabic word for storm is *haboob*," Saskia said, "but I think that's a kind of sandstorm. It might be *aasifa.*"

Later in the evening we lost power. The snow and the wind were battering the windows. Saskia couldn't get a signal on her phone, but reception along the lake was iffy anyway. The landline would be okay, but whom would we call? It was dark, and the snow was pounding against the triple-glazed windows of the reading nook, as if it were falling in chunks rather than flakes. We hadn't closed the shutters, but we couldn't *see* out, only the reflection of our own faces in the glass, and the reflection of the books on the shelves behind us, and the flames in the ceramic windows in the woodstove doors.

The gas furnace was putting out heat, but the electric blower wasn't pushing the air through the ducts. We had plenty of wood, so we didn't have to worry about freezing; and I had three Coleman lanterns, each with two mantels, so we had plenty of light.

During a lull in the storm I went outside.

It was really brutal. Maybe we *should* have gone to a hotel. Ten-to-twelve-foot waves were lashing the beach, crashing against the seawall. I didn't know how much good the rock revetments could do against waves like this. Too late now. I was tempted to go down to the beach. Wanted to see what the lake was doing to the bluff. I was afraid that in spite of the seawall, the waves were chewing up the base of the bluff. I wanted to know. I knew it was foolish, but I felt that it was something I had to do. Confront the storm. Like Ahab. I found the railing for the steps. Tested it. Augie said Eddie had paid $8,000 to replace the old stairs, but I wasn't sure I could believe anything Augie said. One step at a time. When I got halfway down, I discovered that half the stairs — everything below the landing, had been ripped off. I couldn't go any farther.

I started back up, feeling my way, feeling the remaining stairs twisting under my feet. It occurred to me that I'd made a fool of myself. Again. I was on a teeter-totter, like a child, up and down. An emotional teeter-totter. One summer Mamma and I took pictures of all the different stairs within a one-mile range. Old wooden stairs. New metal ones. More than a few in ruins. One had an old trolley track running down from the top of the bluff (to lower groceries, picnic stuff, beer). All these attempts to link high and low, heaven and earth. Sky and Sea. I thought about the enthusiasm and excitement behind all these stairs. Some with landings at different stages, some of the landings large enough to accommodate a screened porch. People imagining how they'd picnic on the beach, carry their baskets down, bottles of wine, pitchers of lemonade, sandwiches, meat to grill. Charcoal.

Looking up, I could just make out Olivia and Saskia, indistinct forms that might topple over with the next gust of wind. They were waving at me to come back. I was almost blown off the stairs. As I kept climbing, I had the sensation of confronting a simple and obvious truth, like a child blurting out an obvious truth about the size of someone's butt. But what was it? The storm let up for a moment. The snow kept falling heavily, but the wind dropped. Almost at the top, I planned to scold Olivia and Saskia before they started scolding me. But then they were not angry; they were exhilarated.

"We closed the shutters," Olivia screamed in my ears. "The wind kept tearing them out of our hands, but we managed to slip the bolts into place."

We fought our way to the front door. We rejoiced in the warmth of the woodstove. I refilled the cast iron humidifier that sat on top of the stove. Olivia poured more wine. I put more wood in the stove. The wind batted the smoke around, but eventually the chimney started to draw again. I was shaping the story in my own mind, turning my foolishness into an adventure. Maybe I'd had too much pinot noir, but I left that out of my story and opened another bottle. Olivia asked me for a copy of Coleridge's "Dejection." I gave her the Christmas present I'd wrapped earlier, a nicely bound copy of Coleridge's poems, Number 15 in the Canterbury Poets series.

"Small square octavo," I said, "original quarter vellum, green cloth boards, brown morocco label, flower stem decoration to spine in gilt, boards ruled in gilt, top edge gilt. Corners of boards bumped and rubbed, label lightly rubbed, boards very faintly marked, slight loss to board gilt, tiny loss to initial blank and closed tear to one leaf (page 135). A very good copy."

Saskia laughed. She was sitting on the couch, her bare feet on Booker's back. "Are you trying to sell Mom the book?"

"That's enough," she said. "Is that for my

tombstone?" She laughed. "Do I need to wash my hands before I open it?"

"It would be a good idea."

"Pay attention to Gabe," she said to Saskia. "You'll learn something." I was glad to see that her spirits had lifted.

When Olivia returned with clean hands, I adjusted one of the Coleman lanterns. Olivia sat at one end of the library table; Saskia and I sat next to each other on one side. Olivia found what she was looking for and read aloud, though she hardly looked at the page. In the poem "Dejection," the speaker anticipates a storm coming, but laments his ability to respond, the loss of his imaginative power. Olivia was a good reader and threw herself into it, like an actress with a script.

O Lady! we receive but what we give,
And in our life alone does nature live:
Ours is her wedding-garment, ours her
    shroud!

That's the fear, isn't it, I thought. That there's nothing really *out there* except what we project. We think we're looking out a window, but all we're seeing is our own reflection in the glass. The storm is just a storm. It doesn't mean anything. We've lost our power to invest nature with joy. But as the speaker in the poem listens to the wind, he regains his power. Perhaps without realizing it. I wasn't sure, but I thought maybe Olivia was regaining her own imaginative power.

"If 'Ours is her wedding-garment, ours her shroud!' " I said when she'd come to the end, "then there's nothing at all 'out there.' "

"It's our power to project that counts."

On that note, Saskia decided to go to bed. I'd gathered extra blankets. We would keep the bedroom doors open to get heat from the stove, but it would still be cold by morning.

In the night, Olivia came into my room. When I felt her nudging my arm, I thought it was Booker, who sometimes jumped up on the bed in the night. She lay down beside me. Booker was sleeping on his blanket between a large wardrobe and the door to my study. Olivia was very passionate that night, and I thought she was incorporating the sounds of the storm into our lovemaking, or the sounds of the poem — the "rushing of a host in rout," the "groans of the wounded, a rushing crowd, tremulous shudderings"; and in the end, a "tender lay . . . of a little child, Upon a lonesome wild, not far from home, but she hath lost her way."

In the morning, before Saskia came down, Olivia and I drank coffee in the kitchen. I let Booker out. "Gabe," she said, very businesslike. "Do you still want to marry me?" She didn't look at me. I could see that she wanted to say more but was having trouble. *Great sex is not the same thing as love,* I thought. *Though it's close.*

The power had come back on and the furnace fan was running, but I was still tending a fire. I went outside and opened the shutters. When I came back in, the sun had laid down large rectangles of light on the floor.

"I feel better," Olivia said. "A lot better. It's a miracle, really. Are you mad at me? For last night? What I want to say . . . is . . . that I feel revitalized after the storm. It is a miracle. Like Coleridge in 'Dejection.' He gets his power back. The storm jump-starts his Imagination."

"The great esemplastic power?"

"Gabe, don't make fun of me."

We heard Saskia's footsteps on the stairs. "You guys look so serious," she said. "Am I interrupting something important?"

"I'm propositioning Gabe, but he doesn't know it yet, or else he's pretending not to hear me."

"Congratulations."

I was suddenly overwhelmed. Something inside me pressed against my chest. At first I thought it was anger, but then I realized it was happiness.

We were snowed in, and I was glad I'd traded the old van for a Jeep Wrangler with four-wheel drive, like Anne-Marie's, but with four doors. Augie called as I was pouring coffee, regular coffee, and looking out the kitchen window at a foot of bright snow.

"You still there? Didn't go into the lake? The National Weather Service reported twenty-foot waves up at St. Joe, winds up to fifty knots."

"Still here," I said. "You're up early."

"I'm an old man. It's part of the deal."

"The house is still here."

"You check for damage?"

"The stairs are gone. At least halfway down. Or up."

"They're the first to go. Come on out. Coffee. I want to talk to you about something."

"Not Eddie again?"

"No. Something else. I lost some money at the Casino. I'm gonna need some help."

I pretended not to hear him. "What am I going to do about the stairs?"

"This morning? Nothing. But I can make a call, give you a name. Nobody's going to do anything till spring. You can forget about that. But I need you to stop by."

"How am I supposed to get down to the beach?"

"You're not *supposed* to do anything. There's not going to be any beach left. That storm shifted it over to Indiana. You'll just have to wait till another storm shifts it back."

"A reverse storm?"

"Something like that."

"You still want your house back?"

Augie laughed. "The sun is shining. What kind of coffee do you like? Forget I asked that. They can make a decent cappuccino. I had to buy the machine myself. Gaggia. There's a woman here, Barbara. She's on her toes. I'd marry her if I were a young man like you."

"We're snowed in."

"We? You got a woman out there?"

"Two of them."

"That real estate woman?"

"Someone else."

Then you're doing better than I am."

I went outside to call Booker. When I came back in, Olivia was paging through the Coleridge. She read the poem again while I cooked bacon and poached eggs. After breakfast we sat around the table and drank more coffee in white ceramic cups.

No newspaper this morning — too much snow. Yesterday's newspaper was still half open on the table, along with a jar of marmalade and our eggy plates.

"It is a miracle," she said. "I feel wonderful."

I thought she was right. I thought we all felt revitalized. Even Booker, who'd been out playing in the snow and was now banging at the door.

Saskia got up to let him in.

It was nice to be snowed in. For the morning. Everything stopped. Everything was quiet. We didn't have to do anything.

By afternoon we'd been plowed out, not just Pier Road but our drive as well. We drove into town.

We had an espresso at Innkeepers and walked through the new shop, which was coming right along. Olivia loved it. She explained the software we'd need to keep track of everything. Software that could distinguish between used books, rare books, and new books too, just by reading an identification number.

When we got back to the house, Olivia touched everything. The Magnum pepper grinder, the dirty espresso cups. As if she hadn't seen them before. The little silver spoons from Italy. She felt the fabric of her blue cloth napkin.

"I had days like this when I was a little girl," she said. "My mother would take me out of school and we'd sneak off and go to a movie or go kayaking on Fidler Pond. It was wonderful."

I still wasn't sure what had happened, or where we stood. Had she really been propositioning me when Saskia interrupted us?

Olivia wanted to go to church on Christmas Eve. "Reverend Sarah," I warned her, "is very attractive, but very intense."

"Does she wear a collar?"

"Not exactly. I think she modifies her blouses so they have a kind of collar look. Don't call her 'Father Sarah,' though. She's ruffled some feathers. Some members of the congregation think she ought to stick to saving souls, ministering to her flock — instead of worrying about the dune mining and the radioactive water leaking into the lake. Salvation versus social gospel. I think she's a force. Unpredictable." Olivia tossed her head, shook out her hair.

I remembered Christmas Eve with Dad in Hyde Park. Then waking up in the morning and Olivia gone, but then hearing her voice in the kitchen.

It was a short service, and I was glad. I thought of the long services at St. Tom's on Kimbark, which I'd sometimes attended with Mamma. I'd run my finger down the program and think we were almost at the end, but then we'd hit the "sermon." I always forgot about the dreaded sermons.

Sarah preached a sermon on Christmas Eve, but it was a good one. "I'm going to keep it short," she said. "I'm not going to scold you for spending too much money on presents, or for drinking too much, and so on. I'm just going to remind you that you can't always get what you want. And that that's probably a good thing. Some of you will remember the song. Nineteen sixty-eight, the Rolling Stones with the London Bach Choir. It marked the end of the sixties, and that was probably a good thing too. At least that's what my mother used to say. She loved that song, used to play it all the time. But I like the song because it sums up the spiritual life. Getting what you want isn't the end. It's the beginning."

After we exchanged the Peace, Sarah blessed the bread and wine; we recited the Lord's Prayer; and Sarah invited us to share the consecrated host and the wine. Olivia was holding my hand. I felt a little tug, a sly invitation to take communion with her. But I stayed put — Saskia too — and sitting there in the darkened church, I realized that Olivia was embarking — had already embarked — on a spiritual journey. And then I realized that I was embarking on a spiritual journey too, but I had no idea where I was going.

"Are you all right?" I asked when she got back to the pew.

"You can't always get what you want," Sarah said to me as we shook hands in the narthex. She looked at Olivia and Saskia. "But sometimes you can!" And to Olivia, she said: "And you must be the fair Ophelia."

"No, I'm the fair Olivia."

"Sorry. Well, welcome. And you must be?"

"I'm the fair Saskia," Saskia said.

"Well, doubly welcome. I hope we'll see you again."

"I'm here to stay," Olivia said. "At least for a while."

"Does that mean I'll be seeing you for some premarital counseling?" She laughed, to indicate it was a joke.

"That's not a bad idea," Olivia said. She

laughed too. "Gabe's never been married before."

"Neither have I," Reverend Sarah said, "but I've got plenty of good advice."

Whoa whoa whoa, I thought. I wanted to slow things down a little. Most of what I knew about marriage I'd learned from the advice columns in the newspaper, and from *Anna Karenina,* and from occasional glimpses into other people's marriages — couples I knew who could go for two or three days without speaking to each other. But on the other hand —

I kept my mouth shut.

On Monday morning, before heading back to Chicago, Olivia helped me set up a Skype interview with Adam and Carla, who came as a pair. They'd be in Marcus's office at six o'clock that evening.

Olivia downloaded Skype onto my computer and added Marcus to my contact list. Then she added herself and Saskia. "All you have to do," she said — words that always made me freeze up. *All you have to do is drag the icon over to —*

All I had to do was find Marcus's picture on my contact list, click on the little green call button and select video call.

I followed the steps. "Nothing's happening," I said.

"That's because Marcus isn't expecting a call this early. He probably isn't even in his office yet. It will work tonight, trust me."

At seven o'clock, I dialed Marcus's Skype number and there they were, two beautiful young people, Adam and Eve before the fall — hungry bright young booksellers in love with each other and in love with books. Adam, who was from the North Side of Chicago, had attended the University of Michigan in Ann Arbor, where he'd had a work-study job in Special Collections, and had been working in the rare book department at the Strand, and Carla was a St. Anne alum from Detroit who'd been working for Marcus. Both were generalists with strong backgrounds in American and European history and in British and American literature. They'd met at CABS — the Colorado Antiquarian Book Seminar — and both wanted to come back to the Midwest.

"I always take a book home with me after work," Carla said. "It's like having a new lover every night."

"What about Adam?" I asked.

"We always look at the book together," she said, "figuring out how we'd describe it, how we'd price it."

I made them an offer and they accepted.

XVIII. PREMARITAL COUNSELING

(MARCH 2011)

On Ash Wednesday, Olivia and I knelt next to each other in front of the high altar at St. Anne's, our arms touching, to receive the ashes. Olivia asked me to go with her, and really there was no reason not to: "For dust thou art. And unto dust thou shalt return." Who could quarrel with that? But I wondered if she was experiencing the same thing I was, namely, the slight pressure of Reverend Sarah's thumb on my forehead, the grit of the ashes. Or was she experiencing something more?

On Friday, we met with Reverend Sarah in her study for a premarital counseling session. Olivia had put her condo on the market, and she and Saskia had moved her clothes and books to St. Anne in the Jeep. Saskia and Nadia were going to stay in the condo till it sold. We hadn't said anything to them about premarital counseling.

A small wood fire was burning in a small

coal fireplace. It was a good working study for an Episcopal priest, faded but elegant — a threadbare oriental carpet on the floor, a big desk, shelves lined with concordances, a Latin Bible, church histories, a dozen works by C. S. Lewis, a copy of Skeat's Chaucer next to Tolkien's edition of *Gawain and the Green Knight.*

Sarah came in with a teapot and three cups on a tray. "I always think tea is better than coffee for talking about marriage."

"There's a dark side of marriage, don't you think," Olivia said, "that needs to be plumbed. That's what we need to do now, in a safe place — at least I hope this is a safe place — before we take the next step. I want to understand something about myself before I make another mistake."

"Safe as houses," Sarah said. Pouring tea into cups, not mugs.

But it didn't feel safe to me. "Exciting," but not "safe." Too much going on. Happening too fast.

"Here's the usual drill for premarital counseling. We don't have to stick to it, but it will give us an overview of the terrain, like a contour map: communication, sexual difficulties, child rearing, substance abuse, financial problems, anger, infidelity. Any place you'd like to start?"

343

"Gabe's a little shy in bed," Olivia said, "but he's learning."

"Whoa," I said. "Maybe I just haven't had as much experience as you."

"Wait wait wait," Olivia said. "I was just kidding."

"Let's start over," Sarah said. "You're both a little nervous. That's par for the course."

"I'm sorry," Olivia said.

"You don't need to be sorry," Sarah said, "but let's stay focused. You're going to love each other for your kindness and your generosity, for your smarts and your bedroom tricks, for your good will and your sassiness . . . But you're never going to love each other for your selves alone. Only God can do that." She paused to sip her tea. Olivia put her hand on my arm.

"That's the difficulty, isn't it," Sarah went on, smiling as if she were revealing a secret: "You will never love each other for your selves alone because you will never see each other as you really are. It's like trying to see the dark side of the moon. The moon doesn't rotate on its axis, you know. We always see the same face. Actually, over a period of time the edges of the far side can be seen due to libration — a kind of rocking motion. That's what we're trying to do this afternoon. Rock the moon so we can see a little of the dark side."

"I'm not so sure," Olivia said. "I think Gabe has seen me as I really am. I think he's gotten a good look at my dark side."

I started to protest, but Sarah shushed me. "Let her finish."

"We were in love my last year at the University of Chicago. I let him think we'd get married — eventually — because I half believed it too. But then when I was at Yale, I stopped answering his letters. I started sleeping with one of my classmates, and then another. They were just boys. They wanted me to clean their rooms. Do their laundry. We'd rub up against each other till — till it was too late to stop, but it didn't mean anything . . ."

"Until David," I said. Sarah held up a hand to tell me to butt out.

". . . and then with my professor. I completely lost my head. His wife found out. He dropped me, but it was too late. He lost his job, denied tenure, landed on his feet in Ann Arbor. I came back to Hyde Park and Gabe gave me a job. He wanted to take up where we'd left off, but I didn't want to be rescued. I went out with other men, but not Gabe. But then Gabe was there in the delivery room when my daughter was born. David — my ex-professor, ex-boyfriend, ex-

lover, I don't know what to call him —
didn't even know I was pregnant, but then
when David got divorced — this was six
years later — I went back to him, and we
got married. After a year, we were both
unfaithful to each other. So I guess I don't
have a very good track record. And now I've
lost my job, my daughter's a lesbian, and I
don't know how I'm going to pay her tuition
at the University of Chicago, or for her to
go to Jordan. I've been sick and I'm going
to lose my insurance. And Gabe's taken me
in. He probably thinks I trapped him and
now he feels sorry for me and doesn't know
what else to do. I'm sorry I've made myself
so unhappy, other people too."

"Gabe," Sarah said. "Do you feel trapped?
If you do, now's the time to get it out on
the table." Olivia started to cry. I moved to
comfort her, but Sarah stopped me. "Just
let her cry. And don't start crying yourself.
That would be too much."

"I thought you were going to say something about God," I said to Sarah.

"I was, but then I changed my mind. I'll
let God speak for himself. Or herself."

"I was sick when Saskia and I came to St.
Anne just before Christmas," Olivia said.
"That was the night of the big storm, and
the storm was like the storm in Coleridge's

'Dejection.' It restored me. I think that was God's way of speaking to me. It *was* a miracle. I should probably make a special offering."

"Well," I said, "it wasn't *really* a miracle. Ovarian cysts usually just go away. That's what the doctor said. And now you've been diagnosed with non-Hodgkin's lymphoma. And non-Hodgkin's lymphomas have a natural tendency of recurrence and remission."

"I refuse to entertain the idea of non-Hodgkin's lymphoma. What kind of a name is non-Hodgkin's lymphoma?"

"Non-Hodgkin lymphomas are any kind of lymphomas that don't involve Reed-Stromberg cells."

"You've been searching the Net," Sarah said.

"What does Reverend Sarah say?" I said, not looking at either woman. "If it's a miracle, won't the Church have to authenticate it?"

Sarah laughed. "There are miracles and then there are miracles."

"And?"

"Let me tell you a story: A woman was unhappy in her marriage. She believed that her husband didn't love her anymore and loved other women, so she went to a sorceress, and the sorceress told her to bring her a consecrated communion wafer. The woman was afraid, but she did it. She kept the wafer in her mouth after receiving it at mass and took it out later and wrapped it up in a cloth and took it to the sorceress, but on the way, the wafer started to bleed and she panicked and went home and hid it in the bottom of a trunk. That night she and her husband were awakened by a bright light coming from the trunk. It filled the whole room. The woman confessed, and she and her husband knelt and prayed till morning, and then they called for the parish priest."

"This happened when?"

"In Portugal, in twelve forty-seven."

"And you believe this?"

"The bloody host is still there, in a monstrance. The blood is still liquid and the host looks like real flesh with delicate veins in it. I've seen it. Last summer. In Santarem."

"You went to Portugal?!" I asked.

"Why shouldn't I go to Portugal?"

"I don't know. No reason. I guess I've never met anyone who's been to Portugal."

"Santarem. On the Tagus River, about forty miles from Lisbon."

I felt that I'd been catapulted into a different world. "I still don't know *exactly* what the doctor told Olivia," I said to Sarah. "Did he use the words 'clean bill of health,' for example? Did he use the word 'remission'? Did he say 'non-Hodgkin's lymphoma'? I try to look inside her head, but my X-ray vision doesn't work."

"It doesn't matter now, Gabe," Olivia said. "I'm all right."

Sarah started to explain that the Episcopal Church doesn't have anything comparable to the Roman Congregation for the Causes of Saints, which authenticates miracles.

This was more than I'd bargained for.

"Gabe," Sarah said, "what would you like to say to Olivia right now?"

"Right this minute? I don't think I should say anything. I keep thinking that all of a sudden I know the truth about love, but then there's always some other truth coming along behind that truth. Like one appetite coming along right after another, each one different. You're hungry, you're thirsty, you're horny, you want some ice cream, you want a drink, you're tired. It never ends. When she got on the Lakeshore Limited — in Union Station in Chicago, going to New Haven — and I saw her face in the window, I thought I understood the truth about love. It's not something you can put into words. It's something you experience in your whole body. And then when she came back to Hyde Park, right after the shop was bombed, and I saw her reflection in the broken glass in the window on Fifty-Seventh Street, and I thought I understood; and then when I held her daughter in my arms right after she was born — it was better than holding the pipe bomb that I'd carried out of the shop earlier that year, two days after the first bomb, and I thought I understood; and then when she told me that David's divorce was final and that she was going to join him in Ann Arbor . . . every time I thought I understood the truth about love, but it was always new, always painful. But then when Saskia called just before Christmas and said that Olivia was sick and that Borders in Hyde Park was closing and asked if they could come to St. Anne for Christmas . . . I almost said *no.* I thought the truth was always something new, but at that moment it seemed like it was just the same old truth over and over again, not really a truth at all, just the same old story over and over. Olivia never wanted to make another mistake. Fair enough, but why was I always the mistake she didn't want to make? That's what I don't understand."

Sarah laughed.

"Stop it," Olivia said. "This isn't a joke."

"You're right, Olivia," Sarah said, "and you were right when you said there's a dark side to every marriage. Something that needs to be plumbed. But I hear worse every week. A lot worse. Infidelity is part of the dark side, but it isn't the darkest thing. And it's not really the issue here."

"And what is the issue?"

"The issue isn't infidelity; the issue is accepting love. Don't worry about what you deserve. Just allow yourself to be loved."

"Are you saying we need to forgive each other?"

Sarah laughed. "Don't worry about forgiveness," she said. "Forgiveness will take care of itself."

"Do you think we're going to have more problems than ordinary people?"

"Olivia, there are no 'ordinary people,' there are just people, like you and Gabe. A lot of couples can tolerate each other only when they're *in* love. And then down the road they have troubles that are a lot more serious than yours. Now here's the way I see your situation: Olivia, you don't want to be rescued. You're afraid that you're not bringing enough to the table. I think you need to swallow your pride. Here's a man who has loved you all his adult life. Now you're living together like husband and wife

351

in a beautiful house on Lake Michigan. You're going to be the IT person at a brand-new bookstore. Gabe says you know how to set up a software program that will tell your computer everything you need to know every time you sell a book. It will even post the books on different websites for you. And you're bringing your s*elf* to the table. Your wonderful sassy passionate self, with a wealth of sexual experience. You know what my grandfather used to say? 'You take the cookies when the cookies are passed.' It's like divine grace. It's on offer right now. You can choose to accept it, or you can reject it. You can choose to be happy, or you can choose to be unhappy. You're lucky to have that choice. Not everyone has it."

"Was your grandfather a priest?" Olivia asked.

"He was an auctioneer."

"I thought he was a bishop?"

"That was my other grandfather. And Gabe, I say the same thing to you. You've loved this woman all your adult life, and now here she is, opening her arms to you. She loved another man more than she loved you, and she caused him a lot of grief, herself too. So what? That just shows how hard she can love. And she spread her legs for other men when she wouldn't spread

352

them for you. Get over it. You had no claim on her. You weren't married, you weren't engaged, you hadn't plighted your troth. You know what this tells me? It tells me you were special. It tells me that she put you in a different category from these other men. So I say unto you: Put your resentment aside, count your blessings, and take the cookies when the cookies are passed."

"Beh, ce l'abbiamo fatta, sani e salvi," I said on the way home. *"Well, we made it through, safe and sound."* Olivia laughed. "Do you want to go to a justice of the peace? There's one on Schoolcraft Road. Or are there more depths that need to be plumbed first?"

"I think we've reached bottom," she said.

I turned onto Schoolcraft Road, but we didn't stop at the JUSTICE OF THE PEACE sign by the side of the road.

"You know something," she said. "I love who I am when I'm with you."

"Who is that?" I asked.

"I guess we're going to find out," she said.

"And you'll get yourself checked out, right?"

"Gabe, I'm fine. There's nothing to be checked out."

"But you're going to see Dr. Matthews again, right? You're going to do it for me.

And for Saskia."

"Okay, okay."

"We'll make a little vacation out of it, stay at the Quadrangle Club, eat steaks at Charlie Trotter's or a *bouillabaisse* at Spiaggia."

At the depot, young mothers were drinking coffee on their way to shop for clothing for their children at Ducklings; a beautiful painting of a child was on display on an easel in front of the art gallery with which we shared a wall.

Chas. Johnson & Son, Ltd. Antiquarian Booksellers was taking shape. Our old partners desk was in place on the old telegraph bay, which would serve as our office. Adam and Carla were arranging books on new shelves in our main gallery, which would be locked. If a customer wanted to look at something, whoever was minding the shop would simply unlock the door and let him or her in. If you're going to sell books online, you can't afford to have browsers taking books off the shelves and moving them around and putting them back in the wrong place, because when an order comes in over the Internet, you have to be able to put your hands on the book right away. If you can't find the book, you'll get a black mark for "fulfillment failure." Too many fulfillment failures and you'll get kicked off the site. Olivia had her own agenda. She wanted to put her mark on the shop. She wanted to be sure that a reader entering the shop could find a copy of *Anna Karenina* — not the first English translation for $5,000, just a good modern paperback — or Isaac Asimov's *Guide to Science,* or Thomas Kuhn's *Structure of Scientific Revolutions,* or Darwin's *Descent of Man;* or Keats's or Auden's *Collected Poems* or Eavan Boland's or Gwendolyn Brooks's; *Peter Rabbit* and *Pinocchio;* Julia Childs' *Mastering the Art of French Cooking* and a selection of Italian cookbooks; a selection of good mysteries: Rex Stout, Michael Connolly, Donna Leon, Walter Mosley, and Sherlock Homes, of course. Tony Hillerman, P. D. James, Sara Paretsky, Sue Grafton, Marcia Muller . . . "You could have a whole shop devoted to mysteries," she said. I didn't remind her that Murder One, on London's Charing Cross Road — a shop devoted to mysteries — had recently closed.

"It's not a good idea," I said, "because it means we'll have to have someone in the front of the shop at all times, someone who could be cataloging books or photographing their jackets, or putting them up online, or blogging about them, or tweaking the website."

"Look at them," Olivia said, brushing aside my objection and pointing at Adam and Carla. "You and I look pretty good. You're handsome and I'm good looking. Still pretty firm, pretty vigorous, pretty sexy. But next to them . . ."

"It's okay, don't you think?" I said. "One generation flourishes, another passes away."

"Are you trying to tell me something?" she said.

"Probably," I said, "but I'm not sure what it is."

Two Sundays later we drove into Hyde Park. There was still plenty of snow cover. I stayed at the Quadrangle Club, but Olivia had to go into the hospital that night.

On Monday and Tuesday, they ran a battery of tests, and on Tuesday afternoon, Dr. Matthews sat us down in her office. Dr. Matthews was wearing gray slacks and a white blouse. Olivia was in a blue silk dress the color of a summer sky. I was wearing jeans and a turtle neck. She told us that Olivia had been diagnosed with indolent NHL, non-Hodgkin's lymphoma.

"A lazy cancer," I said.

"There's nothing to be done right now," she said. "Watchful waiting is the key, and regular checkups."

Leaving the hospital, I was at a loss, but Olivia seemed relatively cheerful. We stopped for a sandwich at the Medici, and then headed out on Stony Island. She waved for catfish and screamed for ribs as we passed Moo & Oink. The sky was dark and heavy, like the future. There were no stars, no moon. The flare stacks along the Skyway were burning off excess gas, like the fires of Mordor.

By the time we got to the Indiana line, she had laid out an agenda. She was going to sign up for the confirmation classes at St. Anne's. She was going to stop tweaking *Varieties* and get the manuscript in the mail to Johns Hopkins. She was going to become a vegetarian. She was going to give up alcohol. She was going to meditate. She was going to renew her virginity and go on a retreat before the wedding in July. Reverend Sarah had given her some literature about a convent near Grand Rapids. She was going to talk to Cleatus about stabilizing the bluff. Then in December, we'd visit Saskia in Amman and spend Christmas in the Holy Land. Nadia would know how to get to Jerusalem. Carla and Adam could mind the shop.

"What if they want to go home for Christmas?" I asked.

"They are home," she said. "But I'll speak to them."

By the end of the week, Saskia had talked to oncologists — not just to Olivia's doctor at Bernard Mitchell but also to doctors at cancer treatment centers at Northwestern and at the University of Michigan Hospital in Ann Arbor — and she'd Googled a dozen NHL sites on the Internet. What we needed to do, immediately, was assemble a team of specialists: a hematologist, a medical oncologist, a radiation oncologist; we needed more tests — biopsies, blood tests, CAT scans, PET scans, MRI scans; and then we needed to consider treatment options: chemotherapy, immunotherapy, radiation therapy, or a stem cell transplant. Possibly surgery, though not if the cancer was outside the limbic system.

She couldn't understand why her mother refused to cooperate, why her mother didn't want her bone marrow aspirated or her lumbar punctured. Why she didn't want to try chemotherapy, immunotherapy, radiation therapy, or a stem cell transplant.

XIX. Confirmation
(MARCH 2011)

"You have to trust a man named Cleatus," Olivia said as we heard Cleatus's truck pull into the drive. "You know he's on the vestry."

"Of course I trust Cleatus," I said.

"He knelt next to us on Ash Wednesday," Olivia said.

"I know that," I said. *"Dust thou art, and to dust thou shalt return.* But it makes me a little self-conscious. Doing business with someone after you've knelt next to him."

"You knelt next to me," she said. "Don't worry about it. Sarah says he can do anything." She was standing at the sink, looking very domestic and very sophisticated at the same time, an apron protecting her new Anne Klein dress.

I got up to open the door. Cleatus came in and sat across from us at the kitchen table. Olivia closed a cupboard door and poured coffee. Cleatus, big and burly, fiddled with his glasses.

"Augie says . . ." I said.

"I know what Augie says," he said. "He show you those old photos of the men putting in the seawall? They came on a boat from Chicago with a pile driver. Now you've got a good seawall. Half-inch steel. Can't get that anymore. That makes a big difference, but the problem you got right now is not toe erosion, it's groundwater erosion. Groundwater discharge from the bluff face. From above, not from the lake. What we call 'perched water' — groundwater that's accumulated above the water table in the unsaturated zone. That water's running underneath your house. That's where your problem is.

"What we've got to do is get rid of invasive plants, especially buckthorn, and restore the native vegetation — wild rye, Joe Pye weed, blue flat, dogwood. June grass and lake sedge on the slope where they'll get full sun. We can stabilize the stream bank with native plants and boulders so it will carry the water around the house and into the creek that runs through the state park. You want to get rid of that perched water. A vertical well, probably two, to pump the water out and into the stream. And a passive well drilled into the bluff face."

"What's wrong with buckthorn? I kind of like it."

"Buckthorn." Cleatus shook his head. "Know your enemy. Buckthorn is like kudzu. It takes over everything. It shades out the native plants that control insects and stabilize the soil. Nurseries aren't allowed to sell it anymore, but there are still a lot of buckthorn hedges around. You can't cut it out because it'll just come back angry. What we'll do is lop the plants off about six inches off the ground and cover them with black plastic bags. The roots will stay in the ground but they won't germinate. That helps control erosion. Then we broadcast seeds of native plants, up here in the yard and right over the edge of the bluff, and cover them with erosion control blankets so the seeds can germinate. They put their roots down under the blanket and grow up through the matting. You want to slow down the flow of the surface water."

"How much is this going to cost?" I asked. The money from the November auction at Swann's had finally arrived, so I wasn't worried. But I wanted to know.

"Not as much as having your house slide into the lake."

"When can you start?" Olivia asked.

"Couple of weeks."

"Can you build us some new stairs?" I asked.

"I can do that too."

I admired men like Cleatus, an older type, like Grandpa Chaz, men who knew how to do things, how to adjust your carburetor, or get bats out of your attic or rats out of your basement, how to seat a toilet or install a new soil pipe or tuck-point your foundation. You'd see their trucks parked in front of the big houses in Hyde Park — CONTRACTORS.

Two weeks later, I came home from the shop, where Adam and Carla and I had been putting together our first online catalog. The yard was full of police cars. Well, three police cars. Local. State. Sheriff's. Olivia, who'd been at St. Anne's with Reverend Sarah, was standing next to a bright red drilling machine talking to a state trooper, holding Booker on a leash. Booker was straining to get at the hole. Two shallow wells had been dug to pump out pockets of "perched" water. A dowsing rod had been used to locate an underground stream. Olivia, I learned later, had been trying the dowsing rod when the digger had uncovered two bodies.

Olivia and the state trooper and a couple

of policemen were looking down in the hole. A police photographer was trying to keep them away from the hole so he could take pictures.

I left the Jeep in the drive and joined them.

A couple of bodies. Or rather, a skeleton and something that looked like a body lay side by side in the hole, about a foot apart. Bits of cloth clung to both. I knew right away who they were. Or what they were. The New York hit men who'd come to kill Eddie. Augie never told me Eddie had killed them. What he'd said was, "Eddie sent them away." I was never sure I could believe Augie, but now . . . I didn't say anything, but I was thinking, there might be more! Two more. And there probably were, though they didn't turn up that afternoon, and I didn't mention the possibility.

"Looks like they were killed with a shotgun," one of the policemen said, though I wasn't sure how he could tell. "Slugs. Something busted up their ribs pretty bad."

Will they find the slugs? I wondered. *Do slugs bear the same kind of distinctive marks as bullets? Does it matter? Were the slugs from the same gun? Or two different guns?* I pictured Augie and Eddie at the bedroom windows at the east end of the house, or running out of the side doors with shotguns, or waiting in the trees. What about the dog? Augie said they'd turned the dog loose.

The bodies were twenty or thirty feet from the house, but they could have been dragged after they'd been killed.

Where would I wait if I knew someone was coming to kill me? How would I know? Would someone tip me off? Or would I just know? What if I didn't know someone was coming to kill me? Would I be prepared? How would I know what to do?

I made a couple of omelets for supper. As we ate, Olivia kept saying how terrible it was, but I could see she was very excited. Some real evil had gotten loose in our backyard. Was this a rent in the cosmic fabric? she wondered. Was it a sign of a "rebellion" against God's plan?

I took a more down-to-earth, Aristotelian point of view. I wanted to divert this stream of thought, the way Cleatus was diverting the underground stream that was causing toe erosion. "Life's already a muddle," I suggested. "You don't need to complicate things."

Olivia covered her omelet with hot sauce. She wanted sensation rather than thought.

"Life's muddle," I said again. "I don't see evidence of anyone rebelling against the cosmic order here."

"But tearing up something. Doesn't it make you think of a rent?"

By the time the sun had finally disappeared, the two bodies had been covered, and the police presence was gone, except for one unlucky policeman who was still there to protect the crime scene. I was glad when he came to the door and interrupted us. He wanted to explain how he thought it happened, though it was hard to be sure now — no weapon, no motivation, no timeline, no witnesses.

"Mr. Palmisano . . ." he said. "His uncle was Eddie from Chicago."

"Right," I said, "a virtuoso with a machine gun."

We didn't invite the policeman to wait in the kitchen because by this time we were eager to get our own bodies into bed. Through the open window, we could hear the police radio squawking and talking. It added to the excitement. Olivia was very sexed up that night. More so than usual. I think she wanted to show me that she could still surprise me. In fact, she surprised me all the time, but this time I think she surprised herself too.

Two days later the landscape crew was able to get back to work. The buckthorn stumps had been wrapped in plastic bags that made you think of rows of graves in a military cemetery, but black rather than white; the perched water was being pumped into the stream. The old streambed had been diverted so that it joined a larger stream in the state park, and the new streambed had been reinforced with rocks. The ground had been covered over with native plants. Erosion control blankets had been draped over the steep slope of the bluff.

Augie called. "You send the police out here to arrest me?"

"Did they arrest you?"

"No, but they wanted to."

"What'd you tell them?"

"What could I tell them? The big cop had a face like a *budino*."

"A 'rice pudding,' " I said.

"That's what I just said."

"You could tell them what happened."

I could feel Augie shrugging his shoulders. "Maybe it was the Finnish guy."

Augie wanted to come out to take a steam. Olivia nodded her approval.

"I'll come and pick you up."

"Nah," he says. "I'll get the van to bring me. I'm in a wheelchair today, since I saw you. My hip."

I started the sauna. By the time Augie arrived, it was up to 120. When it came time to disrobe, Olivia helped Augie. She was a natural helper.

"You're a beautiful woman," he said, not glancing at her sideways, but looking her straight up and down.

"So," Olivia said, spreading out her towel on one of the benches. "Tell us everything. Did you kill those men?"

"Me? I wouldn't put it like that."

"How would you put it?"

"They came to kill Eddie. Eddie sent them away."

"So it wasn't the Finnish guy?"

He shrugged. We watched the fire take different shapes. Elemental. Fire Earth Air Water. We listened too, to the noise the water made when it hit the hot rocks, as if the rocks were spitting at us.

"How did they get under the ground?"

"That I don't know. Eddie talked to them and they went back to New York. That's what I thought."

"Then Eddie shot them?"

Augie threw up his hands to indicate that he knew nothing. But Olivia kept after him. "Maybe *you* killed them, to protect your uncle?"

"You're worse than the police," he said, and then he said: "I asked the driver to take

367

me past that new store of yours. The old depot. I remember sometimes the girls would come down on the train and Eddie'd send me to meet them at the depot."

"We're going to have a section on local history. Maybe you should write a book. About Eddie and about your good life with Eddie."

Augie laughed.

"I did some digging at the library," I said. "And there's lots of stuff online, you know, more than I told you before. The police know about Eddie."

"Eddie was always good to me. Took me to Al Capone's going-away party. I was only seven years old."

"I thought you were three or four, and that he told you about it later."

"I got a snapshot somewhere. Eddie was my mother's brother."

"Sister Sarah, from the church. Nice-looking woman. Drops in every now and then. She's like you. Wants to know all about the old days."

"It's *Reverend* Sarah," Olivia said.

"Like those guys who got drowned in their own wine vats. Eddie didn't have nothing to do with that. That was a different Eddie. That was Eddie the Clutching Hand. That's what they called him. The Clutching Hand.

'Cause of the way he'd grab on to your shirt when he was talking to you and not let go. Eddie Campanello, that was his name. He was friends with the guy who used to run boats from the old harbor, it was a natural harbor then. They'd run a fast boat up the river to Capone's farm, where they made the booze. Take the booze out to the big boat. Six barrels at a time was all they could handle. Take it out to the big boat, then Chicago. Told everyone it was from Canada.

"You want to know about real evil?" Augie leaned forward, as if about to impart confidential information, but I thought maybe his back was hurting, or his shoulders.

"He was a real bastard, Eddie the Clutching Hand. Bought half a dozen good horses and insured the hell out of them. Then he bought half a dozen hackers, locked 'em in his barn, doused them with kerosene, and set the whole place on fire to collect the insurance he took out on the Thoroughbreds. That's real evil. Eddie — Eddie, my uncle — told him he'd kill him if he ever harmed another horse. And he did. That's the only way you can deal with some guys."

The temperature got up to 160, plenty hot for me. Augie told me to adjust the baffles on the stove that transfer the hot exhaust right to the rocks. We sat quietly for a while, the temperature stable at 160.

"Eddie used to put his hand on my shoulder," he said to Olivia, putting his hand on *her* shoulder, "and it was like he was saying, *La vita non è inesauribile? Non è bello essere vivi?*"

"That's what Gabe says too," she said. "He must've heard it from you."

Palm Sunday is the longest service of the year. The weather was lovely and we processed around the church. After the procession, Olivia was confirmed. After the sermon, the bishop called the candidates by name and asked them to stand and repeat their baptismal vows. Sarah, Olivia's sponsor, walked with Olivia up to the bishop. The bishop laid his hands on each candidate in turn, in accordance with the ancient entry rite into the Church. He dipped his right thumb in the Chrism and made the Sign of the Cross on Olivia's forehead, and Olivia, along with seven teenagers, was sealed with the Gift of the Holy Spirit.

XX. The Gettysburg Address

(JUNE 2011)

We attended Saskia's commencement on June 11. Afterward, at the Medici, Saskia tried to persuade her mother to see her doctor again, but she didn't have any more luck than I did. Olivia said she couldn't go till after the wedding. Saskia and Nadia were going to take the train down on Friday for the Grand Opening.

Olivia slept in the backseat on the way home. In the morning, Pentecost Sunday, she read the Old Testament lesson — Genesis 11:1–9, the Tower of Babel. "You've got to admit," she said afterward in the car as we were going over the LaSalle Road Bridge, "the Book of Genesis has got some great stories: the fall, the murder of Abel, the flood, the sacrifice of Isaac."

"In my opinion," I said, "none of these stories reflect well on God. Think about the Tower of Babel: human beings cooperating, working in concert toward a common goal,

371

and God can't stand it. He's frightened. 'Let's go down and mess up their language,' he says. 'If they all speak the same language, there's no telling what they could do. What *they* could do.' "

"But Pentecost repairs the damage," she said. "The Holy Spirit descends into the apostles and enables them — and others in the crowd — to speak in tongues and in foreign languages."

"But who caused the damage in the first place?" I asked. "And when it was over, could the disciples speak languages they hadn't known before? Could they speak Greek? Persian? Hittite? Assyrian? Sumerian? I don't think so."

"I'll have to ask Sarah," she said.

"Maybe we should slow down a little," I said. Olivia had missed two appointments with her doctor at Bernard Mitchell, and in fact had taken *all* her appointments off the table till things got settled at the shop, till she'd fine-tuned the software and optimized the website for mobile apps and tweaked the metrics that would track key performance indicators. And now she had a deadline coming up to get the manuscript of *Varieties* off to Johns Hopkins.

"I'm alive, Gabe. I don't want to slow down."

"You're like Booker," I said. "Always straining at the leash."

"Booker doesn't need a leash," Olivia said, "and neither do I."

In a short ceremony on the night before the opening, Reverend Sarah blessed the shop and the rare book room and the cataloging room and the reference library, and the office, and the eight hundred or so used books from The Warehouse that Olivia had put together in the front. It was late, and we were exhausted, and in the morning Olivia felt feverish, achy. I brought her some ibuprofen and persuaded her to stay in bed. I'd been half awake for almost an hour, listening to the news, which was not good — roadside bombings in Afghanistan and Pakistan, the Chicago Teachers Association gearing up for a strike, a congressman posting pictures of his penis on the Internet.

I brought Olivia a soft-boiled egg in an egg cup and strips of buttered toast and a glass of orange juice; Booker and I drove into St. Anne, parked across from the marina, and walked along the boardwalk to enjoy the boats with their funny names. My favorites — the two boats that Olivia and I had seen on our trip to St. Anne after Dad's memorial service — *Wet Dreams,* a ketch from Watergate, Illinois, and *Miss Behaving,* from Orion, Wisconsin — were now docked next to each other, between *At Last* (Chicago) and *She Got the House* (Chicago). And I thought about the story I'd told Olivia — about the couple we'd seen silhouetted in the window of one of the condos on the St. Anne Peninsula, on the other side of the marina. And I wondered what had become of them. And I wondered what would become of us.

As I entered the shop, I wondered if God would object to the work we'd been doing: working in concert toward a common goal. Had we frightened God? Because we'd been too happy? Or because we'd been too busy to think about being happy? Working twelve- to fourteen-hour days. The shop full of young people — young people in love — Adam and Carla, Saskia and Nadia on weekends, laughing and joking, drinking beer at a table out in the corridor. And Booker, sticking his nose into everything.

The depot itself was quiet, like a cathedral, the only sound the brrr of the big espresso machine at Innkeepers. The counter people moved silently — priests preparing for the early morning mass.

Amy Marckwardt, a St. Anne's student in a blue shirt and a white apron, was watching me from behind the counter, meeting my gaze, as if she had a secret she wanted to communicate.

She brought me an espresso without asking, though Innkeepers wasn't open yet. "I saw your books in the window," she said.

"Find anything you fancy?"

"I might ask my grandmother for something. I have all the Beatrix Potter books, but I'd like to have a first edition."

Hmmm. *Ten thousand dollars,* I thought. But you never knew. Well, I probably knew. "You know," I said, "that Beatrix Potter couldn't find a publisher for her stories, so she published them herself."

"Maybe I'll try that," she said, "with *my* stories."

I drank the coffee, put the cup and saucer back on the counter, walked down the concourse, and crossed the aisle to admire the first editions of familiar children's books in our display window: *The Tale of Peter Rabbit* and *The Story of A Fierce Bad Rabbit;* the Pooh "Quartet": *When We Were Very Young, Now We Are Six, Winnie the Pooh,* and *The House at Pooh Corner.* Laura Ingalls Wilder's *The Little House on the Prairie* with the original Sewell and Boyle illustrations. Frank Baum's *Wizard of Oz* with all twenty-four color plates, like the one I'd given to

Saskia on her birthday a few years back —
before *Charlotte's Web* but after the Pooh
books. These were titles that I'd hand-sold
when I started working in the shop after
Mamma went away, and I had a strange
sense that I'd circled back to the beginning
of my life as a bookseller.

I deactivated the alarm and entered the
shop. The books were on the shelves. Every
book inventoried and shelved according to
the semi-rational taxonomy we'd used on
Fifty-Seventh Street. Olivia's website was a
knockout, an invitation to a feast. The new
software had passed every test, though it
was hard to imagine all our data stored in a
cloud. Olivia tried to explain, but I couldn't
get past the image of lateral filing cabinets
floating around up in the sky.

Olivia had left her mark on the shop. I'd
thought it was a bad idea and we'd had a
proper quarrel, but the result was summoning: seven Jefferson bookcases to your left
as you entered the shop held paperbacks
and hardbacks, used: "The Modern World
in 100 Books," "100 Scientific Classics,"
"100 Great Novels," "100 Great Poets,"
"100 Great Children's Books," "100 Great
Cookbooks," "100 Great Mysteries." Nothing over $10. Delilah would keep us sup-
plied with books from The Warehouse.

Olivia had left her mark on me too: I didn't think twice about sitting down at the computer on our partners desk in the office and typing in our URL and summoning up our unpublished website from the Cloud, like a medium summoning a spirit from the Great Beyond. The site was not live yet, but I cycled through HOME, ABOUT US, OUR STAFF, OUR HISTORY, CATALOGS, BROWSE INVENTORY, ASK A QUESTION, and CONTACT US.

By five o'clock, the concourse was full of people waiting for something to happen. The *Gettysburg Address* — in a display case on a small table in the atrium — gave them something to look at, and they began to file by, silently, like people filing by an open coffin at a visitation, pausing briefly to contemplate the mystery and then moving on.

I guess that made me the undertaker.

I wanted to shout at them: *Talk among yourselves.*

At first, the different contingents — new money, old money, no money, African-American, the Vitale clan, summer people, new condo owners, townspeople, fruit growers, academics, Mayor Toni and the city attorney, several Caxton Club members and other collectors, a handful of antiquarian

377

book dealers from Chicago and Ann Arbor and Lansing and Detroit. Adam and Carla were glad to shake hands with John King from Detroit and Brad Jonas from Powell's in Hyde Park. These groups were like the circles in a Venn diagram, with only a tiny area — the *Gettysburg Address* — in common where all the circles overlapped. But once the waitstaff from Stefano's arrived and began pouring glasses — not plastic cups — of prosecco and passing around trays of bread and marinated olives, prosciutto and thin slices of Parmesan cheese — the circles merged into each other till there was just one circle. The *Gettysburg Address* remained at the center, no longer a dead body at a visitation but a baby at a bris or a christening.

Toni made the rounds, touching everyone on the shoulder. When she touched my shoulder, I said to her, "Toni, buy something, you got me into this." And she said, "You want me to spend thirty-five K for the *Gettysburg Address*?" And I said, "Yes. Somebody's got to, it might as well be you." Though I already knew that Ben Warren was going to buy it for the college library. I was giving him a dealer discount, of course, even though he wasn't a dealer.

"How about *Shipwrecks of the Great*

Lakes?" Toni said, touching my shoulder again. "The author lives in St. Joe. You should get him to give a reading here."

I was glad to hear a train pulling in, bringing Saskia and Nadia and a new contingent of commuters from Chicago. Booker started to moan. I refused to interpret it as a "sign" because he did it every time a train blew its whistle at ninety-six decibels, two longs, a short, and a long. Fortunately the freight trains had been routed east of town.

"Where's Olivia anyway?" Toni said. We listened to the train as it slowed to a stop on the other side of Duval Street.

Saskia and Nadia were also on the train. Olivia must have met them at the station. I'd been worrying about her all day, but when she came into the shop, she didn't look like someone with an "indolent" non-Hodgkin's lymphoma. She looked like a million bucks — confident, stunning in an apricot-colored lace shift dress with a soft shimmer to it. Her hair was pulled back like a French woman's, but her face didn't have the hardness that you'd expect in a French woman. Her face was open and radiant, as if she had just come off stage and was ready to kick back and have a good time. She looked like someone arriving with good news, like someone who knew what she wanted to do next. I felt the same way, could feel exactly what she was feeling, could think exactly what she was thinking. *We're confederates,* her smile said — accomplices, partners. Everything's going to be okay. And she was right. I was unpardonably happy.

A few minutes before six o'clock she tapped her glass of San Pellegrino with a spoon from Innkeepers. We were about to go online.

She told people to open the browsers on their cell phones and their tablets and go to www.ChasJohnson&Son.com.

People murmured.

"Are you ready?"

Standing next to her, I watched her finger hover over the PUBLISH button on her iPad screen, as if she were about to detonate a bomb. I held my breath, waiting for the explosion. She touched the screen, but not much happened. People stared at their smart phones and their tablets.

"You're going to have to refresh your screen," she said, not breaking a sweat, "or close the page and reopen it." Pretty soon a collective gasp, or series of gasps, rolled down the corridor, like waves breaking on the beach. Some people (of course) had trouble, but Carla and Adam were there to help. I didn't have my iPad with me, but Augie had his, and I looked on with him as he clicked on different links.

"Here's you," Augie said, holding up his iPad, "in that red fedora. It suits you." He was wearing a coat and tie, standing in his walker next to the *Gettysburg Address,* feeding bits of prosciutto to Booker. "You know," he said to me confidentially, "all you had to do was sell a dozen books like this and you could have given me a decent price for my house."

I called to Saskia. "Bring this old man a glass of prosecco, will you. And a handkerchief to dry his tears."

She brought a glass of prosecco. When she left, Augie said, "How old did you say she was?"

"Twenty-one. She's got a boyfriend," I said. "I mean a girlfriend," I corrected myself. "Not exactly out of the closet, but the closet door is open. I already told you."

"I forgot." Augie nodded. "Too bad."

Saskia and Nadia were both dressed in attractive white V-neck blouses that they wore over skinny jeans.

Olivia joined us, pausing long enough before the display window to admire herself in the glass before turning and smiling a slightly different version of the smile she'd given me earlier, one full of promise.

Toni was there talking with Sarah. "Buy something," I said to them.

About ten minutes later, Carla gave a shout. Someone had ordered a book online. "Somebody bought the *Gettysburg Address,*" she shouted, out of breath.

The sale of the *Gettysburg Address* unlocked something in people's psyches. The *Gettysburg Address* and the prosecco. More orders started coming in. Olivia, I knew, had asked a few friends to place orders, but there were some real orders too. Everything seemed like a bargain after the *Gettysburg Address.*

"How does it work?" Toni asked me. "You just click 'Add to cart' and put a thirty-five thousand dollar book on your credit card?"

"It all happens in the Cloud," I said.

"You can do it if you've got a fifty-thousand dollar line of credit," Olivia said.

"What kind of credit card has a fifty-thousand dollar credit limit?"

"Ask Ben," Toni said, "or Mrs. Marckwardt."

"But usually," I said, "someone who's going to lay out that kind of money for a book will have a conversation — several conversations — with the dealer first. And then probably send a check."

I was glad to see local people spending money. Olivia went back to the electronic cash register–computer at the front. Carla and Adam were entering sales on a couple of iPads in the main gallery. Everything was interconnected. I hadn't really expected to sell many books, but Jonathan Krause, who had an antiquarian bookshop in Detroit, bought the first edition of Ring Lardner's *Regular Fellows That I Have Met* that was in the window. Emily Perkins — I know her name now — laid out $3,700 for a first printing of *The Sun Also Rises* with "stopped" on page 18, a printing error or "issue point" that guaranteed that this was a true first edition. It was going to be a birthday present for her husband and she wanted to leave it in the shop and pick it up later. "A bargain," I said. "If it had a fine dust jacket, it would go for a hundred thousand."

"I've added it to my cart."

"You could just pay at the cash register," I said.

"It's easier this way."

Anne-Marie was watching us. I turned to her: "It's always nice to see you," I said.

"Likewise."

She extended a hand, and I shook it, and I understood that she was someone who had come into my life for a little while, just when I needed her, and I hoped that she felt the same way about me.

"How's your translation coming?"

"Slowly," I said.

Reverend Sarah, always the good shepherd, joined us. We chatted for a few minutes until another woman came up to us — a grandmother whose name escaped me, though Olivia and I had been introduced to her after coffee at St. Anne's. Sarah let me dangle for a few seconds before introducing us. Mrs. Marckwardt. She was interested in the children's books and thought she might like to start a Beatrix Potter collection for her granddaughter. She wanted me to show her *The Tale of Peter Rabbit* that was in the window.

"Does your granddaughter work at Innkeepers?" I asked.

"Yes, she does."

"She pulled an espresso for me this morning before Innkeepers was even open. Going to be a writer?"

She nodded. "Children's books. I've read all the Beatrix Potter books to her a dozen times."

"The copy in the shop is the first trade edition, not one of the two hundred fifty copies privately printed for family and friends, but still very expensive. You might want to talk it over with your husband."

"I don't have to talk anything over with my husband," she said. "He has to talk things over with me! Besides, he's dead."

"It's a lot of money. It'll be here tomorrow. Probably. You want to be sure you know your own mind."

"But will there still be prosecco tomorrow?" She laughed.

"I'll set a bottle aside."

I was asking one of Stefano's waiters to fill Mrs. Marckwardt's glass when a middle-aged man in a business suit started waving an e-reader around as if he were brandishing a pistol. He had a glass of prosecco in the other hand, not his first glass either. "He's the man," Mrs. Marckwardt whispered, "who wrote to the newspaper advocating a bookless library. He'd like to consign printed books to the dustbin of history. He wants the public library to be an 'information mall.' Virgil Stevens. His grandfather started Stevens Hams. He's loaded."

"Look," Kindle Man — aka Virgil Stevens — shouted. "I've got the *Gettysburg Address* right here, and it didn't cost me thirty-five thousand. He started to read: " 'Four score and seven years ago . . .' I've got five different versions here. Didn't cost me a dime. I didn't even have to cross the street." People stepped back, clearing a space, as if it were a street fight.

He was a man who instantiated all my fears. About my vocation. About life in general. I knew how to deal with this kind of person, but suddenly I was very tired, didn't feel like explaining, didn't feel like launching into an *apologia pro vita mea*. But I did what I had to do. I stepped up to the plate, positioned myself at the entrance to the shop, next to the *Gettysburg Address*.

"Mr. Stevens," I said. "If you're one of those people who think books — I mean books as physical objects, not 'texts' — should be consigned to the rubbish heap of history, then there's not much I can say to you, but I think you've failed to understand that people don't just read books. They live with books. Books become part of their lives. They loan books to their friends. They give them to their children, to their friends and lovers. They borrow books. They collect books. They arrange books on their shelves, and then they rearrange them. Nothing is more beautiful than a room full of books. Nothing. They inscribe books to their lovers and to their husbands and wives, they inscribe them to their children and to their parents. The book as a physical object is the end product of a long and complicated process that has a long and complicated history going back to the clay tablets that filled the Royal Library of Ashurbanipal.

"Think about your own library. Every one of those books has its own story to tell. You start with a few books, and then you add a few more every year. After a while you have a personal library, a library that tells your story in a profound way. And it's right there for you. On your shelves: the books you read as a child, if you're lucky enough to still have them; the book your mother gave you for Christmas the year your father died; the books your dad left behind in his study, the books that named your experience, the books that opened your eyes."

I wasn't sure I should go on, but I didn't know how to stop. "Books are physical objects, like bodies. They carry identifying marks the way your body does — like the mole on your arm, or the shape of your nose, or the scar on your body when you fell and skinned your knee, or the scar when you had your appendix removed. A book has a smell. My grandfather could identify hundreds of books by their smell. Put your nose in an old book and inhale. It's been touched by human hands. It puts you in touch with the physical world, with a time before all things became electronic. Do you know what Reynolds Price said about his copy of Milton's *Paradise Lost,* a copy that had once belonged to Milton's daughter, who wrote out her father's words because he was blind?" I waited a couple of beats. "He said it was like the apostolic succession. He was touching the hand that touched the hand that touched the Hand.

"That's what you're touching when you hold a book like this one." I unlocked the display case and took out the *Gettysburg Address.* I opened it. I hefted it, as if I were trying to guess its weight. I was the only one who knew that Ben Warren was the one who had bought the book for the college library. Except Ben, of course, and Ruth MacDonald.

I examined it. "Forty-eight pages," I said. "Eighteen sixty-three. About nine by six. It's in a cloth slipcase. It's the first time the *Gettysburg Address* was published in book form, though there were earlier accounts printed in different newspapers, and a pamphlet called *The Gettysburg Solemnities,* and there's a Lincoln holograph in the Smithsonian. There are five holographs, actually. They'd set you back six figures.

"You have to remember that Lincoln

wasn't the main speaker in the cemetery that day, four months after the battle at Gettysburg. His name isn't even on the title page. The main speaker was Edward Everett, the most famous orator of the time. He spoke for almost two hours. The *Washington Chronicle* printed Everett's entire speech, verbatim. A couple days later it mentioned the fact that President Lincoln had also given a speech.

"When you hold a book — this book — in your hand," I said, "you're touching an older world." I walked toward him, holding out the book. "Go ahead," I said. "Touch it."

He was reluctant.

"Touch it, Vern," Toni said in a loud voice.

He finally touched it with his fingertips.

"Now touch your Kindle," I said. "Feel the difference?" I was on familiar territory, and the longer I went on, the more my enthusiasm energized me. "The physical book itself, nine inches by five and five-eighths inches, creates a frame. You can feel how the publisher's lettered wrappers have been worn and see the publisher's ad at the back. You'll notice that Lincoln's name does not appear on the front cover. You can touch a world in which Lincoln's two hundred seventy-two words were tacked on, almost as an afterthought, to Everett's 'Great Oration.' You can read what Everett took two hours to say, and then you can read what Lincoln said in two minutes.

"Don't be too sure you would have given Lincoln the prize. In fact, no one paid much attention to Lincoln's little speech till the centennial in 1876. Except Everett himself, who wrote to Lincoln the next day: 'I should be glad, if I could flatter myself that I came as near to the central idea of the occasion, in two hours, as you did in two minutes.'

"This book has more stories to tell. If you open it to the title page, you'll see that this is an inscribed copy, given by Everett himself to his son William, who was a student at Harvard, in 1863, shortly after it was published. It's a line from Pericles's funeral oration, written in Greek and then in English: 'If then we prefer to meet danger with a light heart but without laborious training, and with a courage which is gained by habit and not enforced by law, are we not greatly the better for it?'

"Later William gave the book to the library of the Adams Academy, where he'd been a student. Here's what *he* wrote below his father's inscription:

memoria temporis tenebrosi MDCCCLXV.

Eighteen hundred sixty-five. That's the as-sassination —"

"Okay, okay," Kindle Man interrupted. "But what about the picture book of Indians you've got on the table inside. A hundred thousand dollars! Isn't that a little steep?" I knew from his body language and from the way he enunciated each word — "Isn't. That. A. Little. Steep?" — that something powerful was stirring inside him, anger or indignation or maybe resentment, or even shame — and that he didn't want to let go of his end of the stick.

"Just take a minute," I said, "to reflect on the fact that last year the New York Yankees paid CC Sabathia twenty-three million dol-lars for throwing a baseball about three thousand times. Last March a painting of the United States flag by Jasper Johns was auctioned off at Christie's for one hundred six million dollars."

I paused a minute to let these figures sink in.

"The book you're talking about," I said, "is very rare. There are only half a dozen copies — maybe not that many — that have all eighty plates plus the frontispiece. You can see the binder's label on the front paste-down. This is the first major American color plate book about Native Americans. Not only portraits, but descriptions of the different treaty sites. The chief you see pictured there is Me-No-Quet, a Potawatomi chief. Lewis painted him at the treaty of Fort Wayne in 1827. You may know that the Pokagon Tribe that operates the Casino right here in St. Anne is a band of the Potawatomi. Now wouldn't it be nice to keep this book right here in Saint Anne. In fact, I'd like to suggest that you consider buying it for the Ogden Collection. My grandfather bought this book at an estate sale in Lake Bluff in 1931. No copies have been sold at auction since the Siebert sale in 1999. All eighty of Lewis's original portraits were destroyed in the Smithsonian fire of 1865, so this is it. One of five or six complete copies. It could be put on display in the rare book room at the college library with a little plaque identifying you as the donor."

Kindle Man — Virgil Stevens — started to protest, but Toni interrupted him. "That's an excellent idea, Virgil. You could sell that big Seaton Trawler of yours — which you haven't taken out in the water in five years except to put it in dry dock — and buy the *Aboriginal Portfolio* AND the *Gettysburg Address,* and enough high-end rare books to build a fine collection, and still have enough left over for a cup of hot chocolate at Innkeepers."

That silenced Kindle Man, at least for the time being. But the funny thing was, I knew that Kindle Man was right. Not one hundred percent right, of course, but right enough, and I knew that he'd exposed to the light the central mystery of our trade. Martin Luther was right too, at least when it came to rare book dealers: we are justified *sola fide,* by faith alone.

On the way home, I was very happy. I'd drunk most of a bottle of prosecco at the post-opening rehash, and Olivia was driving. Saskia and Nadia were in the backseat. This was not the first time I'd felt we had reached our destination. But then — and I shouldn't have been surprised — because not for the first time, Olivia seemed to think that we were at a way station, that we were just setting out, that we still had a long way to go. She was still entertaining the idea that we could visit Sasky in Amman in December and then spend Christmas in Jerusalem. "Nadia knows how to do it," she said.

"You've already talked to her about it?"

"I'm still awake," Nadia said. "You take a combination of taxies and buses," she said, "or there's some kind of express bus. You have to cross the river on the King Hussein

Bridge, though they call it something else now. There's an Episcopal Church in Amman, and one in Jerusalem."

"Can't you fly?" I asked.

"Yes, but you'd have to fly to Tel Aviv."

We were too tired to start planning a trip. "Did you notice," Saskia said, "that some of the people who were right there in the store bought books online? They could have asked to see the book and handed over their credit cards."

"Easier just to click 'Add to cart,' " I said. "Maybe they didn't want to put down their glasses of prosecco. How much are we paying Stefano's, by the way?" I asked, turning to Olivia.

"Don't worry about it," she said.

We drove past the college on LaSalle Road till it dead-ended and then cut over to Schoolcraft and then right onto Pier Road.

That night Olivia put on a sexy teddy that she wore when she was feeling especially amorous. Cobalt blue.

There was a bridal book on her dresser, open to a collage of elaborate dresses and brightly colored orchids on long stems. "I'm thinking," I said, "maybe we should pull back a little. Maybe something smaller and quiet. You don't want to wear yourself out."

She shook her head. Her shiny black hair

fanned out on the pillow. "It's a celebration, Gabe. I want to praise the Lord with trumpets and lutes and harps; I want to praise him with tambourines and dancing, strings and pipes and cymbals. Loud clashing cymbals."

"Him?"

"Well, him or her. Besides, everything's set. Augie's going to give me away. Delilah's going to stand up with me."

"Are you going to wear white?"

"I might."

"Are you still planning to renew your virginity?" Actually, I didn't think this was a bad idea. I was having trouble keeping up with her.

"Yes," she said. "But not tonight. Tonight I'm black but comely." She crooked her finger at me. A gesture that never failed to arouse me.

She stretched her arms up over her head, lifted her knees, and spread them. " 'Let him kiss me with the kisses of his mouth,' " she said, as if she were speaking to someone else — the Lord perhaps. " 'For thy love is better than wine. O I am black but comely, O ye daughters of Jerusalem, as the tents of Kedar, as the curtains of Solomon.' "

Later I lay next to her with one arm over her. I could tell she was awake, and I tried to stay awake with her. Not talking, just being there. I was a little frightened.

Mrs. Marckwardt did come back. Not the next day, but the following Monday, and we talked about how you build a collection. Well, one way. You start with a copy of a book you loved as a child. Then a first edition of the book. Then you keep your eye out for a signed copy, and for other books by the same author, and pretty soon you have a collection. I told her she should talk to Susan Reynolds before she took the plunge. Susan collected local authors — Sandburg, Ring Lardner — and books of local interest — histories of Berrien County, Fenimore Cooper's *The Bee Hunter* — set in Kalamazoo — books about shipwrecks on Lake Michigan.

"I know Susan," she said. "I will talk to her, but she's out of town right now. That's why she's wasn't at the opening."

Normally I'd have waited till the check had cleared before handing over the book, but I decided to take a chance on Mrs. Marckwardt.

When Olivia made it clear that she was too busy with wedding plans to keep a long-standing appointment with her doctor at

Bernard Mitchell, I drove over to St. Anne's Episcopal and spoke to Sarah. "She's doing too much," I said. "She's exhausted but she can't slow down. It's not just the shop — the meetings, the demonstrations, the petitions, working full time. She's managing the whole operation. It's no joke. The software keeps track of the inventory and the website. But it's very complicated. At least she's sent her manuscript off to Johns Hopkins."

"She told me about the multiple orgasms."

"Is this something we should be talking about?"

"You find that frightening, don't you?"

"I'm not complaining."

"Then what are you doing? Most men would give their eyeteeth . . . Don't you read the advice columns? Don't try to tamp this down."

"Sarah," I said, "I've always thought of you as a stabilizing influence."

"And now?"

"I think something's wrong. I think she's getting her energy from the cancer, from something growing inside her. Not from God. From the cancer. She refuses to see her doctor. She's just missed another appointment. The doctor's going to write her off. We were going to go up on the train, stay at the Quadrangle Club in Hyde Park."

Sarah touched me. "I'm sorry. I didn't mean to joke about it. But how do *you* know where her energy is coming from? You don't get energy from cancer." She took a deep breath. "Gabe, you've known her longer than I have. But I love her too. She's so . . . so . . . full of life and spirit. You don't want to tamp that down. I could see her as a Saint Teresa in ecstasy. Have you seen the Bernini in the Cornaro Chapel?"

"Yes," I said. "I know what you mean. Coital intoxication. Olivia opens her mouth like that. It just kind of sags open."

"Well, that too. But that's not the whole story. Renewing her virginity before the wedding — and yours — will be good for both of you. The retreat too. I'd like you to support her, encourage her. She's afraid, you know, afraid you'll turn your back on her."

"Turn my back on her?" I was astonished. "Why would I turn my back on her?" I asked, "but a retreat is the last thing she needs. What are they going to do to her?"

"They're not going to *do* anything to her. It will be a quiet time. A time to listen. A time for her to be quiet and gather her strength — to slow down, if that's how you want to understand it."

"What about the wedding plans?"

"We'll take care of it, Gabe. You and Saskia and I can manage."

"She and Saskia are barely on speaking terms. Saskia wants her to see her doctor."

"Then you and I will do what needs to be done."

XXI. The Wedding

(JULY 2011)

The wedding was scheduled for July six-
teenth, which did not, as far as I could tell,
correspond to any significant celestial or
liturgical events. Olivia left for her retreat at
the beginning of the month. Reverend Sarah
drove her to an Episcopal monastery near
Grand Rapids. Saskia was seriously annoyed. But Olivia's condo had sold, which
was a relief, and Saskia was coming to stay
with us till she left for Jordan.

Good things were happening. Mrs. Marckwardt bought *The Tale of Benjamin Bunny*
and *The Tale of a Furious Rabbit* to go with
The Tale of Peter Rabbit; online orders were
steady; we were starting to put together our
first printed catalog; and I'd acquired Stella
Graham's "working library" from her husband, Donald, who owned the Toyota
Agency in Michigan City, Indiana, just
across the state line. Stella was an old
customer who had published four or five

chapbooks and, at age seventy-eight, a book of poems — *Games of Chance* — that had won the Society of Midland Authors award for poetry and was getting some good reviews. After her death, we'd acquired her "working library" — about seventy-five hundred books in addition to her own manuscripts — consisting of first editions of early work by contemporary women poets, hundreds of letters, and hundreds of literary journals, and hundreds of chapbooks, many of them signed. It also included forty shelves of cookbooks and an extensive collection of books on the history of the Upper Midwest.

Adam was networking with old customers and had made our presence felt at the Chicago Book and Paper Fair, and then again in the Twin Cities, where he'd acquired almost four hundred ASEs (Armed Services Editions). If we put them together with the ones Dad had accumulated during a short stint in the Merchant Marines, right at the end of the war, we might have a complete run. The individual books wouldn't bring high prices, but a complete run would be something else. He'd be representing us in Boston in November, California in February, and New York in March, as well as at local fairs in Lansing and Ann Arbor.

Carla had started blogging — one book a week — with *The Tale of Peter Rabbit.* A first edition, first printing, would sell for about $70,000. Our copy — Mrs. Marckwardt's copy actually — was a first commercial edition that we'd priced at ten thousand. A bargain. Carla laid out the familiar story of Peter Rabbit appearing in an illustrated letter that Beatrix Potter wrote for the son of her former governess when he was sick; of the privately printed editions, which Beatrix Potter paid for herself; and then the first commercial editions, with thirty-one colored illustrations, of which our copy was a good example. Carla included several of the illustrations on the blog — Peter helping himself to lettuces and French beans and then some radishes in Farmer McGregor's garden, Beatrix Potter's portrait of herself as Mrs. McGregor, which did not appear in later editions. And the all-important (for collectors) page 51: "Peter gave himself up for lost and *wept* big tears." In later editions, "Peter gave himself up for lost and *shed* big tears." The blog ended with an invitation to anyone who had a copy of *The Tale of Peter Rabbit* with "wept" instead of "shed" on page 51 to contact the shop, and a note saying that our copy had been sold to a private collector.

And the frosting on the cake was that the summer people, desperate for something to read, wandered in and bought detective novels and cookbooks and books of local history. We had to scramble to keep the shelves stocked with books from The Warehouse.

I thought Olivia would be very pleased when she got back from the retreat. But, in fact, I had been right to worry about her, and when I saw her get out of Sarah's dark blue Alero, I swallowed hard. Her shoulders were sagging; she was holding on to something — her large Italian purse — as if it were too heavy to carry. Her eyes were as dark as if she applied kohl. She'd lost weight.

"Didn't they feed you?" I asked.

"Mom, what's the matter?" Saskia said. "What's happened to you?" She turned her anger against Sarah, though I *knew* she was angry at me too. "How could you do this to her? She needs to see a doctor." She turned to her mother: "What did they do to you?"

"Don't scold me. I'm just tired, Sasky. That's all. I just need to lie down for a while. Please. Don't turn your back on me, not now."

Saskia and I got her into bed. When we

came back down, Reverend Sarah was waiting for us, but Saskia asked her to leave.

Olivia rallied the next day but was very irritable, consumed with details about the wedding that distracted everyone from the real drama: the florist couldn't come up with the wildflowers that Olivia wanted; Stefano was planning to serve a red wine with the salmon at the reception instead of pinot grigio; Olivia had lost so much weight that her rings had to be resized, her wedding dress altered. She couldn't sit still.

When Marcus arrived, he assured me that it was always this way before a wedding. He and I would drive into town and see about different flowers; he was quite sure that a light red wine would make a perfect pairing for a meaty fish like salmon, but he would speak to Stefano about it at the rehearsal dinner; we'd take Olivia into town with us and have a drink somewhere while the jeweler resized the rings. It was really quite a simple matter. He'd spoken to Reverend Sarah, who would take in the darts just above the waist on Olivia's dress, a simple white sheath.

In the morning, Marcus and I went fishing on a charter boat and came back with six large chinook, which we took directly to

Stefano's. We ate some lunch at Stefano's and drank some wine and talked the easiest talk of all, book talk.

By five o'clock, the church was full of friends and well-wishers from the congregation, Signora Vitale and her four sons, collectors and customers too. Marcus stood next to me in the front of the church. Augie managed to walk down the aisle with Olivia, following Delilah. Augie gave Olivia away and sat down by himself in a pew at the front. Olivia did not promise to "obey" me, but we promised to honor and cherish each other; Reverend Sarah pronounced us husband and wife. "You see," Marcus whispered in my ear after I'd kissed the bride. "It all worked out." I had to agree.

On the church lawn, we enjoyed a simple but elegant reception. Marcus proposed a toast, and the Vitales uncovered the antipasti — prosciutto, olives, and cheese — and served prosecco and Lachryma Christi, which went down very well with the chinook, which Stefano grilled right in the churchyard.

About eight o'clock, I drove Augie back to The Dunes.

"She looks like hell," Augie said. "What are you gonna do?"

"I'll figure out something," I said.

He snorted.

When I got back to the house, everyone — Marcus, Sarah, Saskia, Carla and Adam, Delilah and her husband, Jack — was sitting on the deck on the north side of the house, drinking the last of the wine. Delilah was reading an advance newspaper account of the wedding in which every single detail was wrong. But it didn't matter. Olivia had already gone to bed. Booker had gone upstairs with her.

When I went upstairs, Booker was asleep next to the bed, one hind leg behind the other, Olivia was lying on her side. She'd left a half glass of prosecco on the side table. Her underwear had been wadded up on my side of the bed, along with a lace chemise. Her high heels poked out from under the sheets. I took her shoes off and lay down beside her. She wasn't asleep; she was crying into her pillow. When I put my arm around her, she pulled away.

"What's the matter?"

"I don't have anything left to give you," she said. "Nothing."

"You're overtired, that's all."

"That's not all."

"Can I get you something?"

"What?"

"I don't know. Wine? Tea? A sleeping pill?"

She shook her head, still turned away from me. "I'm so sorry. Sorry for everything."

"You don't need to be sorry for anything."

"Let's not talk," she said.

I kept my arm over her for a while, as if that might dispel the shadows, and then she said, "Say that poem that you say in the shower every morning. The one that's taped up on the refrigerator."

" 'At Least'?"

"I don't know what it's called. Just say the ending."

" 'I hate to seem greedy,' " I said. " 'I have so much to be thankful for already. But I want to get up early one more morning, at least. And go to my place with some coffee and wait. Just wait, to see what's going to happen.' "

"That's what I want to do, Gabe," she said. "Tomorrow, and every day from now on. Get up every morning and go to our place with some coffee, and just wait to see what's going to happen."

I thought it was a good plan. As least I couldn't think of a better one.

XXII. The Regatta

Everyone had an agenda. Reverend Sarah had an agenda. "Jesus commanded his followers to go out and preach the kingdom and heal the sick," she insisted. She'd called to see how Olivia was doing.

"I don't know what to say to that."

"We should take her up to Kalamazoo to see the bishop, start a dialogue with the Healing Touch Spiritual Ministry. It's a Judeo-Christian perspective, Gabe. Nothing freaky, just rebalancing the body's energy, assisting its natural healing processes, building a bridge between the Church and the World. I can call and make the arrangements. I've already talked to the director."

"I'll talk to her about it," I said.

"Seriously, Gabe," she said.

"I hear you."

"I don't think you do," she said.

Saskia also had an agenda. She'd been surfing the Web and had discovered a miracle drug that was being used in England to treat both HL and NHL — Hodgkin's lymphoma and non-Hodgkin's lymphoma.

"A cancer patient in Manchester, England, was given two weeks to live. He had seventy tumors. They gave him something called Brentuximab Vedotin. It flushed the cancer out of his system. He's fine now. It's a kind of antibody that targets the cell membrane. It destroys the cancer cells from the inside. *I* can't explain it, but the thing is, it works. It's been granted accelerated approval by the FDA. We may not be able to get it here, but we could go to England. It works for anaplastic large cell lymphoma. I don't understand why she won't even think about it."

"Your mother's not about to start taking some miracle drug. One miracle was enough."

"But it didn't work."

"I'm not so sure," I said.

David had an agenda too. The strangest agenda of all. He kept calling. He was taking part in a test in Ann Arbor. The government had shut down all research in the seventies, but now things were changing. Psychedelics were back in the frame. He could try to get Olivia into the program. Or he could maybe get his hands on some psilocybin. He was sure he could, in fact.

"Are these tests," I asked him, "being conducted by scientists at the University of Michigan?"

"Not exactly, but some of the scientists are connected to the U of M."

"That's what I figured."

"It's mostly just psilocybin, from mushrooms. It's been used since prehistoric times in religious rites. Psilocybin semblance. Liberty caps. You know. *The Doors of Perception*? Used in a lot of Native American religions . . ."

"Aldous Huxley," I said. "You want to buy a copy? I'll sell you a signed copy for two thousand dollars."

"Ordinary consciousness gives us only a small fraction of what we can perceive."

"And how is this going to help Olivia?"

"It's the ultimate Romantic trip. Wordsworth getting high on Nature, but a hundred times more powerful. 'That elevated mood in which the burden of the mystery is lifted.' Let me talk to her."

"Maybe later." *Maybe never.*

"You chop them up and put them in a teapot with boiling water and some lemon juice and let it steep for about thirty minutes. Or you can get it powdered and take it in a gel cap. That's what they give us in the study. And a little ginger to prevent nausea. There's a questionnaire, too, that they want you to take first. I know it's got to be tough right now. I think this could help. It could help you too. It can be a little scary, but I could come down and walk you through it. Help you to experience the scary parts as pleasurable. Let me talk to her."

"She's asleep right now."

"Tell her to call."

"I'll give her the message," I said.

"I could FedEx you some," he said. "I don't understand why you don't want her to try it. It's just like LSD, only much safer. Huxley wanted to administer LSD to terminally ill cancer patients to make dying a more spiritual experience. He even had his wife inject him with LSD on his deathbed."

"David, she doesn't want it."

"I need to hear her say it. Let me talk to her."

"She's asleep now." *Fuck off.*

"At least show her the questionnaire. You have to take it online. I sent her the link. I'll send it to you too."

What about the dog? Did Booker have an agenda? His agenda was to go out and rendezvous with Whitefoot and Barley in the morning and then to stand by Olivia's bed with his chin resting on the covers, and then, if she gave him the signal, to climb up on the bed and lie down next to her. He had his own blanket, in a corner, which he would drag up onto the bed and wrap around himself. He could do it in two or three seconds, leaving his head exposed so Olivia could scratch the top of his head or run her finger around the clockwise whorl on the side of his neck.

At the beginning of August, after a difficult week, Olivia declared her independence. She was not going to go up to Kalamazoo to see the bishop and get in touch with the Healing Touch Ministry; she was not going to go to England to undergo a series of injections of the miracle drug, Brentuximab Vedotin. She was not going to start drinking tea laced with psychedelic mushroom powder. She had her own agenda. "We need to start getting up early," she said, "or earlier, and go to our place with a cappuccino. And wait to see what happens. We said we'd do it, and now we've got to really do it."

"Okay," I said. "Let's do it."

In the morning, the LED display on the alarm clock read 4:30. Olivia was already awake.

"I feel better already," she said. "But you'll

412

have to run interference for me."

"Will do," I said.

It was 5:30 by the time we'd eaten boiled eggs and gotten ourselves arranged on the balcony outside our bedroom. Well before first light, well before the birds. The weather had been hot, but it was cool now. I made two cappuccinos in Duralex glasses instead of cups and brought them out on a tray, with sugar and a little Ghirardelli cocoa powder, and little glasses of sparkling water. I'd tried to make a leaf on the top of each cappuccino, the way the baristas do in Italy. I wasn't very successful, but the glasses were beautiful anyway, with the dark chocolate sprinkled over the milk froth, and the little silver spoons that I'd bought in Rome when I was living with Franco Arnulfo, and the folded paper napkins. No e-mails, no computers, no telephone. Just the two of us, trying to stay in the present moment. I was happy, but not sure how to show it.

"What shall we talk about?" I said.

"The geraniums need to be deadheaded," she said.

We'd planted the geraniums in June, in two window boxes that hung over the railing.

"Do you want me to do it now?"

She shook her head.

There's always a kind of awkwardness about deliberately setting out to "talk." When someone says, "We need to talk," you know it's not good. And maybe that's the way we felt now. Setting out to talk as opposed to just talking.

"We don't really *need* to talk," Olivia said, lifting her shoulders. Not-talking was hard too. But after a while, thoughts started to bubble up, like messages at a Quaker meeting.

"The manuscript of an unfinished Jane Austen novel," I said, "was auctioned off at Sotheby's. *The Watsons.* The reserve was two hundred thousand pounds, but it was knocked down for nine hundred ninety-three thousand."

"Who bought it?"

"The Bodleian."

"Have you read it?"

"Another lovable but flawed heroine."

"I'm sure she'll discover her flaw and become a better person by the end."

"Except it doesn't end."

She laughed. "I had a dream about Jacques Derrida," she said. "I'm sitting in one of the little classrooms on the third floor of Linsly-Chittenden Hall. In the old campus."

I'd been in New Haven at the Beineke and

the William Reese Company, though I couldn't place Linsly-Chittenden Hall. But it didn't matter.

"We're sitting at a long table with some people and Jacques Derrida is there, on my right. He's wearing a blue sweater, and he gets up and swings his arm way out, as if he's reaching out to shake my hand, and he says, 'I undermined your first point, but probably in a way too subtle for you to understand, but your second point was a good one.' And he shakes my hand and then leaves."

"You should put that in your book," I said.

"Too late," she said. "It's in the hands of the copy editor."

The silhouette of a large ship had appeared on the horizon. I could barely see it with the binoculars.

"I'd like to see them take a man off one of the big ships and put another up on board. Like in the poem. Who are the two men? Who's the one they take off the ship and who's the one they put on board?"

"I think they take the captain off the ship and put the pilot on board to bring the ship in. Or maybe it's the other way around. The pilot takes the ship out of the port and then the pilot boat brings out the captain and he gets on board, and then the pilot boat takes the pilot back to the pilot station. Something like that."

"What kind of a boat is it?"

"Maybe an ore boat," I said. "I can't see the lights anymore. The sun's coming up."

"What's 'ore' anyway, and where are they taking it?"

"It's a mystery."

"Just because you don't know doesn't mean it's a mystery."

"Like the pipe bomb in the store," I said. "No one ever figured that one out. Maybe the night watchman kept him from trying again, but the FBI thinks he made it to Iran."

"Look," she said, "a sailboat. We're not the only ones up early this morning."

The boat was tacking into an offshore wind, sails filling and then emptying out as it came about.

"I love to watch them," she said.

"We can watch for the regatta on Labor Day weekend," I said. "If we're lucky, we may catch sight of some of the boats from here. They leave St. Joe on the second leg in the morning and get to Michigan City — I don't know, probably seven or eight hours. There are about ninety boats. I missed it last year. I don't remember what I was doing."

"I'd like that," she said. "If I'm still around in September."

"What about the pilgrimage — going to Jordan in December and then Jerusalem?"

"I feel like I'm already there, in the Holy Land."

Booker stopped to say hello on his way down to the beach, where he was joined by Whitefoot and Barley. They ran back and forth along the edge of the water, they chased each other in circles and jumped over each other, and then Booker herded them into the trees.

"It's like Wordsworth," I said. " 'Our souls catch sight of that inland sea . . . and see the dogs sporting on the shore.' "

She laughed. "It's 'immortal sea,' " she corrected me: " 'Though inland far we be, Our souls have sight of that *immortal* sea.' "

"I like 'inland sea,' " I said.

"Another sailboat," she said, raising an arm to point. "Do you still know how to sail?"

"It's been years," I said. "But maybe it's like riding a bicycle. I looked at some sailboats when I moved down here."

"I think you should get one. Carla and Adam are sailors. They could help you pick out a boat. You could go out together. Maybe we could all go together."

417

"We could charter a sailboat," I said. "They've got two-hour charters throughout the day. And there's a sunset cruise."

"I could drink another cappuccino," she said. "Are you allowed to have two in one hour, or do the Italians have a rule against that, like not having a cappuccino in the afternoon?"

"You can have whatever you want," I said.

"You'd make an excellent barista," she said. "Why don't you bring up the paper so I can look at the schedule for day cruises? I think an hour would be my limit."

The next morning I explained the previous day's mysteries. "Ore is stuff from which you can extract metal. The ship was the *Calumet,* and it was huge, longer than two football fields, but it wasn't an ore boat. It could haul more than a thousand semi-trucks. It had picked up a mixture of limestone and dirt in Marblehead, Ohio, unloaded half of it in Marysville, Michigan, and the other half in Sarnia, Ontario. It picked up limestone in Meldrum Bay, Ontario, and took it to Grand Haven, which is not that far away. Fifty miles. It unloaded the limestone at a power plant and then went to South Chicago to pick up a load of coal. It was on its way to South Chicago

418

when we saw it yesterday. It's going to unload the coal today in Green Bay, Wisconsin, and then load limestone at Port Inland, Michigan. And then take the limestone to South Chicago and pick up another load of coal."

"And how do you know this?"

"I asked Jack Donnelly, the harbor master. He likes to keep an eye on things."

"See," she said, "not so mysterious after all."

I also explained the second mystery: "When you're on the high seas," I said, "the captain's the boss. His word is law. But when you're entering or leaving a port — or a river — the local pilot takes over. There's also a docking pilot, who directs the tugboats, and then a harbor pilot, who takes the ship out to open water."

"But what about taking a man off the ship and putting another up on board?"

"Here's what happened — at least I think it's what happened — when I came back from Italy on a student ship one time. When the ship left the harbor in Genoa, the pilot was in charge. Then a boat brought the captain out to the ship. So the captain got on board and then the boat took the pilot back to the pilot house. Then in New York the pilot boat brought the pilot out to the ship and picked up the captain and took the captain back to the pier, and the pilot brought the ship into port."

"Another mystery solved."

We'd gotten up early. Booker didn't join us till shortly after first light. I gave him his breakfast and he went out to join Whitefoot and Barley on the beach.

"I want you to tell me something you've never told me before," Olivia said. I thought that what she really meant was that she had something she wanted to tell me.

I thought for a minute. "I got a letter from my mother after Dad's death," I said. "After the shop closed."

"Gabe. You didn't! What did she say?"

"Not a lot. She was sorry to hear that Dad had died and that the shop had closed. She said she was happy. The funny thing was, she said she was living in Florence, not Rome. But she didn't explain."

"Did you answer it?"

"No. I was still angry. How could she leave us like that? And not a word of apology in the letter."

"Calm down, Gabe. It's all right. It doesn't matter now. But you have to answer it. You have to."

"You're right, and it doesn't matter that David invited his first wife to come and live

420

with you, and it doesn't matter that he's got another wife now."

"You're right, Gabe. It doesn't matter. But I want to see the letter, the one she wrote."

"It's in Italian."

"You can read it to me in Italian, and then translate it."

"We'll see."

"I want to see it, and I want to look at the mystical experience questionnaire David sent."

"Do you want to try the psilocybin?"

"Just the questionnaire. It's in my e-mail somewhere, but I think he copied it to you too. Isn't that what you said? We could take it together."

"You have to look at it online, on a web-site. They've fixed it so you can't print it out."

"We can bring out my laptop and we can look at it together. It might be fun. Maybe tomorrow."

"Look," I said. "*Two* sailboats. Do you suppose they're the ones we saw yesterday? They each have two sails, but they aren't quite the same. One of them has two masts. That makes it a ketch."

She held out her hand for the binoculars, but she couldn't hold them steady enough to see the boats. "The geraniums keep getting in the way," she said.

"I think the other one's a sloop," I said. "But it's hard to tell."

We watched till they disappeared over the horizon. "They must be going somewhere, Michigan City, or Chicago. That's how you can tell the earth is round. Ships disappear over the horizon." I put the binoculars down on the little table. "What about you?" I asked. "Do you ever wish you'd learned to sail?"

"I am learning to sail. I'm sailing right now." And then she said, "Did you look for your mother when you were in Italy?"

"I was in Rome most of the time, living with Franco Arnulfo and his wife, who had a big shop on Via Condotti. It was Dad's idea. I could polish my Italian and apprentice with the 'dean' of Italian antiquarian rare book dealers. I always looked for Mamma on the streets, and I went to the Ufficio Anagrafe but she wasn't listed as 'Johnson' or 'Bennison.' That was her maiden name."

"What was the name of the man she ran off with?"

"Rossi. Do you have any idea how many Rossis there are in Rome? Thousands."

We sat for a while, watching the sailboats till the dogs finished up their games and the beach began to fill up with summer children and their mothers or baby sitters, and Booker appeared on the balcony. He sat next to Olivia, who fed him some treats that she kept in an old pill container, and we were joined by Saskia, who was going down to the beach for her morning swim.

"Have you guys reached any conclusions?" she asked.

"Not yet."

"Do you think you will?"

"I'm sure we'll come up with something."

"How about Brentuximab Vedotin?"

"Give it a rest, Sasky."

On our third morning, Olivia said she'd had a dream about my mother. She, my mother, had come into our bedroom and was sitting on the edge of the bed.

"How did she look?" I asked.

"She looked good," Olivia said. "Beautiful."

"She was beautiful. And smart too, and she had a charming accent."

"Did she say anything?"

"She said something that sounded like what you said after we had our premarital conference: *sani e salvi,* something like that."

"Sani e salvi," I said. "We made it through

safe and sound."

"I want to see the letter. I want you to read it to me this morning."

The letter was in a box on a shelf in my study, a big orange and black box marked LETTERS, big enough to hold legal-size paper. It was filed under M. It was a light green *aereogramma* with three decorative edges.

I showed it to Olivia. *"Caro Gabriele,"* she looked it over before handing it to me. I read it in Italian, and then I translated it.

31 agosto 2009

Caro Gabriele —
I was sorry to learn that your father died, and that you had to close the shop. I heard about it from the book dealer in Piazza Santa Trinità — Sig. Ungaretti — where I sometimes stop to chat and to smell the old books. It's always very sad when an old bookshop has to close. It's happening here too.

I never thought I'd be living up north. We have a lovely apartment on Via Fiesolana, right in the center, but I don't think I'll ever get used to the food. They don't put salt in the bread, you know, but there's a Roman bakery in Piazza

Ciompi where you can get *pane salato,* and a trattoria on Via Verdi where you can get *carciofi alla giudia* and *spaghetti cacio e pepe,* like I used to make for you.

I don't want you to worry about me. I'm Piccarda, not St. Teresa. Any more happiness would be wasted on me. The only thing that might make me happier would be a letter from you.

— Mamma

As I was reading the letter, I could picture my mother sitting on the edge of my bed the night before she left, and I could hear her voice too, *"Mi trovo un po' in difficoltà." I find myself in a little trouble.*

"Have you answered the letter?"

I shook my head. "I don't know how she can be so happy after what she did. Besides, I didn't know what to say. I meant to write, but I kept putting it off, and after a while . . ."

"I'm happy," Olivia said. "After what *I* did."

"You didn't abandon your husband and your son."

"No," she said. "But listen, Gabe." She stopped and took a deep breath. "I'm going to tell you something I've never told anyone, not even David." She paused for breath.

"You already told me. About giving David the 1820 Keats I gave you for Christmas."

"Something else."

"I'm bracing myself," I said.

"I'm the one who called David's wife and told her about our affair."

"You're full of surprises, aren't you. Why did you do *that*?"

"Because I was in love. I thought I could explain it to her. I thought when I explained it, she'd step aside. But she wouldn't listen. She went crazy. I caused a lot of pain, Gabe. And then when they got back together, I thought I was off the hook."

"But you weren't."

She shook her head. "It never goes away, and now it's part of who I am. If I were an alcoholic in a twelve-step program, I'd still have to make amends, wouldn't I? Isn't that one of the steps? But I wouldn't know how to do it."

"And you're okay now?"

"I'm okay."

"You weren't okay when you got back from that retreat."

"That's because I didn't understand what was happening when I was there. We had to be quiet all the time; we couldn't talk to anyone, not even at meals. I've never been so lonely, so frightened."

426

"What *was* happening?"

"I was learning to turn towards the dark, toward the sharp edge, instead of backing away from it."

"And you're happy now?" I said.

"I'm happy now," she said. "I'm happy because you're here with me and because we're being carried by great winds across the sky. Remember when we saw that painted on the side of a VW van, on the Outer Drive?"

"I was with Dad when that happened," I said. "We were on Stony Island, not the Outer Drive."

"Well," she said. "You must have told me about it. And I need to lie down now."

When I got to the shop that morning, a man was waiting for me. I was expecting a collector from Indianapolis who wanted to look at our copy of *Tortilla Flat* — not the ASE copy that had been on Dad's bed when Olivia brought over the spinach lasagna from the Medici — but a signed first edition, first printing — Covici Friede Publishers, New York, 1935, in fine condition with the original dust jacket, also in fine condition.

But it was David. We'd never met. But I knew right away who it was. He looked like

427

me. Brown hair a little too long, jeans, retro glasses in metal frames, sleeves rolled up to his elbows.

"I had to come," he said.

"I see," I said. And I did see, though I wasn't exactly pleased.

"I brought some psilocybin," he said. "I know you didn't ask for it, but it could be important. It's LSD, but much safer. Used by Native Americans. It would be good for you too. I could walk you both through it."

"Haven't we been through this already?"

"I'm not leaving till I talk to her."

"I can't leave the shop now," I said. "I'm expecting a man from Indianapolis."

"I know how to get to the house," he said. "I looked it up on the Internet. I brought capsules," he said. "Easier than chopping them up and putting them in your tea. As long as she can swallow."

And something snapped. No, "snapped" is the wrong word. More like "let go." Like a downrigger releasing the lead weight when a fish strikes. "Okay," I said. "I'll be home early afternoon."

The man from Indianapolis showed up an hour later. He already had a first edition of *Tortilla Flat,* but his wasn't signed and didn't have a dust jacket. He had an interesting list of books he wanted to trade for our signed copy, which I'd priced at seven thousand, but he didn't have the books with him, and I told him I'd have to see the books myself. Or I'd send Adam, who was going to an estate sale in Indianapolis at the end of October, after the Michigan Book and Paper Show in Lansing. I introduced him to Adam, and then I sat alone in my office and wondered about the truth about love as I imagined David and Olivia together in our bedroom.

Where was Montaigne when I needed him? Probably snoozing on the sofa up in my study. I sat alone in my office for a while and then drove home.

The trees had turned Pier Road into a dark green tunnel, but I could see Saskia, sitting on the lowest limb of the copper beech tree where Pier Road became our driveway, her back against the trunk. She was chewing on a lock of her own hair and didn't wave. She'd inherited her mother's high cheekbones and wide mouth and long fingers which were gripping her knees, and I realized that she was twenty-two, the age the age Olivia had been when we set up the Orwell exhibit. Like Olivia, she'd always been so sure of herself, but she wasn't sure of herself now. I saw her as a tiny baby, five minutes old, and my arms remembered how heavy she'd been, dense. I saw her as she had been when she came into the shop on Fifty-Seventh Street to do her homework — fifteen years old, just starting to develop a secret inner life — and I saw her as she was now, perched in a tree like a wild bird, and I saw her as I hoped she would be in the future. Happy, confident, unafraid. But she wasn't happy, confident, and unafraid now.

"Your dad here?" I couldn't see David's car from where I was at the end of the drive.

Saskia didn't answer: "She's going to die, isn't she?"

"Yes."

"She won't listen."

"This is about the miracle drug, isn't it?"

She indicated that it was by moving her arm. Like flapping a wing.

"Do you know — Dr. Kerry says you can't have those injections till you had at least two courses of chemo. The list of side effects is a mile long: neutropenia, neuropathy, fatigue, nausea, anemia, upper respiratory tract infection, diarrhea . . . That's just the beginning."

"I know that," she said. "But it might not be the same in England."

"You have your agenda, Saskia. Reverend Sarah has her agenda. And your father has his agenda."

"And you have your agenda too. You want her to die."

"Is that what you believe?"

It took her a long time to answer. "Not really," she said. "But it's hard to see her just passing right through our lives like this."

"We're passing through her life too," I said.

"I hadn't thought of it like that," she said. "But what should we do?"

"I think that what we can do for her now instead of fighting against her is just keep our eyes open, look hard, try not to miss a thing. Our ears too. Let's listen to her and smell her and touch her so we can carry that with us."

"You left out 'taste her,' " she said, and I understood that she was passing the torch of anxiety on to me. "When did you become so wise?" she said.

"Me?" It was my turn to laugh.

In the kitchen I fixed a sandwich and drank a beer, which I didn't usually do in the middle of the day. And waited, letting the truth about love sink in. I waited till David came downstairs. "You've got to talk to her," he said. "She could take the psilocybin right now. You could take it too. I'll stay right here to talk you through it."

"David," I said. "How about a liverwurst sandwich?"

"Liverwurst? Now?"

I knew what he meant. He was on the edge of tears and I was offering him liverwurst. I put an arm around his shoulder. "Why don't you take Saskia to lunch. She knows where to go. You can go to Stefano's, or you can grab a hamburger at Atkinson's." I guess you could say that I was glad he'd made the trip from Ann Arbor, but Olivia's spiritual journey was going to come to an end without the help of psilocybin, and I was going to travel with her as far as I could go. In the end, though, she'd have to go on alone, like Everyman in the old play.

Dr. Kerry came to see her later that afternoon. He had come to St. Anne the year before Mamma went away. He'd treated us for poison ivy, summer colds, a broken arm. He sat on the edge of the bed and explained what we could expect. It wasn't going to be the encounter with pure being that David had put on the table, but it was something like that.

"You're going to be tired," Dr. Kerry said. He'd driven out to the house. "You're going to sleep most of the time. You're going to lose your appetite. Your breathing will become irregular. You'll probably experience many emotions, strong ones, and may have hallucinations, or maybe I should call them visions."

"Do you think I'm doing the right thing?" she asked. This was the only sign of doubt, hesitation. She was sitting on the edge of the bed; Dr. Kerry was sitting next to her. I was standing with my back against the wall.

"Well, you've already done it," he said, taking her hand in his, "if you mean what I think you mean."

"I do."

"It's the difference between Socrates and Jesus. You know Plato's *Phaedo*?"

Olivia nodded.

"I'll bet they made you read that when you were a freshman at the University of Chicago."

She smiled. "For Jesus, Death, with a capital D, is the great enemy, something to be conquered."

"And for Socrates?"

"I've read the *Phaedo*," Olivia said.

The doctor touched her forehead with the palm of his right hand, as if checking for a fever, and then he released her hand. "You never knew Gabe's mother, did you? She was here the year I came to St. Anne. She had a bad case of poison ivy from squatting to pee in the woods. I fell in love with her,

433

but so did everybody else. I was sorry she went away."

"Gabe's going to write her a letter," Olivia said.

"Tell her I said hello," he said to me.

Olivia had good days and bad days. We were still watching things happen and trying to reach our own conclusions, but we no longer tried to spin our stories to make them count in the larger scheme of things. We stuck to small stories — about what was going on at the shop, online sales, the new online listings, our first printed catalog (which was selling well), the new IT person, Carla's weekly blogs, Adam's plans for the Boston Book Fair, the dogs who'd started dropping by the house in the afternoon to visit with Booker — not just Whitefoot and Barley but two or three other dogs too; Signora Vitale's youngest son, who'd gone to live for a year with relatives in a small town on the coast south of Naples; and Saskia (of course), who was pining for Nadia, who'd gone back to Amman for the last weeks of summer; the conviction and sentencing of Barbara Duncan, the town controller, who'd siphoned off almost $30 million of village funds over a period of twenty years and built a nationally renowned horse-breeding operation west of town.

"Astonishing," Olivia said, more than once. Shaking her head. "How could the town have that much money in the first place?"

"It was Toni," I said, "who figured out what was going on. You want me to read the article?"

She shook her head.

On the day of the second leg of the regatta, Saturday, September 3, we got up a little earlier than usual. Booker was still asleep, lying on his side in the closet, an ear flopped over one eye. We let him sleep and went down the stairs and drank our coffee in the reading nook, where we had two comfortable chairs. The weather was too cold and rainy to sit out on the balcony. We couldn't see past the second sandbar. We had the radio on. On Friday, at the start of the first leg, two sailboats had almost collided leaving Chicago, and one had almost crashed into the stone water treatment plant. The regatta had almost been canceled, but most of the boats made it to St. Joe by Friday afternoon.

The boats were expected to leave St. Joe about at 9:30 on Saturday morning for the second leg — St. Joe to Michigan City. We might see some sails in early afternoon, but only if the weather cleared. We sat outside. It wasn't really cold, but it was chilly and Olivia was wearing a warm coat over her sweater.

"We could drive over to Hesston," I suggested, "to see the Annual Hesston Steam and Power Show. Grandpa Chaz always liked to go. A sawmill, steam traction engines, antique farm machinery." But Olivia wanted to do the mystical experience questionnaire instead. She had the URL for the website. I had it too, in an e-mail from David.

"You ready to take it?"

"No, Gabe. I want *you* to take it."

"Me? I thought it was for *you.*"

"I don't need it."

"What do *I* know about mystical experiences?"

"That's what we're going to find out."

"Livy, David wanted *you* to take this."

She shook her head "He thought *you* ought to take it. Psilocybin too."

"Me?"

She laughed. I typed in the URL and had a look at the introductory quotations from Rumi and Einstein about the unity of all things: that there is a pure consciousness, that the observed and observer are one, and so on. We rushed through the preliminary questions — age, gender, body type, household income — to get to the good stuff. By this time I was curious. Was I thinking or hoping, that something was going to be settled? Was I worried that my mystical experience rating would be below average? Or above average?

"Once you answer a question," I said, looking at the instructions, "you can't go back and change your answer. You can only go forward."

"Like life," Olivia said.

I read the questions aloud. Most of them were variations on a theme: *Have you experienced the insight that "all is one"? Have you experienced pure awareness/being, beyond the world of sense impressions? Have you experienced with certainty an encounter with ultimate reality (in the sense of being able to "know" and "see" what is really real) at some point during your experience?*

Possible answers to these questions were:

a. Never
b. So rarely I can't be sure
c. Occasionally
d. Often
e. Very often
f. All the time

"I'm clicking 'Never' for the first one," I said, "though I might have clicked 'All the time.' " Olivia waited for an explanation. "Well," I said, "everything is made of the same stuff. Our fingernails are stardust. That sort of thing. But I don't think about it very often. It's not something I really 'experience.' "

Have you experienced pure awareness/ being, beyond the world of sense impressions?

"I'm going to say 'Occasionally.' " Olivia wanted an example. "Watching the dogs play on the beach? Or how about 'longing'? Does that count?"

"What are you longing *for*?"

"Just longing."

"Let's count it."

Have you experienced with certainty an encounter with ultimate reality (in the sense of being able to "know" and "see" what is really real) at some point during your experience?

"All the time," I said.

Olivia laughed and then started to cough. "Keep going," she said, and coughed again.

"How about this one? *Have you ever experienced the belief that you, as your separate individual self, are all-powerful?*"

"What are you going to check for that one?"

"All the time," I said.

"I think you just flunked the test!"

"I don't think this is the kind of test you can flunk, but I might be wrong."

Let's keep going. *What do you think you'll see at the end,"* she read, *"once you realize you can't turn back?"*

I was surprised by the change in tone — a shift to a different register that I didn't care for. "How should I know?" At that moment I looked up. A sailboat was emerging from the fog — first the prow, then the jib, then she slowed as the keel buried itself in the sand. "Look at that," I said. "A sailboat. I think I'm having a mystical experience right now. "Do you see it too? My God, it's grounded on the sandbar, the second one."

Olivia turned her head to see it. A sailboat had run aground on the second of two long sandbars that run parallel to the beach. You can wade out a long way on these sandbars, but you have to watch out for riptides. The water gets backed up behind the sandbars, then rips through, creating a channel as the water rushes back into the lake. The boat had keeled over. The sail was smacking the water.

I dialed 911, handed the phone to Olivia, took off my shoes, and rushed down to the beach. It was cold, starting to rain, the wind was exploding in gusts. Three people in the shallow water were wading toward shore. The woman in the middle had a blue windbreaker pulled up over her head. It didn't seem like enough people to crew a sailboat, but I couldn't really see how big the boat was.

The first thing I heard over the wind as they came out of the water was a string of curses. The man was shouting, cursing the weather, cursing the weather bureau, cursing the water, cursing the commodore, cursing his wife and his son, cursing another couple who had backed out of the second leg at St. Joe because of the bad weather.

"Hey," I say. "You're going to be all right. You're alive." *Che bello essere vivi,* I thought. The wife was trying to calm her husband down.

"Son of a bitch. I've been running this race for fifteen years and I'm not going to quit because of a little bad weather."

"You stupid asshole," his wife shouted. "You call this a little bad weather? I told you we shouldn't go without Bucky and Sonia."

"Fucking cowards. They shouldn't have agreed to crew if they were going to be scared off by a little bad weather."

"You call this a little bad weather."

440

The son, in his early teens, was crying. "Can we talk about this later?"

"Goddamn GPS went out," the man said to me. "We didn't know where the hell we were. You couldn't see a goddamn thing."

"We listened on the radio," I said. "A lot of problems. Two boats almost collided in Chicago on Friday. Five-foot waves."

"Our GPS went out," the man said again. "We couldn't tell where the hell we were. You couldn't see a goddamn thing."

"You don't need to swear all the time," his wife said.

"Jesus Christ, listen to you. I'm going back out to see what the damage is."

"You're not going anywhere."

"I think your wife has the right idea," I said.

The man turned on me, his face contorted. I thought he was about to cry. We clumped up the beach to the stairs. By this time I was soaked too, just as if I'd been out in the boat. "Let's get into some dry clothes," I said.

Saskia had collected towels and sauna robes and a pile of dry clothes from our different closets, and they changed in our bedroom. We got the wet clothes into the washing machine to spin dry before we'd put them in the dryer. Saskia offered to make tea.

By the time the tea was ready, the three sailors, in warm robes, had calmed down. The boy had stopped crying; the husband had stopped cursing. We sat in the living room with the radio on. The husband talked animatedly. He had been doing this regatta for fifteen years. The first time he'd done it with his father and his uncles. This was the first time with his son. "But it won't be the last."

The son sat on the floor with Booker.

The wife worried about missing the big party at the Michigan City Yacht Club. "A regatta is a race wrapped in a party," she explained. But I didn't think her husband was interested in the party. He kept twisting in his chair, trying to get his body to understand what had happened. I could see that he was embarrassed. He was the captain, and he'd run his ship aground. And I felt a kind of pity for these people. The man had shamed himself in front of his wife and son, rammed his ship into a shoal, if you can call a sandbar a shoal. But even as I was feeling sorry for the man, I was conscious of my own happiness. Even though Olivia was dying, I was happy. *Had I experienced with certainty an encounter with ultimate reality (in the sense of being able to "know" and "see" what is really real) at some point during this experience?* Maybe. Maybe not.

We sat in the living room. I kept checking the dryer. The rain had stopped. We could see the boat, on its side. The man wanted to go out to the boat, maybe get the GPS, assess the damage, maybe push it off the sandbar. But this wasn't going to happen. The wife called her sister in Michigan City, asked me for directions. I said it would be easier if I took them into town. We could meet at the Shell station at the stoplight on Duval and Madison.

We had to wait a little longer for the clothes to dry. I got tired of waiting and took them out of the dryer. They were still a little damp, but dry enough.

"What about the 911 people?" I asked as we were walking out the door.

"They stayed on the line," Olivia said, "till I could see the people walking out of the lake."

When I dropped them off at the Shell station, the man got out his wet billfold and offered me a hundred dollars for my trouble. I shook my head. He insisted. It was his way of taking charge. I took the wet hundred dollar bill and put it in my back pocket. I could feel the dampness as I drove home.

When I got back, Olivia and Saskia and I had a drink and spent the rest of the afternoon trying to figure out what had just happened, trying to reach our own conclusions — as Olivia liked to say — and I thought we were getting close. But we couldn't quite put our conclusions into words. "I've been thinking about that last question," I said. "*What will I see at the end, once it's clear that I can't turn back?* Maybe I'll see the sailboat emerging out of the fog. I'd like that. But what if I see that dysfunctional family, and hear them too? That wouldn't be good."

"If it's at the end," Olivia said, "you'll be *on* the sailboat, not on the shore. You'll be leaving the shore behind, heading out into deep water. Besides, you're not close enough to the end to know what's you'll see."

"What about you?"

"I don't know. Maybe I'm not close enough either."

"What about you, Saskia?" I asked.

"I think you're both a little bit crazy," she said. "I'm going into town to get some fruit and some more lettuce and a bottle of pinot grigio. All I want for supper is a big salad. You want me to pick up anything else?"

We shook our heads. "We'll probably take a nap," Olivia said.

■ ■ ■ ■

The next morning was beautiful. The great inland sea was as flat as one of the pancakes I'd fixed for our breakfast. According to the radio, the sailboats in the regatta were becalmed in the harbor at Michigan City, waiting for wind. But the copyedited text of *Varieties* had arrived in the night, attached to an e-mail, so we had other things to think about. Olivia was overwhelmed and pretended to be upset by the hundreds of notes, corrections, and queries that filled the margins in tiny print. "I'm supposed to accept or reject every change by clicking 'Accept' or 'Reject.' I can't write a single sentence that this woman doesn't want to correct. I can't get a single endnote formatted to suit her." But she couldn't conceal her pleasure in the fact that someone was paying such close attention to every single word she had written. "I've got my work cut out for me."

Olivia and I were paging through the file on Olivia's laptop and drinking more coffee when Saskia joined us on the deck with a couple of cold pancakes on a plate. She was wearing a light robe over her swimsuit. The three of us sat in silence for a few minutes, watching two large men from the St. Anne Marina maneuver the abandoned sailboat out to deeper water and harness it, stern first, to their power boat. We kept our eyes on the two boats till they disappeared, and then we watched the dogs roughhousing on the beach.

"Reached any conclusions?" Saskia asked.

"I thought we were pretty close yesterday," I said, "but then . . . it's like trying to reach the horizon."

Saskia, who didn't drink coffee, went down to the beach for her morning swim.

"Why didn't you tell her about the manuscript?" I asked.

"I just want to savor the news for a while," she said, "before going public."

We watched Saskia wade out past the sandbars and then plunge in. She was a strong swimmer, but when she swam out farther than usual, I started to get a little nervous. What if she kept on going?

But then she turned and waved.

"That's a good sign," I said. "It means she's going to turn back."

Olivia shook her head. "It means," she said, "that she wants us to be happy."

The sun, which had come up over the dunes behind us, had turned the rims of our white china coffee cups into ovals of yellow sunlight. An off-shore breeze had begun to ruffle the surface of the lake. The boats would be leaving the harbor in Michigan City. And I thought that these were good signs too. And I realized that we *were* happy, at least as happy as we were ever going to be.

XXIII. The Buffalo
(SEPTEMBER 2011)

Reverend Sarah continued to hover around the edges of our lives. Sensing a battle, I tried to keep her away from Olivia, but she was insistent, like a horsefly, biting and stinging. That's what it felt like. She needed to intervene, to do something. She'd given up on a visit to the bishop, and wanted to administer "last rites." Not right away, but when the time came. "You've got to understand that. When it's time, I'll need to administer extreme unction."

"She doesn't want extreme unction," I said.

"How do I know what she wants if you won't let me talk to her?"

"Sarah," I said calmly. "You've put enough ideas in her head. If we'd taken her to Bernard Mitchell instead of letting her go on that retreat, she might have had a chance. I never should have let her go."

"You didn't 'let' her go. She decided that

that was what she wanted to do and she went. Besides, you know she wouldn't have gone back to Bernard Mitchell. You know that. She chose a different path, Gabe. Death isn't the worst thing. But I think she took us both by surprise."

"Right. It's just like walking through an open door."

We were standing on the balcony. The lake was calm. The weather chilly. A sloop was tacking out of the marina.

"She's having visions," I said, regretting right away that I'd said it.

"There, you see."

"They don't make a lot of sense. I don't know if they're waking dreams or visions." I didn't tell her about the dream about my mother, but I told her about the dream she'd had about Jacques Derrida: the classroom at Yale, the blue sweater he was wearing, swinging his arm, telling her she couldn't understand him, shaking hands with her . . ."

"Who's Jacques Derrida?" she asked.

"Olivia says he's the source of a lot of dreary French theory that has yet to shed light on a single poem or story. As far as she was concerned, he was the devil."

"Go to hell, Gabriel Johnson. Don't you dare make fun of her like that." She started to cry. "Death is like an open door and you're standing in the way, just like you're standing in the light. Blocking the light."

I was in the process of discovering here just how angry I was. "I think you should leave now."

"I'm not leaving till I talk to her, or are you afraid to let me see her?"

"Why would I be afraid?"

"You tell me."

"All right," I said. "Five minutes."

"Alone."

What was I afraid of? Another dark sermon? Another expulsion from the Garden? Another Flood? Another Tower of Babel? Another sacrifice on Mount Moriah?

Five minutes went by. Slowly. Enough time to poach a large egg.

Sarah came out and left without saying anything. I could see that the fight had gone out of her.

I went in. Olivia was shivering. Cold or afraid? The room was warm, but her shivering had nothing to do with the temperature of the room.

"It will be all right," I said. "Like walking through an open door." And she started remembering doors at Yale, like the door to the Berkeley Common Room, doors and more doors, the doors on Wieboldt Hall at the University of Chicago, the doors at Rockefeller chapel and at St. Anne's Episcopal, and the doors of restaurants where she'd eaten, the little white portico over the black door at Mory's in New Haven, the door at Stefano's on Merchant Street, the door to the Medici, with that 1327 over in the tympanum. "What happened in thirteen twenty-seven?" she asked.

"Thirteen twenty-seven is the street number," I said.

"Oh," she said.

We tried to remember all the doors in the house on Blackstone, but there were too many to count from memory, and I was glad when Saskia came into the room and sat down on the edge of the bed. "What did Reverend Sarah have to say?"

"She wanted to administer the sacraments."

"This afternoon?"

"No. Later. When the time comes."

"What did you say?"

"I said I felt like Emma Bovary," Olivia said, "after she was dead, with the priest sprinkling holy water around the room and the chemist pouring chlorine on the floor."

"So Sarah's the priest?"

"Right."

"Who's the chemist?" Saskia asked.

451

"*You* are!"

"Shit. Me? Who's Gabe?"

"I'm not going to be Charles Bovary," I said. "Don't even think of it. I told her about your vision or dream of Jacques Derrida. She thought I was making fun of you."

"You know what I've figured out?" she said. "It was Jacques Derrida all right, but he looked like Professor Weaver. What a lovely man. Professor Weaver, I mean. I took both his Shakespeare classes. He lived across the street from you, didn't he, on Blackstone?"

"Across the street and a little farther north. I told her you thought Derrida was the devil, and she got mad."

Olivia tried to laugh. "Did you tell her about the other visions?"

"Just the one."

"Dr. Kerry said I'd 'see' things."

"Do you want to see him again? Dr. Kerry, I mean. Not Jacques Derrida."

She shook her head and sank back into her pillow. "No, but he was right. I do see things. Last night I had another dream. This one was really strange. I'm walking down Pier Road toward the highway and I see a buffalo coming out of the state park, that's how I know it's not a real buffalo. Buffalo don't live in the woods, do they? Anyway, I can still see the big shaggy head. It's huge. I'm frightened. I've got the camera but it's tied to a rope, and I whirl it around my head, thinking I can drive the buffalo away, but it keeps coming toward me."

"The plains Indians thought that the buffalo was a symbol of abundant life," I said. "If a buffalo reveals itself to you, it's a good thing. You shouldn't try to push it or shove it away. You should take the easiest path. That's what the buffalo does."

"How do you know this?" she asked.

"George Catlin," I said. "*The Manners and Customs of the American Indians.* I'm not sure I've got it exactly right, but close. We have a copy in the shop. I'll bring it home tonight."

"I was trying to drive it away," she said.

"But it kept on coming, didn't it?"

"Yes," she said, "it kept right on coming at me."

"And then?"

"I just realized that this is what I'll see at the end, once it's clear that I'm not going back. I'll see the buffalo, but this time I won't try to drive it away."

"Mom, you should probably rest now."

"Birth and death are a lot of work," she said. "I don't know which one is harder." She paused. "Saint Teresa in ecstasy. That

453

was another one, not last night but a couple nights ago. Gabe was touching me with your little vibrator. I've never been to Rome, never seen the Bernini statues, but I've seen pictures. That was all I needed then. Just the tip of the vibrator, and then I was walking down Fifty-Seventh Street and Jock Weintraub drove by and waved."

"You used my vibrator? Mah-ahm!"

"You shouldn't have left it on your dresser."

"It was in the drawer."

"Maybe it was, I don't remember. Never mind. It doesn't matter."

"I thought Weintraub didn't know how to drive," I said.

"He could in my dream."

"Mom," Saskia said, "you never told us what happened on that retreat."

"I told Gabe," she said. "I learned to turn towards the dark instead of away from it, turn toward the sharp edge."

"It didn't do much good, did it?" Saskia said.

Olivia adjusted her pillow a little. "Well, it's hard to know," she said.

"Why is it hard to know? You looked terrible when you came back."

"You know the tree of the knowledge of good and evil?"

"The apple? Or probably a pomegranate."

"I think that the most important knowledge comes at a price," Olivia said, "and once you've got it, you can't go back. You have to pay the price. It's experiential. Like sex. No one can explain it to you, and you can't — you can't just tell someone, can't just explain it. I think that's what happened to me. It's something I can't put into words. The words get all tangled up."

"For example?"

"That's my point. I can't put it into words. But it wasn't what I was expecting. Maybe it never is. It took me a while to digest it, or come to terms with whatever it was. But I understand now why Abraham never spoke to his wife again after he almost killed Isaac. What could he say?"

"Of course he couldn't speak to her again," Saskia said. "He was ashamed of himself."

"He wasn't ashamed of himself," Olivia said. "He was ashamed of God. And the Tower of Babel. Everyone working together. How often does that happen? I understand that too. God gets frightened. That's why he stirs things up. I see that now. Do you think that's what happened? Do you think God would be frightened if we all worked together? I think God is frightened right now.

He can't control things anymore. He can't control *us*. He can't stop us from loving each other. Look how many times he's tried."

Saskia kissed her mother. "I'm going downstairs to read. Call me if you need anything."

Being alone with someone can be more intense than being alone by yourself. That's how I felt when Olivia disappeared into her *self*. Or wherever she went. Maybe it wasn't into her *self* but into some spiritual realm. Sometimes she came back exhausted, and sometimes refreshed.

She thought a lot about doors and asked me to read and reread Sandburg's poem "Circles of Doors," which is not like anything else Sandburg wrote. I opened the curtains and let in a shaft of warm light.

"Don't stop," she said.

I kept on reading: "hearing, Sometimes her whisper, I love him, I love him, And sometimes only a high chaser of laughter, Somewhere five or ten doors ahead or five or ten Doors behind . . ."

I couldn't go any further. I sat down on the edge of the bed and massaged her feet.

Sometimes we shared things you'd think a person couldn't possibly share. Dangerous

456

knowledge that we could have used against each other. We weren't speaking anyone else's lines. Not Montaigne's, not Wordsworth's. Just our own. Unscripted.

One night she asked me to play my guitar. Booker was there, and she encouraged him to climb up on the bed so she could press her hand on the top of his wedge-shaped head and feel him stiffen his neck and press back. I no longer played much, never really mastered the tremolo, but I took my guitar out of its case and got out *The American Songbag* from a shelf in the living room that held my guitar music. I opened it to the first song: "I'm goin' away for to stay for to stay a little while, But I'm comin' back if I go ten thousand miles." Too sad. I put the guitar away.

Olivia asked if I'd answered my mother's letter, and I told her no, and then she said, "I'll leave this place and I'll go ten thousand miles, but I won't come back in a little while. I won't come back at all. I'll leave you and Saskia and Booker, and I won't remember you at all."

"But we'll remember you," I said. "That's the way it works."

"I understand that now," she said.

That was the best I could do. *That's the way it works.* I'd absorbed plenty of wisdom

457

about death from Montaigne and his Stoic mentors, but what does he do when his friend, La Boétie, is dying? He doesn't know what to say, so he starts quoting: Terence, Horace, Virgil, then Terence and Horace again, then Catullus. And really, he falls apart. I had to check a similar impulse in myself — an impulse to start quoting Montaigne. But what did I want to say myself, unscripted, unrehearsed? I was thinking that now at last I understood the truth about love. Once again. But what I understood now was that it isn't something you can put into words.

How many times I'd thought I'd understood this truth, and I didn't see how there could be any further truths beyond what I understood right now. But maybe that's always the way it works. There are always further truths no matter how far you go. I didn't see how I could go any further — making love to Shirley and then having a drink with Dad, putting Olivia on the Lakeshore Limited, seeing her reflection in the broken glass at the shop . . . I ran down the whole list in my mind.

"You forgot something," Olivia said, as if she'd been privy to my thoughts all along, or maybe I'd been speaking my thoughts out loud without realizing it.

"What's that?"

"Wiping my forehead when I was in labor. Do you remember?"

"Of course I remember."

"But you never forgot Shirley, did you?"

"No," I said. "I guess you never forget your first time."

"I forgot *my* first time. But I had a lot of first times. They all seemed different at the time, but looking back, I think they were all the same. I never told you. I didn't want you to think I was . . . whatever. Besides, I always thought that God was watching me. That's why I always wanted a sheet over me. At Yale . . ." She started to cry and smile and laugh at the same time.

"Look," I said. And then I said it again. "Look." I couldn't think of anything else to say that would explain it. "Look. Look. Look."

I let her cry for a while. "Let's just keep on doing what we're doing," she said, "and reach our own conclusions. One more morning. At least."

XXIV. EPITAPHS
(SEPTEMBER 2011)

We continued to go to our place with some coffee. Olivia brought down her laptop and started to respond to her editor's notes and queries, but she didn't have the energy to keep at it very long. We didn't talk much. We watched the waves and tried to determine if every seventh wave was bigger than the other waves; and we watched the gulls and the terns and the dogs and the children playing on the beach as summer started to fade away. Olivia slept most of the time, and in her sleep she continued to dream about the buffalo. Sometimes she saw it down on the beach, playing with Booker and Barley and Whitefoot. Or coming out of the sauna, or just poking around in the yard. "I take pictures in my imagination," she said. "I wish I could show them to you."

I went to the shop every morning, after we'd had our coffee on the balcony, and worked on our new catalog. Adam and

Carla were doing most of the heavy lifting. Adam had his ear to the ground and his nose too, sussing out estate sales, keeping in touch with our old network of collectors and dealers, showing our wares at book fairs. Our online business was good; Carla's video blogs were attracting followers across the country; we'd hired a professional photographer to photograph the books for the catalogs and the online website — no monoliths, no distracting backgrounds, no distracting optical effects, no knickknacks, no Renaissance perspective studies — just long focal length shots to minimize keystone distortion.

Olivia's "100 Greats" didn't bring in a lot of money, but they brought people into the depot in the afternoons — townspeople, students, and faculty from the college. Innkeepers had set out bistro tables along the corridor and it was a pleasure to see customers sitting at one of the tables turning the pages of a recent purchase. I took photos to show Olivia. She herself was slipping in and out of time. Sometimes she seemed to be talking to herself, or to some unseen companion. Her lips moving. I'd paged through our copy of Catlin's *Manners and Customs.* Catlin's documentation of the great buffalo herds was impressive, but I

couldn't find exactly what I was looking for
— about what it meant for a buffalo to appear in your life. Maybe I couldn't find it
because I'd made it up, I couldn't be sure,
but I thought I could find something like it.
Maybe when there was more time.

The fall equinox slipped by us before we
reached any definite conclusions. We'd
reach *some* conclusions, of course, but then
there were always *more* conclusions to be
reached.

We were reading the 1805 *Prelude* in the
Salincourt Edition. The book was on Olivia's lap when I came into the room with a
cup of tea. "Crushed red morocco over red
cloth boards," she said, "like your Montaigne. Raised bands, floral designs in the
spine compartments and marbled end papers."

"You get an A for descriptive bibliography," I said. I sat down on the bed next to
her and took the book out of her hands.
"Do you want a pain pill?" I asked.

"I just want to investigate the pain," she
said. "I want to interrogate it. It's not that
bad."

We were reading Book I, "Childhood," in
the 1805 text, and I could hear time passing as I read. It sounded like the waves lap-

ping the beach, like the lines of the poem. I skipped ahead to one of her favorite passages, one of mine too, because it reminded me of the times we'd skated together on the Midway.

> Not seldom from the uproar I retired
> Into a silent bay, or sportively
> Glanced sideway, leaving the tumultuous
>   throng,
> To cut across the image of a star.

She raised her hand, as if we were in a classroom. "Did you know," she said, "that in 1799, it's the *shadow* of a star, in 1805 it's image, and in 1850, it's the *reflex* of a star?"

"Hmmm," I said. "I like *reflex*. How about you?"

She didn't answer. I kept on reading.

> That gleamed up on the ice. And
>   oftentimes
> When we had given our bodies to the
>   wind,
> And all the shadowy banks on either side
> Came sweeping through the darkness,
>   spinning still
> The rapid line of motion, then at once
> Have I, reclining back upon my heels,

Stopped short — yet still the solitary cliffs
Wheeled by me, even as if the earth had
   rolled
With visible motion her diurnal round.
Behind me did they stretch in solemn
   train,
Feebler and feebler, and I stood and
   watched
Till all was tranquil as a dreamless sleep.

I massaged her feet for a while, till she
went to sleep. I pulled the covers back over
her feet, not realizing at the time that these
were probably the last words she would ever
hear. At least she never really woke up after
that. But when she died, two days later, her
head was cocked, as if she was still listening. Her eyes were open. There was still
some blue in them. And I thought that she'd
seen the buffalo. And then I thought that
not only had she *seen* the buffalo, she *was*
the buffalo — not just the *sign* of abundant
life, but abundant life itself. And I hung on
to this thought for about an hour before
calling Carl Abrams. We had a plan, but now
that it had happened, I wasn't sure it would
be okay to leave her overnight.

"Nothing will happen," Carl said. "Nothing much. But it'll be easier if we do it now,
before rigor sets in. I'll come down later.

Give me an hour. I've got some business at the home in St. Anne anyway. I'm sorry, Gabe. I'm going to need a death certificate from Dr. Kerry, but you don't need to do anything right now except crank up the air conditioning. You can close her eyes if you want to." I pulled the lids down with my little finger. "But just be still for a while. Give yourself an hour." I was reminded of the advice I'd heard Delilah giving to someone on the phone.

"Crank up the air conditioning. I'll bring some dry ice over. In about an hour. We'll wash her and you can leave her where she is overnight, but she's got to be refrigerated or in the ground by tomorrow afternoon if you still want a green burial. I've got all the permits."

Saskia and I helped Carl wash the body. "It's a good thing to do," Carl said, and maybe it was, but it was hard. I could feel the grief sinking into me, with no words to contain it. I couldn't stop thinking of Olivia as the person she had been until a few hours ago, and not the leaden weight in the bed where we'd made love and read to each other and fallen asleep in each other's arms. And as we swabbed her mouth out with vinegar, these two realities became harder to reconcile. Trying to think of them was like trying to force two magnets together, like the little black and white dogs I played with as a child. Of course, when you turn one of them the opposite way, they snap together: *No motion has she now, no force, She neither hears nor sees; Rolled round in earth's diurnal course, With rocks and stones and trees.* It was unbearable. I didn't understand how she could have loved this poem.

We wrapped bricks of dry ice in thick cotton towels and put them in the bottom of a long wicker basket. We wrapped Livy in a light linen shroud and lifted her into the basket.

The next morning, about an hour after first light, Sarah stopped by to see Olivia. When she realized that Olivia was dead, she wanted to administer extreme unction. I almost sent her away, but then I asked if she'd like to sit with us for a while, and she did. The three of us sat in silence till the sun rose over the dunes. Sarah pulled back the shroud and kissed Olivia's forehead and said good-bye. I pulled the shroud back over her face, which looked the same. The dry ice that Carl had positioned under her neck and back was still smoking or steaming. The air conditioning was on full blast and it was chilly.

Booker dragged his blanket out of the closet and jumped up on the bed.

About 9:30, Saskia went for a swim. I watched her from the deck and waited till she turned around and headed back to shore.

Carl and his assistant came over about ten o'clock. We drank some coffee and then they loaded Livy into the removal van and drove off.

I wanted to go to The Dunes and speak to Augie, but I didn't want to leave Saskia alone.

"I'll be all right," she said. But she was crying as she drank a cup of tea.

"You won't swim out again?" I was afraid to ask, but I had to. She shook her head.

Augie was in his chair. The TV was on low. The picture was clear, but I couldn't see what it was, couldn't understand.

"Augie," I said. "Livy's dead. *È morta.*" I put my hand on his shoulder. "Last night. Saskia and I washed her body. Now she's nothing. A rock or a tree. But it was good to touch her. I'm sorry now I didn't help wash my dad, but I'll do it for you."

"The women used to do that," he said.

"You walk through a door and disappear. You can't explain it. Well, maybe you can. I

467

have a rough idea. You don't die all at once. It's like lights going out when it starts to get dark. No, when it starts to get light. They don't all go out at the same time. The enzymes break down the cells; microbes start to multiply . . ."

There was a bowl of fruit on the table.

"So," Augie said. "It's all over. You didn't call me."

"I'm sorry. I wanted to tell you in person."

"*A tutto c'è rimedio fuorché alla morte. There's a remedy for everything except death.* Your daughter with you?"

"Saskia?"

"You got another daughter?"

I didn't feel like explaining, didn't want to correct him. "She's probably going to Jordan pretty soon."

Augie was eating a ripe peach with a knife and fork. He still had juice on his chin. "You want one?" he asked. I shook my head.

We buried Olivia that afternoon, earth to earth, the first green burial in the St. Anne cemetery, in a new section at the back. A reporter was there to cover the action. Carl had called in some favors and twisted some arms to get the permits. Augie rode with Saskia and me in the limo. Reverend Sarah said a few words and we went home.

468

Montaigne has a lot to say about death, but I don't think he got it quite right. The problem isn't your own death, it's the deaths of other people, people you love. He should have figured that out after the death of La Boétie. Maybe he did.

I was glad that Saskia was with me. In St. Anne. She wasn't sure of her plans, but I knew that there were good things in store for her. She knew Arabic, for one thing. That gave her a leg up. She didn't have to be in Amman till the middle of October.

After the simplest of all funerals — Sarah said a few words — Saskia and I went down to the lake for a swim. The water was very cold. An east wind had blown the warm surface water out. Cold water from the depths had moved in to replace it. After a short swim, we walked along the beach all the way south to the Loft and I told Saskia about coming here with her mother, back in 2009. She remembered calling her mother, calling her on her new cell phone, and her mother telling her she was having a dirty weekend. "You were with her then, in the car. When I called."

I nodded.

She thought she might forget about Jordan and go to grad school in linguistics, but by the time of Olivia's memorial service, she'd gone back to her original plan.

The memorial service, at the end of the week, was at the cemetery. About a hundred people gathered at the grave. And Booker, who ran back and forth, interrogating, looking for Olivia. I was surprised to see so many people from Reverend Sarah's protest groups, and so many people who'd met Olivia at the children's story hour she'd organized at the library; and people from the church, and customers who knew her at the shop. David was there too. I didn't notice him at first. They all had something to say, and by the time we were done, I realized that Olivia's footprint in St. Anne was bigger than mine. And in a funny way this lifted my spirits.

Sarah said a few words about Olivia's spiritual journey. How the nuns at the Episcopal monastery near Grand Rapids had been praying for her. She read a card from the Mother Superior. David spoke too, about her love of Nature. And he recited the poem that was always on my mind:

A slumber did my spirit seal,
I had no human fears;
She seemed a thing that could not feel
The touch of earthly years.

No motion has she now, no force,
She neither hears nor sees;
Rolled round in earth's diurnal course,
With rocks and stones and trees.

Augie spoke too. He was nervous and spoke in Italian without realizing it. *"Lei potrebbe far sentire un vecchio di nuovo giovane." She could make an old man feel young again.*

Afterward we went back to the house for a drink: Saskia and Sarah and Augie and David and Delilah and I. Augie had brought a bottle of homemade limoncello, which we drank in our Duralex glasses.

"Why is the lake so blue?" Saskia asked after a while.

"Because," Delilah said, "it's reflecting the color of the sky."

"And why is the sky so blue?"

"When I was a kid," I said, "I used to see ads for *The Book of Knowledge* that promised to explain why the sky was blue. I suppose we could look it up in *Wikipedia*," I said, but no one really cared.

Saskia wanted a sauna. She'd become quite the expert and offered to get the fire going. She and Olivia and Sarah had taken saunas together; and she and I and Olivia and Augie had taken saunas together; and

Olivia and Saskia and I. But it would be the first time for this particular combination, which included David and Delilah, Adam and Carla.

Saskia got up and stood with her hand on the doorknob of the door that opened out onto the south side of the house. I think we all felt a little awkward, but no one wanted to say "no." It was embarrassing to say "yes" and just as embarrassing to say "no." Maybe "self-conscious" rather than "embarrassing."

I poured a little more limoncello into our glasses, and Augie cautioned us against drinking too much before a sauna.

Saskia went out to start a fire.

"I got an e-mail yesterday," I said, "inviting me to enroll in a program that would enable me to reach my highest potential. There were two parts to it: physical cleansing (eliminating toxins) and discovering my inner warrior."

No one wanted to know more.

When Saskia came back in, she looked around and said, "Did I miss my cue?" After about half an hour she went upstairs and came down with a stack of Turkish towels and a couple regular bath towels and was the first to slip out of her clothes. She wrapped one of the towels around her —

472

young, confident, beautiful, sad. Reverend Sarah was the last. She stretched and shook out the muscles in one leg, then the other. Like a runner before a race. She was beautiful too. In fact, everyone was beautiful.

We sat in towels for another fifteen minutes, and then we took turns showering in the outside shower. Booker went down to the beach. We wrapped our towels around ourselves again, entered the sauna, took off our towels and sat on them, not looking at each other. At least not directly. Except for Saskia, who sat nearest to the fire, so she could ladle water from a bucket onto the hot rocks, and who looked at everyone. We'd never had that many people in the sauna before. I kept counting and kept coming up with different numbers, usually seven or eight of us, all speaking in such complex counterpoint that it was hard to tell us apart.

"I don't care for that poem. I never understood why she liked it. *Rolled round in earth's diurnal course; With rocks and stones and trees.* It's horrible, brutal."

"Maybe it's going back to Nature, being one with Nature. Who wrote *The Sand County Almanac*?"

"Aldo Leopold."

"Doesn't he say it's comforting to think that our bodies are part of the natural cycle, that we'll decompose and become part of the natural world? That's what green burial is about."

"But what does it all *mean*?"

"What does anything 'mean'? Maybe nothing means anything."

"If nothing meant anything, we wouldn't be sittin' here wringing our hands and cryin'."

"Is that what we're doing?"

"It's an old blues song. 'C. C. Rider.' "

"What do you want to know when you want to know what something means?"

"The meaning of the porter scene in *Macbeth*? What you want to know is, how does it fit into the play as a whole?"

"What does a carrot *mean*? What does a dog mean? What does a person mean?"

"What does first sex *mean*?"

"I don't know about a carrot, but first sex is easy. It means you've turned a corner, crossed a border into new territory. You can't go back. That's what things 'mean' — turning corners."

"Aren't the best things the things that don't *mean* anything? Like dancing. Beauty. Swimming. Mountain climbing. The sound of the waves."

"Fucking?"

"There's fucking and then there's fucking. *You rub your dick back and forth and some stuff comes out the end.*"

"Philip Roth, *Portnoy's Complaint.*"

"Marcus Aurelius. M*ontaigne* quoting Marcus Aurelius."

"That doesn't mean anything by itself. But you fuck your neighbor's wife and you could fuck up your life. Her life too. You might find that you've turned a corner. That would *mean* something."

"Or your neighbor's husband."

"Or maybe it was a wonderful experience and you never tell anybody about it, but you think about it for the rest of your life, whenever you're feeling sad — and then you feel happy."

" 'No motion has she now, no force, She neither hears nor sees; Rolled round in earth's diurnal course, With rocks, and stones, and trees.' Olivia must have thought it was okay."

Saskia ladled some water on the hot rocks, and we were enveloped in a burst of steam. The temperature was up to 140. We were quiet for a while.

"At one with Nature."

"You gonna ask me about my plans for the summer?"

475

"You going back to Italy?"

"Eddie and I — probably not going to make it back now."

"I'll be in Amman, Jordan, in the fall, working in a palace. Working for a prince."

"We're going to miss you."

"I'm going to read Montaigne."

"You've already read Montaigne."

" 'Philosophy is learning how to die.' "

"That's Cicero, not Montaigne. Montaigne quoting Cicero. You know Al Bernstein got rid of his all his books, everything. He's already gone to Israel. He wanted me to find someone who'd keep his collection together. Give it to a library. These things can get complicated. I arranged a deal with the Holocaust Museum in Chicago."

"I'm going to visit all the places my mother lived. She was born in Fayetteville, Arkansas. Learned to play the violin. Played all over the country. My dad heard her in South Bend, Indiana. She was playing with the Notre Dame Symphony . . ."

"And I'll bet he said, 'That's the woman I'm going to marry.' "

"How did you know?"

"I could see it coming a mile away."

"You think your old car will make it?"

"I have faith."

"When will you be back?"

"I'm not coming back."

"You got another parish?"

She shook her head.

"You're just . . . leaving?"

She nodded.

The temperature was up to 150.

"When he rolled away the stone, Jesus erased the line between the living and the dead. Before that, there was a river dividing the two worlds. You had to take a boat."

"Flannery O'Connor. 'A Good Man Is Hard to Find.' "

"And now you think it's a round trip, *andata e ritorno*?"

"Not exactly."

"Maybe he made a big mistake."

"Well, it was a gamble."

"Jesus didn't move the stone. I thought it was an angel."

"The young man at the tomb was *not* an angel. He was just a young man."

"What was he doing there?"

"That's the question, isn't it."

"It was called a 'golal.' The stone was. Mark says it was 'exceedingly great.' What's really strange, though, is the absolute unbroken silence concerning a spot that must have been a very sacred place to thousands of people, the circle of the Christian believers themselves, and outside the circle too. It never became a sacred site. Unlike the cenacle. You can still visit the cenacle, but nobody knows where the tomb was."

"What's the cenacle anyway?"

"The upper room where Jesus and his disciples ate their last meal."

"But Olivia's still dead!"

"What are you going to put on her stone?"

We thought for a while as the temperature kept rising. We looked up at the big thermometer on the wall. Up to 160.

"Don't put any more water on the stones."

Saskia ladled more water anyway and another blast of steam filled the little sauna house.

" 'Rolled round in earth's diurnal course, With rocks and stones and trees.' "

"It's too brutal."

" *'Nella sua voluntade è nostra pace?'* "

"In his will is our peace? I didn't know you were religious."

"You got to be at my age."

"How about something from Shakespeare: 'There is a special providence in the fall of a sparrow'?"

"It's getting hot in here."

"Don't say, 'It's like a sauna.' "

"Does it get this hot in Jordan?"

"It's like this every day. In summer. It gets

478

pretty hot. Actually it's often one twenty, but that's out in the desert."

"The legal limit for a sauna is a hundred ninety-four degrees. In the United States and Canada."

"That's almost boiling."

"It feels like it's boiling now."

"When you need me, put your arms around anyone and give them what you need to give to me."

"Too sappy."

"It's *not* sappy.

"Pretty hard to get all that on a tombstone."

"How about 'carried by great winds across the sky'?"

"That's an Ojibwa saying. She'd like that."

"That was a plaque on the wall of Tony Soprano's hospital room."

"Tony Soprano?"

"A TV show, a kind of soap opera."

"Oh."

"It's still pretty good."

"You know, the last two months have been really hard. But right now I think they were the happiest time in my life. I was happy, and I didn't know it. Can you be happy and not know it? I mean happy and sad at the same time?"

"Do you think you'll look back on this

moment, sitting here, and realize that you were happy?"

"I think so, but 'happy' is not the right word. It's hard to believe it right now."

"I think Mom was happy too. She was happy, and I tried to spoil it. I couldn't just let her be, and . . ." But she started crying before she finished the sentence.

"Maybe the word we're looking for is *ol-bios,* 'fortunate,' or *eudaimon,* 'flourishing.' "

"How about 'blessed'?"

"That's better."

Saskia continued to cry. Augie reached over and put his hand on the top of her naked thigh. She put her young hand on top of his old one, and then after a minute or so she stood up. The rest of us stood up too and put our arms around her. It was awkward at first. There were too many of us. We had trouble adjusting our arms. And then all of a sudden it wasn't awkward. Our bodies, slippery and shining with sweat, wanted to press together, to touch each other, as if each body wanted to touch as much of the other seven bodies — or was it eight? — as possible. As if we were trying to confirm the four-color map theory. Or maybe disprove it.

Everyone's flesh touched everyone else's.

Old flesh, withered and dry; young flesh, nubile and firm; mature feminine flesh, ripe; and middle-aged masculine flesh, hard and firm. As if we were becoming one body. We gave to each other what we needed to give to Olivia, but we didn't stay that way long. It was too intense and suddenly we became self-conscious.

"It's getting hot. We need to get out of here."

The big thermometer read 170 degrees. It felt just right, beyond mellow. Saskia closed the vents on the stove. We wrapped our towels around ourselves.

"Baruch dayan emet," I said as we stepped out of the sauna into the middle of fall. "Blessed is the true judge. That's what should go on her tombstone."

481

XXV. The Cemetery
(OCTOBER 2011)

I drove Saskia to O'Hare on Saturday, October 15. By the time we got to the Illinois state line, she'd pretty well convinced herself that she was making a mistake, that she didn't want to leave Nadia, who was starting her senior year at U of C; but when I asked her if she wanted me to turn around, she laughed and said "no." We stopped at the Lincoln Oasis for a bite to eat. Her flight wasn't till eleven o'clock. We sat next to each other in the International Terminal till she thought she'd better go through security. I couldn't go with her any farther so we hugged each other and tried to keep from crying. I waited in the terminal till her flight was called, and then I drove to the Quadrangle Club in Hyde Park to spend the night. Dad's tombstone was in place, and I wanted to see it in the morning.

I was at Oak Woods Cemetery when it opened at eight o'clock on Sunday morning. Five minutes later I was standing at Dad's grave on Sunset Drive.

CHARLES JOHNSON, JR.
1931–2009
SPINE A LITTLE DARKENED AND
FADED IN PLACES.
CORNERS SQUARE
BUT RUBBED THROUGH.
FRONT INTERNAL HINGE CRACKED.
BINDING SOMEWHAT LOOSE.
SOME FOXING THROUGHOUT.

I had plenty to say, but I kept my mouth shut. I'd come to listen.

What did I want? What was my agenda? What was I trying to accomplish? What did I want to happen? Why was I here? What was I listening *for*?

I suppose I was listening for the kind of approval I'd heard all my life. From Dad, from Mamma, from my teachers, from Grandpa Chaz too. I suppose I wanted a sign of some kind. Dad would be pleased that I'd finally married Olivia, and I thought he would approve of the new shop even though he'd advised me to sell everything and live life instead of reading about it. And I thought that he and Grandpa Chaz would approve of the decision — which Adam,

Carla, and I had made at a "visioning" session shortly after Olivia's death — to donate Grandpa Chaz's Americana to the Ogden Collection at St. Anne, a tax-deductible gift that would really put the Great Lakes Study Center on the map — and that would offset our taxable income for the foreseeable future.

But I was listening for something more too, not a voice from beyond the grave, but for something not quite me, something distinct from my own imagination. "He that hath ears to hear, let him hear," Dad liked to say when I wasn't paying attention while he was explaining the issue points in one of his Modern Firsts, or an unusual cancel in a nineteenth-century novel. I could almost hear him say it now. Almost. But not quite. I was paying attention, and I had ears to hear, but the only thing I could hear was the early morning rush of traffic on Cottage Grove.

I had work to do at the shop, and I'd had a condolence call from Olivia's editor at Johns Hopkins, who thought that between the two of us we could deal with the rest of the copy editor's queries. I thought so too and was anxious to get started. But instead of going straight home, I drove back into Hyde Park

484

and had a cup of coffee at the Medici. I walked down Fifty-Seventh Street to have a look at the old shop. Looking through the dirty windows was like looking back for traces of my old life. But the shop was still empty. I walked down Blackstone, past the Davises, past the Gridleys, past the Harringtons. The ginkgo in front of the Harringtons had dropped its leaves, but the maple trees were still showing yellow and red and orange. It was nine o'clock in the morning. Mrs. Al-Dajani was sitting in the sun on the steps of our old house, on the east side of the street, enjoying a cigarette, and it made me think of Olivia and Dad smoking in the warming house; it made me think of Olivia and Father Gregory lighting up in front of the administration building at Cardinal Newman College; it made me want a cigarette myself. I wasn't sure what I was doing, or what I wanted to do.

I stopped in front of the house to admire Grandpa Chaz's crabapple tree, which was turning from orange to bronze. Mrs. Al-Dajani looked at me. Curious. A large dog was curled up in a spot of sunlight next to her. I wasn't sure she'd remember me, but she did. "Mr. Johnson," she called out.

"Mrs. Al-Dajani," I said. "You remember me?"

"Of course."

"I just had a cup of coffee at the Medici," I said, "and thought I'd walk through the old neighborhood. I was out at the cemetery earlier. My father's grave. My grandfather's too. And my grandmother's."

"Of course," she said again. "You were all in the bookstore business together. And now you live in a wonderful house on the lake. We hear all about you from Nadia Tal-houni." She stubbed her cigarette out on the step and cupped the butt in her hand. "My grandchildren won't allow me to smoke in the house," she said, smiling.

"You know Nadia?"

"Of course. We know all the Jordanian students. And Saskia too — your daughter, or your friend's daughter. She speaks very good Arabic. Better than our son. We were very sorry to learn of her mother's death." She said something in Arabic and then translated: "May her spirit remain in your life."

"I took her to O'Hare last night," I said. "She's going to stop over in Paris for one night, so she won't get to Amman till tomorrow morning. Nadia's parents will meet her at Queen Alia Airport. We're going to meet

486

up in Rome at Christmas and then go to Florence to see my mother."

"Florence is lovely at Christmas," she said. "And now you're on your way back to Michigan and you thought you'd like to see your old home."

"Yes," I said. "I like to imagine that you're happy in this house."

"Very happy," she said. "My husband just left. He'll be sorry he missed you. My lazy granddaughters are still asleep."

"You have three children," I said. "If I remember correctly."

"A son and two daughters. Our older daughter's two girls are here for the weekend while their parents are taking a little vacation. With another couple. They all live in Elmhurst. Our other daughter lives in New York. Our son's a surgeon in Minneapolis. They'll all be here for the holidays."

A girl, about thirteen or fourteen, came out on the porch in her pajamas, letting the screen door slam behind her.

"Nina," her grandmother said. "This is Mr. Johnson, who grew up in this house."

"Good morning," I said. "Nina was my mother's name."

Nina rubbed her eyes.

"Go upstairs and tell your lazy sister it's

487

time for breakfast." To me, she said, "Would you like some coffee? I've already made it. This morning I'm making a traditional Jordanian breakfast for the girls. Would you like to join us? Za'atar. Thyme and sesame seeds, with some labaneh — strained yogurt."

I said that I would but that I didn't want to impose. But of course she wouldn't accept that as a good reason. The dog, Omar, followed us into the house. A very large dog. I thought Arabs didn't like dogs, but what did I know?

There was a grand piano in the large bay window, and a very large doll house on a rectangular table. Nina wanted to show me around. There was a stack of New Yorkers too, on a coffee table, and an Arab-language newspaper.

In the kitchen, Mrs. Al-Dajani poured small cups of bitter coffee from a thermos and offered a plate of sweets to counter the bitterness.

The girls stopped petting Omar long enough to ask for cereal instead of za'atar, but Mrs. Al-Dajani just laughed at them, and they ate the za'atar without complaining — flat bread dipped in olive oil and then sprinkled with a mixture of thyme and sesame seeds and then toasted, dipped in some kind of yogurt. It was delicious.

"I used to eat breakfast here every morning," I said to the girls. "I used to sit right where you're sitting. My mother was Italian and just drank coffee in the morning, coffee and milk, but she always fixed eggs for me and my father, and my grandfather. Soft-boiled or poached. Never fried, except on holidays.

"You see those beautiful flowers in the yard? My grandfather planted those flowers. He dug up some bulbs from the side of the road in St. Anne, Michigan, where we used to go every summer, and then every three or four years or so he divided them, and then when he got too old to work in the garden, my dad planted some late-blooming varieties so we could still enjoy them in the fall." Most of the daylilies were dead, but the late-blooming varieties were still displaying bright colors, and I thought for a minute that I had stepped outside myself and that I could hear them, red and yellow, purple and orange.

"He planted that crabapple tree in the front yard too," I added. "You'll have to prune it in winter," I said, "after the first hard frost."

"My husband's very good at pruning," Mrs. Al-Dajani said.

"Are you happy in this house?" I asked her a second time.

"We're very happy here," she said.

"Then I'm happy too," I said.

"Would you like to see your old room? It was in the front of the house, right?"

"I've seen what I needed to see," I said. "I don't need to see it."

I left the Al-Dajanis at eleven o'clock and drove straight home, picked up Booker at Ben Warren's, sat down in my study, filled my fountain pen — the one with the green cap and the italic nib — and answered my mother's letter. I told her everything, and by the time I'd finished, the sun was going down and I had a cramp in my hand. Booker and I drove in to the post office to mail the letter, and on the way back we stopped at the cemetery. No tombstone yet, but I could see it in my imagination. Marcus had written it out in Hebrew and told me to have the stone cutter call him if he had any questions:

ברוך השופט האמיתי

BLESSED IS THE TRUE JUDGE

ACKNOWLEDGEMENTS

In July 2016 I attended the Colorado Antiquarian Book Seminar. I entered with one set of questions, and left with a very different set. When, on the very first day of the seminar, I showed a tentative financial plan for my fictional bookstore to one of the faculty, he said: "You have to know how to sell a hundred thousand dollar book. No one here has sold a hundred thousand dollar book." I knew right then that I was in deep water.

How *do* you sell a hundred thousand dollar book?

Love, Death & Rare Books explores this and other equally troublesome questions, and I would like to thank the faculty at CABS, as well as the following booksellers and librarians, who offered advice and encouragement along the way: Lorne Bair (Lorne Bair Rare Books), Bill Butts (Main Street Fine Book), Sharon Clayton (Seymour Library, Knox College), Jeff Douglas (Seymour Library, Knox College), Ken Gloss (Brattle Book Shop), Brad Jonas (Powell's Books Chicago), Rob Rulon Miller (Rulon-Miller Books), Ernie Quist (Quist Antiquarian), Ben Stone (Stone Alley Books), Doug Wilson (O'Gara & Wilson, Ltd.).

And finally, I would like to thank my first three readers — my wife, Virginia; my long time agent, Henry Dunow; and my new editor, Joseph Olshan — for their encouragement and wise counsel.

None of the above should be held responsible for any errors or misinformation in this novel.

PERMISSIONS

The author is grateful for permission to reprint the following:

of Knowledge, originally published by Prentice-Hall in 1966. The rights have reverted to the author, who died in 1999.

Excerpt from Merrit Malloy's *"Epitaph,"* from *My Song for Him Who Never Sang to Me.* Originally published by the Ward Ritchie Press (1975), and later by the Three Rivers Press (1988).

Image: Melencolia, *Han Sebald Beham, 1500–1550*

ABOUT THE AUTHOR

Robert Hellenga was educated at the University of Michigan, the Queen's University of Belfast, and Princeton University. He is a professor emeritus at Knox College in Galesburg, Illinois, and the author of seven novels and a collection of short stories: *The Sixteen Pleasures, The Fall of a Sparrow, Blues Lessons, Philosophy Made Simple, The Italian Lover, Snakewoman of Little Egypt, The Confessions of Frances Godwin,* and *The Truth About Death and Other Stories.* He lives in Galesburg, Illinois, with his wife and a dog (Simone). Like several of his protagonists, he is the father of three daughters, plays country blues guitar, and has spent a lot of time in Italy.

The employees of Thorndike Press hope you have enjoyed this Large Print book. All our Thorndike, Wheeler, and Kennebec Large Print titles are designed for easy reading, and all our books are made to last. Other Thorndike Press Large Print books are available at your library, through selected bookstores, or directly from us.

For information about titles, please call:
(800) 223-1244

or visit our website at:
gale.com/thorndike

To share your comments, please write:
Publisher
Thorndike Press
10 Water St., Suite 310
Waterville, ME 04901